Praise for
Darkborn

"Alison Sinclair's unique world of two societies, mortally divided by sunrise and sunset, provides a fascinating backdrop for a fast-paced thriller of politics and intrigue. Delightful!"

—national bestselling author Carol Berg

"Alison Sinclair's *Darkborn* plays like a sweeping historical novel in a teeming preindustrial city whose residents are divided into those who can only tolerate light and those who can only exist in darkness. A sprawling cast of characters argue and scheme and practice magic in secret—until a calamitous chain of events reveals the whole city to be under siege from a mysterious and ruthless enemy. Despite swift action, broad conspiracies, and monumental life-and-death stakes, the heart of the book is a delicately rendered love triangle that tracks the human cost of any grand adventure. I can't wait to read the next book about these complex and engaging characters."

—national bestselling author Sharon Shinn

"[A] wonderful read, with an intriguing setting populated by appealing and memorable characters." —Lane Robins, author of *Maledicte*

Darkborn

Alison Sinclair

A ROC BOOK

ROC
Published by New American Library, a division of
Penguin Group (USA) Inc., 375 Hudson Street,
New York, New York 10014, USA
Penguin Group (Canada), 90 Eglinton Avenue East, Suite 700, Toronto,
Ontario M4P 2Y3, Canada (a division of Pearson Penguin Canada Inc.)
Penguin Books Ltd., 80 Strand, London WC2R 0RL, England
Penguin Ireland, 25 St. Stephen's Green, Dublin 2,
Ireland (a division of Penguin Books Ltd.)
Penguin Group (Australia), 250 Camberwell Road, Camberwell, Victoria 3124,
Australia (a division of Pearson Australia Group Pty. Ltd.)
Penguin Books India Pvt. Ltd., 11 Community Centre, Panchsheel Park,
New Delhi - 110 017, India
Penguin Group (NZ), 67 Apollo Drive, Rosedale, North Shore 0632,
New Zealand (a division of Pearson New Zealand Ltd.)
Penguin Books (South Africa) (Pty.) Ltd., 24 Sturdee Avenue,
Rosebank, Johannesburg 2196, South Africa

Penguin Books Ltd., Registered Offices:
80 Strand, London WC2R 0RL, England

Published by Roc, an imprint of New American Library,
a division of Penguin Group (USA) Inc.

First Roc Printing, May 2009
10 9 8 7 6 5 4 3 2 1

Library of Congress Cataloging-in-Publication Data

Sinclair, Alison, 1959–
Darkborn / Alison Sinclair.
p. cm.
ISBN 978-0-451-46270-1
1. Magic—Fiction. 2. Twins—Fiction. 3. Good and evil—Fiction. I. Title.
PR9199.3.S5324D37 2009
813'.54—dc22 2008046235

Set in Garamond
Designed by Alissa Amell

Printed in the United States of America

Darkborn

One

Balthasar

The knock on Balthasar's door came as the bell tolled sunrise. For Imogene's Darkborn, it was the hour of criminals and suicides, the hour of violence or desperation. In this civilized city of Minhorne, the ancient law of succor was half forgotten, and many might not have opened the door to an unknown's knock at the brink of dawn.

Balthasar Hearne was not one of those; he hurried to the door and pulled it open, heavy as it was. On the step stood a lone woman muffled in a thick traveling cloak. He sonned no carriage at her back, no living movement within his range except two cats and a small indistinct fluttering of birds. This close to sunrise the street was quite deserted. "For mercy's sake," the woman begged breathlessly, "let me in."

He could already feel the sting of imminent daylight on his skin. He stepped back and she stumbled heavily over the threshold, pulling away from his steadying hand and fetching up against the little hall table. "Oh, sweet Imogene." She panted, leaning hard on it with both hands. "I thought I would never reach here in time. I thought I must surely burn."

He shut and locked the door against the day. There was nothing else to do. Left outside, she would burn to ash in an instant at sunrise, as would he. That was the Darkborn's legacy of Archmage Imogene's Curse.

Her heavy cloak had snagged and was dragging one of the ornaments on the table, and Bal reached out and freed it before it fell. It was one of his wife's favorites, a horse with its foal pressed to its flank. He held it cradled in his hands as the woman straightened with an effort and turned to face him. He felt her sonn sweep over him, shaping him for her perception: a plain, slender man a little below average height, decently but not fashionably dressed. Certainly not as befitted the husband of a duke's daughter, if she knew whom she faced. He returned the sonn, delicately, as one must, to respect the modesty of a lady. Her small face was puffy above the fur trimming of her cloak. Her little gloved hand reinforced the clasp. She was still breathing hard. Like most women of the aristocracy, she was unfit for walking any distance, though she seemed unusually distressed. He wondered what had brought her here unaccompanied. It augured not well, for either of them. Her reputation would suffer, and his marriage, if gossip placed them together through the day.

The bell fell silent. In a few minutes, the sun would rise. They were trapped here, together, until nightfall. In the meantime his manners reasserted themselves. "The sitting room is in here." He gestured her toward it.

She did not move. "Don't you remember me, Balthasar?" she said in a clear, sweet voice. "Am I really so much changed?"

He sonned her again, but the voice had already told him, that musical inflection. "Tercelle Amberley," he said flatly.

"Yes," she said, smiling. "Tercelle Amberley. It has been a very long time."

The echoes of his sonn faded, leaving him in the grainy haze of all the reflections of random vibrations around them. He was ashamed of himself for feeling as he did. It was not her fault that he had tried ten years or more to forget his brother and everyone associated with him.

She directed her next splash of sonn at the hallway, a lady gracefully sidestepping awkwardness. "Your home has not changed at all," she said. "Yet you married well."

"My wife and I have a family home elsewhere," he said, trying not to sound curt. His domestic arrangements were none of her business.

She heard the curtness; he heard her take a heavy step forward. "Balthasar . . . Balthasar, I would not have imposed on you were I not in desperate need. I truly believe you are the only one who can help me."

The last he had heard of Tercelle Amberley was the announcement of her betrothal a year ago to Ferdenzil Mycene, heir to one of the four major dukedoms, and the hero in the campaign to subdue piracy in the Scallon Isles. Quite a coup for the daughter of a family that had scrambled their way into the nobility a scant three generations ago. The Amberleys had major interests in armaments and shipbuilding, which would attract the heir to the most expansionist of the four major dukedoms even more than the lady's sweet face and social polish. The betrothal, Bal's contemporaries said, was one of the many signs that boded ill for the independence of the Scallon Isles. Bal could hardly imagine how Tercelle would come to need to throw herself on the mercy of an obscure physician-scholar, even one married to the archduke's cousin. Or rather, he could hardly imagine any good reason for her to do so.

Years of training in courtesy prevailed. "Please"—he extended his arm toward the receiving room—"do sit down."

She paused on the threshold, and in the reflections of her sonn he perceived the salon's shabbiness, the best room in a house of impoverished minor nobility. He had another home, true, a fine home to suit the lady he had married, and even though it had been bought and paid for with her inheritance, not his, when she was there, he felt it home. When she was not, when she and the children went to one of her family's estates, he returned here. And no, this house had not changed; if anything, it had become shabbier than when Tercelle knew it. She had made no secret of her disdain then, during her long flirtation with his brother. Bal wondered if Lysander had known how little chance his suit had had, even then. He wondered what he knew now.

She walked into the center of the room and turned with some small effort of balance. "Have you ever heard from Lysander?"

"No," Balthasar said, suppressing his slight disturbance at having his thoughts echoed so deftly: Of course she would be thinking of Lysander, facing his brother. She was no mage.

She sonned him, a delicate lick of vibration. "Are you still angry with him?"

"Leaving," Balthasar said, "was the best thing he could have done. For us, his family, and for you."

"How harsh," she said in her breathless lilt. "I never thought you would become so unforgiving a man. You were always so gentle. And you adored Lysander, as I did."

True, he had, once. "Please, Tercelle, why have you come?"

There was a silence, and then a rustle of movement. "I need your help." His sonn caught her as she shrugged the unhooked cloak from her shoulders and let it slide to the ground.

Somehow he was not entirely surprised to know that she was pregnant, though he was disconcerted by how large and low she was carrying. She must be very near her time.

But her fiancé had been gone over a year, harrying the Scallon pirates and conducting diplomatic forays into the neighboring island kingdoms to advance the dukedom of Mycene's claim on the isles, their territory, and their exports of exotic fruit and spices.

"The child is not your intended's," he said, keeping all tone from his voice.

She scowled that he should say it. She reached back and lowered herself awkwardly into a chair he had not offered. "If he learns of this child, the best that will happen is that he and his family will repudiate me. The worst is that he would kill me." She shifted her belly on her lap with a grimace. "I'd rather be dead than cast aside."

"How is it," Balthasar said, "that no one has told him?"

"When I knew I was with child I sought to lose it. I tried all the means I could discover. I even contrived a fall from a horse." He was silent, remembering the aching devastation of Telmaine's one miscarriage. He and Telmaine had walked around the house like souls in purgatory. "It didn't work. But I had the excuse to go away, to live as an invalid until my time came."

She pressed a fist against her abdomen, grimacing. "I . . . lay with him but four times. It was the last . . ." She could have given him the date, the hour, he knew. He felt compassion for her in her fond folly, despite his dislike of her and the danger in the situation for himself. Ferdenzil would surely believe she had sought the aid of her lover.

"He would tap on the door to give me warning, and then I would tap back and go into the next room and wait, and he would come in . . . Sometimes I wanted to lock the door; once I did and then I unlocked it again . . . I could not do otherwise. And it was in the day he came, always in the day."

Bal frowned. Ballads and broadsheets told of Lightborn demon lovers, crossing the sunset to seduce Darkborn girls. The stories were absurd, since the Lightborn could no more abide the darkness than the Darkborn the light; such was the nature of Imogene's Curse. Part of his irregular physician's practice was treating people, usually young women, with a dangerous obsession with the Light: Lightsickness, it was called, a delusion that could end in an impulsive, fatal stepping into sunlight. He wondered why Tercelle would tell him a story they both knew was impossible.

She heard the skepticism in his silence. "He came from the Light, I tell you," she cried out. Sonn showed her pulling herself forward in the chair. "That's why I came to you. You have friends among the Lightborn. *You* can take the child, whatever it is. And if it cannot go back to the Light, then there are places where yet another bastard will hardly pass notice, places *you* know."

Ah, there was that, if he set all the rest of it aside. The demimonde, the Rivermarch, where fallen women, mages, and criminals gathered to ply their disgraceful trades. The rejected of society gathered there. He had worked at a demimondaine clinic as a student, and still did when Telmaine's aristocratic family left him, and her, in peace—and the physician in him did not like the appearance of Tercelle. He wondered how far she had come on foot. Coach drivers insisted on being under cover before the sunrise bell began to toll. He stood up. "Tercelle, the rest of it can wait. You are here now, and you have had a hard walk for a lady in your condition. You should rest now."

He showed her to his parents' room, which he had kept well

aired since their deaths six years ago. It had an ample four-poster bed, the bed in which he and his brother and sister had been conceived and born, the bed in which his parents had died within weeks of each other. She had brought nothing with her, so he offered her a nightgown that had been his mother's. He found a jug of water, a glass, and a bowl for her bedside, and said that he would leave the door ajar so that she might call on him at need.

He went quietly up the stairs to his top-floor study. As soon as he opened the door, he knew that Floria White Hand was in her *salle*. He could hear the soft-footed shuffle of her solitary practice from behind the wall. Nothing rested against that wall, not table, not bookshelf. Much of its length consisted of two layers of heavy paper, sandwiching a fine metal mesh that was proof against accidental perforation. The remainder was an extension of the bookcase, and set into that was a low cabinet with a lightproof door, a *passe-muraille*.

Elsewhere in the sundered lands, the Lightborn had their perpetually lit towns and cities and the Darkborn their perpetually darkened underground caverns and aboveground keeps. Here in Minhorne, Darkborn and Lightborn lived side by side. The streets were the Darkborns' by night, the Lightborns' by day, and each race had its private spaces for the hours its members could not be outside. This row of terraced houses abutted another row adjacent to the Lightborn prince's palace. It was not a fashionable address amongst the Darkborn, but for the past five generations Balthasar's family and the Lightborn family of White Hand swordsmen and assassins had lived in amity and trust, as demonstrated by this paper wall. Were the wall to be torn, the light by which Floria lived would burn Balthasar to ash. As a youth, Balthasar had enjoyed an intense infatuation for the unattainable Floria, expressed only in abundant daydreams, poetry, and words, at least until he had met Telmaine. Floria had abetted his courtship of his future wife with an enthusiasm that was, in retrospect, unflattering. His young self *had* been rather slushy, and with maturity—and marriage—he had learned to keep his feelings to himself. He in turn had carried messages through the night to abet her rise in her prince's secret service.

Floria said, "Bal? That wasn't Telmaine's voice, was it?" He was not surprised she had heard, even through the closed door. Her hearing was not a Darkborn's, but for one of the Lightborn, it was uncommonly good. She cultivated her senses, she said, as she did everything that helped her survive and prosper.

He sat down in the chair nearest the paper wall, his arm laid on the armrest so that his fingertips would rest against the wall. She could not see him—she could never see him—and with the mesh he could no longer sonn her through the wall. Telmaine had insisted on the mesh before she would even bring their firstborn into the house.

"It was Tercelle Amberley. She was courted by my brother, once." He told her what had brought the lady to his door. Beyond the paper wall, he could hear the distinct sound of her sharpening a stiletto.

"I mislike this," she said. He heard her set aside the stiletto and begin to pace, the pacing broken with small shuffling fencer's steps. Unlike Darkborn women, who cultivated decorative repose, Floria was seldom still, always testing her body, refining her physical skills.

"I can't understand why she should tell me such a ridiculous lie."

"To avoid telling you a revealing truth, such as the father's name," Floria said tartly. He heard her take up a practice rapier, the distinctive rattle of the swords in the rack. He envisioned her as she prowled the room, stalking the mannequin. There was a *shush-shush* of soft soles, the thud of a blade driven home. "Take my advice and get her out of here as soon as night falls. She'll have somewhere she can go: She didn't travel all the way from her obscure country estate today. She'll have had some plan to cover not finding you here, or your not taking her in. Even if it's merely a fanciful story to cover her follies, she's betrothed to Ferdenzil Mycene, and the risk of his knowing of this is high, too high. The man's dangerous, and he would have society's outrage on his side. He'd expect her to bolt to the father of her bastard, and you are the brother of the man she was once pursued by. Think of Telmaine and your daughters, if you have no care for yourself."

Floria, Bal reflected, was an expert with sharp objects. And gave good advice, even if it was advice that he doubted he could follow.

He said, "Floria, there have been mages trying to reverse the Curse for two centuries. Is it possible that someone has succeeded?"

"Do I hear one of the Darkborn talking about mages?" she said dryly.

"Yes," he said patiently. She well knew he did not share his people's prejudice against magic. Even without his family's generations-long association with the Lightborn, who had preserved and elevated magic, his own sister's choice would have forced him to confront any unthinking assumptions. Indeed, he had a trace of magic himself, though in him it was manifested only as uncommon diagnostic acuity; he could not read thoughts with a touch, the way even the weakest true mage could. His sister, Olivede, could, and more, and at the age of twenty had chosen to leave respectable society to live among the demimonde as physician and magical healer. Magic aside, she was a better midwife than he, and he would have to get word to her that he was likely to be calling on her services soon. Tercelle's child appeared very large for a small woman to deliver easily.

A shuffle of feet, the soft, rhythmic thump of a lunge, recover–forward, lunge sequence. Her *salle*, she had told him, was a hall of mirrors, strong reflectors of light as all hard surfaces were reflectors of sonn. She and her master-at-arms were the only people she permitted in it; given the danger to the paper wall of an uncontrolled blade, he was glad of that, though he was sure that, fond as she was of him, it was less for his benefit than hers. She needed her secure and private retreats in a dangerous profession in her prince's dangerous court. Neither Lightborn princes nor their White Hand guardians expected to die of old age.

"The prince has increased the reward for the breaking of the Curse. Fifteen thousand in gold. Of course," she added, "the amount is irrelevant. Anyone who can break the Curse would claim the princedom, archdukedom, and all the island kingdoms and shift the balance of the world."

"Do you think it can be done?"

"We've been trying for the better part of a thousand years and we still do not understand all of it. Without full understanding, we have no hope of counteracting it. And doing so would take an Imogene and her followers, twenty-four eighth-rank mages all mad with sacrifice. Those it didn't kill, it ruined, but they had lost everything else to their war; none of them cared to live any longer. To undo something with that much emotion in it would take equal numbers with equal power and equal compulsion." He heard her rubbing her hands together. "It was a more passionate, more barbarous time. We are civilized." Her voice, as ever, was ironic.

"I have the impression," he observed, "that you think the breaking of the Curse after all these centuries would not serve us well."

She snorted; this was an old gambit. They argued hypotheses with as much changing of places as in a galliard, though he tended to optimism and she to pessimism. "Bal, first off, you have an archduke and we a prince. Only one would rule in the end. You expect your women to be beautiful ornaments, and punish them when they are not. The first gallant who decided that a Lightborn woman was as available as any whore would learn otherwise at the point of a stiletto. You have denigrated magic as feminine irrationality and are now endeavoring to suppress it entirely. We school our magicians to their fullest potential and regard an untrained mage as a danger to be contained. Need I go on? We are better apart. Send that woman away; you owe her nothing." She finished her exercises without speaking again, and went out.

He sighed. Debt was not the point. Tercelle's unborn child was. Seeking distraction, he went to the bookshelf. He rested his hand briefly on a stack of minutes from the Intercalatory Council of Interracial Affairs. Both Bal and his father had been called to serve multiple terms on the mixed council that—through a paper wall—negotiated conflicts between Darkborn and Lightborn interests in Minhorne, everything from land development to road repair to the Lightborn's wish to regulate Darkborn mages. He was due to serve another term this autumn, but conscientiously followed the proceedings between his terms. Which were, due to the current chairman, as dull as they were important. Bal guiltily shifted his hand and pulled down one of his father's favorite travel histories.

He was deep in a two-hundred-year-old account of a journey to Pelalethea, the largest underground city of the Darkborn, two weeks' hard travel into the eastern mountains, when he heard Tercelle call for him.

His diagnostic acumen had not deserted him. He found her as he had expected, doubled up and outraged by the cruel presumption of pain. He ran back to the study to leave a note asking that Floria get a message to Olivede for the night, and then set about making Tercelle as comfortable as he could and gathering together what he would need to deliver her child.

The child was still unborn when Olivede arrived promptly after nightfall, striding into the room with unfeminine vigor, shedding her cloak and setting down her doctor's bag. She was three years his elder, as slender and nondescript as he. Her expression, habitually guarded against the insults of the world, was warm to his sonn.

"Floria passed on your message," she said, and bent to brush her lips lightly across his cheek. He welcomed the kiss; they had long ago come to terms with her mageborn ability to discern his thoughts with a chance touch of skin on skin. She did not comment on what else Floria had said, or ask any questions.

"Hello, Tercelle," she said, making a matter-of-fact claim to familiarity.

Tercelle sonned her, and turned her head away. Olivede was beyond scandal: a woman physician, a practicing mage, and a respected citizen of the demimonde. "Don't touch me," Tercelle said through her teeth.

Olivede pulled a pair of fine gloves from her bag. As a mage-healer, she wore gloves not only for sanitary reasons, but so as to signal no intention to intrude upon her patients' inner life. Bal, understanding magic, knew she did not need them: She had the strength and training to contain her touch-sense without them, and she had sworn vows that further restrained her. But the gloves were a necessary concession.

"Don't be silly," she said crisply. "I'm not going to learn anything from you that you don't tell me aloud. Bal," she said, briskly, bending over the straining woman, "do make yourself useful elsewhere. I'll call you if I need you."

The night dragged on. Between spells of bitter silence, Tercelle groaned and cursed the Sole God and her careless lover, though never by name, Bal noted. Olivede offered the comforts of her magic; and Tercelle, predictably, declined, no doubt repelled as much by the thought of what she might reveal to the mage's touch as the notion of the magic itself. It was well into day when, from his exile in the study, he heard an infant's cry rise over Tercelle's hoarse shriek.

Olivede's voice called, "Bal, I need a hand here!"

Olivede was stooping over the bed, reaching between Tercelle's drawn-up knees. She said, without turning her head, "We've got twins here. Mind that one." Within the crib, a baby twitched in its blankets, hastily wrapped and laid aside. He slipped his hands beneath it and lifted it from the crib to the dresser, catching up a pad of folded towels. Behind him, Tercelle screamed through clenched teeth, and Olivede said, in a tone of utmost concentration, "Just one more now."

Balthasar unwrapped the baby, setting aside the damp blanket, and rubbed the tiny, naked body dry, playing his sonn lightly over it so as to match impression with feel. It appeared to be a healthy baby boy, somewhat small, as twins usually were, with normally flexed limbs and a round, soft belly. His features were normal, though his eyes, unusually for a newborn, were wide-open. Bal wondered if they appeared large because of that. He reached across the baby to lift a soft cloth, and as the cloth passed close above his eyes, the baby blinked.

He could so easily not have noticed, he thought later. A few seconds later and he would have heard the first cry of the baby's brother and turned his head. Or he could have muted his sonn. Or he could have noticed but not wondered. Except he knew about Lightborn senses and reflexes. He had heard Tercelle's extraordinary story. He flicked his finger close to those wide eyes and the baby started and blinked again. He sensed no sonn, which was not unusual: Sonn might take several weeks to establish.

When younger, Bal and Floria had spent hours trying to explain to one another their unshared senses. To her, a world assembled solely from the echoes of unseen sound—as the Darkborn understood their unique gift—was as incomprehensible as one revealed by light was to him. Theories of sound were fundamental to Darkborn science, whereas theories of light were, and always would be, a fringe interest. Bal could hardly imagine color, or transparency, or the reflections of glass in water. Floria struggled to explain the existence of horizon, sky, *stars*, to Balthasar, whose immediate awareness extended only to the limits of sonn, at its most forceful, a city block.

"Balthasar," Olivede said in some exasperation. "I asked you to *help* me, not play patty-cake, and I hope you haven't forgotten how quickly they get chilled."

He finished wrapping the first baby and returned him to the crib, where Olivede had set the second one while she delivered the placenta and began to clean the exhausted mother. The second was also a boy, smaller than his brother, with a tense, anxious expression on a face that seemed no larger than a prune and almost as creased. Bal crooned to him as he dried and bundled him, his sonn playing lightly over the infant's form. As the infant relaxed, his eyes opened wide, fixing on Bal. Bal hesitated, then moved his hand suddenly before the baby's eyes, and the child started, a small convulsion, and began to cry. Bal gathered him up, murmuring apologies. Holding him, he crossed to the fire, which to his sonn was an indeterminate shimmer of turbulent echoes, and a potent heat across his face. Fire, he knew, gave light, though firelight alone was not enough to sustain the Lightborn or burn the Darkborn. He found a taper from the kindling and held it into the flame, and then, crouching, pivoted to put his back to the fire and raised the taper, holding it away so that heat would not betray its presence. The baby did not react, its face still toward Bal, its anomalous eyes wide. He raised the taper higher and sonned a twitch in the skin around the eyes, as though the eyes had moved. He dared not sonn deeply enough to discern the movement of muscles behind the tender, thin infant skin.

"Balthasar, what *are* you doing?" his sister said.

The baby turned his head toward the taper.

It could, Bal thought, have been a twitch or a reflex. Slowly, he lowered the taper and the head turned further, before the baby lost interest and turned back to . . . stare? . . . at Balthasar's face. With a slightly unsteady hand Bal tossed the taper into the fire and stood up.

Tercelle lay with her head turned away, her hands on her flattened belly. The air was thick with the smell of blood. Olivede was stripping off her soiled gloves. Within the crib, he sonned movement, a small arm already working itself free of its swaddling. He crossed to offer his finger to the little hand, which closed on it as lightly as a flower, the skin as dry and intact as a Darkborn's should be in darkness. He cleared his throat.

"I believe," he said, "they may be sighted."

Balthasar

"Sighted," said Floria, a soft, fascinated sibilant. "Yet are unaffected by the dark . . ."

Balthasar and Olivede listened to her light, restless footsteps, a few paces, a *passe-avant*, a few more paces, several advances. "Is it so impossible?" Bal said, half rhetorically. Olivede's confirmation of his observations, and reluctant agreement with his interpretation, had left him shaken.

"Not that I know of," Olivede said. She sat weary and straight-backed in their father's wide leather chair. "I know of no instances of a child born sighted among us. Do you know any of a child born blind among you?"

Floria paused. "I am not a physician," she said—disingenuously, Bal thought, for her profession required a physician's knowledge of injury and poison. "But the prince's physician makes a study of abnormalities and has a record, and blindness is not listed as a congenital defect. We can become blind through trauma or disease."

Bal had one of his grandfather's textbooks open on his lap, along with several of his own that he had already ransacked, and was scanning the perforated pages with his fingers. "From comparing descriptions of anatomy we know Darkborn are all born without the nerves that in Lightborn lead from the eyes to the brain—optic nerve atresia—and with extra bundles along the tracts of the olfactory and laryngeal nerves to conduct nerve impulses required for sonn, and there's altered laryngeal morphology to allow production of the frequencies used for sonn. . . . Infants tend not to cast for the first five or six weeks of life, though they learn to perceive passively from birth."

"So . . ." Olivede said thoughtfully. "It is likely that Imogene's Curse also includes this blessing: that the Lightborn child will not be born with sonn nor the Darkborn with vision. I wonder where in the Curse that is laid out, and I wonder what other patterns of health and illness are embedded in the Curse." She tapped the rim of the glass against her teeth; it *ting*ed softly.

"Olivede," said Floria, "what do you hear of a third race in Imogene's Land, a race of people who can come and go as they will, in light and darkness?"

"Who might have both sight and sonn . . ." Olivede said, picking up her thought. "Very little. Stories, of course. There are the forerunners, our ancestors from before the Curse. And the Outlanders. Those two are scientific fact."

"But the forerunners are gone, and the Curse claims any Outlander who comes within its range," Bal said. "Its range has not changed for centuries; it shows no signs of weakening."

"And there are," Olivede said reluctantly, "the Shadowborn."

That checked him. Shadowborn were the other offspring of the great divisive magic, the grotesque life-forms that emerged from the devastated lands around the mage's last stronghold to maraud in the Borders. Whether they were produced by the Curse itself, or by some corruption in the land and its wildlife resulting from that ancient war, nobody could be certain, and polite society did not speculate. Bal had never encountered a live Shadowborn, and never wished to. Large, preserved specimens made their way from the Borders for public display and spectacle; the smaller, and the more grotesque, came to the Physicians' College and the College of Natural History for study and dissection. He could not imagine that these tiny, healthy infants could be Shadowborn.

"It may be," Floria said, "that there is more to their father's heritage than sight." Her voice had that particular light, careless tone he had learned to distrust. "We could test it," she said. "I have a needle and a lamp. If I were to perforate the wall, it would cast a very fine beam directly onto a small area of skin. We know that that would not be immediately fatal—"

"No!" said Bal. Exposure to such a narrow beam of light might not be fatal, but it caused excruciating burns. Disturbed Darkborn mutilated themselves thus; he had treated several cases. Imprisonment outside in a perforated box was still legal as an execution method, barbarous as it was. The last person so executed had been a mage convicted of sorcerous harm.

"It would settle the matter," Floria said, sounding mildly surprised at his outburst.

"Have you ever come close to the Dark, Lady Floria?" said Olivede. Bal knew the answer; Floria had once been trapped outside at sunset long enough to feel the life start to seep out of her, the substance of her body begin to unbind itself. Dissolution was as painful to the Lightborn as immolation to the Darkborn.

Olivede took Floria's silence as her answer. "I do not know how they treat infants in the Light. But they do not torture them here." The sunset bell began to toll, and she got to her feet. "I must go, and I may not be back tonight. I have work to do among my own patients. I will make arrangements for the children, as you have asked me to do. I will also consult my brother and sister practitioners on the question of the children's sight; that may take a day or so." She smiled a little, ironically, at her allusion to the other mages in the terms of the polite society she had abandoned. "Tercelle will no doubt leave the moment she musters the strength; until then she should feed them—if she will." By her manner she thought not. Balthasar agreed. Tercelle had not once cast sonn over her infants.

When his sister had gone back to her work and Floria to her bed, he went down to the kitchen, where the fire was smoldering in the stove. In their beds beside the warm stove, the newborn twins slept. He sonned them lightly, so as not to wake them. Perhaps, he thought, he should have let Floria try her experiment. He could not know at present that they would grow to manifest sonn. Perhaps the pain and scars of a burn would be a small price to pay to be spared the certainty of a life needlessly spent in darkness and fear of the sun.

What selfish brutes adults are, he thought, leaning close to listen to the feathery breathing beneath the rasp and crackle of the fire. Neither their mother at her pleasure or their father at his had given the least thought to the children that might come of their union. Illegitimacy would have been hardship enough without their mother being the betrothed of Ferdenzil Mycene and their father . . . whatever he was. He wished he dared keep them, to protect them, and devoutly hoped Olivede could find them a kind and flexible-minded guardian.

He drew up a rocking chair beside them, sat down, and in a very few motions was asleep, as exhausted as he had been after his own daughters' births.

He was awakened by Tercelle groping her way around the kitchen. She was wearing another of his mother's nightgowns, and moved hunched over and as though every step hurt. He got quickly to his feet. "Tercelle, you should not be up."

She said sullenly, "I was hungry. I called you. You didn't come."

He apologized and found her a cushion to sit on while he brewed the tea and turned on the gas to grill the toast himself. Her sonn rippled around him, soft and persistent, muddying his impressions; he realized that, sonning him, she need not turn her head toward the cradle.

"What time is it?" he said, disoriented.

"The sunrise bell will be tolling in less than two hours. When will your sister be back?"

"I'm not certain. She said maybe not tonight." He laid down toast, teapot, and tea, and poured some for both of them. In the crib, one of the babies squirmed and smacked its lips. He said diffidently, "They may be hungry."

"They're quiet yet," she said indifferently. "So she will be taking them."

"She'll be making arrangements. As you asked." She had also insisted that she did not want to know where, or have any further contact.

"I need to send a letter," she said, and produced it from her sleeve, a neatly sealed envelope with a neatly punched label, likely written before she even arrived on his doorstep. "If you could get someone to take it before light."

With a suppressed sigh he yielded, got up, turned some coin out of the jar he kept for errand money and fares, picked up the whistle, and went out onto the front steps. There was a message boy loitering with his bicycle at the end of the terrace in hopes of such custom; he hopped aboard and came swift as a swallow to the distinctive sound of Bal's whistle. He read the address to the boy, knowing that he might be illiterate. Bal could not help noticing how very close it was to where Telmaine's family lived, when they were in town, the house he had besieged to win his bride, and when he climbed the stairs it was not steadily; he could not concentrate on the complexities of sonn for missing Telmaine, missing her so intensely it hurt.

"I have sent your letter," he said to Tercelle.

"Good." She smiled at him for the first time. "I have poured some more tea for you. Yours was getting cold."

The tea was stronger than he liked, bitter with tannin and a strange, musty aftertaste; it was probably damp, or older than he thought. He had become too used to having servants take care of these things, in Telmaine's and his household, so in summer he was always finding himself with moldy bread or sprouting potatoes. He added extra honey to disguise the taste, unable to be bothered to get up and make a fresh pot. He had a second cup, which tasted much better, and a thick slice of toast with honey. She sipped fastidiously, despite her discomfort and bedraggled state. The babies seemed to have resettled.

He found that, despite his best efforts, despite his knowledge that this was extremely rude, he was having difficulty remaining awake. His last awareness was of her lifting the cup carefully from his hand and saying, "It's all right, Balthasar. You just sleep now."

Balthasar

The sunrise bell woke him. He struggled up through heavy sleep and an incoherent half dream. Telmaine was on his doorstep, pounding on the door, begging to come in. He was angry; she had stayed too late at the dance, abandoning herself to the frivolities of the life she had supposedly set aside, and so he was going to refuse her and let her burn away. Then suddenly he knew he must go to the door, must let her in, but he could not move. He heard his own slurred cry of anguish. A draft gusted around his ankles.

The last brought him to his feet, staggering. His head swayed from side to side, sonn snarling and fracturing, table and stove and sink and crib all reeling around him. Empty kitchen. Silent crib. He turned toward it, lost his balance, and caught himself with a hand on the crib and a hand on the stove. Pain shocked him sober. He was in the kitchen; he had been there with Tercelle; he had fallen asleep, not willingly, and now the kitchen and crib were empty and the back door open. And the sunrise bell tolled.

By habit, he caught the key from the hook as he stumbled through the door, thudding one shoulder against the lintel with bruising force. She was outside in the high-walled, narrow little garden, arranging bundles on the wide bird table, sweeping it clean with fastidious little motions of her gloved hands. She was fully dressed, even to the cloak she had arrived in, and the cloak swung distractingly, dizzyingly, as she sensed his sonn and turned.

"It's for the best," she said, after a moment.

He swayed on the threshold, key in hand. Then he fumbled behind him, found the handle, and pulled it closed behind him. She started toward him as he jammed the key into the lock, still moving like a drunken man. The burned hand hurt, but he got the key turned, out of the lock, and sheltered behind his back as she threw herself on him.

"Are you mad? Unlock this door." Even in her terror, there was an overtone of imperiousness and incredulity, not so much at the outrageousness of this act, but his impudence. "Can't you feel the sun?"

Not yet, but soon. Soon the pain would begin, and then the agony. The possibility that he would penetrate the greatest of all mysteries in no way stilled the hard beat of his heart. He had thought to have much longer before this to enjoy this life. Nevertheless, he kept his voice level; though his words were slurred, he fought to make them an intelligible slur. "We have time to talk."

"Talk about *what*? I'm only doing what I must!" She tried to lunge around him to grapple the key from his hand. Her weakness was a match for his ataxia; they crashed together against the door, the key still in his possession. He thrust her back with a most ungentlemanly shoulder; she staggered a few paces, half bent over, clutching her abdomen.

He took a deep breath, trying desperately to clear his head. "Think about this," he said, words slopping in his mouth. "You are grown—going to be Duchess Mycene. I am nobody. Would anyone believe . . . *me* if I said those babiesh were yours?"

She sonned him hard, judging his nearness to collapse. "Balthasar, at least open the door and we can talk about this in safety."

"Not," he said, "until you promish—promise."

"If you do not open this door, they'll die too."

"Them, you, me. All together." There was no need to elaborate. She was far more adept at the reckoning of that scandal than he.

"You were always sentimental." He said nothing, but whatever she sonned in his face made her say, tight jawed, "Damn you, I promise. Now give me the key."

There was something wrong with that idea, and though he couldn't work out why, he followed his instincts. "You get'm," he said. "I'll 'nlock door." He leaned against it. She swept her sonn around him, and he had the sense that he could hear her mind working. "Get them," he said, "or I drop d'key down drain." The drain was as close to him as the rocks lining the flower beds were to her. She turned and lurched to the bird table and clumsily gathered up the infants. She had unswaddled them, leaving them naked to the rising sun. That removed any desire he had to laugh at the shambling comedy he made.

As she started back, he twisted the key in the lock and fell across the threshold, knowing he risked having her slam the door in his face if she preceded him. He pulled himself up the edge of the door as she crossed the threshold herself, with a snap of sonn strong enough to stun anything sober, never mind drugged. He threw his weight against the door, slamming it closed, and the key clattered on the floor.

The babies hardly stirred as she dumped them side by side into the crib and turned to face him, one hand on the wall beside the stove to support herself, the other on her abdomen. "How do I know I can trust you?"

"Tha's part of trust," he said, with more bite than he intended. "Not knowing." He wished she were a man; he did not know how to measure that calculating sullenness. If she were a man he would never have had to go to these lengths—but if she were a man she could have overpowered him in the garden and left him to burn with the twins.

He had to keep moving to stay awake. He circled to the side of the cot to sonn the babies. "Gave'm the same thing's me?"

She was still and silent and angry.

"Coulda killed them."

She tossed her head a little. "Would that have mattered?"

He felt nauseated with the effort to remain standing. He might have thwarted her for the moment, but she was still a danger to these, her infants.

"Ferdenzil would strangle me in our marriage bed if he knew," she said in a low voice that trembled.

"That's not right," he said earnestly. "'S'as wrong as killing the children. That's why I promishe—promise. Never say. Never."

"And how will you account for your having them? Have you thought of that?"

"Found on doorshtep. Traditional. Just babies," he said drunkenly. "I had babies."

The tolling of the sunrise bell stopped; they were once more trapped together. She said bitterly, "You're a sentimental fool. Lysander always said you were."

And then she was gone. He could not track sound well enough to know where, but it would not be out the front door, not now. He gathered up the drugged babies. Up the stairs to the study, opening and closing his burned hand on the swaddling so that he felt as if he were gripping barbed wire. Keep him awake. Where was she? Had she given up? No more than he. This was the most perilous part of it. He must leave the door behind him as he crossed the room to lay them down on the chair, side by side. Then back across the vast empty plain of room to swing the door, to turn the key in the lock. On the far side of the paper wall, he could hear Floria at her morning exercises, the soft whispering shuffle of footwork. He fell halfway to the wall. Had a drugged nightmare of falling against the wall, falling through the wall, falling burning into her presence. "F'oria."

Silence. "Bal? Balthasar? What's wrong with you?"

He crawled toward the wall, toward the *passe-muraille*, mumbling his story and fighting the heaving in his stomach, which occurred in countertime to the heaving of the floor. "Hel' me, Floria."

She rapped hard on the wood of the cabinet. "Bal, don't fall asleep! Keep talking to me. Musty, you said, and in tea. Mother of All Things Born, I wish I had a sample."

"Washed up," he said, with an inordinate sense of pleasure at a word he could slop all over. "Washed all up," he repeated. "Shh, shh."

"No, don't shh," she said. "Keep talking," and this time he heard her footsteps recede. He leaned against the corner, hand against the paper wall, imagining he could feel the burning light on the other side. It was not dreadful, but warm as firelight.

"Balthasar!"

He lurched awake, a vile sensation. "Yes."

"I've made up a stimulant. It's in the cabinet. Drink it."

He fumbled the glass two handed from the recess, and explored getting it to a mouth that seemed to belong to an unrelated body.

Finding it at his mouth, he groped it between his lips, drank. "Nishe taste."

"I studied the blending of tastes from a master chef. Comes in useful." She let a brief silence elapse. "Keep talking to me. You should feel an effect very shortly."

Already a jagged clarity was growing in him. His sonn refocused, he crawled over to the babies and with one clumsy hand tucked their blankets around them. By the time he had finished doing that, the clumsiness was gone; his hand moved in sharp jerks and trembled when it was still. His other hand he held against his chest, curled; as her antidote stripped away the stupor from his mind, it stripped away all muffling of the burn.

"What about the babies?" he said.

He heard her breathe out in relief at the change in his diction. "You can't give them anything while they're drugged. Think about it, Bal. They could breathe it in." He thought about it. "All you can do is keep stimulating them, make sure they don't go so deep they stop breathing. I'm sure you know better than I do."

"Floria, thank you," he said, though he shivered at intervals.

"You should let me take care of this woman."

He went still; his thoughts snapped and flew apart. He couldn't even find the word *no*.

"No one has ever fed you poison before," she answered his silence. "I don't know what is going on here, and I don't like it."

"And rather than find out . . ."

"I never tried to hide what I am," she said. "A dangerous friend, and a deadly enemy." There was an unsettling amusement in her voice. "I value your friendship enough to let myself be bound by your morality in this."

Shaking with fine tremors, he studied the twins for a moment, and then picked up the one whose breathing was weakest, wincing at the pain in his hand. He settled the limp infant on his shoulder and began to rub its back. He felt frighteningly fey, ready with hysterical laughter or murderous rage at the twist of a thought. "Floria," he breathed. "What is this you've given me?"

"Something the Prince's Vigilance uses to keep us alert and give us a fighting edge," she said, and his heightened senses heard undertone and meaning to the undertone even before she said, "In case you needed it."

A shudder went through him at that, at the realization of what he might do if danger threatened him, under the influence of this drug, and with the realization that Floria well knew this.

"Bal, are there any weapons in the house? Any pistols, rifles, crossbows, longbows, daggers—"

"No!" he said.

"There are other things that can be used as weapons," she said steadily. "You may need to think about defending yourself."

He tried to read, but his concentration was gone, his thoughts uncontrollable and all spiraling down into violence. Sometime in that interminable day, he heard the door handle turn. His heightened hearing was almost as acute as sonn. On his shoulder, a baby slept, walnut-size fist jammed against its ear, breath barely tickling Bal's skin. There was a moment's silence, and then he heard something softly probe the lock. He laid the baby down on the chair, silently, and slid down to a crouch in the middle of the floor. His lips drew back from his teeth in a snarl. His sonn swept the room, hunting. He found what he knew was there: the smooth-handled letter opener Telmaine disliked for its length, its sharpness, its danger to the children, the fact that it had been Floria's gift to him. He crept up to the desk and drew it out, fitting it into his hand with no sense of incongruity or clumsiness, and listening to the scratching at the lock. He did not have the experience to know whether it was expert or not, whether it represented a true threat or simply a last attempt to overcome an obstacle. It did not matter. He had a knife in his hand and an anatomist's knowledge. He would use them both.

"Tercelle!" he cried sharply, in warning.

The probing stopped. No voice called from the other side of the door. He envisioned her standing there in her velvets, with . . . what in her hands—a hairpin or a hat pin, perhaps, but what else? A knife? More poison?

It was a long time before he could trust himself to lay down the knife and lift the baby. A very long time.

Two

Telmaine

Lady Anarysinde Stott perched on her sister's bed to observe the last of her toilette. "Why *must* you wear those long gloves, Tellie? They're *so* unfashionable."

Telmaine Hearne smoothed the silk of her gloves, which reached almost to her shoulders, and groped on her dressing table for a buttonhook. She could not imagine how she could have brought so many bottles and baubles for four days' stay, even one at the archducal summer palace, even for an occasion when everyone who counted in society would be attending. Two months away from her frugal, tidy Balthasar had produced a sad backsliding.

"Bal says that what becomes a beautiful woman is always in fashion," she told Anarys, retrieving the hook at last. She used it to fasten the last of the pearl buttons and settled the full sleeves over the cuffs of the gloves, ran her fingertips along the lace of the neck, higher than fashion now permitted. She turned to her sister, shaking out and spreading her full skirts. The gown was new, expensive—dear Bal would never know how expensive!—and in the splendid height of fashion. "What do you think?"

Her sister's sonn pinged off her. "You're beautiful, and you always will be." Anarys sighed.

Telmaine rustled over to kiss her lightly on the cheek. She remembered being sixteen, the sheer interminableness of the year before she was presented to society, before she could veil her head as a grown woman, before she could be courted—and poor Anarys seemed to be a late bloomer, still flat chested and growing out of her clothes. The gown that so became Telmaine would have hung on her like a sack.

"Give yourself time, my dear. It will come."

She straightened up with the certainty that Anarys planned to creep downstairs later, before the sunrise bell, when wits were beginning to blur with fatigue and wine, and when the sonn of matrons and chaperones was wearied. She suppressed a sigh, balancing duty against discretion. "You be careful, Any-any," she said, tilting up her sister's chin with her gloved finger. "Have your fun, but remember that reputations are very easy to lose, and very hard to regain, and not all young men can be trusted."

Anarys sulked. "How do you *know* these things? You weren't perfect, either. You met Balthasar in secret."

"I was lucky," she said. After all, it *was* luck that Bal's friends had chosen that particular summer night to scramble over the garden wall of her family's city home and join, uninvited, the masquerade held for her seventeenth birthday. "I was lucky that he really is as special as I thought he was when I met him."

Her sister tucked her knees up beneath her, kneeling in a billow of skirts. "Did he really come to your party dressed as a Lightborn?"

"Oh, yes." Remembering that extraordinary figure by the bookshelf, a slight young man in a densely embroidered tunic and woven hose that, but for the length of the tunic, would have been indecent; odd, narrow, ornate shoes; and a huge, wonderfully absurd hat with a bedraggled plume. "I couldn't decide whether he was lurking by the bookcase because he knew how out of place he seemed, or because he was shy. Of course, now I know the attraction was the books."

"And you asked him to dance." Anarys sighed.

"Yes," said Telmaine a little wryly. Her mother and aunts had garrisoned her with a veritable regiment of suitable suitors. Of these, a couple frightened her; some merely bored her; the rest did and would stifle her. So when the musicians started to play the first of the traditional three ladies'-choice dances, she had bolted to the oddity standing by the bookshelves.

"I scared the life out of him, too," she said, smiling.

When he took her hand uncertainly in his to guide it to his shoulder, according to the new—shocking, to her mama—style, his hand was trembling. She had smiled reassuringly at him and placed his hand, quite deliberately letting it brush the bare skin of her shoulder. He started to apologize, and then she pulled him onto the dance floor, understanding for the first time the girls who flaunted their young men like prizes won. She had touched the sweetest, brightest mind she had ever sensed, and she had found the man she would marry, whether he was duke, servant, musician, or mage.

Anarys sighed again.

"Just you be careful," Telmaine said. "Remember the things I've told you about. They don't just happen in the demimonde. They happen among people like us."

Anarys pouted. "Mama would *swoon* if she knew what you'd told me."

"Mama," Telmaine said, "is a dear woman, and very sheltered. She cannot tell real dangers from minor social inconveniences." She felt a little guilty saying that; her mother did not have her insight into men's intentions. "I've told you things I think every young girl should know."

"They're not *nice*."

Telmaine settled her veil on her head, securing it with pins and folding it carefully back from her ears, as today's liberal custom allowed. Bal would not have it any other way. "It is the way things are."

There was a crisp rap on the door, and their elder sister bustled in without waiting for permission. Merivan was a tall, perpetually discontented woman of thirty-one who sought an outlet for her abundant energies in childbearing; after six children, she was again with child, though not yet so conspicuously as to have to retire from society.

"Good evening, Merivan," Telmaine said pleasantly. "I trust your digestion has settled?"

Merivan raised a hand. Telmaine braced herself for one of Merivan's pat-slaps, but all her sister did was reach up and tug Telmaine's veil forward. "You sonn like a demimondaine in that dress," Merivan said sharply, while Telmaine sensed her usual mixture of envy and censoriousness through the brush of fingertips. "And your conversation is vulgar."

"I am twice a mother myself, Merivan," Telmaine said peaceably. "I know the way of it."

"And these absurd gloves of yours. Really, Telmaine, if your husband is so expert with disorders of thought, why can he not do something about your phobia about diseases?"

Telmaine's teeth set, but she kept her tone light. "Because it troubles neither myself nor him if I wear unfashionable gloves, and our family has always enjoyed excellent health, perhaps because I *am* so careful."

"I cannot understand how you can tolerate him working in that *clinic.* Surely he's in contact with all kinds of disease."

She suffered Merivan to take her arm and steer her from the room, where her sister promptly revealed her real intent. "What have you been saying to Anarys? Some of the things her maid overheard, I scarcely credit."

"She needs to know these things. There are men even in society who will take advantage of innocent girls."

"Oh, Telmaine. You have gone coarse. This is precisely what we feared would happen when you married that—"

Telmaine jerked her arm away. Merivan could say whatever she pleased about Telmaine, but she would not criticize Bal. "I am going to say good night to my little ones."

"You spoil them," Merivan complained. "You should have more; then you would not cling—" She stopped, stifled a burp, and pressed her hand to her stomach.

Telmaine pitied her. Merivan had a fine mind; she could argue Balthasar to a standstill on the need for social rules, conventions, the stifling of individual urges for the common good. As Balthasar said, she had sacrificed herself to her ideals, denied herself any intellectual outlet but marriage, childbearing, and the cultivation of her children's minds and morals. She did not cling to her offspring; she marshaled them like a diminutive army in training.

"Meri," she said mildly but firmly. "Bal and I will raise our children in our own way."

When she entered the nursery, her daughters scrambled away from the muddle of little ones in the ornate playhouse and scampered to her. Six-year-old Florilinde chattered in one ear about the horseless carriages that some of the guests had arrived in—she was fascinated by all things mechanical—and five-year-old Amerdale babbled in the other ear about the birds in the aviary. Telmaine kept one arm loosely around each supple, squirming child while they clutched at her with their little hands, and with each touch on skin, their thoughts ran like clear streams through her mind. Amerdale's were like Balthasar's, open, endlessly curious. Florilinde's were muddied by traces of jealousy, like puffs of mud cast up from the river bottom.

The only time Telmaine had said to her nurse that she knew what people were thinking when she touched them, she had been reduced to tears by the woman's dismay, horror, and fear. Those had made a far more indelible impression on her than Nurse's shocked, "Please, Lady Telmaine, don't *ever* say something like that. It's not proper. It's . . . *magic*." Magic, she had understood even at Amerdale's age, was wicked. Magic was what had happened eight hundred years ago, when the Darkborn were made unable to live in sunlight. Magic was what happened in the part of the city where girls like her did not go. Magic was what the Lightborn did on the other side of sunrise. Later, from an ill-punched pamphlet of her brother's called "Profane and Ekstatic Magiks"—which she had no business reading or he having—she had learned what she was: a touch-reader, as even the least powerful mageborn were, and learned what men thought a touch-reader could do. And later than that, she had realized that most men thought any woman should be a touch-reader, able to know and satisfy their every whim before they uttered it.

That had embittered her, once. Now it only saddened her. No wonder men held it as an ideal—women too, in their way. They were all so locked up in the prisons of their own thoughts, doomed never to know one another's truths. And at the same time, they were terrified of having their secrets known and revealed, so terrified that magic must be denigrated, denounced, enclosed within the demimonde. Above all, it must never, ever enter the receiving rooms and dance halls of society. Even at five years old, she had understood that no one must know about her.

But magic had its compensations. She need never mistake anyone's intentions, never fear their deceit. She could make the most important decision of a woman's life with confidence, and enter marriage secure that she had chosen well.

She answered her daughters' excited questions about the ball, her dress, whether the archduke would be there, whether she would dance all night, impressions formed by a mélange of nursemaids' gossip and the romantic stories told little girls. She cuddled and kissed them and told them to be good and do what the nursemaids told them to. This she particularly directed to Florilinde, who was beginning to understand the social order and explore what she was and was not allowed to do to the nursemaids. Then she left them, waving over her shoulder, and set her gloves to rights, smoothing them all the way up onto her shoulders. Despite Merivan's accusations, her gown was perfectly decent: high necked, the bodice closed, the least possible skin exposed to a chance touch. But it was in the new, lighter style, not so many layers of cloth, less exhausting to wear. In polite company, it was more than sufficient for modesty, even without the dense lace of her undergarments.

Now, Lady Telmaine Stott Hearne thought and, smiling—for herself, not for anyone observing—started down the stairs. Though she did not, and could not, live this life forever, she enjoyed her summers, and she was glad her father had extracted this promise from Balthasar, that she would spend summers among her family.

Her father had taken his time to make up his mind on Bal's suit. Bal proved to be neither duke, servant, musician, or mage; he was a young physician-in-training, of old though impoverished and eccentric family, and descended from the archducal line itself through a succession of daughters and younger sons. Of his family, he was the respectable one. His sister had not only trained as a physician herself, but was an acknowledged mage. His older brother had vanished years ago; society had largely forgotten him, and Bal never spoke of him, though he thought of him, and Telmaine knew more of Lysander Hearne than she ever wanted to. Bal's principal blemish, as far as society was concerned, was his relationship with the woman behind the paper wall, Floria White Hand, spymistress and assassin to the Lightborn princes, and his involvement in the council that mediated affairs between the two peoples. Society much preferred that the Lightborn, with their violent customs, shocking mores, and cultivated mages, did not exist. For all his personal virtues, Bal certainly wasn't the safe, aristocratic husband that her family wanted for their daughter.

Her mother and brother objected, wheedled, and dangled inducements. It turned out to be surprisingly easy to defy them, in one respect, for if she would not say, "I do," then they could not make her marry. She could not but know that her mother truly desired that she marry happily in addition to well. Her brother was not much concerned with her happiness; she was a woman and her happiness was irrelevant, as was his own. He was insecure, terrified of his own inadequacy as lord and heir, and thus desperate to gather around him all the proper relationships, friends, behaviors. She pitied him, but she would not let him trap her.

She neared twenty-one, unmarried. She watched her friends blossoming, even the ones whose marriages were compromises, or surrender, or—she could not but know—mistakes. Time only firmed her resolve that hers would be none of those. In the third year, her father suddenly gave his permission, and it was her turn to blossom, and then discover that marriage was far more complex and satisfying than the novels said. A month after her wedding, his secretary found her father dead in his study. An aneurysm, one that the doctors had told him could rupture at any time. His permission was his last gift to her.

She floated down the stairs, luxuriating in the familiarity of the sounds of music and many voices blending together, sounds that for her entire life had meant anticipation, excitement, and romance. Even more so now that marriage and motherhood had liberated her from the marriage stakes, and now that as a woman married to no one in particular, she need not engage in the political intrigues of the high families that aligned themselves around the four major dukedoms. She need not speculate how far Ferdenzil Mycene's territorial ambitions might extend beyond the Scallon Isles, or that the Duke of Zegravia also had designs on the isles but was being thwarted in their advance. She need not listen to whispers about the archduke's younger half brother and spymaster, Vladimer, and whom he might now be investigating. She need simply enjoy herself.

The sudden cascade of sweet metallic chiming startled her. She cast her sonn over the display automaton standing in the center of the great hall. As the Darkborn repudiated magic, they had embraced technology as a replacement. Boys of the aristocracy studied engineering and mathematics at the ducal schools, and the cleverest young men continued their studies at the university. Fashionable salons discussed the latest developments, and progressive girls' schools and governesses argued for women's right to study these marvels. A mechanistic art was all the fashion, moving sculptures artistically arranged to challenge the mind with the complexity and fineness of the machinery and please sonn and ear with the frequencies. Telmaine privately found the art tiresome; she'd rather hear living musicians, and she had no interest in studying a piece exhaustively to appreciate how neatly each minute cog fit into each minute wheel.

She did not notice the man standing half behind the structure, still amongst all the shimmer of interference and small rippling movements. Feeling the brush of her sonn, he stepped clear of the automaton, and his sonn swept over her more forcefully than was polite. She felt her skin heat at the sense of exposure, and hoped that none of her family was nearby. Since her marriage, they did not trust her to remember her station and properly remind others of it; they would feel obliged to make a fuss that would embarrass her more than this boor.

The boor was not a tall man, and appeared all the more squat for being so broad in the shoulder and long in the body, though his plain dress jacket was well tailored. The shirt and trousers underneath were equally, almost defiantly, plain. He was not young and life had not been kind to him. Two parallel scars ran from the side of his mouth to his chin, real, untidy scars, not the duelist's marks affected by a certain set among the young men. The deeper of the two pulled his mouth slightly awry. His nose was upturned, the nostrils wide, rippling a little as she approached. Her mouth set. She had encountered that gesture among the women-peddlers in the demimonde, a vulgar, demeaning insult to virtuous women.

She stopped before him. "Your sonn, sir, needs be muted."

The challenge startled him, but his voice was deep, soft, and courteous, and he dipped his head. "I am sorry, m'lady. I . . . I am too used t'rougher and more dangerous places."

It was a more civil response than she had expected. His accent was Borders, mitigated, she thought, by travel. "May I have your name, sir?"

"So you may set your husband on me?" he said dryly, then, in a conciliatory tone, "I am Baron Strumheller. Ishmael di Studier."

She caught her breath despite herself; this was not merely one of the formidable border barons, who held the fringes of the civilized lands against the Shadowborn, but the most notorious of them all, the celebrated Shadowhunter. Ishmael di Studier had made his name—and, she presumed, collected those scars—killing monsters. He'd only lately begun moving in society circles, and then seldom.

"I expect," she said, recovering her poise, "that usually ends any conversation."

He stepped back and bowed in the old courtly fashion, hand to heart. "I hope not, m'lady," he said formally. "I do apologize if I have offended you. Might I know your name?"

She hardly heard that for realizing that the hand he held to his heart was gloved, a long glove like a falconer's. It was not the fashion for men to wear gloves indoors, any more than it was the fashion, just now, for ladies to do so. She remembered one of the reasons for his notoriety: People said Ishmael di Studier was a mage.

She pushed down her alarm, saying briskly, "I am Lady Telmaine Stott Hearne, sir. Wife to Dr. Balthasar Hearne."

He bowed again, hand at his side. "M'lady Telmaine. I know something of your husband. We have a mutual acquaintance in the Lightborn Mistress Floria White Hand."

"Like draws like," she said tartly. It was irrational to be jealous of a woman one's husband could never touch and barely sonn, but there it was.

"I will take that as a compliment," he said. "The Lady Floria is said to be a fine swordswoman—she would be a fine swords*man*, if she were male."

"It must be an agreeable sensation," Telmaine returned, "to be able to decide what you will take as a compliment, and what you will take otherwise. To trust so in one's competence."

"M'lady, y'need no special competence for that. You need only character. Competence only means that you do't with more or less safety. Setting aside safety, then you may take or reject compliments as you please."

Somehow this reminded her of meeting Bal for the first time. Not that they said the same thing, the shy scholar and this Shadow-hunting baron, but that they said the unexpected thing, and neither could be readily provoked.

The automaton commanded their attention with a jubilation of arpeggios. The baron sonned it and snorted softly, unimpressed. That raised him a little in her estimation. Then he returned his attention to her and set his heels together, dipping his head. "Pleased t'have met you, Lady Telmaine. Mayhap I might hope t'dance with you later this evening."

And he left without waiting for her answer. She did not sonn after him, but still the echoes of others' overlapping sonn built a suggestion of easy, powerful movement. She sensed she had been rebuked, though she was not sure for what.

A dress rustled behind her. "Telmaine!" She turned and sonned a young woman clinging to the banister, mouth wide, lacy veil slightly askew. "You can't *possibly* dance with him. Have a care for your reputation!"

"Sylvide!" The woman slithered down the steps and rushed into Telmaine's mannerly embrace "like two roses kissing in the wind," as her deportment mistress, an aspiring poet, had styled it. "Dearest Sylvide, how long have you been back?" Sylvide's husband had been sent as envoy to the contested Scallon Isles five years ago.

"A month ago, and then we all came down with this dreadful

feverish cold, and the baby—you know we were blessed again, six months ago?—the baby was so sick, and we've all been so low. Dansin still has such a terrible cough. . . . If this is the summer, I *shudder* to think of what the winter will be like: I've become so used to the *warmth*. But how are you? The last time I visited you, before we left for the isles, you were at home."

"Five years ago," Telmaine agreed. "Just before I was blessed with Amerdale. She's five, and a delight. They both are."

"And where is that quietly fascinating husband of yours?"

"Up in the city," Telmaine said, with a trill of laughter. Sylvide, feather-wit though she might seem, had the redeeming virtue that alone of all Telmaine's friends she had wholeheartedly approved of Bal from the moment they met. Sweetness recognized sweetness. "Father made me promise that I would join the family for three months of the year. Bal and I came together until I was blessed with Flori, but Bal was miserable. He has no frivolity in him, and my family behaved im*poss*ibly. So now we all come down for a little while, just long enough to dispel any gossip"—or hopes of an estrangement—"then Bal goes back to the city and I stay. I dance my shoes to tatters, stay up all day if I please, and sleep half the night away, and have all the indulgences my frivolous heart desires. He lives in his parents' old house and immerses himself in his scholarship, gets up before sunset, eats whenever and whatever pleases him, spends nights *and* days up at the Physicians' College debating microbes and the unconscious mind and all the latest passions in his profession." She need not mention Floria White Hand, or the clinic in the demimonde. "And when we go back to the city it's like being newlyweds again. And how is *your* husband? Is he glad to be back? Is he getting a better position?"

She caught, with her sonn, the creasing of Sylvide's brow. "You have not heard?" her friend said in a low voice. "He was forced to resign: Ferdenzil Mycene wanted his own man in. If Dani had not gone willingly, he would have found himself in some kind of disgrace. His uncle is furious at him." Dani's uncle and patron was a younger son of the Duke of Zegravia, an ambitious man who used up his tools and blamed them for their failings, in influence no match for the son of the Duke of Mycene, rival to the archduke, and his ambitious son.

She said, "But you don't want for a living—"

Sylvide tossed her head. "Oh, we don't want for a living. We could be gloriously idle all our days—but that's not what Dani wants."

Telmaine said, "I will speak to my brother. He has the Duke of Imbre's ear." Imbre had no love for Mycene, and did not approve of Mycene's expansionism, and she thought he would help a victim of Mycene's ambition. But she did not say so. Dani had all the prickliness of a man whose aspirations exceeded his abilities, so let him think he had been helped out of merit, and not because he was wronged. "But I'm going up to the city in two days' time. When will you be coming?"

Sylvide grimaced again. "If we came up to the city, we should stay with Dani's family, and his mother would find some way to blame me for his losing his post."

"If you came up to the city, you should stay with us. We have plenty of room, *and* Bal would surely persuade Dani to write a monograph about the islands, which would keep him from fretting and would help his career. We might hear nothing of the men for days on end, but we have ever so many ways to amuse ourselves."

Sylvide smiled. "Dear Telmaine, what a good idea. I shall put it to Dani. He likes Bal. And you, of course."

And I will not let him try my temper, Telmaine resolved. Dani was easy around Bal not only because Bal was adept in making him so, but because he found nothing to envy in Bal's ancient, extinguished lineage. He was not easy around Telmaine, not only because she was richer and more highly born, but—and this was much less forgivable—because she had married beneath her station. She represented an unwelcome possibility: that of social descent. Why Sylvide should choose to wrap her cottony good nature around the spiny climbing vine that was her husband, Telmaine did not know. Except, as Sylvide had more than once insisted, Dani needed her.

"You know Ferdenzil's betrothed, don't you?" Sylvide said. "Tercelle Amberley, of the armaments and shipbuilding Amberleys. She used to keep company with your Balthasar's brother, or so people said."

"I've met her, but I've never met Lysander Hearne," Telmaine said, to close any further discussion of him. If this were an opera, and she one of those turbulent heroines, when she met Lysander Hearne it would be with a loaded pistol for the wrongs he had done her gentle husband. But she was not, and she hoped Bal's brother would never return from his exile.

Sylvide wrinkled her dainty nose. "Nasty little nouveau riche. She and Ferdenzil deserve each other. But it's *tragic* to think what he'll be able to do in the isles with access to her family's money and factories. They'll build ships and arm them for him."

"But surely," Telmaine said, "putting down the piracy is a good thing."

Sylvide leaned close to her. "Tellie, putting down the piracy is an *excuse.* I won't say it doesn't happen, but the dukes of the isles are well aware of the effect it has on trade and shipping, and it's in their interest not to let it get out of control. Ferdenzil and his father *want* the isles—not just the Scallon Isles, all the little island dukedoms.

They'll swallow them up one by one. And then they'll swallow up the archdukedom."

Politics was the last infection Telmaine had expected Sylvide to contract. She shrugged her shoulders under her elegant gown. "And what can we women do about any of it?" she said lightly. "Damaris notwithstanding, we have no say." Lady Damaris, only daughter of a minor duke, was campaigning for women to have the same inheritance and political rights as their brothers. Telmaine couldn't think of anything more tedious; she knew how his work in the Intercalatory Council wore on her Bal, and stole time and energy from the medicine and scholarship he loved. She was glad she need have no part of it.

"Come into the ballroom," she said, and turned her friend toward the door into the ballroom. "You won't have danced any of the new waltzes. Mind you, they won't be the very newest; those are considered too shocking for the archducal residence. I'm told the chaperones carry canes with rulers on the end, and they push these between the dancers to make them move to a proper distance. . . ."

Ishmael

Ishmael de Studier, Baron Strumheller, leaned his back against one of the carved columns along the side of the ballroom and settled into stillness, observing his surroundings without sonn. It was a hunter's skill, to perceive without offering others the chance to perceive one in turn. Though he was more accustomed, he thought wryly, to doing this in the open air, and interpreting the subtle intelligence of nature: whispering leaves and grasses, rustling small animals, and stray odors carried on the wind.

There was no subtlety here. Music from the small orchestra

bounded from the raised half balcony to reverberate beneath the domed ceiling. Dresses swished and rustled; shoes clicked and squeaked on the wood inlay and tile of the floor; glasses clinked on glass tables and silver trays. Men's and women's voices lapped against one another, and bright female laughter chimed with a sweetness as cultivated as the scents that wafted in from the garden. The air was thick with the colognes worn by women and men alike, the aromas of wine and spices that lingered on breath and hands, and the odor of bodies in joyous or frantic exertion. The revelers battered one another with sonn, desperate to resolve the last detail of fashion on those around them, the least hint of straying interest from those with them. The dance floor was a stirred miasma of interlaced echoes in which he might briefly perceive the sweep of a woman's dress, or the turning line of a man's flank and leg, before each was folded again into the acoustic shambles. Around the edges of the dance floor, the watchers cast out brilliant bursts of sonn at the dancers and one another. Young girls or young women too shy, plain, or overchaperoned to make desirable partners. Young matrons enjoying the last of society before their latest pregnancies confined them. Older matrons whose pleasures had given way to the satisfaction of judging others' pleasure. Among the men there were those too clumsy, corpulent, or timid to dance, or doomed instead to dance attendance on the whims of a wife or aunt. And, of course, those awaiting their moment.

He smiled a little, and admitted to himself that he was loitering here in part in expectation of summons and in part because he knew that Lady Telmaine was out there, somewhere. He was waiting to learn the bare sketch of her shape, as he would any rare creature that had caught his attention. But what he would do then, he did not know. Most of the rare creatures whose shape and habits he learned he then hunted to kill. And he could hardly walk up to her and say, "By the way, my lady, do you read people's thoughts when you touch your skin to theirs?" could he? The question would cause a social outrage more profound than if he had asked her how she preferred her husband to make love to her. He could only interpret the unspoken messages of her appearance. The unfashionable gloves that rode snugly up to her shoulders. The gown, high necked but entirely lacking the encrusting of embroidery and gems that a woman especially concerned for her modesty would adopt. And a vibrant social confidence perceptible even at a distance, that might be merely the glow of a happy matron, but might be something else, the surety of a mage to whom no secrets were hidden.

He knew other mages, most of them men and women who, wherever they had started out, had come to inhabit the demimonde with the other useful pariahs from polite society. Many were more powerful than he, able to transform their own and others' vitality to greater effect, but others were like himself, with only enough ability to ensure their estrangement from society. He had never met a mage who maintained a comfortable position in high society. He had never known such a thing was possible. His own father had certainly not believed it so, when he cast out his sixteen-year-old son to live or die by his own wits.

Far more likely, his impression of her was a fantasy born of his own loneliness.

Ish felt a light brush of sonn, smelled a trace of a particular spicy cologne worn by no one else in the room, and turned his head in the direction of the man who had just reached his side. He did not need sonn to recognize him, not with that cologne clinging to him. The man bowed and murmured, "He will receive you now."

Ish trailed behind the aide, weaving through the decorative columns and the other wallflowers. Sonn brushed him peripherally, curiously; out of habit, he remained alert for threat. None came. An ornamental column adjacent to the arch of the door made a small awkward space, cramped for one, never mind two. His escort slid a key into the lock of the small door in the wall and opened it inward. Ishmael followed him through, closing the door firmly behind him and ensuring that the lock slid home. Back against the wall, he eased along the narrow corridor to pass through another door of its ilk, between two bookshelves.

In the center of the room, the archduke's half brother lifted his head from a game board he was contemplating and sonned him. "Thank you, Pasquale. Ishmael, do come and appreciate this."

Ish sonned the array of carved counters. There were two different sets of patterns, and two different faces. Intricate rules guided the allowable juxtapositions. He knew enough to know that here was a game well under way. Otherwise nothing. He was no game player. Perhaps because, as one of is few friends had remarked, if he could not sonn the pulse of a carotid artery, he did not find it a challenge.

"Here," said his host and preceptor, leaning forward and turning one counter so that the complementary symbol was uppermost. Ishmael silently pointed out the other four that would be affected. "Ah, but then . . ." Vladimer leaned forward, and his long, bony fingers flicked a spreading wave of counters all the way to the periphery. "And now . . ." He reversed a single counter and traced the wave's collapse. "I have not found any other combination that allows so drastic a change in fortunes." He lifted his head, frowning. "You appreciate that, don't you?"

"Now you've shown me, aye."

Vladimer brushed him with a light sonn, with head tilted as he weighed this answer. "Ah, well, even so. Will you have something to drink?"

"Watered wine, my lord, thank you." A man might try to match drink-softened wits with the archduke's spymaster, but a wise man did not try to do so twice, and a fool would not be granted a third chance.

Vladimer moved out from behind the table, leaning on his cane. To this day, Ishmael had no idea whether his need for it was real, habitual, or affected. Vladimer had suffered a near-fatal carriage accident at the age of nineteen—one Ishmael well knew to have been no accident—and since then he had lived in retirement, at least as far as society was concerned. In reality, he maintained a vast and diverse network of contacts that included everyone from border barons to former labor agitators, from high-class madams to public agents. Like his elder half brother, the archduke, Vladimer had inherited their mother's ascetic bony face, with its broad forehead, wide cheekbones, and hollow cheeks, which was as deceptive of his nature as it had been of hers. The archduchess had been notable for her luxuriousness, her gambling, her political intrigues, and her many lovers, both as matron and widow. Nonetheless, her husband, no fool himself, had loved her for some of those things and tolerated the rest. She had had the discretion, at least, to bear her illegitimate son a full two years after her husband's death. Rumor had it that his father was the young, unmarried Duke of Mycene, who would later father Ferdenzil; if so, neither family had acknowledged it. Her son Vladimer had her skill at gambling and delight in intrigue, but as far as anyone could tell, he took neither women nor men to his bed.

Vladimer eased himself down into a chair and gestured for Ish to sit. They waited until Pasquale served the wine. "So," Vladimer said amiably, "it would seem that the settled life is finally starting to agree with you. You've lost that gaunt and witchy aspect you had when we first met. And your tailoring's better. You may still be shaped like an ape, but at least it's a well-dressed ape."

Since Vladimer had taken a hand in that, as in many other things to do with Ish's acceptance into Minhorne society, Ish merely said, "Glad y'approve, my lord."

Vladimer leaned back. "I do approve; I know the hold that the Shadowlands exert on a man." There was a brief silence, though Ish waited in readiness for what would come next. Vladimer was not above probing deep, though the impersonal *a man* rather than the personal *you* suggested he would not just then.

Vladimer steepled his fingers. He was plainly in a mischievous mood. "So, how goes your search for a bride and mother of your heirs? Be advised that my lovely cousin Telmaine is known to be a faithful wife. Though I'll allow you'll need a wife with character."

So, his encounter with Lady Telmaine had already come to Vladimer's attention. The man was uncanny. He would worry more for Lady Telmaine's sake—if his suspicion that the lady was a mage were correct and not merely the self-delusion of a lonely man—since Vladimer well knew why Ish wore gloves in social gatherings, had Vladimer not been a man who discounted women. As much regard as he had for the archduke's spymaster, Ish very much wanted to be there when some lady of intelligence and character taught Vladimer his error.

"You should dance with her," Vladimer suggested. "Since her husband is not here, I give you my permission, as her male cousin. It might encourage some of the matrons with eligible daughters to come sniffing about. Assuming you do not have some baronial blossom already in mind."

Ish did not know whether to be unerved or pleased. Vladimer—

childless as he himself was—had taken to making pointed comments on Ish's need to marry and ensure his own line rather than leaving the barony to his younger brother. But Lady Telmaine was already married, and Ish knew of no reason why Vladimer should intend mischief toward her, her husband, or, for that matter, Ish himself. Perhaps it was not merely the spiced cologne that was making his head ache.

"I take't," he said bluntly, "you've not summoned me t'Minhorne just to show how well I walk on my hind legs?"

Vladimer's face showed brief amusement. "No, Shadowhunter," he said quietly. "It was to hear your impression of this last summer in the Borders."

There was that title again. It made Ish uneasy, as it had been several years since he had ceased, by his reckoning, to be a Shadowhunter. It was work that had a natural term, and he had been lucky to survive that term. "Quiet," he answered the implied question. "Some herd animals slaughtered, but no people killed outright. Seven people gone, though. All said t'have acted strangely beforehand."

He left unstated his conclusion: that they had been afflicted by the Call to the Shadowlands. Vladimer, to his relief, did not ask him for details.

"And as far as you know, has there ever been a year so quiet?"

"No," Ish said.

If there were another one, he allowed privately, he would go quite mad. He had spent half the summer pacing the halls of his manor house, expecting at any hour a desperate messenger on a blown horse. The other half he had spent on the road. Between visits to his neighbors to review and advise on their preparations, and the long patrols of the villages of his own lands, he must have dragged his guard troop half the length of the entire borders, expecting disaster around every bend. His men had enjoyed their heroes' welcome and the hospitality of villagers in the midst of a fruitful and tranquil summer. He himself had enjoyed the company of a manservant with orders to subdue him by force if he took one step closer to the Shadowlands than he must. If Vladimer thought he seemed less gaunt and witchy now, he must have been in a pitiful state before.

But then, a few years ago he would have taken manacles and chains with him on the hill patrols, so loud was the Call of the Shadowlands on him.

"Ishmael," said Vladimer, sounding dryly amused, "any other one of my brother's lords or barons would have been trumpeting their achievement in pacifying the Shadowlands."

"They'd be wrong," Ish said flatly. For eight hundred years the Shadowborn had raided the Borders and, at times of great unrest, beyond, and nothing that the Darkborn had done had contained them within their own lands. Shadowborn spilled over the borders, hunted, killed, and were killed.

Vladimer smiled thinly. "My sentiment exactly, though do not discount your work in building the Borders' defenses and warning systems. They've not been this strong for two centuries, and I'm glad of it. As the expert on the Shadowborn, why do you think it has been so quiet?"

"Been wondering that myself. Wondering if the Lightborn had done anything."

"You would have sensed anything magical, would you not?"

"My lord," Ish said uncomfortably, "m'magic's nothing, set against some of the Lightborn." Once Vladimer had been convinced that Ishmael would not trespass on his thoughts, his wily mind had immediately turned to the usefulness of having a loyal mage. Some of those uses made Ishmael uneasy in his conscience; others were frankly dangerous. "I cannot say what I would or would not have sensed. I did send a message to a Lightborn mage I know; he said that they'd done nothing to touch the Shadowlands or the Shadowborn. Lightborn don't talk about Shadowborn."

"One day," Vladimer mused, "I will know *why* the Lightborn abandoned the Borders." He waved a long hand. "So they'll be no help. What else?"

"The Shadowborn need t'eat and drink; that we know." He need not spell out what, or how they knew; Vladimer had all reports of Shadowborn incursions delivered to him, and had copies of all the scientific and speculative literature, even the sensationalist broadsheets. Very few of the aristocracy outside the Borders showed any interest in the danger that the Shadowborn posed, but Vladimer, for whatever reason, did. Perhaps, Ish thought, because the archduke's spymaster was, in his detached, intellectual way, the most paranoid individual he'd ever met. Vladimer detested mysteries, and the Shadowborn were a mystery. "Much of the Shadowlands west of the mountains is desert. Some years, even if we dared try t'live off the land, we would not be able to: the heat, the scrub, the lack of water. This was a good year for the hill farms, and the scouts who went into the Shadowlands said that 'twas unusually lush. Perhaps this year the Shadowborn had enough t'eat."

"And on other good years," Vladimer said inexorably, "have they been quiet?"

"No," Ish said reluctantly. "Th'best years for the hill villages are the worst years for Shadowborn."

"Ah. So, this year is different. What else, Shadowhunter?"

Ish's unease intensified—that title again. "We don't know how

Shadowborn breed. Never killed a young one, or one in pup, or egg-heavy. If the breeding failed, that might be it."

Vladimer's fingers drummed lightly on his chair arm. "Still all speculation."

"A dozen scouting parties went into the Shadowlands," Ish said. "One went over two hundred miles inland. They were harassed by the little brutes, but not attacked. It is quiet inside the Shadowlands, as well as outside."

"Two hundred miles in," Vladimer said, "whereas we know the Shadowlands are eight, nine hundred miles wide at their fullest north–south extent. And no one dares eat and drink in the Shadowlands, yet the food and water are not exactly poisonous to us, are they, Ishmael, particularly if one has magic to tell if they can support life or not?"

"It is possible t'eat and live, yes, if it's that or die," Ish said, very still. "But I've a thought that drinking the water and eating from the land brings on the Call."

"You have eaten and drunk within the Shadowlands."

"Yes."

"And returned alive and sane, though afflicted by that same Call. Which you have so far been able to resist."

"My lord," said Ishmael softly, "please do not ask me t'do this."

There was a silence. "I have not yet asked you to do anything. But your instinct is, as ever, right. An old fisherman once told me about this phenomenon, a great wave that sometimes follows an earthquake. Just before the waters begin to rise, they gather offshore, and the sign of their gathering is that they flow back, back from shore. Do you understand what I am trying to say?"

Ish believed he did, and hoped he did not.

After a moment waiting for an acknowledgment that would not

come, Vladimer continued, "The Shadowborn have raided the Borders ever since the Curse was laid, sometimes with great slaughter, but always as single beasts or as small hunting packs. They have never shown any sign of other than instinctual behavior, never any sign of cooperation amongst breeds, and never any sign that they would not prey on one another, given the opportunity. And there is nothing to indicate that this is the way it might not always be."

He pushed himself to his feet, leaning upon armrest and cane, and limped around to the game board. Carved stone squares clicked as he turned them. From where he sat, Ish thought he was recapitulating the pattern that he had shown Ish earlier, when the turn of one square spread a tide of change across the board. "And still I am uneasy. Still I ask myself—and would like to put to you—what would happen if a breed of Shadowborn arose that could dominate all the breeds of Shadowborn? What do you suppose would happen if a breed of Shadowborn arose that had the intelligence, cunning, and ambition of men?"

That was a nightmare that, even in his most hopeless hours, Ish had never had visit him. It was one of those moments when he was grateful not to live in Vladimer's head.

"Envision an army, Ishmael, made up of scavvern and glazen and led by . . . one like our own Ferdenzil Mycene, perhaps. Envision that sweeping down from the high passes into the Borders. And *then* say, 'Do not ask me to do this.' "

He heard the soft thump of Vladimer's cane as the archduke's spymaster moved to sit down opposite Ishmael.

"I know what I am asking of you," he said, almost gently, "and I also know that if you were any other man you would think me quite mad to be more concerned about this than the intrigues of Mycene in the Scallon Isles, or half a dozen other schemes by prodigiously capable men of high and low birth. But you have spent your entire adult life hunting these creatures and training others to hunt them. *If* the reason they are not raiding is not because they have enough to eat, and is not because there are too few of them, but is because something or *someone* within the Shadowlands is gathering them up, then I *must know*. And there isn't a scout or Shadowhunter who knows those lands better than you do, and is a mage besides."

"No *living* Scout or Shadowhunter," Ish said harshly. "It is not," he continued in a lower voice, "that I do not know the need, my Lord. I do. But t'go across the Border—I can do enough to keep me on this side, but I know of no way I could scout the heart of the Shadowlands and not lose myself."

Vladimer nodded acknowledgment, but continued his own argument. "Even if nothing is happening, even if this is a natural fluctuation in population—assuming that anything to do with the Shadowborn can be called natural—I want a way to know what is happening inside the Shadowlands. I want you to find me that way. For ten years, I have relied upon your experience in dealing with this particular grave threat. I am relying on you once more. So, if you are willing, I would like to try an experiment, attempt a different solution."

Ish gave a tight smile. "As long as it leaves me in no worse case than I am now. Though I suppose if I failed and followed the Call, I *would* answer your question, though you'd never be knowing the answer."

"I do not use my agents that way," Vladimer said, in mild reproach. "The idea I have had is this: The husband of the lovely Telmaine—the one she wed to the consternation of all her relations—is a physician with a professional interest in disorders of the mind, particularly disorders of self-control: addictions, compulsions, Lightsickness. He has lately come to my attention through one of his successes: Guillaume di Maurier." The young man was one of Minhorne's more notorious rakehells—and a valued window into Minhorne's underworld for the spymaster. "Furthermore, Hearne's sister is a known mage and he maintains a warm relationship with her—to the scandal of his in-laws, I might add. There are more eminent and experienced physicians, but those facts incline me to think there might be none more able to help you. I instruct you to consult him, to lay your experience out before him. I will not send you to certain failure and death"—Ish noted the order of exclusions—"but I *need* that intelligence. I do not like this silence."

"I understand," Ish said heavily.

"I thought you might," Vladimer said, unsmiling. "As I have discovered to my own cost, your reward for service is to serve again. So I suggest you go and dance with my pretty cousin, and make your arrangement to meet her husband. I want those answers, Ishmael, but I'd prefer you come back safe with them."

Telmaine

After several dances, Telmaine pleaded fatigue and joined Sylvide in a place just inside the archway to the main ballroom, adjacent to a little alcove that was a favored—if obvious—hiding place during children's games, as well as one of the entrances to Lord Vladimer's private study.

"Do tell me why my reputation is in danger from dancing with Baron Strumheller?" she said lightly, judging the question within the bounds of a lady's interest. Sylvide's family's lands were far south of the city, with only the Strumheller barony between them and the Shadowlands. "I've heard about him, but nobody said anything about his being a great seducer, not like Lord"—and she leaned close to murmur the name into Sylvide's ear.

But Sylvide did not squeak with scandalized glee. "Tellie, this is serious. Baron Strumheller's a *practitioner.* There's no telling what he could do if he *wanted* a woman."

Practitioner being the current euphemism for mage. Telmaine's gloved hands worked on her fan. She wanted to know more about Ishmael di Studier, but she did not want to hear more about what Sylvide thought mages might or might not do. It was a topic she had learned to avoid.

Sylvide whispered, "His father threw him out and *disowned* him because he actually wanted to *study* magic. He took to Shadowhunting because it was the only way he could live. He came back years later, when there was a glazen marauding in the Borders. People say he blackmailed his father into reinstating him, before he'd help them kill it. He's been into the Shadowlands dozens of times."

"I thought people who went into the Shadowlands too often either went mad or didn't come back at all."

"My brother knows someone who's ridden the hill patrols with him. He has himself chained to his bed at night, so he can't rise in his sleep and follow the Call from the Shadowlands."

Telmaine shied. The conversation had taken a disturbing turn. She sonned quickly about her and was relieved to discover that no one seemed to be taking any particular interest in it.

Sylvide clutched at her arm, her expression anxious. "Now I've shocked you."

Telmaine drew a deep breath of the close, overperfumed air. "I've heard all about obsessions and compulsions from Bal. It makes me uncomfortable to hear about them, but that's because . . . well, he tells me it's because I empathize with people who cannot remain in control. Which I think makes me sound better than I am because . . . it is rather horrible, isn't it?"

"It *is* horrible. Men and women disappearing, and then the *things* that come out of the Shadowlands. I don't know why we don't just leave the Borders, the way the Lightborn did."

The deep voice behind them said softly, "And you'd be leaving your family's lands so easily, Lady Sylvide, that you would tell others t'do so?"

Sylvide gave a little shriek that was half sonn that outlined the broad figure of the baron as he emerged from Lord Vladimer's private door. "And before you chide me once more about manners, Lady Telmaine," the baron said, "I believe th'dishonors are about even."

He started to move past them, and she realized that, gruff composure in his voice notwithstanding, he was greatly shaken. Moved by an impulse of curiosity and compassion, she laid gloved fingers to his sleeve and found that he was actually trembling. What would frighten a man with a reputation for courage acknowledged even by his enemies? "Are you all right, Baron Strumheller?"

His sonn washed over her revealingly. Telmaine said, firmly, "You *must* mute your sonn, sir! You're not in the Borders now. Someone will call you out for it, which you would richly deserve, but then you would probably kill them, which would be grossly unfair." She rapped his forearm lightly with her fan. "Come. You promised me a dance."

"Tellie!" Sylvide hissed.

She flipped her fan toward Sylvide and tucked the baron's hand firmly into the crook of her arm, turning them toward the dance floor. She was aware of waves of sonn spreading over her, of whispers moving outward.

"Why are you doing this?" the baron said in a voice pitched just low enough for her to hear. She noticed he moved with assurance, even without casting. She was impressed. Her brothers, as mad-for-hunting adolescents, had practiced the skill, with much crashing into lintels and falling over ornamental tables.

"I have a soft heart." Which was true enough. Like it or not, she was aware of the pain of those excluded from society. Where she could without insulting them further or endangering her own secret, she tried to ease their struggles, using her own high position and many connections to introduce them to suitors, friends, and patrons. Of course, the usual people she reached out to were girls handicapped by an absent or embarrassing family, or awkward, gifted young men from the provinces. Not a man a decade her senior, with lands more extensive than her own family's, and a formidable reputation besides.

Still, what was done was done, and need never be repeated.

She yielded to his lead, at first tucking her toes back warily, but he moved lightly and turned her deftly, dancing in a formal style that was at least fifteen years outdated. She concentrated on relaxing, so that he would relax in turn. He was taking her injunction against sonn quite literally, and she realized that as well as other people's sonn, he was using the small shifts in her own body language to steer by. As to the sniffing, it seemed he had not intended to insult her beside the automaton; he must be used to interpreting his surroundings by smell as well as sound and sonn. He was indeed like a wild creature.

When the music ended and he turned as though to leave, she caught his arm. "Do stay, please," she said. "You have no idea what a pleasure it is to dance with a man I can trust not to tread on my feet."

Her sonn caught an expression of wary amusement on his face. "M'father ensured I had all the proper accomplishments," he said.

The music began once more. She waited, not responding to something that was surely a lure inviting her to flinch, or to pry. After four bars, aware they were becoming conspicuous, she took a half step closer, and he took hold of her and began to lead.

Dancing, she had become aware of a trace of Vladimer's distinctive cologne. "You were talking to Lord Vladimer just now, weren't you?"

He tensed, but did not break step. She turned her body slightly, and he steered her away from her sister-in-law, who was casting pointedly in their direction. She said, "I recognize that cologne. I found my way into his study back there when I was a little girl, playing hide-and-seek with my ducal cousins. He terrified me out of a year's growth when he caught me, though now that I think about it, he was but twenty-one years old then."

Her skirts swung across a fellow dancer's legs, reminding her that she could not concentrate only on him, as she wanted to. He felt her twitch, and played a burst of sonn over their surroundings that would not have penetrated gauze.

"What did he do to upset you?" she said.

His sonn brushed her face, which showed, she hoped, an expression of ladylike concern. "My lady," he said, "don't you think that an intrusive question?"

"Yes," she said. "But Vladimer is my cousin. I respect him, and I know how important he is to the archduke and to the state. But if you do not know him well, he has peculiar humors, and I would not like you to take them ill."

He relaxed slightly. "I've known Lord Vladimer—and his humors—for years. If you'd be reassured by it, *he* told me t'dance with you. Thought it might help my marriage prospects if I showed myself tame."

"Gracious me! With all due respect to my cousin, I am not sure I would take any advice *he* offers on the subject of matrimony. He's expert in withering hopeful buds. He doesn't trust women, which isn't surprising. His mother was notorious."

"My lady," he said, after a moment, "if you hope t'show me the bounds of polite conversation, you have me more confused than ever."

Telmaine flushed. "You're correct, sir. It is my turn to beg your pardon."

"I think," he said, steering her in another turn, "we should not keep tally. We seem t'bring out the worst in each other. But as for Vladimer, I had not thought of it in quite that way, but that may well be the way of it."

She drew breath to ask about the baron's own mother, who was so far absent from his conversation, but realized it might be a question he did not want to answer.

"I'm supposed t'present myself t'your husband. By Lord Vladimer's orders."

He might have spoken lightly, but the renewed tension in him told her otherwise. She could not but grow apprehensive; the attenuated tie of blood, as well as her insignificant womanhood, might grant her some immunity from Vladimer's machinations, but her husband was not similarly protected. She could not keep the tension from her own voice. "Why has Vladimer ordered you to meet Bal?"

The music ended with a prolonged rallentando. This time, the baron offered her no chance to linger, but steered her firmly toward the side of the dance floor, and, under cover of the stir of dancers bustling off and onto the floor, said, "He thinks your husband might be able t'help me with that affliction your friend spoke of." He stepped back, bowed decisively to her, and withdrew into the echoes. She fanned herself briskly, indicating to all that she was not interested in observing his departing back. How *would* the Shadow-hunter react to Balthasar, gentle, scholarly, and inexorable when he thought there was need? Thinking of her husband made her feel obscurely guilty. Foolish, since she had danced with the baron but twice, publicly sanctioned. She closed her fan and smoothed her sleeves and gloves and waist, removing all impressions of his fingers. That done, she maneuvered around the perimeter of the dance floor, murmuring greetings to the people who greeted her—whether slightly frostily or curiously, but too well-bred to question her—or in friendship.

An elderly dowager, sitting amidst a small court of her relatives, accosted her. "So you got young Ishmael di Studier dancing, did you?"

Xephilia was the elder sister of the archduke's mother. Their rivalry for the late archduke's hand and heart, in which they had used every wile and abandoned every scruple known to woman, was a forty-year-old scandal. Telmaine suspected it had been immensely entertaining to the spectators.

"Sit down by me, Telmaine." Xephilia shooed away the granddaughter seated beside her. Telmaine slid into the chair with a mixture of obedience and curiosity.

"Old-fashioned style, but he still dances well, doesn't he?"

"My toes know it," Telmaine said demurely.

"Mm." Xephilia leaned closer. Society of forty years ago had considered her the beauty, not her sister. "You do know why he wears those gloves, don't you?"

"I assumed that they were the fashion down in the Borders," Telmaine said airily. "Either that or he's got clammy hands."

There was little of an old woman's wavering in Lady Xephilia's sonn. "You aren't that naive, girl. He wears those gloves because he can read thoughts with a touch. You'd be well-advised to remember that when you're dancing with him. And you might be advised to leave your own pretty arms bare, as long as he's around to remind people of things they'd rather not think about."

Telmaine's mouth was suddenly as dry as the Shadowlands. She managed not to clutch at her fan or her arms. "It's . . . because of my phobia," she said. "Without the gloves I'd not be able to enjoy—"

"Oh, don't fret about it, girl. We know you. It would be best if you could, that is all; you should get your husband to pay some attention to you, professionally as well as as a woman. And as to di Studier, the man couldn't help being born the way he was; I'll grant that. But he should have let matters be over the barony. How he imagines he might continue the line, I don't know. What girl would marry him?"

"It isn't inherited," she said. And if the gods heard no other prayer of hers, let them hear that one.

"Not if we don't let it be," Lady Xephilia said crisply. "Ishmael di Studier shouldn't wed. The barony should pass to his brother, as it was meant to. It will in time. Di Studier won't be able to resist the Call indefinitely, living in the Borders."

The callousness shocked her enough to make her forget her own personal danger. "You'd approve a man going to a horrible death, just because he's a mage?"

"There's no 'just' about it," the old woman said sternly. "Mages are as dangerous as Shadowborn. So don't you go making him one of your projects, girl."

In the main hall, three light-timbred bells began to peal, sweetly penetrating. It was the warning for those guests who did not wish to stay throughout the day that the last safe hour of night was approaching. In the height of summer most of the guests did stay, night being far too brief for proper revelry. Now that summer was sliding into autumn and the nights were lengthening, some would choose to leave, and others would seize the chance to take in the air and scents of the garden while they could. Telmaine rose—not, she trusted, too hastily—and excused herself, saying that she must go and catch a breath of air before the sun rose. The folds of her dress hid her clenched hands. *Poisonous, dangerous old woman!*

She gathered her skirts to her and stepped sideways through the door, using the spill of sonn only to let her step around the guests on the balcony. She risked a soft sonn-cast over the stairs and grass below, so that she would not collide with anyone, and then ran down the stairs. A backward cast picked up the couple standing entwined, pressed back in one of the decorative alcoves beneath the stairs. Sensing the sonn, the woman twisted to place her inamorata between herself and the garden. Telmaine had already recognized her second cousin, in ardent embrace with a man not her husband. She sighed. Parthenalope's behavior was scandalous, but her husband's was little better. He drank and she strayed; she strayed and he drank. When she was in their company Telmaine did not need to touch them to feel their mutual revulsion and yoked despair.

She turned away from the adulterous couple, moving quietly across the grass toward the pond. In late summer, the nights were long enough to lose all the day's warmth, and the air, scented as it was, was chill. Her foot crunched softly on the pebbles as she reached the path around the pond, and she rocked back on her other foot, still placed on the quiet grass. Then she took her foot off the pebbles and turned, slowly moving parallel to the path, using sonn, scent, the feel of the ground under her shoes, and her familiarity with this garden. Unlike the gardens of some other great houses—her own family's included—the layout of this garden had not changed in a hundred years. Here were the linked ponds, with their languid screen of willows, and here the flower beds, with their extraordinary flowering of night blooms from Imogene's land and even beyond, and here the hedge around the maze, from behind which she suddenly heard her husband's voice.

"How was I supposed to know she would come here?"

She went still, listening with all her disbelieving being as the whisper hung in the air. A moment passed, and from behind the hedge the whisperer spoke again.

"How was I supposed to know about the child? She never told me."

Not Bal, couldn't be Bal; she could not imagine scholarly, scrupulous Bal declaring, "How was I supposed to know?" in that defensive whine. And a child—whose child?

"You've been unforgivably careless," a woman's voice murmured. Telmaine shivered, not knowing why.

The man with Bal's voice said, with an urgency bordering on panic, "I'll take care of it. I promise. I'll take care of it. Please."

There was a considering silence, and the husky, almost expressionless voice said, "Ensure that you do. Now, go."

"Are you—"

"I've more to do here. Go."

Telmaine heard a crunch of gravel to her left as the man hurried out of the maze, tripping in his haste. The woman growled softly under her breath, a sound almost animal in its timbre. She did not move, did not sonn after him, waiting, as the *crunch, crunch* of feet on gravel faded. Telmaine remained unmoving, pressed against the hedge; she was not even sure she was breathing; she was so dreadfully cold and strangely light-headed. Leaves crumpled under her hands; twigs and leaves jabbed her cheek and ear. She did not know why she did not want to be perceived, only *that* she did not want to be perceived. She listened, almost with her skin, as the woman emerged and turned toward the great house with barely a sound even on gravel. She thought she felt, or fancied she felt, the hem of the other's skirt breeze past her own, but surely not; surely she would have been sonned. She heard the woman pause just beyond her, and the tiny snap as she freed her skirt from a thorn.

Laughter chimed from the direction of the house; light running footsteps sounded on the path; fractured sonn washed over her. She readied herself to be discovered, and turned in time to perceive the exchange of sonn as the woman swept her skirts aside to pointedly avoid two hectic young girls, one of whom was Anarys. She thought the woman's hand reached out to tug brusquely at Anarys's slipping veil as sonn faded.

Anarys gave a little cry. Telmaine's sonn leaped out, resolving the girls, standing bewildered in the path. Of the woman, there might have been a vague movement, close to the limit of her perception, but nothing else.

Telmaine hurried forward to meet the girls. "Tellie," cried Anarys guiltily, and fussed her veil over her head. "We just wanted to go out in the garden—we so seldom get to be in the garden at this time."

"Anarys," she said. "The woman who went past you—do you know who she was?"

"What woman?"

"What do you mean, what woman—she pulled at your veil."

"It was the wind that pulled at my veil!" Anarys cried.

"There was a woman on the path just now."

"I didn't meet any woman," Anarys said, and her sixteen-year-old friend shook her head emphatically.

Telmaine had no way to remove her long gloves unobtrusively, to let her intrude upon her sister's thought to detect the lie—or whatever lay behind the denial. Unless Telmaine herself were somehow deluded, dreaming. She took control of herself, aware that the chill had faded; at least she could get the girls in, safe, and maybe later she could ask Anarys again. "You should go in. The sunrise bell will be sounding soon."

"No, it won't," said Anarys, emboldened to impertinence by her friend's presence. "The inside bell goes off half an hour before that; it's just been a few minutes."

"Anarys," Telmaine said, "you're not supposed to be outside in the garden at this hour. Please go inside."

"Why are you outside?" said Anarys, but the brass had worn off her challenge.

"None of your business," Telmaine said, growing angry with a fear she did not understand. "Please go inside, or I will tell Mama—both your mothers."

The two girls turned as one, Anarys flouncing and Jaquecynth trotting along beside. "She's meeting a lover," Telmaine heard Jaquecynth declare, loud enough to be audible. Telmaine pressed a gloved knuckle to her lip, ready to stifle a sound that might be a giggle or a sob. Was it possible that two clever teenage girls could be made to forget an encounter? Or were they lying, and if so, why should they lie? Telmaine had heard no words exchanged, not even a murmur of promise or threat. Who was the man who had sounded so much like Balthasar, in timbre and pronunciation, and so little like him in speech and manner? Why were the woman's soft voice and muted manner so terrifying, both to the man and to her?

Her heart rate had barely begun to slow when she sensed someone behind her. She whirled, loosing a snap of sonn that crisply outlined . . . Ishmael di Studier.

Mortally embarrassed at having committed the very impropriety she'd first accused him of, she made a tiny sound and pressed her gloved fingers to her lips.

"It's all right, my lady," he said, a smile in his voice. "I am sorry I startled you."

She lowered her hand, slowly, and flicked a tiny, timid burst, which showed his square face and skewed smile. "Oh, dear," she said.

His smile broadened. Blood surged to her face, mingled mortification and renewed fury. He had no business embarrassing her like this. "You *did* startle me!"

"I should be most glad you were not armed, then," he rumbled.

She stood breathing quickly for a moment, cold air catching in her throat. In a smaller voice she said, "I am sorry."

"So we are quits on that particular offense as well."

"Quite . . . quits. Baron, did you sonn a woman on the path a little while ago?"

"A particular woman?"

"Yes. She came from the maze, encountered two young girls, and went on into the house, I think, though I cannot say for sure. I did not sonn her clearly myself, and I would very much like to know who she was."

"I cannot say I did," Ishmael said. "You're troubled about something."

"Is it possible—" Telmaine said, and then stopped, shocked at herself. No woman of society should ask whether something could or could not be done by magic; no woman of society should be in the least interested in magic. She found that she was plucking at the fingertips of her gloves, with no idea whether it would be worse if he told her she was raving, or took her seriously. "Never mind. It's . . . it's nothing. It must be getting close to the sunrise bell." She started to move, realized he was not accompanying her, stopped.

In his soft, slightly abashed rumble he said, "You should go in first; I will come once the bell rings. There are malicious tongues about."

She halted and turned to face him. "Did you hear her?"

"Lady Xephilia? Th'words, no, but I know the tenor of it well enough."

"I was furious at her," Telmaine said.

Sonn licked gently across her face. "Why so?" he said curiously, and as well he might, as she had spoken with more vehemence than she could readily explain. She was not going to tell him Lady Xephilia preferred that he should suffer an unknown but likely horrible death rather than live in society as a mage. She was not going to think what Lady Xephilia would consider a suitable fate for Telmaine.

"No need t'be upset on my account," he said. "I've built a thick skin over the years. Takes more than words to draw my blood these days." With a smile in his voice, he added, "Annoys them no end, that."

"You just go on annoying them, then," she said, as lightly as she could.

"As you command, m'lady. While we have this moment, I understand you and your daughters will be taking the train back to Minhorne. Might you accept me as escort? I'd thus mix pleasure with the duty laid on me t'present myself t'your husband."

Common sense warred with rebellion, caution with impulse. She had always been exquisitely careful around acknowledged mages, hiding her own secret behind social prejudice. She could easily refuse to travel with him, because of his reputation. But she had danced two dances with him, and he would need to meet her husband. And she would not let the Lady Xephilias of the world rule her.

The sunrise bell began to toll, startling her. She blurted out her answer before she could change her mind. "Of course I will. It is an eminently sensible arrangement."

Her sonn caught an ironic slant to his smile. "My pleasure, m'lady. Now, please, you must go in."

She put a gloved hand on his arm. "Don't wait too long."

"I've the rising of the sun in my bones, Lady Telmaine. No sunrise bells in the wilds."

Three

Balthasar

On the other side of the paper wall, Floria did her morning exercises, while Balthasar read the proceedings of the latest Intercalatory Council meeting and tried not to doze off. He was still weary with the aftereffects of Floria's stimulant and two days caring for Tercelle's abandoned twins. Sighted or not, they had the same imperious helplessness of any newborn, and as briefly as they had been in his life, they left a hollow in his heart with their going. Now he listened for the sound of a carriage and the excited chatter of two little girls, knowing that if he did not hear it soon, he would not be hearing it tonight. Telmaine would not bring the children out so near to the sunrise bell.

When the doorbell rang, he was on his feet before he realized it could not be Telmaine; she had her keys. Fleetingly, he was tempted not to answer it, but then carefully laid the papers aside and went downstairs. He had no more than unlatched it when the handle twisted under his hand and the door was hurled open by a man's greater strength, throwing him back against the hall table. An ornament brushed his leg in falling and smashed beside his foot. By then, the two men were in the hall, the larger pinning him against the wall. "Where are the brats?"

He cast sonn, gaining a blurred impression of a stranger with a thick neck, square features, damaged ears, before a fist drove into his lower belly, doubling him over. "None of that," his assailant ordered.

He hung in the man's hands, retching, shocked into paralysis by the violence that had come without forerunning threat or warning.

The second man spoke, his assumed Rivermarch accent not quite masking the distinct aristocratic tones that Bal loved to hear from his wife. "Get him inside. We don't want to be sonned from the street."

He tried to draw breath to call for help, but could manage no more than a half cry before the heavy door slammed. He heard broken porcelain crunch under heavy feet.

"Now, Dr. Balthasar Hearne, this can go easy with you, or it can go hard. Where are Tercelle Amberley's infants?"

He straightened up, struggling against fear more than against pain, because he knew that to defy them would be to invite more violence. "I do not know what you mean," he said, his voice shaking.

He heard the creak of a heavy jacket, and his sonn burst out involuntarily to catch the man who held him drawing back his fist and the other reaching out to stay his hand. "Not yet," said the aristocrat. "Not quite yet. We will search the house, and perhaps we will find what we need, or perhaps we will find something that proves to the good doctor that he cannot lie to us. Hood him."

They jammed a hood over his head, muffling sonn and disorienting him. They lugged him from hall to receiving room to kitchen, thrusting him face-first against the wall while they investigated cupboards, drawers, and cubbies, anywhere that might conceal a newborn child. They found the crib pushed back into the cupboard beneath the stairs, but Bal had drizzled dust from the unemptied dustpan over and around it, craftily enough to deceive Telmaine, never mind these two. They were rough in their search, but not wanton, and that gave him a modicum of hope that they would treat him no worse than they did his household. Perhaps they might yet be persuaded that he knew nothing, that their information was tenuous.

The search ended, as he hoped it would, in the study. There was no sound from behind the paper wall, but keen-eared Floria would surely have heard the incursion into his home. He heard the aristocrat's footsteps move over to the wall and linger, as though he were examining it, and then return to Bal. "As I said, this can go easy on you, or it can go hard."

"I have no idea who you—" Bal said.

"Very hard," said the aristocrat.

The first man drove a fist into Bal's back, above his kidney, and he thudded to hands and knees. The pain and the need to breathe consumed him for an interminable length of time. He fought not to call out Floria's name, not to plead for her aid. If she could do something from behind that wall that could not be breached, she would.

"Again," said the man above him, he did not know which of them, but in answer a boot plowed into the front of his ribs, and he found himself lying on the floor without a recollection of having fallen, clawing at the boards in his struggle for air.

"Just tell us where Tercelle Amberley's bastards are," said the man, his true tones more marked in command.

Balthasar curled up, his one feeble strategy to protect himself. He heard heavy feet moving around him. "Not about the head," the man with the cultured voice said. His voice came closer as he crouched. "Tercelle Amberley gave birth to twin boys here. You had the disposing of them. Where did you send them? Did that sister of yours take them?"

"I haven't . . . met T-Tercelle for . . . years," Bal said, his voice a thread.

"Again," said the interrogator. The kick jarred his whole body; ribs cracked and breath went out of him in a strangled scream. "He," the speaker said, "could break your spine with one move. You'd end your days a cripple."

"I . . . don't . . . know," Bal gasped.

"Then we'll wait for your pretty wife and daughters."

His body answered for him. He started to drag himself up, rising from hands and knees, before his torturer planted another kick in his abdomen, leaving him once more in a retching huddle.

"There," the aristocrat commanded, directing the toe driven again into his rib cage, the heel brought down on his hands and wrists and ankles, each blow well spaced to allow for the question, "Where are they?" until his, "No, no, no," was sobbed through his teeth, more plea for cessation than refusal. They did not stop to discern the difference; they battered him until, beyond speech, he writhed like a crushed worm against the base of the paper wall.

"Stop," said the aristocrat. He felt the hood jerk from his head, and sonn lash his face. "He said this one was soft."

"He's faking."

"He's not— Who's that?" There came a small sound, neither thump nor slash, overhead.

Floria's voice said distinctly, "The White Hand." It was her mortal challenge, her last declaration to the men and women she killed. The aristocrat stooping over him shrieked. One of them kicked him again, but it was a glancing blow, and there came a second cry, higher and hoarser. ". . . shoot and we'll burn . . ." "We're burning anyway—" "Stop! Stop, Lightborn! You're killing us." He heard them scrambling away from him, and felt the fever of sunrise on his skin. He felt her spring over him to harry them out the door in pitiless, miraculous pursuit. He struggled to raise his head, to make the last thing he sonned be her, but he was too weak to do more than roll it, and his sonn was a whisper. He heard her say from beside him as he lay against the paper wall, "Bal, Bal, please talk to me!" Burning, he thought, was not so terrible after all.

Telmaine

At the train station at Bolingbroke Circle, Telmaine had second thoughts that had nothing to do with the propriety of allowing Ishmael di Studier to escort her through the city so he could meet her husband and lay his case before Bal.

"Is that thing . . . magical?" she said doubtfully, pulsing sonn over the conveyance in which he proposed they travel.

"Not in the least," Ishmael di Studier said cheerfully. "I admit the design is based on the Lightborn horseless carriages, which are, but the engine burns a mixture of alcohols and petroleum. We are experimenting to find the best possible mix."

She had not expected him to share the fashionable mania for machinery, given his disdainful response to the display automaton. Yet here he was, showing off a polished and decorated *machine* that was clearly his pride and joy. The thing was like a low open coach, except that there was no horse and it had grafted onto the rear a casing that he claimed housed the propulsion mechanism. Above the axle and between the wheels ran a bundle of piping. She sonned it dubiously, trying to convince herself that it was no more than a single small, trackless train engine, while Amerdale clutched her skirts and Florilinde sidled closer to the thing, fascinated. The baron had spent much of the train journey exerting his charm on them, to good effect. "*Papa* would like this," Flori said slyly.

Telmaine surrendered. Balthasar would indeed like it. Sunrise was approaching, and she could not risk having to take shelter with Ishmael, of all people. She said briskly to her daughters, "Then do get in."

"Need t'prime the engine," the baron said, which he did with a vigorous pumping motion on a lever in the front of the car.

The racket was astonishing. "Heaven's heart, Baron! Can you even hear to sonn . . . ?" Amerdale had her hands clamped over her ears, and even Florilinde's expression was dubious.

"Pardon?" the baron bellowed back.

"Can you even hear—" she tried again, although she felt her point amply illustrated.

"Not th'same frequency!"

That might be, Telmaine thought, maneuvering her skirts, but the whole neighborhood was still going to know they had arrived.

They started with a lurch. Telmaine, watching the baron over her shoulder, thought that, compared to driving a carriage, steering seemed a remarkably onerous procedure involving levers and pistons and a large wheel. The baron plied them like an organist playing a fugue with more enthusiasm than skill. At least so close to sunrise the streets were largely empty, though Ishmael seemed oblivious to the occasional shying horse and cursing coachman. She hoped the children were similarly oblivious. Their vocabulary was quite diverse enough.

It wasn't a relaxing trip, with the noise, the starts, the stops, the sudden swerves and jolts that threatened to pitch her and Amerdale on the floor and tumble the incautious Florilinde into the street. Still, it was swift; she could say that for it. She was surprised to sonn a carriage standing at their front door. The baron deftly pulled in behind it, and the sober horse did not bolt, though it stamped restlessly.

When the baron turned off the engine, she thought she had gone deaf.

"Papa!" cried Florilinde, and scrambled down from the car. "Papa, sonn what we came here in!"

The baron came suddenly to life. "Hold her!" And she sonned on his face the expression that he must wear as a Shadowborn charged out of the brush, as the door opened and two men came reeling out. Both men had narrow, oozing brands across faces and chests. They blasted her with a shock of rude sonn, making her blanch. "Who . . ." she began.

Ishmael di Studier vaulted from the carriage, snatching at Florilinde. His hand closed on the child's collar and then the other man swung at him with something like a black sock. With a crack of weight on bone, the baron went to his knees. But he was no sooner down than he was dodging sideways, and Telmaine heard the swish of the sap as it missed its second blow.

"Mama!" screamed Florilinde as the first man snatched her up.

Another blast of sonn, directed at her, which must have stripped her practically naked. He said, "We get Tercelle Amberley's bastards, Hearne gets his daughter back. Tell him that."

And they ran for the coach. Florilinde thrashed futilely in her kidnapper's arms. "Mama!" Telmaine slithered from the carriage and scrambled after the coach as it began to move. She came close enough to clutch at a wheel that tore itself from her hands as the coach inexorably gathered speed.

She turned wildly to find Ishmael leaning against the carriage. "What are you standing there for? We have to go after them."

The baron was sweating with pain, supporting his left arm against his body. "Can't drive," he said hoarsely. "Need both hands. And we must tend t'your husband."

She dithered in a torment of indecision, and then pulled the daughter left to her from the carriage, holding her smotheringly tight as she ran up to the door. Her feet crunched on broken ornaments, her skirts snagged on an overturned table. Amerdale sobbed, clinging to her. Into the receiving room, into the kitchen, into the pantry, out into the garden, her panic mounting. Dimly, over Amerdale's sobs, she could hear another voice, like an echo.

"Lady Telmaine!" She whirled. Ishmael di Studier stood bracing himself in the doorway. "He's upstairs," he said, more quietly. "Can't you hear?" So prompted, she could hear the voice of Floria White Hand, crying her husband's name.

Balthasar was in the study, lying curled up against the paper wall. At the sound of their arrival, Floria's voice demanded, half a hiss, "Who's that?"

The baron answered for them both. "Ishmael di Studier, mistress. Baron Strumheller, and Lady Telmaine Hearne."

"Baron Strumheller, thank the Mother. It's Floria White Hand," the Lightborn assassin said. "What's happened to Balthasar?"

The baron went down on one knee. He grimaced and set his teeth on the fingertips of the glove, pulling at it, finding it too new to yield. "M'lady," he said, "help me get my glove off."

Telmaine ignored him. She fell to her knees, spilled Amerdale from her arms, and stripped off her own traveling gloves, reaching for Bal, feeling chilled and clammy skin, and *pain-pain-pain.* She screamed and snatched her hands back, clenching them against her stomach and doubling over with the reverberations of his agony. Di

Studier muttered, "That answers that," and reached out to grip her wrist in his. "Where is he hurt?"

She could not answer. She had no sense that there had been any one place. Just *pain-pain-pain* that seemed to soak the very air.

"Need my glove off," the baron gritted. "Now!"

Amerdale grasped his glove with her little hands, pulling with all her strength; belatedly, Telmaine helped, unaware of his thoughts, hardly aware of a sense of presence, like a bank of glowing embers. The baron laid his bare hand on Bal's throat. "Pulse is there, but he's in a bad way." He slid his hand around to press gently on Bal's stomach. Bal moaned. "He's got a belly full of blood. They've burst something—spleen, curse it."

His tone told her the worst of it. Telmaine struggled to her feet. "He needs a doctor!"

"One of your leeches would kill him," Ishmael said. "Mistress White Hand, as you value this man's life, I need a spicule, strongest charge you've got. I'm a first-rank mage, not much, but this man's dying on us."

She heard Floria's feet running from the room.

"Lady Telmaine, sit down on the floor," Ishmael said brusquely to her, "before you faint. I'll do what I can."

She huddled down beside him and wept for her losses and her own uselessness. Amerdale crept to her, clinging and whispering, "Don't cry, Mama."

Floria returned and slammed something into the *passe-muraille*. "Di Studier! Here's your spicule. Can you handle it?"

Amerdale scuttled away from Telmaine's embrace with a tearing of hem and pulled open the door, returning with something in a small velvet bag. Telmaine roused herself to reach for it at the very moment the baron said, "Not you!" She felt a sudden jolt, a lightening of the pull of the earth on her bones. The baron's sonn jarred her, his expression unfathomably appalled. "That's done it," he said in a strange voice.

"Di Studier, what is it?"

He didn't answer Floria, but took the bag from Telmaine's hand and upended it, using his teeth, to spill a little shard of stone no longer than Amerdale's finger into the palm of his hand. His fingers closed on it a moment; then he shook his head. "Curse it," he said to her, and without apology.

"Di Studier, what is it!?"

His sonn swept over her again. "How do you feel, m'lady?"

"It doesn't matter," she said—thinking, *I shall* not *faint now*. "My husband needs help."

"That he does." He drew a deep breath, then said distantly, "I don't believe we closed the door."

"The *door*? What has the door to do with it?"

He did not answer. She heard his footsteps leave the room and go unsteadily down the stairs. It made no sense. She brushed trembling fingers against Bal's forehead, feeling a wavering presence, and pain that came and went, came and went with each shallow breath. Outside, the sunrise bell began to toll, the beginning of their day's confinement. All hope of outside help would go at its silence. Still, as she touched him, she felt herself begin to settle, just a little, to earth. And it seemed that his presence wavered less, and his pain eased a little.

The sunrise bell's tolling stopped. The baron's footsteps returned. He set a case—a gun case, she realized—down inside the door, and his sonn swept over her. Then he sighed, and knelt beside her and took her hand, which had been stroking Bal's forehead, and forced it down to the place that was seething with pain. She tried to free herself, but he pinned her hand in place, his touch conveying *strength-resolution-irony* . . . and potent fear. His whisper was harsh and steady. "Th'way this works is y'feel his pain, and send your healing into it. Feel what is wrong in him, feel what is right in yourself, and use that to make it right in him. Can't explain it any clearer. Can show you, though."

"Di Studier," Floria said, "what's going on? Isn't the spicule enough?"

"Hush, mistress. Now, Telmaine," the baron murmured. There was nothing seductive in the murmur, or in the pressure of the large, warm hand over hers. She felt a gathering of energies, a focusing of resolution, and then a sudden heat in her fingers and lightness in her bones. She gasped, suddenly realizing what he was about. "Yes," he whispered, breath warm on her ear. "I know what you are. Only way t'do this now. Listen to me." With his deep, almost breathless whisper and with his thoughts, he pressed pictures into her mind that were like and very unlike the diagrams in the books that Bal studied, because the diagrams, no matter how beautiful, were inanimate, and Ish's voice was alive. And as counterpoint and undercurrent, the words and images and sensations passed between them, and she could feel, she could *feel* Balthasar's torn blood vessels and broken bones weaving together as though drawn by the finest thread.

Abruptly the baron said hoarsely, "That's it, I'm done; I've no more," and he pulled their hands from Bal's side, and her bones turned suddenly and irrevocably to lead, and she herself slid against the base of the paper wall.

She had no idea how long she would have lain there, but that she heard Bal's whisper: "Telmaine."

She levered herself up and snapped a sonn in the direction of his face, making him frown with the force of it. His answering sonn was as weak and unfocused as his voice. His breath was foul, stale with old blood; she fought not to gag. "Mmm," he breathed, "I've missed you so," and dropped away from her into unconsciousness or deep sleep. She started to sit up, but she never completed the movement. Her last awareness was of a strong hand easing her down beside her beloved, and a sense of the warm embers of a spent fire.

Ishmael

The effort of settling the lady beside her husband made Ishmael reel; kneeling, he rested his cheek on the gritty hem of her skirt, half wishing that the small sun in his shoulder would flare and turn him completely to ash and out of his misery. Working a healing—working any magic—magnified any physical weakness in a mage. His cracked collarbone had broken entirely, and he had the sick feeling that an infection had seeded into it. And he'd thrown himself into the healing against all caution, even when he realized she wasn't the first- or second-ranker he'd assumed. What by the Drunken God of All Follies did he think he was *doing*, aiding an untrained mage with her strength in a healing that would have taxed four of him?

"Who'ze Drunk God of Follies," said a small voice. He pushed himself painfully upright, and sonned Telmaine's younger daughter sitting upright amongst her mother's skirts like a baby gannet on its nest.

He hadn't realized he had muttered aloud. "My patron deity," he allowed. He'd long since given up addressing prayers either to the Mother of All Things Born, goddess of forerunners, Lightborn, and mages, or to her usurper son, the Sole God of respectable Darkborn. His patron deity might be imaginary, but to Ishmael, he sufficed. He was certainly the only entity who might understand predicaments like this.

Amerdale sonned him, a fast, firm train of pulses, and declined to talk theology. "What did you do to my mama?" she demanded suspiciously.

Ish gathered his syrupy wits, thankful that Hearne's daughter was not a stroppy little boy, ready to back the demand with fists and weight. Of course, a chatty little girl brought her own problems. The child had witnessed everything that had happened, and would no doubt comment on it to her father.

Who—unless he was much mistaken—had no idea his wife was a mage.

Well, he'd deal with it then. "Your mama needs to sleep," Ish said. "She was helping me help your papa." If Balthasar Hearne had the wit to realize a healing had been worked on him, Ish could always claim to have drawn on Telmaine's vitality. That should be enough to annoy a doting husband into losing command of logic.

"You're not a doctor," she declared with the absolute authority of the small.

"No, but I've cared for people with hurts like your papa's." Most of whom died, Ish privately noted.

"Papa *is* going to be all right."

"I hope so," Ish said truthfully. He and Telmaine had managed to seal off the bleeding from Hearne's spleen, and reduce some ugly bruising on his kidneys and lungs. Hearne's broken ribs were now merely cracked, though they wouldn't hurt any less for it. They'd even managed to shift much of the internal hemorrhage back into his bloodstream. And the assailants had left his face and head alone, presumably so he could speak. Whatever the reason, Ish was relieved, since he doubted he and Telmaine could have addressed a head injury, even given his experience. Balthasar Hearne was still in a precarious condition. And right now, Ish himself couldn't have cured a fleabite.

"Are you going to make these men give back Flori?"

"Yes," Ish said, starting to feel slightly beset—he hadn't much experience asserting himself against small children. "I am that."

"Ami," spoke up Floria White Hand from the other side of the paper wall, "it is daytime just now, so *I* am searching for your sister. Would you like something to drink?"

She considered that. "I'm thirsty," she allowed.

"Wait a moment," Floria said.

A glass was poured; there was a pause, and then the door to the *passe-muraille* was slid open and shut. Amerdale spared him another scowl before she deigned to accept the offering. She was truly thirsty, judging by the way she slurped at the glass. Ish managed not to lick dry lips in envy. He suspected he knew what was coming. His conscience niggled a little; he doubted that Floria's troubled her at all.

Amerdale thrust the glass at him. "More," she demanded, and abruptly dropped onto her bottom. She pulled herself over onto all fours and crawled back to her mother's side, where she settled, head down, rump up. Bracing his useless arm, he eased over to nudge her onto her side, retrieve a fold of Bal's blanket, and tuck it around her. She must have her mother's temperament, he decided. His ill-formed sense of Balthasar was of someone more diffident—though with some sinew to him, to have withstood that beating without breaking.

"Is she asleep?" Floria's voice said after a moment.

"Sound asleep," Ish said, stirring up his muddy wits again to something approaching fluid. "I'll take a glass of that, if you would, minus the sleeping draft, but with anything you have for pain. I caught a sap on the clavicle, and the healing's done it no good." He didn't need to explain further; as a Lightborn, she knew the physical penalties of magic.

He heard another glass being poured, and wondered how one weighed the recklessness of taking a draft from a premier Lightborn assassin against that of aiding a powerful untrained mage in a critical healing. "Knew you knew Hearne, here," he remarked. "Didn't know this was a twinned house." Nor did he think that one of the Lightborn Prince's Vigilance would assent to share a paper wall with any Darkborn.

"It's of very long standing: five generations. We don't advertise. Less controversial that way, and safer, though in truth the danger in a breach is more to Bal than myself." She hesitated. "I heard him speak. Is he—"

"What I can, I've done," Ishmael said. "He'll take more healing, or be a long time laid up, but he'll do till sunset."

"Thank the All-Mother," Floria said quietly. "Baron Strumheller, you have earned my abiding gratitude. Balthasar Hearne is one of my oldest friends."

If he had heard those words spoken in such a tone by a Darkborn woman, restrained as the tone was, he would have said there was more to the relationship than that.

"I'd rather hear an explanation," he said, making his way back to the *passe-muraille*. "This isn't a simple robbery."

"If I had one, di Studier, I'd gladly give it, and let you take it back to your Lord Vladimer. As it is, you can take back only a mystery."

Retrieving the glass from the lighttight cabinet, he settled his back against the leg of the heavy armchair. "What is't you know?"

While he sipped—and felt the infernal little sun slowly dim—she told him of the birth of the two sighted infants, of their mother's attempt to murder them and then Bal, and of her escape. Balthasar's sister, the healer mage and midwife, had taken the children away last night, and this night two men had arrived to threaten Balthasar, and then to beat out of him the children's whereabouts.

"What in perdition did you do t'drive them off?" Ish said, setting aside the question of whether he believed such an extraordinary story.

"Pricked the wall with a needle and shone through a torch. Light travels in straight lines." So that accounted for the burns across the men's faces. "I risked killing Bal, I know, but he'd have been dead anyway." She paused, controlling her voice, he thought. "Now, your turn," she said. "Did you draw on Telmaine? It certainly sounded like it."

"Yes," he said, having considered and readied the lie. "I had to. I couldn't use th'spicule as well as I should. Not got th'strength."

She sighed. "Baron Strumheller, if it worked, then no apologies are needed. Bal will understand the magic but not the drawing—he has very few of the prejudices of his class—and Telmaine will likely forgive the drawing but not the magic—she has all the prejudices of hers."

"M'work's been worse met," Ish said, in a dry tone that she would surely misconstrue. "Now, going back to these children—never heard of such a thing."

"Not even amongst the Shadowborn?"

Unusual, he thought, to hear a Lightborn mention the Shadowborn. The Lightborn had abandoned the Borders some five hundred years ago; no one knew why. The best explanation he had heard was that the aura of Shadowborn magic made the Borders uninhabitable. Even he, weak mage though he was, could sense the chilling, repellent aura of it, if the source were close enough.

He reviewed the parade of monsters from a quarter century's Shadowhunting. "Sighted creatures—birds, dogs, lynxes, and th'like—don't sonn. Most Shadowborn sonn—some don't. We've not been so worried about the ones that don't sonn; they're th'easier to kill, hunting at night." He considered this uneasily. "Y'believe this, about th'sight."

"From Balthasar, yes," she said.

Which told him more about Balthasar Hearne. Intrigues amongst the Darkborn nobility might be vicious, and drive men to suicide or murder and their families to ruined desperation, but those were the exceptions; by and large, even the most savage skirmishes were conducted with words. Whereas the Lightborn prince's father and granduncle had both been assassinated, that being the usual way of deposing a weakening or unpopular prince. Members of the Prince's Vigilance were not known for trust or, for that matter, sentiment.

"Have y'taken this up with your mages or scientists?"

"Not yet," she said grimly. "I thought it a curiosity that could be examined at leisure."

He appreciated that. "Have y'any sense or word of any kind of magical aura about the children?"

There was a brief silence. "I have no such sense, no. Baron Strumheller, I am needed at my prince's court. I will have a watch put on Balthasar's house, since I mislike the notion that these infants' father might have come through the day."

"Can't say I care much for it myself," he rumbled, ruminating upon that silence, and whether her words meant no more or less than she said—that *she* had no such sense. She had changed the subject with unusual alacrity.

"I will also send a message to Balthasar's sister, to make sure she is warned. I'm certain she'll come here as soon after sunset as is safe."

"I'd be glad of that," he said. "She's a solid third-ranker. I'll be glad of anything else you get to know. Lord Vladimer has no liking for tales that are short on meat and long on stuffing."

Balthasar

Balthasar Hearne woke to the tolling of the sunset bell and the feel of a wooden floor underneath him. He was confused. He thought he had gone home from the college, and even if he had not, the last time he had fallen asleep in the library he was an overworked student, and then he had dozed off with his head on a desk, not the floor.

There was a woman sleeping beside him: He could feel her warmth and smell her perfume. He smiled slightly, deciding that this was one of those revealing dreams where one found oneself doing something indecent in a highly improper place—something that one school of his profession argued indicated repressed desires. He was no doubt about to discover three or four of his most feared and respected preceptors arrayed in armchairs around him. Very likely, he thought hazily, one of the occupants of the armchairs would prove to be his father-in-law.

But when he managed to raise his head, he sonned only one figure, a broad-shouldered, scarred stranger, sitting in Bal's own familiar armchair beside the paper wall in his study. Bal started to raise himself, and was stopped by an eruption of internal agony. He gave a choked cry, and the strange man dropped quickly to one knee beside him, bare hand spread over his abdomen in a disconcertingly familiar manner. The pain eased appreciably.

"Take it from someone who has collected th'odd beating himself," the man said in a dry rumble, "the less you move, the less you will hurt."

"Beating . . . ?"

"Aye, Dr. Hearne. Those two bravos in here last night. Cursed near beat you to death, if you'll excuse my Lightborn. Took one of the most powerful magical spicules I've ever handled to pull you back from the edge. You've a debt to your Lightborn friends you'll be some time repaying. So just you lie still. When we get some reinforcements we'll be moving you t'somewhere more comfortable, and then we can deal with the rest of it."

If the pain was reality, then the woman . . . "Telmaine . . ." He strained to lift his head without using his trunk muscles, and this time the stranger eased his hand under his shoulders and supported him so that he could sonn Telmaine's crumpled shape and the much smaller form of Amerdale. He tried to pull himself up further, and groaned, and the stranger eased him back onto the floor. "Florilinde . . ." he protested. "Where's Flori?"

"Aye, she said you had too much wit for your own good," the stranger murmured. "Best you go back to sleep now." Bal felt a callused hand brush his temple. He recognized the touch of a healer mage as the stranger pressed him down into sleep.

Ishmael

"Bal," said Telmaine Hearne, stirring in the shambles of her skirts. Her sonn, wavery with sleep, brushed him, just raising his fingers from her husband's temple. "What are you doing?" she said, her tone sharp with suspicion.

"Putting him back t'sleep," he said, with no apology in his voice.

He settled back on his heels, assessing the extent of her recovery. "If you can wait t'go back to sleep youself, I need t'talk to you before Mistress Floria returns."

Reluctantly, she tucked her husband's hand away under the blankets, stroked her daughter's hair, and with a great effort pushed herself to her feet and followed him out of Bal's study. Out on the landing there was a little curtained alcove with two chairs pushed haphazardly back into it. He pulled the door to, until he heard her draw breath to protest.

"We'll hear them from here," he said quietly.

She sank into the chair and drooped there like a drought-ridden plant. Years of rigorous deportment training could not overcome the debilitation of body and spirit that came with such a healing. He eased the other chair as far back as it would go against the curtain, acknowledging his own weariness. He had tried to rest, but the pain in his shoulder precluded that.

"All Mistress Floria knows is, I was the one healed your husband, using th'spicule. All you did was lend your vitality. That's all anyone need ever know, from me."

"Thank you, sir," she breathed. "Bal . . . does not know."

As he had thought. And who was he to say she was wrong? He remembered her sweeping through the illustrious ducal gathering, entirely at ease in such company, spilling the largesse of her self-confidence. He said, "M'lady, that's remarkable that nobody knows. A mage as strong as you are is rare." He paused, and with the habit of honesty that grew between mages said, "I envy you."

"Envy me!" Her sonn washed across his face, revealing that he was quite serious. And then she leaned forward and began to cry, stifled, almost inaudible sobs. He took her wrist in his gloved hand and held it until she spoke.

"If I could give it all to you," she said in a thread of a voice, "I would. Let me go."

He heard more than one meaning in that. He let her go and leaned back. She drew a deep breath and straightened. "And as to my control, clearly you know nothing of a woman's life."

She did not understand, he thought, though perhaps she would have said the same of him, each of them with a different meaning. "Your husband would have died without it," he reminded her.

She straightened and then leaned wearily back in her chair. Let the echoes fade between them. "Why were you afraid?"

Of course she would have sensed that, given the circumstances. Her voice had an undertone of merciless challenge about it. *There*, it said, *convince me that magic has any good in it, if you were afraid.*

"My lady, it's etiquette among"—he rejected *mages* and *our kind*—"people like ourselves not to mention chance-gained knowledge, unless there's need, or two people are close." He raised his hand as she drew a quick breath, choosing to assume she would apologize rather than deny the intimacy. "We're not keeping tally, r'member. . . . And you have the truth of it: I was afraid. You've that much more power than I do—fifth or sixth rank, I'd say, to my first—and you're untrained. You could have drained me to a husk t'give to your husband, and there'd have been nothing I could've done t'stop you."

Her breathing was harsh. "Then why did you do it? Does the magic . . . demand its expression?"

"Not so as to make a man lose what common sense he's born with, no," Ishmael said wryly. "Y'need never use your power—" At her quick-drawn breath, he said roughly, "Don't shy from it, m'lady. Your power's real, and it's yours. Y'need never use it in a way that seems wrong to you." There were qualifications to that statement, but it would stand for now.

"I don't want it," she said sharply.

"I know," he said. "But you have it."

"Take off your gloves," she said suddenly.

"What—"

"Take off your gloves." With swift, jerky motions, she snatched off her own. "Give me your hands. I want to *know* this man who knows the worst of me."

He gripped the chair arms. "No," he said. "My lady, no."

Her small, bare hand trembled between them. It was not her power he feared. His first fear, the fear that had driven his refusal, was that what she learned from and of him would repel her. His engagement in his power, his years as a mercenary Shadowhunter, his encounters with the Shadowborn, and the Call that twisted and hauled on his very core. His private sins and torments were reasons enough to dread her touch. But there was a greater fear: that if she pressed touch on him, despite his express refusal, he would know that he had misjudged her. He would know that he could not trust her to wield her power well.

He said intensely, "Lady Telmaine, you should not *want* t'do this."

Then she shuddered, revulsion crossing her face, and snatched back her hand and thrust it into her glove as though it represented some indecency. "I'm sorry," she said. "I'm sorry."

He did not want her restrained in her power by revulsion, but by common sense and courtesy. He said, "We Darkborn mages have our own authorities, m'lady, for all that they're hardly recognized either by our own state or th'Lightborn. We've got to govern ourselves, or suffer the Temple's justice. I'll not claim we're all perfect, but we can't but know th'pain of others, and want t'ease it if we can. You're that way yourself: Y'can't tell me you didn't dance with me out of kindness."

From the study, Balthasar Hearne moaned in his stupor, and she rustled to her feet and went quickly past Ish to go to her husband, to soothe him, no doubt, with her touch. He wondered whether Hearne or their daughters had ever known a day's illness or suffering before this. He doubted, somehow, that they had, but it was too soon to make her aware of it.

He did not expect her to return, and decided he would wait for the sunset bell and leave as soon as someone she could trust arrived. There were still things she had to know about her power and its obligations, but he could only hope that they could wait until she was less fragile.

He started out of a still and amorphous reverie at the sound of a rustle of a hem and sonned her sharply, too sharply, perceiving something of her shapely private form beneath her graceful dress. She said, "Mute your sonn, sir!"

"I'm sorry, m'lady. You startled me."

"Did I?" She spoke with an effort. "Good."

"Take care how you spend your energy," he warned, hearing the fatigue, knowing its source.

"It is mine to spend."

He smiled thinly; he had answered so with equal arrogance, and less cause, before bitter experience taught him otherwise. He gestured her to the chair. "Thought you'd've lain down by your husband and gone back t'sleep."

"Did you? You might have been done with me; I certainly am not done with you. What do you know of all this? What has that woman told you? Who did this to him, and why? *Where is my daughter?*" Her sonn stung him, but it was a genteel sting, nothing like the raking that she no doubt intended it to be. She was too well-bred to use or even know the full power of her sonn.

He honored her intent, nevertheless. "This is what I had from Mistress Floria. Two nights before last a woman came t'your husband's door just as the sunrise bell tolled, begging t'be let in. Her name was Tercelle Amberley."

A soft indrawn hiss of breath, her posture intent, but no words. He waited a moment, then continued, "She was great with child, a child she said was fathered by a lover—not her betrothed—who came to her in the daytime. Her pains began before the sunset bell and she gave birth to twins. Your husband thinks the babes were sighted, like Lightborn. Th'mother tried t'expose the children at the next sunrise, which your husband put a stop to, and at sunset she left the house. Your husband's sister took th'infants yesterday, promising t'find them a home. I heard from Mistress Floria that Mistress Olivede had a visit at her clinic from a pair of rogues like the ones who set on your husband, who met a sorry welcome. Unfortunately, they were rousted before she'd a chance to know it was other than an attempt at robbery, or she might have sent warning. She'll be here as soon as it is safe to travel."

A sharper hiss of breath.

"I can call in one of your leeches, if you'd rather," he said uncharitably. Did she imagine that nonmage physicians could have kept her husband alive? "I doubt they'd do him any harm, with you there."

"Go on," she said, ignoring the provocation.

He subsided. It was unfair to blame her alone for the prejudices of her class. "That's the sum of it. I'll be glad to lay it before Lord Vladimer, let him find the pattern in it."

"By all means, entertain Lord Vladimer with your mysteries," Telmaine said. "But I have to find my daughter."

"I've not forgotten the little one. Come sunset, if Mistress Floria's part of it has not borne fruit, I'll be speaking to a man who knows the underworld. We can speak to the public agents, too, if you'd like."

"And have it appear in the broadsheets?" she said. "My family would never forgive me."

As one who had provided ample fodder for the broadsheets' excesses, he could sympathize. "Notorious Mage Baron" was his usual sobriquet, interspersed with "the Shadowhunter" when he chanced to be in favor. And the ill-paid public agents who were the city's law enforcement supplemented their incomes with sales to reporters.

"I'll have to engage private agents," she said wearily. "Maybe my brother-in-law can help."

Thus a lady prompted a gentleman to take up her burden, he thought, though in truth he'd have needed no such prompting. "Lord Vladimer should have no objections t'my tapping his network for this, and we're as good as any private agents. I'd be cooling my heels until your husband was well, as it is."

"Thank you, Baron Strumheller. You put my mind at ease." She leaned forward, surprising him by offering him a cushion, which she eased under his braced arm, carefully avoiding all possibility of touch. Then, straight-backed, she went into her husband's study and closed the door behind her.

Ishmael

Olivede Hearne arrived almost as the last echoes of the sunset bell had faded, under escort, in a rattletrap carriage pulled by two of the rawest specimens of horseflesh Ishmael had met outside the hill villages of the Borders. She must have left shelter as soon as it was safe to do so. Like Hearne, she was of modest height and build, with an even-featured, somewhat delicate face; unlike him, she had the guarded manner of a woman who lived beyond the pale. Her accent was soft and cultured, revealing her origins amongst the minor aristocracy. She exclaimed in disapproval at finding her brother still lying on the floor, a disapproval mitigated somewhat as she realized how grave were his injuries. Ish settled in the armchair, out of the way. Telmaine stood to Ish's left with her drowsy daughter mumbling in her arms, clearly divided between being close to Balthasar and being too close to his mageborn sister.

Eventually, Olivede stroked Balthasar back to sleep and climbed to her feet. Telmaine shifted closer to Ishmael, though he doubted the movement was conscious.

"I've done what I can," she said. "I asked Magister Kieldar to come, and he can do more. I have a great deal to thank you for, Baron Strumheller."

"We took th'same training and the same vows, Magistra Hearne," Ish said. "But I never refuse a lady's thanks."

"Can I do anything for you?" She gestured toward his shoulder.

"I'd be grateful," he said, though he was aware that Telmaine had tensed, and carefully avoided showing any awareness of her. "Give me a moment," he said, to give himself a chance to settle into a light, meditative state, bringing to the forefront of his awareness an impression of the still water of the lake downhill from his manor just after sunset. That, Magistra Olivede's skill, and the vows they shared would mean that she would sense no more than that impression. The lake was restorative in itself. The touch of her cool hands, dulling the pain to the ache of a fresh-healed break, was pure bliss. "Magistra," he said, leaning his head back, "if I thought you'd take me, I'd propose t'you."

"You were starting a fever," she said dryly, and brushed the fever neatly aside, like an efficient housekeeper with a feather duster. He sneezed, either at the touch of magic or the comparison. She waited a moment—for a resurgence of fever, or proposal, perhaps—and then eased his collar closed and left him to button his shirt, turning to Telmaine. "Telmaine, how are you?"

"I am . . . as well as can be expected," the lady said with a brittle smoothness.

The exchange told Ish a great deal about the relationship between sister and wife: civil, but not confiding or close. How could it be otherwise, when Telmaine so feared discovery? Olivede stroked her little niece's hair, and Telmaine did not stiffen or protest. The touch, tendered to her daughter, connected them.

"What do you know about this?" Telmaine said at last. "Where are these infants of Tercelle Amberley's?"

"By now," Olivede said, "I don't know. As soon as I found out about this, I sent word that they should be moved as soon as possible."

Telmaine breathed, "I would trade those children for my Flori in a heartbeat."

There was a silence; the warning, or ultimatum, was understood. "Telmaine, we're going to move Bal to a bed. You can put Ami down as well—in your room, if you'd rather not leave her."

Ish said, "You'll be well guarded, m'lady. You have my word on that."

She nodded, turned, and rustled out.

Olivede pressed her fingers to her forehead. "Baron Strumheller, what do you know about this?"

"Only that it has something t'do with those twin infants of Tercelle Amberley's. I hope your word was a strong warning. Someone wants them, and likely wants dead anyone who knows about them."

She drew a deep breath, twisting her hands one in the other. "My brother is not equal to this—he is a gentle man. Not unworldly, but not . . . I know I have no claim on you, that Balthasar has no claim on you, and that the mage's vows do not tie your other skills to service, but in the name of justice and protection of those who cannot protect themselves, will you help?"

"Aye," he said easily. "That's already long decided."

She had brought with her three of the irregulars whom the mageborn in the demimonde employed for protection, when their own skills did not suffice. She pressed all three, and Telmaine, into service as orderlies, helping to move Balthasar Hearne onto a stout rug and carry him through to his bedroom. She and Telmaine stayed to settle him, and the three men drifted back, one to guard the outer door, and two, both of whom Ish knew slightly, to speak to Ish in the study.

From them, Ish learned details of the thwarted attack on Olivede, and from that, Ish had little doubt that that attack would have ended like the one on Balthasar, or worse. "She needs to stay elsewhere, next day," he said. "Well away from her usual goings. And she needs t'be guarded. She mustn't send any more messages after th'twins. Everyone along th'trail needs to be guarded, and anyone close to her. They've taken Hearne's daughter, so that shows their thinking. I want you to put out a description . . ." He described the kidnappers, pulling details out of his memory that he had not been aware of noting during their brief, drastic encounter. "Hearne may be able to give us more, by and by." He would not need to be strong enough to talk; glimpses of memory or nightmare would be enough for the touch-reader.

Olivede Hearne showed herself a woman of impressive common sense, capitulating without argument to his advice that she not follow her usual rounds. She grasped immediately that she could bring harm to the very people she wanted to help. She would stay, she said, to care for her brother. Which eased one set of worries and created another, because it made it more exigent that this household be well protected. Olivede had her magecraft, and her three guards. By contacting Vladimer's other agents in the city, Ish could raise a layer of more potent temporal protection around the family.

And if those failed, there was Telmaine, whom no enemy could anticipate. How close was she to realizing that she could as readily maim and kill as comfort and heal? If she did, did she have any sense that with her strength she need not touch to kill? He thought not: She had experienced her magic only as expressed by touch, and kept it stifled within her skin. Yet if she were the last one standing between murderers and her husband and daughters, she would use everything she had and was against them. And she would not know how. If she attacked with magic she would try to do it through touch, and there would be a knife in her heart or across her throat first.

Should he tell her that it might be done? Could he try to teach her how, though the actual doing of it was beyond his own strength? The vows that he had taken when he had committed to his own training had bound him to do his best for any mage he discovered, and placed no constraints on what he might teach them so that they might make the best lives they could in a world hostile to them. Though he would answer for what he taught and how it was used until his students could answer for themselves. He would teach her to use a gun, if he thought she needed to know. Why might magic be different?

He was not a great thinker, and so he could only accept that to him it was. He might be awed by and attracted to her, but he did not have the core-deep sense of her that would let him trust her. He wished, now, that he had taken her bare hand in his, for he would surely have come away with the knowledge that would have let him decide. But he had not.

He heard, but did not appreciate, a soft footstep and a rustling hem on the stairs—neither was a threatening sound. A man's voice did command his attention. He came quickly to his feet and was out the door. From the distorted images of their sonn, he perceived the two figures confronting each other before the door, the irregular, a broad and rather shy young man, nevertheless barring her exit. Telmaine was saying, "I *am* going out. I have to find my daughter."

"Lady Telmaine," Ish said, startling them into a double ping of sonn that caught him midway down the stairs. He brushed them lightly in return, the lady's upright, shapely figure in the coat, gloves, and veil she had arrived in, and the young man, intimidated but equally determined to do his duty.

"I am going to find Tercelle Amberley," she said. "I will not leave my child in this odious captivity one minute longer. My husband, if he were able, would go, but since he cannot, I must."

Ish made a swift decision. "I'll go with the lady. We will be back as quickly as we may. Before we are, there will be a guard on this house, but until I'm back, please don't be thinking that anyone you sonn is friendly. I'd not let anyone even as near as the steps without Magistra Olivede's say-so." He ran a hand around the jamb of the door, measuring it and finding it solid for a domestic door, though unlikely to resist a determined assault. It would take someone more mage than he to reinforce it, inanimate as it was.

Telmaine flinched as the door closed behind her, her expression wavering, briefly heart-torn and then resolute. She started briskly down the stairs, pulling out a little whistle, on which she blew a clear arpeggio. A cabdriver at the stand at the end of the street flipped his reins and started his cab toward them.

"How are you thinking t'find her?" Ish said as they settled inside. "If she was far gone with child, she'd not stay with family or friends, or anywhere that she'd chance meeting them."

Her lips thinned. "I have a notion," she said, and leaned out of the window to call an address up to the driver. It was on the other side of the city, in a neighborhood known for its new wealth and decadence.

"And that is?" Ish said, as the carriage began to rumble and rock down the street.

"Not yet," the lady said, and leaned back, folding her hands in their gloves, the image of contained preoccupation. But a moment later she said, "Balthasar's brother, Lysander Hearne, left her a house."

So there was the connection that had brought the lady to Balthasar's door on the eve of her confinement. He tried to recollect what he knew of Lysander Hearne, but could remember only that the man had disappeared some sixteen or seventeen years ago, before Ish himself came to the city.

"How well," Ish said, choosing his words carefully, "do you know her?"

"Not in that way," Telmaine said, almost as though the knowledge were carnal. "Through society. Her family members are the most arrant social climbers."

He said in a measured voice, "M'lady, you've heard my and Mistress Floria's thoughts, but you've not shared yours. What's between the lady and your husband that could draw him into this?"

"Nothing's between them," she said, her small mouth firmly closing on the last syllable.

"Lady Telmaine, it needs no touch-reader to know you're lying," he said. She caught her breath and he gave her an edged smile, the smile telling how utterly irrelevant were the standards of society, where telling a lady she was a liar was simply not done. "Lady Telmaine," he said softly, "mayhap you'd sooner not know because the knowledge offends you, or the way you came by it offends you. But your husband was nearly murdered last night, and your daughter was stolen."

"Brute," she said in a shaky whisper. "I cannot tell you."

"Who'd you want to protect more than that man resting back there in the shadow of death, or that little girl out there alone?"

"Brute!" she said more loudly, and pressed the knuckles of both gloved hands against her lips, shuddering with stifled sobs.

He sat back, grim of face and heart. He had delivered the most telling stroke he knew, hurt her cruelly, and she still would not tell him.

They rode the rest of the way in silence, of voice and sonn.

Telmaine

With the jolting of the closed carriage, her exhaustion, and the baron's harrowing at her conscience, she felt quite ill by the time they alighted in front of the ostentatious house Lysander Hearne had bequeathed his paramour. The heavy, musky-sweet scent of the blooming night roses nearly completed her undoing; in a cold sweat, she pressed her fingers to her upper lip and willed her stomach to stop heaving. If Ishmael sonned her, she wasn't aware of it, but she abruptly felt his gloved hand on her wrist, pulling it down, and felt the lip of a flask pressed against her mouth.

"Drink," he said.

She drew a breath to protest, but what she smelled was not liquor but something herbal. She let herself swallow. "It's an old Southern Isles remedy for seasickness," he said. "I'd to take th'coastal steamer up from Stranhorne, and though it's mere fancy that a mage can't cross water, I'm a Borders man, blood, bone, and belly."

Mint and astringent, it did help. She nodded acknowledgment of the fact, carefully concealing her horror at the mere thought of traveling by sea. No doubt, like her husband, the baron could discourse endlessly on the detailed maps, the clever navigational devices, and the extensive system of warning bells on coasts and rocks that enabled Darkborn to venture on the waters despite the limitations of sonn. No matter. She had never set foot on a boat, and never would.

He let her precede him up the steps to the elaborately decorated door and stood at her shoulder as they waited to know whether anyone would respond to the ring. A footman opened the door.

"Tercelle Amberley, please."

"Lady Tercelle is not receiving—"

"Tell her Telmaine Hearne requests an interview, concerning a favor that her husband Balthasar did Lady Tercelle."

The door closed in their faces. She was aware of Ish's attention to their rear, of his casting a crisp yet delicate sonn to either side along the street. The moment before the door opened, his head turned back, though she had heard neither voice nor footstep through the door. His acuity was unnerving—was it magic?

She would be ill if she thought too much of magic, though as the footman ushered them across the hall, she itched to free her hands from their gloves. Had she been alone, or in the presence of someone ignorant of the meaning of the gesture, she would have.

She did not need Ish's hunter's senses to know that the big house had been long unoccupied and barely reopened; all she needed were a chatelaine's. With its wide central stair, the hall echoed to sonn, all the muting hangings and decorations removed to be stored or displayed elsewhere. Most of the furniture in the large receiving room was still draped, and the room smelled of dust and aged dried flowers. Tercelle Amberley sat on one of the chairs, wearing a loose morning gown that flowed from the yoke and would conceal her milk-laden breasts and thickened waist. She had changed very little over the years, Telmaine thought: still the same little droplet face that could sparkle pertly or crumple piteously. "Lady Telmaine," Tercelle said with a tremor. "Do come in. Take a seat. And introduce me to your gentleman friend."

As an insinuation, it was a shaky effort; perhaps it was merely habit.

"Lady Tercelle Amberley, Ishmael di Studier, Baron Strumheller."

Tercelle extended a hand that trembled slightly. "Forgive me, Baron Strumheller, I have been—" And then she froze, jerked her hand back, and froze again. Telmaine realized then that Ishmael had slipped his glove off.

And that Tercelle Amberley knew what that implied.

Telmaine recovered her wits enough to summon a social laugh. "Baron Strumheller, I fear that your reputation has preceded you."

Tercelle panted. "I'm so sorry. I've been so very nervous lately. I'm sure it's nothing, only . . ."

Telmaine regarded her with head cocked slightly to one side, assessing strategies.

Ishmael di Studier, his expression wry, drew his glove on and held out his hand to receive Tercelle's. When he stooped, he brushed air with his lips.

"Where is my daughter?" Telmaine said.

"What? Your daughter?" said Tercelle.

Her confusion seemed genuine. Telmaine did not trust it. "Yes, mine. You may not care for your sons—"

"Voice down," rumbled the baron.

"—but be assured that Balthasar and I care for our daughter, and we will stop at nothing to find her."

Tercelle snatched back her hand from Ishmael. "The woman's mad. I have no sons." She caught up the bell sitting beside her. The baron intercepted her as she started to ring it, muffling the bell with his gloved hand. "M'lady, we need your help."

"If you are trying to blackmail me, I warn you, my betrothed—"

"Is as ruthless as any man alive," Ish said, "aye, and y'might rightly fear for your life. But Balthasar Hearne nearly lost his last night, and the same men who beat him almost t'death stole his daughter from his doorstep. Were they your men?"

"Of course not! Why would I risk—" She stopped.

He nodded approval. "First rule of intrigue—the less done, the less tracked. So, if it wasn't your doing, whose was't? Who knew you were with child?"

She pressed her fingers to her face. "For pity's sake," she whispered. "Not here." She tugged to free her hand and the bell, and the baron let her go. The tintinnabulation of the little bell owed as much to the involuntary tremor of her hand as to any deliberate movement. The footman's prompt appearance justified their caution.

"Mercury," Tercelle said, "tell Idana that my guests and I will be going up to the roof garden for a little while. I think Baron Strumheller might be more at home in a more . . . natural environment," she said, with one of the most perfect parodies of a snide society lady that Telmaine had ever heard.

Telmaine's sonn caught the bobble in the footman's throat at the mention of Ishmael's name.

They trailed their hostess up to the roof garden she spoke of. Her maid followed, a sweet-faced, very fat girl who huffed behind them to the last, narrowest flight, and then sank, panting, down on the lowest step at a signal from the lady. Leaning heavily on the banister, Tercelle led them on. Behind her, Telmaine ungloved with two swift yanks and bundled her gloves into her reticule.

On the roof garden the baron sonned around himself at once, another sequence of overlapping bursts that somehow penetrated without being conspicuously forceful. Telmaine was coming to realize that, in the wilds, at least, the baron was a master with sonn. His last burst caught her, poised with ungloved hands; she perceived his very slight nod.

Her turn. She swept down on one knee and caught up Tercelle's icy hand in both of hers. "Please," she said, "*please*, you must help me. They've stolen my daughter."

Images, phrases, impressions tumbled into her mind. The exhaustion and discomforts of a woman one day from childbed, bone-deep weariness, aching breasts, cramping womb, raw genitals. As raw was the memory of writhing agony, the helplessness, the humiliation. Telmaine gasped, losing her own coherence of thought. "Who . . ." she breathed, and remembered lying tense in bed, expectant, disbelieving, thinking, *Why?* The question always silenced by kissing, fondling, driving all questions away on great surges of molten ecstasy. A man's erect member, sonned as though she were bending to kiss it. His nipples, his neck, his broad back. Heat surged through her body, and she was no longer sure whether the body was her own or Tercelle's.

"Uh-oh," she heard the baron say, and the woman's erotic memories were suddenly snuffed out of her awareness as he shucked her hands from the lady's and caught the lady by the elbow and waist and half carried her the few steps to a bower with chairs. He settled her down solicitously and pressed her head forward. Shortly she struggled upright, saying, "No, I'm all right. For pity's sake, sir, no one must know."

Feeling dizzy and light in the bones, Telmaine got to her feet and picked her way over to stand in front of them.

"You should rest," the baron said. Telmaine noticed then that he, too, had removed his gloves.

Tercelle, unnoticing, began to weep and rock. "He will know, he will most certainly know, when we come to our marriage bed. And I don't know, I don't understand . . ."

Telmaine believed her and, for the first time, pitied her. "Please," she said simply, "do you know anything that might help me find my daughter?"

"No," said the lady, sobbing more loudly. "No, I know nothing."

"Shh," said the baron. "Does anyone else know of this?"

She sniffed, calming. "My maids, Idana and Maia. They have been with me since . . . since I first came out."

"And you trust them?"

"This would have been impossible without them. Maia is very like me in appearance, and she rides well. There will be people who say I rode out after sunset every night until we left for the city. And you met Idana—Idana is a delightful girl, but she has a terrible taste for sweets. If pressed, she will say that she went to visit Dr. Hearne because she thought he could help her with her difficulty." She stopped. "I trusted my life to them."

"Very good," the baron said quietly. "Then in a few weeks, after you have healed up from the childbed . . ." He leaned forward and murmured briefly in her ear. Her mouth fell open. "You are not the only lady with an indiscretion in her past," he assured her. "But right now, you'd best go somewhere better guarded than this, somewhere where people do not expect to find you. Balthasar Hearne all but died last night, and it may be that by coming here, we have put your life at risk."

"I don't . . . I can't—"

"It is your choice," the baron said. "Nevertheless, I do advise it. Now Mrs. Hearne and I will take our leave."

Telmaine

They climbed into the carriage, the baron moving as though his bones ached. His expression as he settled himself across from her was grim.

"She didn't know anything," Telmaine said.

He stirred himself. "No, m'lady. She didn't. And you pulled on her hard enough."

She frowned, troubled by the flatness of his voice.

"Is something wrong? Is your shoulder hurting?"

"Aye, it is," he said in that same tone. "There's touch-reading, and then there's reaching in and taking. You reached in and took; I had to replenish her, and that costs me. Lady Telmaine, you're a dozen times the mage I am. You have t'be careful."

Hearing her one ally condemn her, for reasons she did not understand, and was not sure she could have helped if she understood, she started to cry.

After a moment she heard him stir and grumble. "Don't do that."

"Why? Are you one of those who can't abide weeping women?"

"No," he said, after consideration. "Though I can't abide those who do it for effect." He lowered his head into his hand and gave an absurdly girlish sob, and she felt a delicate little brush of sonn on her face; he sobbed again, and sonned again, and she could not help it: She giggled, with a little involuntary catch of hysteria. "Why, Baron," she said, "I did not realize you were such a good actor."

He lowered his hand. "I am a very good actor, Lady Telmaine," he said, unsmiling. "As are you."

She rejected the suggestion with a nervous wave.

"M'lady, you have passed for the perfect society lady. Oh, a little radical in her choice of husband, true, but nothing I had heard of you led me to suspect the reality. Until I sonned you coming down the stairs by that ridiculous automaton, with your gloves up to your beautiful shoulders."

"Ridiculous," she said, piqued, her mind shying from the rest of his statement.

"Aye, it was. All that machinery t'do what? Move a single silver ball?"

Telmaine drew a deep, steadying breath, glad of the moment's grace he had given her. "What do we do now?"

"I take you home t'your husband." She heard a rustle of movement as he raised a hand in anticipation of objections. "Telmaine, these are not places a lady should go. And I will need all my wits about me, and you, m'lady, are a sore distraction. I wish I had met you before he did."

"Baron," she said, "if I had met you at the age of seventeen, I would have bolted like a deer."

He threw back his head and laughed, wincing and bracing his arm.

She waited out his laughter, since she had told no more than the truth, chewing on the inside of her lip and listening to the rattle of the wheels on the cobbles, coarser cobbles now: They were out of the fine neighborhoods. She dearly wished she did not feel compelled to ask this of him, but she had to know. "Baron . . . was she . . . ensorcelled?" She was utterly at a loss for polite and innocuous words to describe the memories she had drawn from Lady Tercelle Amberley, and felt almost faint with embarrassment for herself and for the other woman. She burst out, "What she felt for her . . . for her lover. It didn't seem . . . decent. I've never felt . . . didn't know anyone . . ." Her face was burning so brightly she was surprised they were both not falling into ashes.

"People do, m'lady," he said, the low rumble consolingly matter-of-fact. "But you ask a good question, and I think . . ." This came very reluctantly. "I fear it's possible. She had far, far too much to lose by letting herself be taken like this."

"So magic can do *that*."

He was silent, jolting along opposite her. When she brushed him with her sonn, he stirred and said, "What would you have me say, m'lady? That yes, magic can be used to abuse and control people? Done that way, it's called sorcery, and by any measure a crime." He eased forward, wincing slightly. "I'd sooner not frighten you, but it seems I must. Do again what you did then and you risk your gift, your sanity, and mayhap your life. You are not trained, and you are powerful enough to do harm. You drained Lady Tercelle quite thoroughly; without me there to replenish her, you might have sent her into a coma."

"I . . . I never—"

"Hear me out, Lady Telmaine. Have y'heard of the Lightborn Temple Vigilance?"

"Yes, but . . . but they're Lightborn. They have nothing to do with us."

"Not so. There're more and more powerful Lightborn mages than there are Darkborn mages. Mayhap they know how to bring on a child with magic; they don't tell us. The Lightborn Mages' Temple rules magic among Lightborn *and* Darkborn. They don't much care what lower-rankers do; we're often more menace to ourselves than anyone else. But they do care about real power misused. It goes back, all the way back to the Curse and the mages' war before . . ."

He paused, leaning back against the seat. "Y'know virtually nothing of magic, I expect. When we say *power*, *strength*, it's more like *efficiency*. Working magic means drawing on your own and others' vital energy to effect a change in th'physical world. How much y'can do depends. Even now, you'd do far more with your vitality than I ever could with mine. First rank to sixth rank, that's a vast difference. Th'most powerful mages alive are eighth-rank. If you'd known what you were doing, you'd not have needed a spicule to heal your husband. If you wanted to, you could make someone do whatever you wished, or drain them to th'point of death. That's sorcery. If you were caught by the Temple Vigilance, they'd destroy your magic, and mayhap your mind. The stronger th'mage, the greater the risk. I've already lied for you to Mistress Floria. I'd lie for you again. But there'd be a point I'd not be able to go past, even if I wanted to."

Her hands were pressed to her mouth, her mouth open in a silent cry in the dark. She could not even sonn. She felt him take her shoulders in his broad, warm hands. "Take care, m'lady. You've a power and spirit that're beyond price." She felt his lips touch hers.

He released the kiss an instant before she would have pulled away. They rode the rest of the way in silence, and with a proper but not fulsome farewell, he handed her down from the coach and stood guard until she had climbed the steps and opened and closed the door. Through the door she heard the clatter of his carriage leaving, and she braced her gloved hands against the door and leaned her forehead against it. She had never, ever in her life touched someone who could touch her back; never, ever in her life known what it felt like to be known. She knew what it was to be desired, yes: Every time they came together, she drank of Balthasar's desire like a sparkling wine. It was to preserve the heady clarity of that desire that she would not let Bal make love to her after they quarreled, until they had healed the quarrel with words. But when the baron—Ishmael—kissed her, she had felt the pain of his injured shoulder, felt the anger he still harbored, felt his fear, felt his desire like a resinous brandy, felt the aching loneliness of the outcast. Then she had felt his emotions shift as he felt hers in turn, the anger mitigated, the fear falling away, the desire becoming mingled with surprise, the loneliness become a yearning toward her. For a moment, pure revelation of reciprocity had held her, and then she broke away, and she knew that he knew how nearly she had not broken away. Sweet Imogene, what manner of wanton *was* she, with her husband lying beaten near to death upstairs? Magic was as corrupting as everyone claimed.

"Telmaine," said Olivede from behind her.

She turned, at bay. "Don't come near me!"

There was a silence, and then Olivede's sonn brushed her very lightly. "So your errand was not successful. I am so very sorry." She stepped back and gestured toward the sitting room. "My colleagues are upstairs," she said. "You might be more comfortable if you waited here until they're done."

Could the mageborn woman—standing square in the hall, blocking the way to the stairs—sense the wild impulse working in her to scream at them to leave Balthasar alone, to beat or drag them away from him if necessary? She tamped down the scream to a single gulped sob, which reactivated the turmoil in her stomach. There was no baron to offer her his potion—she pushed past Olivede into the downstairs privy. Olivede, blessedly, finally left her alone.

Shaky and purged, she crept into the sitting room and closed the door. She sat, her head back, sonn quiescent, and did not stir as she heard footsteps come down the stairs. Cheap soles, she recognized, cheap soles and the weary tread of a strange man and woman. She braced herself as outside the door she heard skirts rasp and rustle and words quietly exchanged: Olivede, thanking her fellow mages, followed by a low-voiced argument as to whether they should take a cab. She knew what she should do—rise, go to the door, open it, *face* them, offer them money for a cab, offer them her *thanks*. She shuddered; there was that part of her that could not believe that Balthasar was not lying dead, or if not dead, as corrupted as she. And so she huddled in her chair while the argument concluded, with Olivede saying finally, "You *will* take a cab and an escort. I *cannot* let you return unguarded. Baron Strumheller would have apoplexy." A moment later, through the door came a piercing whistle of the most common sort. Telmaine winced at the thought of her genteel neighbors—even the cabdrivers—hearing that. And plainly, the cabdrivers agreed, for the whistle was not followed by the approaching sound of a cab, but by silence and another whistle, and a, "Curse them," from Olivede.

"We should be able to get a cab on the avenue," said the young woman resignedly. "Perhaps I could walk there and bring it back."

"D-do you think"—that was the young guard—"the baron would mind if . . . if we used his automobile? I can drive it. My b-brother builds them."

Telmaine started to her feet, suddenly finding it intolerable that they should linger a moment longer in the hallway of her—of

Bal's—home. Never mind that she well knew that Bal should not likewise find it intolerable. She handed herself from chair arm to chair back and leaned upon the doorknob as she pulled the door open. "I will summon you a cab," she said.

She stepped out into the night air, the young guard at her shoulder, and blew upon her whistle. There was a moment's silence, and then, from the direction of the rank, the jingle of a harness and a cab coming slowly into motion. She waited with her head high, aware that her dress was rumpled and her veil slipping, and refusing to acknowledge either. When the cab drew up and the driver's sonn brushed lightly over her, she lifted her skirts and stepped lightly down to the curb. "You will take the magistra and magister wherever they need to go, please. They have done my household great service tonight." From her pouch she took a half-solar and put it in the coachman's hand; for that he should be prepared to drive halfway to the Borders. Then she turned, and, sweeping her skirts aside, she passed the mages as they came down the stairs. For the first time she sonned their faces, the young woman a young girl, actually, no older than Anarys, though much plainer, and the man well past middle age. Both moved with that bone-aching weariness she herself felt, drained by magic. The man's sonn caught whatever of her unwelcome empathy showed on her face, for he paused, and then said gently, "You have a remarkable husband, Lady Stott. What he lacks in constitution, he makes up for in spirit." He did not sonn her again, so he did not sonn her frozen apprehension of his words. She took the last few steps at a stumbling run, and Olivede and the guard stood aside to let her pass.

"He's asleep," Olivede said, a penetrating whisper, as Telmaine set foot on the stairs. "Don't wake him." Telmaine turned; Olivede spread her hands. "The longer we can leave telling him about Flori, the better. I may be the mage, but I've never been able to keep anything from Bal."

Nor I, lodged in Telmaine's throat, so painfully she thought she would gag on it. Teeth clenched, she pressed on upstairs.

Bal lay on his side, on their bed, his breathing slow and deep beneath the quilts piled over him. There was no dreadful sickroom odor, no fumes of bizarre herbs or potions, just a faint scent of new-cut grass. You had to think to know that it did not belong here, in this small city house. She chose not to think. Very carefully, she drew off her gloves, eased her weight onto the bed, and crept her hand across the quilt to overlap his. Through his skin she could feel how much stronger he was since the last time she had touched him, his breathing no longer an effort against gravity and air, his pain merely monotonous rather than agonizing. He was not healed, but he was healing, and his sweet essence was unchanged. She curled up with her forehead against his hand, drinking in that essence. He did not stir.

Four

Ishmael

Ishmael dismounted from the carriage at an address in the fashionable quarter of town. The hour was most unfashionable, and his dress well behind fashion, but at least after a sleepless, hectic night and day he might be taken for fashionably played-out. He padded up the wide stairs and hung on the doorbell until an impassive manservant admitted him. He handed over his calling token and waited, feet apart and stoic, wondering what he would do if he were denied admission. In this household, a mage's welcome was never certain. But after several minutes, the manservant returned to escort him into the receiving room.

He waded into a miasma of cologne and tobacco so pungent that he fully expected to sonn the reek itself, like fine gauze draping the walls. He sneezed—the jolt to his collarbone!—and applied the brakes to a whole runaway train of sneezes. The room's sole occupant, a large young man in lounging dress, sneered at him from his armchair, enjoying his discomfiture.

Guillaume di Maurier was another dispossessed son of the border baronies, but where Ish's offense was magic, Guillaume's was a career of dissipation prodigious for a man of only twenty-six. Ish had paid to regain his inheritance, paid in blood, grief, friends, and scars both visible and invisible. Guillaume was slouching toward his own redemption, tight-leashed by Vladimer. Like Ish, he was one of Vladimer's irregulars, his specialty the dens of the demimonde. Likely the cologne was intended to disguise the smells of stale hard liquor and smoked intoxicants, presumably against the arrival of one of his patron's more numb-nosed agents.

Ish, far from numb-nosed, had no interest in reporting on the young reprobate, as long as he was sober enough to hear the case and set to work on it. He gave Guillaume the crisp bow of one gentleman acknowledging another, teeth set against the plaint from his collarbone and a new eruption of sneezes.

Guillaume waved a large, soft hand, its nails bitten to the quick. "Didn't expect you at this hour, Strumheller." *Or at all*, his sour tone implied. "You've the likeness of death on the stroll. Lively night?"

"Aye," Ish said. "And not over yet. I've come for your help."

"*My* help?"

"I've a kidnapped child t'find."

"Kidnapped?" This in a metallic tone; languishing no longer, Guillaume pulled himself upright. "Boy? Girl? How old? Sit down."

Whatever his vices and whatever his attitude toward Ish, Guillaume's protectiveness toward children was relentless, for reasons preserved in crumbling broadsheets of twenty years ago and, Ish suspected, in Guillaume's nightmares and drugged dreams. Gil and his two younger sisters had been the victims of a Borders feud, kidnapped, and held for ransom. The kidnappers were killed in ambush, the children's whereabouts still unknown. When they were finally found, the little girls were dead of hunger and thirst, though the boy had, at the end, tried to feed them his own blood.

There had been a mage involved, who had entered the house as a nursery nurse. At the trial of the conspirators behind the kidnapping, she was accused of lulling the household into an unnatural sleep to enable the abduction, and of hiding the children's whereabouts from their rescuers. She was convicted of malignant sorcery and executed by blades of light.

Given that history, Ish could forgive Gil much.

"Girl, six years old. Her name is Florilinde Hearne." He paused, remembering that Vladimer had coupled Guillaume's name and Hearne's, while persuading Ish to seek Hearne's advice. "She's Balthasar Hearne's daughter."

A sharply indrawn breath. "I know that child. Where's Hearne? Does he know?"

"He's been beaten near t'death, and the child was all but torn from her mother's arms."

Guillaume said in a low growl, "Tell me."

Ish did not tender Tercelle Amberley's name, and omitted the fact that her child was twins, and that they were sighted. And, of course, he left out Telmaine's part in healing her husband. The rest he told as fully as he could without compromising any of his elisions. By the time he had finished, Guillaume was pacing and gulping coffee strong enough to rattle a skeleton's bones. Ish had set aside his own cup after a few mouthfuls out of regard for the lining of his stomach and his steady hand.

"Shame you didn't hear the other speak, because if he had maybe you'd likely have heard the sound of good breeding turned rotten. That description sounds like Melchisedoc di Palmar."

"I've heard of him," Ishmael said. A Shadowborn in Darkborn shape, by all accounts.

"I've never known him to prey on children, but I'd not think it beneath him. And I know where to find him, and that's a start." Guillaume drained the dregs and set the cup down with a thud. "Tell Hearne I'll get his Florilinde back if it's the last thing I do."

Even allowing for youthful dramatics, there was deep conviction in that vow. Ish judged it a good moment to ask, "How do you know Hearne?"

For a moment, he thought Guillaume would not answer. Then, "I fetched up more dead than alive in that clinic in the demimonde where he works. My family's physicians had long since given up on me, said I'd be dead in months. Hearne purged me, dosed me, and worked over me for the better part of three nights straight. Then he talked me into letting him try with me. That was three years ago. Some days now when I step out the door, I think there might be a future there. If there is, it's his doing."

"Then he's good at what he does?"

A crisp wash of sonn, a considering silence.

"I've a reason for asking," Ish said. "A personal reason."

"Aye, then, I'd say he's good." He turned away with another careless wave of that large, battered hand. "I'll be going out, but I'll tell Zacharias to make up the spare room. You'll do my reputation as a host no service, leaving here like misery incarnate."

How like Gil, Ish thought, regretting that he would never be able to call this man his friend. "Be careful," he said, bracing his elbow as he rose. "There are a few things I haven't been able to share with you. This could be bigger and stranger than we know."

Gil sneered. "Keep your mysteries, Magister Baron, if you must."

Magister, Ish thought, *indeed.* The suspicion that Tercelle Amberley had been ensorcelled presented him with yet another problem, and one that belonged exclusively to the mage rather than the nobleman or irregular agent. Aspects of Lady Tercelle's experience were too readily explained by magic: her abject enthrallment, and her conviction that her lover came to her through the day. By his visit, he might have set Tercelle Amberley thinking about magical influence, and if that happened, she had already proven herself ruthless in self-defense. If concealment of her childbirth were impossible, she would resort to counteraccusation, and if she did that, with her family and fiancé, more mages than the guilty would fall. Society might disdain magic and shun its practitioners, but that did not mean that it would ignore the threat to its foundations of respectability and inheritance. Mage hunts and mass exposures might be in the past, but he did not want to test how far.

For the moment, however, an old Shadowhunter's common sense prevailed, the wisdom that had taught him that a tired hunter could waste more time by missing a fresh trail than he did by letting it get a little older. He'd had no sleep, he'd been expending magic, and he was injured. He prepared an urgent message to Vladimer's second in the city, asking that a watch be kept on the Hearne home, had it dispatched, and then asked to be shown the spare room. Guillaume's manservant did so, straight-faced. Alas, he and his master were to be disappointed in any mischief meant; it wasn't until Ish woke three hours later that his sonn focused well enough for him to appreciate the bed. The wood of the bedposts was expensive, the carving technique exquisite, and the carvings themselves obscene. That and the memory of that importunate kiss given—shared—in the carriage, were considerable distractions to his efforts to heal his shoulder, although the extra injection of vitality served him well in the end. He washed, pulled his freshened clothes back on, and let the sober Zacharias serve him what he supposed to be this household's idea of a light luncheon, of which he ate half and still felt overfed. Guillaume had not returned.

A cab took him to the edge of the Rivermarch and the household of Magister Farquhar Broome, most powerful of the Darkborn mages. A man of different temperament would have been archmage of the Minhorne mages, but Magister Broome had no talent for leadership whatsoever, and barely enough practical sense to have escaped simple starvation in his early years. His immense natural gifts took him out of the world. Such leadership as there was for the mages of the Rivermarch was provided by Broome's natural-born daughter, Phoebe, and adopted son, Phineas, two fourth-rank mages of strong character and decided—and often contentious—views. What united them, and the two or three dozen permanent members of their community, was a commitment to their kind, as teachers, guardians, and, if need be, judges.

Generations ago this part of the Rivermarch had been an exclusive area for the aristocratic Lightborn. The Broome household occupied two of those houses and still had the plain—to Darkborn senses—frontage and large, framed windows that marked the architecture as Lightborn rather than Darkborn, though the windows had been long since sealed. The front garden, well cultivated and decorous, sloped gracefully down to the river's edge, though it was constant work to keep the shore free of litter from the heavily used waterway. The rear garden, behind very high walls and hedges, was a shambles of experiments in cultivation and manipulation of trees, plants, and flowers, beautiful and grotesque, fragrant and rank, which pressed close around the paths and left Ishmael, even now, thoroughly spooked. Some were too reminiscent of the bizarre and dangerous vegetation that grew in the rare moist areas of the Shadowlands. On his very first visit to the household he'd emptied both revolvers into a bank of semianimate plants, thereby earning the fury of their creator and the worship of the children, who talked for days about how swiftly and thoroughly he'd demolished his targets—and got him labeled a bad influence.

Therefore, he restrained his reflexes as he crossed the garden, waved to the one gardener he recognized—who, he was sure, would rapidly tell the others the essentials, plant massacre and all—and climbed the long stairs to the back door. All across the garden, he had been sensing magic, which for him was accompanied by vertigo, though he'd heard others describing it as heat, a drone, a hum, a sense of lightness or heaviness—how the body translated the sense was entirely individual. As a weak, untrained mage, he had found the vertigo intolerable; he couldn't shield himself against it, and after years as a Shadowhunter, the perturbation of his senses unnerved him. Between the intrusive sense of magic and the distraction of living in a large, roiling household after years of solitude, he had been a poor student, and the more sensitive of his fellow students were aware of the Call, and of his violent dreams, and were disturbed by both. It had been a relief to all when Phoebe Broome introduced him to the man who would become his preceptor, a phlegmatic, misanthropic mage who lived on the far side of the Rivermarch, in the old Darkborn district. Magister Perrin had explored the Shadowlands himself in his youth. He had seldom had a student, had not much idea how to teach a student, but Ish, for his part, had little idea how to *be* a student, so they had improvised together.

The big front hall was much as Ish remembered, walls and ceiling draped with ornamental hangings and rugs, tasteless in their abundance and smothering to sonn. Higher-rank mages forgot what it was to have to rely upon the common senses. He climbed the stairs, keeping away from the hangings: He had heard that the younger mages' love of mischief had crossbred with the prevalent fever for automata. He didn't want to enhance his reputation by assassinating a nest of mechanical spiders.

<Who . . . ? Ugh!> The brief mental touch was one of the children, taking liberties, and regretting them. Ishmael might lack the raw strength to shield himself against mental intrusion, but he could certainly conjure up the imagery to repel intruders, and did so now as an automatic response. Aside from his own preference for keeping his unspoken thoughts to himself, his work for Vladimer brought him into possession of state secrets. If there were any capacity he envied his stronger fellow mages, it was their ability to speak to one another without touching, and without crippling themselves—an ability that would have saved lives in the hunt. When he used it, it laid him flat for days.

He heard a whisper of clothing overhead, and sonn rippled over him. He smiled, recognizing the soft step, the whisper, and the sonn. "Magistra Broome."

"Magister di Studier. Up to your usual tricks, I gather."

She alluded, he hoped, to his moving with a minimum of sonn. He imaged her standing in the doorway to the main hall, which had become the center of the household. She was a tall woman, nearly a foot taller than Ishmael himself, and extremely thin, with a long, narrow chest, and hips that were only slightly broader than a lean man's. Her head was small for her body and surprisingly delicate in its features. In her own household, her preferred attire was a man's jacket and trousers. Ish occasionally wished he could introduce her to a former transvestite burlesque star he knew; Ruther would be enchanted. He hadn't dared; Magistra Broome was not one to offend, and mage or no mage, she had her own brand of conventionality.

Which, it had warmed Ish to discover, did not include hypocrisy about sex. The day before he left the city, returning to the Borders for his father's last rites, she had appeared on Magister Perrin's doorstep. "I don't know when I'll get the chance again," she announced, and made the first move in what he had—embarrassingly belatedly—recognized as a seduction. It was the first time Ish had ever lain with a fellow mage, and it had been even more of a revelation than when he first shed his virginity.

The recollection threatened to bring Telmaine Hearne to the forefront of his mind. That must not happen in this household. The senior mages' control was exquisite and their behavior scrupulous—neither Phoebe nor Phineas would tolerate it any other way—but there were still the students, testing their boundaries. . . . He tucked the memory of her securely behind his barrier image.

Phoebe Broome took both his hands in hers. Like him, and as an example to the younger mages, she wore gloves. In her case, delicate silk gloves, sheathing her slim wrists and long tapering fingers. "I hear you've been moving in elevated circles these days."

He could not help but hear envy in her voice. Of the mages' leaders, she was the one who aspired to recognition from society, while her brother advocated separatism. Ish was quite certain that she would not have seduced him if he'd been a nobody from the provinces.

He didn't begrudge her her ambitions, and at times like this he regretted that he'd never be respectable enough to host a house party and let her inspect the nobility for herself.

"Aye," he said. "Lord Vladimer's done some smoothing of my way, and I've been minding myself."

"No shooting out the shrubbery," she teased. A pause. "You have that air about you that tells me you haven't come to socialize," she said. "We've a problem."

"Why *we*?" he said after a moment.

She gave him a mischievous smile. "Ishmael, Ishmael. As long as I've known you, you've thought it your prerogative to keep your troubles to yourself. Sometimes unwisely so. So, if you're bringing me a problem, it's one that's shared."

"You have the right o' it," he said. "Has Magistra Hearne spoken to you?"

"Olivede? No . . ."

"I'd think she might, eventually," he said, as she showed him into her receiving room. In this huge, haphazard house it was a model of taste and fashion, an expression of her aspirations. She, in her jacket and trousers, might have inhabited a set in an avant-garde comedy. "But there's more parts to the matter that have come to me since." He sat down on an elegantly designed and decidedly uncomfortable chair. "There's been sorcery worked on a highborn lady, causing her t'compromise herself. There may be trouble over it; there may not, since she's bent on keeping it to herself. I've touch-read her, and since she's no mage herself, she had no sense of magic. But her thrall to her lover was unnaturally powerful, maybe, and she believes he came t'her through the day. And I could take no impression of his face."

"Touch-read her unwilling and unwitting," she said, without expression.

"At the time I thought her more villain than victim. There's a kidnapped child that's part of all this, and a man near beaten t'death." He paused. "I think you need to hear the whole of it."

"I think I do."

He began, once again, with Vladimer's instructions to him—which she greeted with some dismay—and his arriving on Balthasar Hearne's doorstep to be met by the stroke of a sap, a felled physician, and Floria White Hand's extraordinary account. He continued through to the interview with Tercelle, and his mandate to Guillaume. He omitted, of course, all mention of Telmaine's magic. There'd surely be consequences if she misused her magic again, but he found he simply could not expose her.

She tapped silk-clad fingertips against her teeth. "Sighted children . . ." she said, with a dread that only now, having walked through the garden, did he understand. There had been early efforts to restore sight to the Darkborn, all failures, and nowadays the manipulation of tissue, other than for healing, was sorcery. Manipulation of plant life was itself barely acceptable. He had not thought of that possibility before. "Oh, Ishmael, you have brought me an ugly one." She leaned forward suddenly. "Promise me you'll carry this no farther. Speak of these children nowhere else. If a mage is responsible, it's worth our peace, everything we've built, maybe even our lives to have it known."

"I cannot promise," he said after a moment. "I don't know where this investigation is bound; I don't know how much of it may need t'be taken to Lord Vladimer. The best I can promise is t'delay if I can, t'let you find the one responsible—if it is a mage."

"Sweet Imogene, what else could it be? This woman, Tercelle Amberley, will she lay accusations?"

"Not unless it would cost her less t'lay them than to keep still. She'd be as much ruined by it as by th'other. But y'need to hold it close. For your own sake, as much as hers."

"I will, believe me." Her face went briefly still. "I've called in my brother, and two or three others."

"I'll leave you to't then," Ish said, rising. "Y'know where to find me."

"Coward," she murmured sardonically.

He shook his head. "Your brother won't believe me; he'll want me touch-read. I'll not allow that. I've told you what I know; you'd best confirm it with others, Magistra Olivede first. I've my own errands to pursue. One thing, though: Florilinde Hearne. I'd be grateful if one or other of you higher-rankers gave a thought to finding her. Magistra Olivede would likely be asking for herself."

"Where are you bound now?"

"Magistra Olivede's clinic. They tried t'set on her yesterday, and failed."

"Take care," she said. "You've nowhere near the power to match yourself against a mage who could alter a child in the womb, and anyone that perverted will not hesitate at murder."

"Nor will I," Ish said. "And I've been hunting perversions these twenty-five years. Good day, Magistra."

"Is it?" she said sourly. With a hand on his arm, she stayed him at the door. "I mean it when I say 'take care,' Ishmael. I've heard about the way you overspend yourself. Mages die doing that. Or their magic never recovers."

He stooped to lift her hand and kiss it, which spared him from having to answer. He knew she was right; he also knew he could be no other way.

He passed Phineas Broome on the stairs. The other ruling mage, being no relative of Phoebe's, was her physical opposite: compact, broad, and muscled, with a face as sculptedly male as hers was delicately female. He was a trained acrobat and dancer, and moved with a compact, springy agility. His sonn was harsh; he scowled as he recognized Ish, but did not speak. He was ferociously republican in his politics. Shortly after Ish had arrived, Phineas had made an attempt to drive him away that had left Ish unconscious for a day and Phineas, to his horror, afflicted by an echo of the Call. His peers had considered that just punishment and imposed no other. Phineas had not left Minhorne since.

No, Ish thought, he'd sooner be out of range before the shouting—audible and otherwise—began.

Back in the old Darkborn section of the Rivermarch, he began his inquiries at Olivede Hearne's clinic, where the abortive attack on her had taken place. Amongst people familiar with mages, he could also ask to receive touch-impressions and swiftly compiled descriptions of the men involved. He didn't know them, but he had little doubt he, or Gil, would find them.

No sooner had he left the clinic than he was accosted by a lanky young rogue who he was sure would have sapped him in a back alley as soon as fulfill his charge.

"I've been half the night finding you," the youth said sullenly.

Ish doubted that; this appearance was much too convenient. But, "Good," he said, "I'd hate to think I was becoming predictable. To what end?"

"Got a note." The youth held up a small envelope, pinching it between his fingers, well out of Ish's reach.

Ish plucked a coin from his purse; they jousted briefly over who should yield and who should receive first. The transaction was completed, and Ish carefully observed the youth's departure. That done, he withdrew to the doorway of a Lightborn shop, closed for the night, set his back against the painted shutter, drew off his glove, and traced his fingertip over the note: *I need your help. Come to where we met before. TA.*

So she had ignored his advice to leave. He sniffed the note, trying to screen out all the pungency of the city. He recalled that she had been wearing a heavy scent when they met, either out of habit or to overlay the lingering taint of blood from the birth. No perfume clung to the note, though no smoke did either. He thought he smelled a little grease, perhaps from his gloves, from working on the car. Touch told him nothing, beyond that the paper was expensive; he wasn't mage enough to gather impressions from the inanimate. The note was forcefully punched, but agitation might be sufficient to make a woman's hand heavy. Nonetheless . . .

He made his way to the rooming house on the edge of the Rivermarch where he had fetched up when he first came to the city, and where he still kept a room. The house was home or sometime home to a random mix of intractable bachelors, homosexuals, bit-part actors, and the occasional fugitive husband. The two old men who owned it were as long married as any elderly couple he'd ever met, and happier than most. And much more interesting, with a life in burlesque and theater behind them, and a keenly scatological interest in politics and gossip. Not to mention their other talents.

"I need to get up to, if not into, a house in the Lagerhans district," Ish explained, sitting in a receiving room crowded with theatrical memorabilia. When he had first washed up here, he was constantly starting, catching movement off to the side as his sonn triggered some shimmering display.

"Lagerhans, eh?" said Ruther di Sommerlin, born Roberd Sommer, once famous in the best cabarets as the Minhorne Lily. In the stooped old man there was still the wraith of the tall, languid stage beauty. " 'Tis a pity you've the body of a troll, my boy. It limits you so."

"Alas, I take after my father, not my mother."

"Most men do." He clucked. "And you don't want one of us to do your errand for you. Poppy could use a little distraction." He shook his head. "The boy's been into the drug again. He's got a terrible hunger."

What the nineteen-year-old had was what might prove a fatal inability to reconcile himself to his own nature. "I'll speak to him when I come back," Ish said. Though he didn't share Poppy's particular affliction, his Drunken God knew he'd tried any number of methods of self-immolation before settling properly into his own skin. Maybe he'd have a word with Balthasar Hearne, too, once the physician had recovered. "It's not that I wouldn't want him on the job, but I don't know what I'd be sending him into."

"You're a good man, for a woman-loving mage," Ruther said. He sonned him once more, with a disgruntled expression. "Best leave you a man. If you were a woman you'd have to be a fat crone."

Ish departed the house in the guise of a lowland provincial nobleman in robust middle age, his hair extended and tied back, and a fashionable tricorne hat perched on his head. He wore a coat with a high waist to hide the length of his torso, and padding to give him corpulence to match his shoulders. Theatrical putty hid his scars, his cheeks were full, he had jowls and a double chin—the better to mask the shape of his jaw—and his hair covered his ears. "Not many people properly notice teeth and you're not in the habit of smiling unless you're at ease. But be mindful." Ruther would not let him choose his own shoes. "You are a prosperous provincial. You'll have shoes that suit fashion and please your vanity, even though they pinch a little. Above all else, they'll remind you not to move like a Shadowhunter on the hunt."

The shoes definitely pinched a little, and with wearing they would pinch a lot. He caught and paid for a cab, though the provincials he had met tended to be parsimonious in small things, and had it let him off at a circular park two or three blocks from the house. Then he started walking, reminded by his nipped heels to put some mince into his prowl. At least as a sightseer he had an excuse to lay about liberally with his sonn, imaging not only the street ahead of him, as a local might, but the housefronts with their main and understairs, the cabs and carriages. He allowed himself to stop and study an engine-drawn carriage as a countryman would, puffing out his thickened cheeks with disapproval at the thought of such a newfangled gadget affrighting the livestock. He also took note of the people who were out and about, though he had to catch himself before he let his sonn become too penetrating for politeness; it would not do to let himself be caught up in some quarrel with an irate male escort accusing him of compromising a lady's modesty. He felt as though he were hunting in dense undergrowth.

Tercelle Amberley's tall house appeared no different than it had earlier, graceful arc of front stairs to wide door, intricate stonework that created shimmering sonn chimeras, frill of growth from the roof garden decorating the upper story. Of late, the fashion was to suspend a decorated fan in the doorway to indicate a willingness to receive visitors, and the private codes conveyed by such fans had helped many an intrigue, both personal and political. The door at number twenty was devoid of ornament, and there was no evidence of anyone being home. He inspected it only slightly longer than he did the house next to it, and then continued his stroll. Two houses down he reached the corner and paused to unfold and finger a piece of paper at some length. A provincial countryman might be prosperous and locally well regarded, but he need not be a great reader. Meanwhile, he listened to his surroundings. That done, he turned and with some perplexity sonned the houses he had just passed, as though it were just entering his head that he might be lost. In doing so, he caught the movement he had heard—someone ducked down on the basement stairs of number twenty. Too swift a movement, he thought, for him to go bustling up with an, "I say, might you be able to direct me . . ." He felt the same stilling within him that was familiar from the Shadowlands, when he sensed danger. It clarified his thinking. He tucked the paper into his waistcoat and went up the stairs to number twenty-four, which did have an ornamental fan mounted and swaying gently in the breeze. He was aware that, shoes or no shoes, he was stepping soft and smooth.

A housekeeper answered; they sized each other up, he, Ish thought, probably deriving less information from the exercise. She was a stout, worldly body who he would have said was proud to know her place and prouder still to have everyone else know it. He produced his laboriously punched paper, and said—in his best provincial accent—that he sought friends who he thought lived in this street, but he must have had their number wrong. He thought it might be twenty. Oh, no, she said, number twenty was a lady who had just arrived, a lady in not very good health.

Ish brushed that aside with his preoccupation with his wish to find his friends. No, number twenty-two was empty; that young family had not yet returned from the seaside. And they were number twenty-four and— No, she did not think anyone in the street had that name, though she did not know number twelve. Had he come so very far?

Indeed he had, Ish said, but he still had time to try to trace his friends, only he must now worry about the sunrise bell; people were not so willing, here, to let distressed strangers across their threshold.

Indeed not, said she, because it was a favorite trick of criminals to obtain admission under pretense of being caught outside at sunrise and then sack the household. Even though this was supposed to be a good neighborhood, some of the visitors were enough to make one think. Only this afternoon she had met a man going into number twenty who was a ruffian if ever she knew one, with great burns across his face.

He was glad that she did not sonn his face in time to catch his expression before he had mitigated it into innocent shock. "Madam, you alarm me," he said, and made his flustered good-byes, bustling down the stairs and heading up the street with his rubber-tipped cane pattering on the pavement. Now he was sweating. Either Tercelle Amberley was a villain, or she was a victim; whichever way the cards fell, this was surely a trap for him.

He never had had any sense. So his father told him, and about that he could not argue. A sensible man would have rattled on out of there in the first cab he called, switched cabs, shed the disguise, gone to ground. A sensible man would have decided Tercelle Amberley was a villain and left her to her well-deserved fate. Ish veered around the end of the row, confronting the stone wall around the rear gardens. He unfastened his padded jacket to free himself for movement, jammed the cane into his belt like a sword. Jumped to get his arms over the top of the wall of the end-row garden and heaved himself up and over into the bushes at the rear. He circled the garden, keeping behind the screen of bushes. On the far side, a small tree offered him a leg up. He imaged the garden with a single cast, this one a mazelet of low hedges and skirt-wide paths around several shallow ponds. He dropped into the garden and ran across it, flicking his sonn before him, skipping over the hedges and jumping the paths. This time, he took the wall at a run and vaulted onto it, coming to a deep crouch at the top. He paused there for no longer than needed for a swift, light lick of sonn, which revealed no one, and he dropped to earth in Tercelle Amberley's rear garden. He drew gun and cane and used the cane on the edge of the garden path to guide him toward the door. His shoes clicked like a soft, soft sonn as he climbed the stairs.

The door was not quite closed. As he eased it open, he smelled blood, and feces spilled in terror or terminal spasm. He eased the door closed and propped the cane against it, and sketched in the room with a bare whisper of sonn.

Tercelle Amberley was lying on the floor, on her back, her legs splayed beneath their heavy, proper skirts in the lax impropriety of death. He went quickly down beside her, pulling off a glove to touch bare skin. She was still warm, newly enough dead as to let him sense the last fading impressions of life. There was no stain or residue on her chest, no sign of a wound from knife or bullet. As his fingers passed over her throat, he felt a sudden intense pressure in his own. Strangled, then.

The cane clattered. The very walls rattled with sonn, the shot that passed overhead as he dropped no less shattering. He fired without turning. The shot struck with the meat-bone thud of a heavy bullet and a punched-out shriek of agony. He heard footsteps in the hallway, and a bullet staved in a panel of the inner door. He threw himself at the empty door, catching up the cane as he went, swung around the lintel, and leaped up onto the wall from the upper step. As another bullet exploded the wall beneath him and sent stone splinters into his arm and wrist, he rolled off the wall into the next-door garden, breaking the cane in two. From the room he had just left, a woman's voice rose in a shriek, "He's killed her, he's killed her." He did not recognize the voice, but she sounded authentically terrified, or well rehearsed. Bent low, he sprinted along the wall, imaging his way to the rear gate with swift, precise sonn. Bullets cracked on walls; over his head, foliage burst. He ducked into the shelter of the gate, briefly paused, tallying bullets fired and time to reload, and then burst out of the gate and down the rear lane in the shelter of the wall in a flat-out sprint. He heard shouts; a last bullet split a flagstone at his heels, and then he turned the corner and was, for the moment, clear. Two more turns, and he was once more mincing down the street in his fashionable shoes, his jacket buttoned and a moue of vexation on his face at the cheap workmanship of the modern cane. Perhaps passersby would mistake the sweat on his face for that of an unfit man on a warm summer's night. He seemed reputable enough to bring a cab to his whistle; keeping his bloodied arm hidden, he climbed aboard.

Ishmael

A brothel on the Rivermarch was an excellent place to go to ground. Men would rather not know their neighbors, and if the ladies gossiped and speculated among themselves, they were an insular little community who seldom felt a need to share their speculations, and certainly not with strangers. Ish had used the Rainbow House before, for those very reasons; and in this case it was close to Olivede Hearne's clinic. He paid for a room to himself for the day, and for hot water and bandages, tea and bread rolls. When he was alone he pulled off his gloves and shirt, and soaked and dressed his bleeding hand and arm. After that he worked off his shoes, inspected his raw heels, wrapped himself in the quilt, and leaned back against the headboard—not nearly as evocative a one as in Guillaume's spare room—to drink, chew, and brood.

This whole grim matter was tangled beyond his wits. He disliked the way it was making victims of people who were not usually victims, the innocent or the privileged. The learned Dr. Balthasar Hearne and his daughter were both, and Tercelle Amberley, whether innocent or otherwise, had been the bride-to-be of Ferdenzil Mycene. The fact that Tercelle had just given birth would certainly be evident to even an incompetent examiner. It would be . . . interesting to track what became known. Assuming Ish survived in freedom to do so, since he had been so carefully dropped into a frame of Tercelle's murder, if not his own. Before he did anything else, he needed to report to Vladimer. He needed Vladimer's wits; he needed Vladimer's protection; and whatever larger game was being played out here, Vladimer needed to be advised.

Eventually the house quieted. Still in his clothes, he rolled himself in the blanket, in the manner in which he had learned to sleep in camp, beat down the overstuffed pillow, and slept.

He woke coughing, smoke acrid in his throat. Rolled from his bed, to thud onto all fours, almost strangling with the force of the cough. Sonn shuddered with the coughing, but beneath the shuddering, everything in the room shimmered in the layered smoke and heat.

He snared the shoes from under the bed, spilled the water pitcher from his table down over his head and shirt, and pressed the soaked shirt to his face to filter the smoke. He was already disoriented. No point feeling the door before he opened it; to open it might be to burn, but to remain was to suffocate.

He did not burn, and the smoke was thinner on the landing. He heard women coughing; men, too. Sonn laced the stairwell. He worked his way down the stairs, halting above the mill of two dozen partly dressed whores and overstayers.

Someone shrieked overhead, a cry far too brief for its intensity. The house shook and scattered stinging debris. A man said near him, in a remarkably calm voice, "Next door's roof must have gone. Whole row must be ablaze. We don't have long."

One of the women said shrilly, "If we go outside, we'll burn."

The man said, "We need to get into the basement. These old row houses used to connect through the basements. Maybe we can make our way ahead of the fire; surely the Lightborn will come to our aid."

There was a moment's desperate babble of hope and despair that the Lightborn were their only hope of succor. Ish did not add to it. The Lightborn fire service would assemble to fight the fire, and the mages themselves would intervene if they could not control the blaze, but it would take time for them to ready the magical forces needed to damp the fire or conjure a rainstorm. Working with the elements was extremely demanding.

The whole mob crowded down the stairs, the madam and the man who had suggested the basement leading, Ish lagging. Without gloves, and with his shirt dragged up around his face as a shield against smoke, every touch would sear him with someone else's terror. Within a press of half-naked, panicking people, he would lose his wits utterly. As the men began to tear away the paneling over the connecting door between basements, Ish probed the recess beneath the stairwell with his sonn. The houses on the Rivermarch dated from the earliest years of the city, when the main streets used by the Darkborn had run underground. With time and the aging of their infrastructure, underground thoroughfares had become more difficult to keep dry, and the Darkborn had become more trusting of the Lightborn's willingness to contain their light and share the streets. Eventually the tunnels were abandoned and the entrances bricked or boarded up. However, over the years, some of the houses on the Rivermarch had harbored trade less reputable than brothel keeping, and some of those forgotten entryways had been reopened. If Ish were not imagining the draft he felt on his sweating skin, then they might be able to get deeper yet and make their way clear of the fire along the old thoroughfares.

Across the room, men's voices cried in triumph and women's

with relief as the panels cracked. Ish, crouching in the recess, sonned them as they pushed through the shattered door. He ducked back out of the recess, meaning to draw breath and call their attention to the other, and perhaps ultimately surer, option—and at that moment, with a great hot thunder, the house above them began its collapse. The ceiling overhead held, for the moment, but a fiery rain of fine debris stung his skin, and something struck him, hard and searing, on the shoulder. Across the room someone screamed, "The door! Bar the door!" In the mad miasma of smoke and dust, he could no longer sonn the other exit. He knew himself committed to one choice or the other now, and made his decision. He ducked back into the recess, strangling on smoke, his head scraping the underside of the stairs. His groping hands met brick, met and measured the cleft; for a moment he thought it could not pass him, stocky as he was, and then he thrust himself into it, trapped heart beating on brick, brick scouring his burned back and shoulders, and hauled himself through with the power of his arms alone. Air blasted past him, dragged by the furnace overhead. He found himself hanging out of the side of a long tunnel, above the rubble that had once sealed the entryway and before that been the stairs up to it. He managed to lever himself out and get his feet under him before he half fell, half skidded down the tunnel's side into the foot of foul water in its base. Its fetor was kinder to his lungs than the smoke, its filthy cold poisonously soothing on his burns. He struggled up to his knees in it, supporting himself on rubble as he drained soundness from his bones into his lungs and throat. Only as much as he dared and not nearly as much as he needed, but still enough to let him get to his feet. He could hear voices, distorted by the tunnel and by a panic mounting toward madness: the other refugees, trapped, or realizing that they could not break down doors faster than the fire could travel. The fate he now realized he had, without knowing it, feared. He started toward the voices, skidding on the slimy, uneven footing of the drowned flagstones. The voices grew clearer, and by that clarity he found another former doorway in the wall. He tried to call to them, but nothing came from his raw throat but a cough that had him tasting blood. The stairs were nearly intact here, so he started up them, when from the far side of the cleft there came a rumbling roar that built until it almost masked the screams, and a blast of smoke and heat through the cleft. He launched himself from the stairs and sprawled his length in the water, scarcely believing for a time that sunlight had not speared through and burned him. The living sounds from the other side continued for a little while longer, though they had ceased to be recognizable as man or woman, or even as Darkborn. He would hear them in his nightmares for much longer still. Shuddering, Ish pushed himself to his feet once more, and made his way onward.

Five

Telmaine

Telmaine woke to the sound of her daughter, her Flori, crying, and to a certainty of horror. There was smoke in her throat, the roar of fire in her dreams. With pounding heart she sat upright on the bed beside her sleeping husband, sweeping the room with her sonn. "Flori . . ." Olivede stirred in her chair beside their bed. Amerdale did not, where she slept curled up against Balthasar, whom she had refused to leave.

"Something's happening," Telmaine whispered. "Something bad."

"I know," murmured Olivede. "I sense it, too." The shared awareness shimmered between them, and then Olivede fully awoke and Telmaine remembered where she was and to whom she spoke. "I must have been dreaming," she said, panicked at so near a self-revelation.

The smoke was gone, the roar of fire gone. Only the presentiment of disaster remained, throbbing like a migraine. Olivede rustled to her feet, shaking out her plain skirts. "You weren't."

"But I . . . I couldn't . . ." Telmaine struggled to cover her lapse, shaken.

Olivede shook her head and said sourly, "Don't be so appalled, Telmaine; you don't catch magic like a cold."

Bal, beside her, stirred and reached out with a wavering sonn. "Telmaine? I feel . . . something . . ."

Olivede leaned over him, fingertips brushing his temples. Bal knocked her hand away. "*Stop* that," he complained, younger brother to older sister.

"You rest," she scolded him, older sister to younger brother, and firmly gathered his hands into one of hers, trying with the touch of the other to subdue him.

"What time is it?" he said, struggling against sleep. "Has the bell sounded?"

"Not—" She broke off.

Telmaine felt a sudden, shocking lightness, as though all her bones had evaporated and her flesh gone to steam, as though she were about to be sucked out of the cracks in the walls and whirled upward into the night. She gasped, feeling that little inhalation lift her from the bed, and gripped the bedclothes to anchor herself. Olivede said, "Sweet—" the remainder of the oath unheard beneath a thunderclap that seemed to split the world from firmament to core. Amerdale's waking shriek was like an insect piping. Screaming, the little girl launched herself over her father's body, toward Telmaine. Telmaine scrambled up on her knees to heft her clear before she did Bal injury, almost overbalancing as she did so. Amerdale wrapped arms and legs around her, pulling on her hair and ears. Olivede was standing half doubled over, with a stupefied expression on her face, her hand still on Bal's forehead. Only when Bal tried to roll onto his back, grimacing in pain from his daughter's jarring, did Olivede start to collect herself. "It's a w-weather-working," she said, voice shaky. "The Lightborn mages have called up a storm. Listen to the hail . . ." And from the outside walls came a sound like that of many small stones.

"Amerdale . . ." said Bal.

"She hates the thunder, poor little one, I know," Olivede said, through teeth that chattered.

"Flori—"

"Flori's next door, Bal," his sister said with a strained self-control. "You always t-told me she could sleep through anything."

Bal was too distracted to recognize the lie. "Why are they doing this?" he said.

"What's wrong with him?" Telmaine said, gripping his hand and feeling his pain and inner turbulence, like the one that threatened to liquefy her bones.

"They're doing a weather-working, the Lightborn. Intangible matter is the hardest of all to influence, so they must have a dozen mages involved. That much effort, that much concentration, anyone with any sensitivity to magic whatsoever will feel."

Another thunderclap. Amerdale shrieked in Telmaine's ear, tightening her stranglehold on her mother's neck. Telmaine rocked her, grateful for the crying, clutching burden, else she was sure she would have lifted into the air and been borne away toward the vortex of wind and power that surged in her awareness. Hailstones salvoed against the outer wall, rattled on the gutters.

Olivede rummaged in her supplies bag, coming up with a hand-labeled vial, which she dumped into a plain mug and added some water to. She propped up Bal's head and held it to his mouth. "Drink. My magic's useless until this is done, but this will help some."

"Have to tell Tercelle, the children . . ." Bal said, moving his head away.

"Little brother, it's done. Drink."

"I didn't tell—"

"I believe you." She pushed the lip of the cup between his lips. "Really, you'd think you were an infant of three." He drank, sputtered, drank again, fluid spilling from the side of his mouth. She forced him to drain the cup and carefully wiped his cheeks. "Now, lie still and let that take effect." She turned back to her bag and busied herself returning vial and cloth. Bal continued to shift his legs, restive with the pain in his chest and abdomen, and his own dim perception of the stour of magic around them.

"You do not know how lucky you are not to be able to sense this," Olivede gritted, making Telmaine start. She bit back a madwoman's laughter, gripping Bal's hand with all her strength, not daring to try to ease him consciously with her own wits in such disarray. "Mama, Mama, Mama," whimpered Amerdale, damp against Telmaine's neck. Olivede sank down, put her head into her hands, and rocked slowly back and forward. The rain drummed on the outer walls.

The terrible turbulence of magic had eased, and the rain lightened to a whisper, when the tolling of the sunset bell began. Balthasar seemed more or less asleep, and Amerdale was quiet, sucking her fist against Telmaine's shoulder. Telmaine and Olivede listened as the bell shivered into silence. Olivede pushed herself to her feet and went to the door. "I have to find out if anyone knows why this working was done."

Telmaine nodded, untwining the arms of her reluctant daughter from her neck to let her settle the child in a more comfortable position.

"Mama," Amerdale said, "where's Flori?"

"Shh," she said. "Shh."

"Is Mistress Floria searching for her?" Amerdale persisted. Telmaine could sense her need to have her world in order.

Through Bal's hand, she could feel his drowsy awareness. She put her mouth to her daughter's ear. "Shh," she murmured. "I don't want Papa to know. Not while he's so very ill."

Amerdale's sonn washed over Bal, outlining him with all the vividness of childhood. The child went back to sucking her fist, her thoughts cloudy and unhappy.

Olivede returned. "Mistress Floria has not come into her *salle*, but I've left her a message. Sparling says that he heard fire bells and fire engines, and I can smell the smoke now. There must have been a fire, though it would have been a very large one to require a weather-working to put it out." She pulled her bag toward her and began going through it by touch. "They said the bells came from the Rivermarch. Telmaine, if there has been a fire in the Rivermarch, I'll need to leave as soon as Bal's properly settled again."

"When can he be moved?" Telmaine asked.

"Preferably not for a few more days, unless he has further magical healing."

Telmaine's gorge rose. "Does he need it?" she said evenly.

"Not to recover, no." A small silence. "I want to thank you," she said. "For allowing us to do as we did."

"I would have done worse than that," Telmaine said, not troubling to regret or moderate her sentiment, "rather than lose him."

Then she felt, from Bal, an abrupt wash of pain and despair.

"They took her, didn't they," he said. "Those men took Florilinde."

For a moment, both women were immobilized by dismay at his realization. Amerdale, stricken by remorse and relieved of the need for secrecy, started to howl. Bal fended off Olivede's soothing mage-touch. "Yes," his sister said, resigned. "The men took Flori to force you to tell them where the twins are."

Through Bal's hand, she felt him make a desperate effort at reason. "Has there been any message?"

"No, but the house is being guarded."

"How is anyone supposed to get to us with a message?"

Telmaine had not thought of that; she floundered, caught between the impulse to order all guards away and to embrace their protection.

"If there's a message," Olivede said, "it will find its way to us. And we'll find her. Mistress Floria's people are searching for her; my friends in the Rivermarch are searching for her; and Baron Strumheller, the Shadowhunter, is searching for her. They'll find her."

"I don't understand," Balthasar whispered, with a helplessness that tore Telmaine's heart. Despite all his years working in the demimonde, despite all his dealings with the disturbed and troubled, he had never lost that purity of spirit that had so captivated her at their first meeting. She, the sheltered woman with the mage's touch, was the one who understood cruelty, evil, hate, and lust.

From downstairs, the doorbell began to ring. Olivede came to her feet, producing one of the baron's heavy revolvers from amongst the cushions of her chair. Telmaine struggled free of Amerdale, admonishing her, "Stay with Papa, but be gentle with him!" Olivede let her go first down the stairs, and stood back as she went to the door, holding the revolver leveled. Calling through the door produced no response; at Olivede's nod, Telmaine opened the door.

Ishmael di Studier stood swaying on the doorstep, soaked and reeking of smoke and burned meat, his shirt shredded and burned off him. She felt his sonn batter her, but so dreadful was his appearance, and so glad was she to sonn him, that her reaction was to clutch at his arms and pull him inside—at which he gave a hoarse cry and began to cough, great lung-wrenching coughs that brought him to his knees on the doorstep. She crouched with him, snatching her hand away from the raw flesh on his shoulder. He gripped her skirts and turned his face into them like a child clinging to his nurse.

"Mother's tears," Olivede murmured, sliding into place at Telmaine's side. She slipped a hand into his shirt, and Telmaine felt the lightness of nearby magic. After a little while Ishmael stopped coughing and the ghastly rasping crackle of his breathing eased.

He said in a hoarse voice, "Th'Rivermarch's burned. The dead—so many dead."

Olivede said, very controlled, "Let's get him inside."

Telmaine did not sonn the other woman, much as she wanted to, to know what kind of expression, what kind of face and manner went with such restraint.

Even with their help, the effort of rising started Ishmael coughing again. Olivede shook her head slightly, privately, and did nothing except help him into the parlor and sit him down on the couch. Carefully, with fingers and delicately probing sonn, she inspected his nose and his throat, and bent her stethoscope to his chest. "Baron Strumheller, is this just smoke inhalation? Did you breathe heated air?"

"The smoke was terrible," he said. "It was all terrible." He started to shiver.

Telmaine said in a small voice, "I'll get a blanket," guiltily pleased that she had her gloves.

"Get my bag as well," Olivede ordered.

Balthasar managed to lever himself up on one elbow as she entered the room. Amerdale pushed one of the fat pillows behind his back. "Telmaine," he said, questioning not her identity but her presence.

"Baron Strumheller," she said. "He's back." Her voice quavered, but surely Bal must not take it as profound relief for the man, only the strain of the situation—and then she thought angrily that, good as he was, of course he would take it as relief for the man.

"Flori," Bal said.

She felt suddenly, desperately sick. So many dead, the baron had said, and the Rivermarch burned . . . and Flori had been crying in her dreams with the smoke. If she had been held in the Rivermarch . . . She stifled hysteria. "She's not with him," Telmaine blurted, and, heart's mercy, she fled her husband lest he say more.

Ishmael was still talking in hoarse, half-whispered sentences of his escape from beneath the inferno, like a man recounting a nightmare. Telmaine stood with hands clenching and unclenching at her sides as Olivede dressed his burns, and his driven recitation halted and stuttered with pain. She listened for any hint that somewhere in this ruin a little girl named Florilinde Hearne might have lived or died. When she could bear no more, she thrust the bag at Olivede and retreated to Balthasar's side, lay down beside him fully dressed, and clung to him around the blankets, sobbing. He stroked her head, silently, and his suffering and helplessness only deepened her despair. She cried for long minutes before she found words. "I can't do it," she said. "I can't do it."

"She'll be all right," he said. "Flori will be all right."

If only she did not know the emotion under those steady words. She raised her head, saying in despair, "Bal, they've burned the Rivermarch. I don't know who they are, but they've burned the Rivermarch. Ish barely escaped with his life. He's terribly burned."

"Not that terribly," said the baron's hoarse voice. She twisted around, the movement wringing a shallow gasp from Bal. Amerdale sonned him and started to cry, frightened. Ish was leaning against the doorjamb. At his side, tethered, it seemed, by Ish's broad hand, was Olivede, who was saying, "I *have* to go, I *have* to go," in a voice quite unlike her own.

"Hearne, Ishmael di Studier, Baron Strumheller of th'Borders, but th'social niceties can wait. We need t'get out of here, get somewhere much better protected than this."

"Baron," Olivede said, "I'm a doctor. I'm needed in the Rivermarch."

He propped himself carefully on his right shoulder, and rolled his head toward her. "Were I t'believe in miracles, I'd call it one that you weren't there last night. Since I don't believe in miracles, I'll remind y'the reason you weren't there last night is because y'were here, minding your brother, who'd been beaten near t'death. Which they are likely to realize, same as they are likely t'realize my bones are not smoldering in the cellars."

"You've no idea there is any connection!" Olivede said.

Bal stirred. "Excuse me," he said. "Might somebody please explain to me what is going on?"

Ishmael di Studier laughed, though the laugh ended in a brief coughing spasm. He wiped his mouth on his sleeve. "Wish I could oblige, Hearne, but my gut's not good on logic. Tercelle Amberley's dead—strangled—and it's only my low, suspicious nature that stopped me from being shot down as her murderer. Nine city blocks are gone, centered on *your* clinic, Dr. Olivede, I can tell you that much. Take it from an old Shadowhunter—and there *are* no other old Shadowhunters—if there's *any* connection between all of this, we're all dead if we stay here. I've been wrong before, mind, but not so I've died of it. Embarrassment's not mortal, whatever they say."

"Tercelle . . . dead?" said Bal.

"What are you trying to do to him!" Telmaine accused the baron.

"Find m'self a sensible ally," Ish rasped. "We need to get out of here, all of us, now."

"This isn't sensible!" Olivede pointed out. "You said you're running on instinct."

"He's not strong enough to be moved," Telmaine protested.

Bal's hand wandered across her bodice, seeking something to grip. "Telmaine, Olivede, I won't risk staying if there's a chance he's right. If we are to save Flori, then we must first save ourselves, and we have Amerdale to think of. I'm sorry"—his voice quavered—"sorry I have brought all this trouble on you—"

"Yes, yes," Ishmael said, "you be sorry, as though I or your sister or your lady would have done otherwise. Get yourselves ready—I need to speak to th'lady next door." He rolled off the doorjamb and lurched down the corridor. Bal held out a hand to his sister, who sat down on the bed on his other side.

"Bal, do you really believe him?"

"I won't take the chance he's wrong. We must be strong and we must be cunning. Whatever or whoever has taken our little Flori, and whatever murdered Tercelle Amberley and may have murdered her little boys—and I don't know how many other people—"

"Baron Strumheller thinks there could be hundreds dead," Olivede said faintly.

His mouth worked for a moment around words that could not come. When they did, his voice shook, for all its resolution. "Whoever or whatever is responsible is an evil that must be fought, and healthy or not, ready or not, we may be the ones appointed. Telmaine, Olivede, quick as you can, collect the essentials for all of us."

He lay on his pillows, directing the flurry of wife, sister, and daughter as they piled carpetbags, clothes, coats, toys, jewelry, books beside him on the bed. He culled their luxuries and even necessities quite ruthlessly, but all the time with one hand on a stuffed bear that Florilinde took to bed with her, and Telmaine knew that nothing was going to shake his conviction that, sun, fire, or murderers, his daughter was coming back to him.

"Imogene's ti—" said Ishmael di Studier, coming through the door with startling energy for a scorched tatterdemalion, and stalling in midprofanity at the sight of the bustle. He rummaged in the pile of clothes, speaking almost too quickly to be understood, his Borders accent even more pronounced. "I need t'borrow a change of clothes so I don't seem as if I've been dug out of th'smoldering ruins." Telmaine wordlessly passed him a jacket and shirt from the back of the wardrobe that had been bought too large for Bal, and that he kept promising to get around to sending to the charity shops. "I need a hat. . . . Magistra, best you go into men's clothing; you'll pass better than her ladyship. Pity you've nothing for th'girl. Hearne, nothing for you t'be but an invalid."

Bal was frowning. "What did Floria give you?"

"Don't worry. When it wears off, I mean t'be near a bed and a large bottle o'consolation."

"You'll need to be," Bal warned.

The baron vanished again, but they heard him pacing up and down the halls, roaming up the stairs. Olivede leaned around the doorjamb and murmured, "He's got his revolvers drawn."

"Just pack," said Bal, sounding worried. At Telmaine's questioning sonn, he said in a low voice, "If she's given him what I think she has, he's ready to fight a Shadowborn army. Don't startle him."

Telmaine packed; Olivede disappeared into the dressing room

with an armful of Bal's clothes, and emerged with her hair wound up under a cap and so creditably like an effeminate young man that Telmaine had to wonder if this was the first time she'd donned men's garb. Ish loomed again in the doorway as she and Amerdale were fastening the straps on the bag. His sonn shimmered around them, unstable as the man himself. "Fine, fine," he approved. He handed the revolvers off to Olivede. "Get th'bags to the door, but don't open it until I'm there. Hearne, are you ready for this?"

"Yes," said Bal. He had worked himself free of the quilts, managing to wrap one rug around himself. Now he slid his legs over the edge of the bed, his face taut with pain.

"No need," said Ish. "But keep your hands off m'scorches." He stooped and collected Bal, lifting him with a grunt and a muttered, "Falling in love with your wife, sir, is bad for a man's health."

"You are *not* in love with me," Telmaine said, after a moment of mortified incredulity that he should *say* it. "I don't like your sense of humor, *sir*."

He gave her a vulpine grin as he carried her husband out the door. She and Amerdale followed close behind, Telmaine hampered by the bags and Amerdale, who clutched her skirts as though she expected Telmaine, too, to disappear. "Where are we going?" she said, but the question went unanswered.

Outside, the rain was still falling heavily, filling the air with fine shifting echoes. The smell of smoke was bitter on tongue and throat. Ishmael cracked a single intense pulse of sonn toward the pavement on either side of them, and went still, listening. Olivede, her back against the door lintel, held one of the revolvers partly sheltered from the rain. Telmaine heard the sound of distant carriages in the rainwashed streets, a slamming door, footsteps fading unchecked in the distance, the song of one of the late birds. Ishmael said, "I think it's clear. Call us a cab." He followed Olivede down the stair, lurching a little, and saying to Bal in a voice that carried some strain, "You'd like my fuel carriage, Hearne, or so your little ones say. Pity she's a rough ride, and conspicuous."

Olivede, who had palmed the whistle, blew it; the cab came quickly, eager for the first fare of the day. With a struggle, Ishmael lifted Balthasar aboard and then bent over, gripping the base of the door, coughing again. Covertly, Olivede extended her hand to soothe him, collecting a nod of gratitude. He hefted up their baggage, wincing as he used his arm, then helped Telmaine and Amerdale inside. Olivede he left to manage herself, as befitted her disguise; she swung aboard with reasonable competence. Ishmael whistled, a distinctive call that sounded almost birdlike, and waved, and a young man appeared from beneath the steps of a house opposite and trotted swiftly over—one of their hidden guardians. Ishmael gave him brief instructions and sent him running off in the direction of the coach stand before clambering into the coach himself. He slammed the door and leaned out the window to pass up their fare and growl instructions to the coachman to take them to the train station, and then fell into his seat, wincing as the cab started to move and he lurched back against the rear of it.

"Where are we going?" Telmaine said again. "Bal's too weak for a long journey, and we're not leaving the city until Flori is found."

"Station's a decoy. We'll be met," Ishmael said, steadying himself by gripping the window.

They arrived at the train station, and Ishmael at that point passed up another fare and gave instructions to another landmark. Two more such legs followed before they were met, on a side street, by two private carriages with a pair of husky coachmen each. She, Bal, and Amerdale were loaded into one, Ishmael and Olivede into another. She fought down the improper desire to beg Ishmael to stay with them. They set off again, she bracing Bal against the rocking, Amerdale leaning against him, clinging to the stuffed bear and sucking her fist. Telmaine didn't have the heart to reproach the child for the reversion to infantile habit.

"How," Bal said, "did you meet Baron Strumheller? Ought I to be affronted?"

She so wished she were an ordinary wife, who need only guess at the pain and grief and worry that he was trying to distract them both from. She stroked his forehead, giving him what of herself she could. "Just a few days ago at the archducal summer house. He offered to escort me here. I'm glad I let him: He saved your life. I hope he hasn't formed an attachment to me; it would be so awkward." Which was a thin, thin expression of her own turmoil.

Bal laughed weakly. "My dearest heart, for a man to form an attachment to you seems to me to be the most natural thing in the world. I'm constantly amazed that you don't have admirers following you around in besotted herds."

"I'm married to you!" she burst out. "Though just at this moment I don't know why! *Why* did you have to take in Tercelle Amberley?" Immediately she felt his hurt and remorse and cried out, "I'm sorry, I'm sorry, I should not have said that."

"It's true enough," he told her in a measured voice. "But I couldn't know then what I know now, and I could not have closed the door against her with the sunrise bell tolling."

"Mama, Papa, *don't fight*," Amerdale appealed.

Bal put an arm around his little daughter and rested his cheek against her head.

"I want Flori," she whimpered. "I want to go home."

"So do I," Bal breathed. "So do I. But, my dear, we have brave friends who are doing everything they can to help us find Flori and go home safely."

Telmaine found herself unable to ease a pain that was as great in her as it was in them. She huddled beside them in the coach in shared but solitary misery.

They changed coaches again in a street she did not recognize. Her protests at the effect of the handling on Bal were silenced only by Bal's warning that she shouldn't draw attention. The coach, though lacking an emblem, was luxurious, well sprung, and large enough that Bal could stretch out along the seat. She sat opposite him, Amerdale curled up with her head on her lap, sonned his face tighten with each jar, and wished that she dared lull him to sleep, as she had felt Ishmael and Olivede doing.

Suddenly Bal lifted his head. "I know where we are," he said, startled. She reached for the carriage shutter to let it down and sonn, but Bal's sonn stopped her. "Best not," he said. "We'll be there shortly, and it might be best that no one sonns who is in this carriage."

"Why? Where are we?"

"The archducal city palace. I recognize the feel of the paving."

"Why . . . !" she said, her first reaction one of pure alarm at the thought of arriving here of all places with her social armor in such disarray. "I've nothing suitable to wear," she protested, though that was the least of it. Bal, her dear Bal, laughed. Immediately his breath caught and he clutched his ribs. "My dear heart," he gasped, "you never change."

"No," she said, "it's—"

"I know what it is," he said gently, reaching a hand out to her. "I know what it is."

She clutched his hand briefly before releasing it to try to put her veil and dress in a semblance of order. Bal did not attempt to reassure her that her efforts would serve. She sensed he understood a little how exposed it made her feel to arrive at the archducal palace as a refugee, trailing an injured husband, a missing daughter, her husband's practitioner sister, and the notorious Ishmael di Studier. Even if Bal had no idea of the depth of the potential scandal around her. He said, "I'm sure we can keep to our rooms for as long as we need."

The carriage described a familiar final curve, made an unfamiliar turn, and drew to a stop. Bal said thoughtfully, "They've brought us to the side door. Must be trying to make sure we aren't observed." She heard orders given and received. She gathered up the sleeping Amerdale, who whimpered a protest, straightened her spine, and prepared to face the haughty servility of the archduke's house staff and the curiosity of his family and other guests.

Telmaine

There was no curiosity. They were shown into a room in a part of the house she had never stayed in before when she had attended events as an eligible ducal cousin. The stairway came off the side entrance but was placed so as not to be immediately evident, and the rooms were secluded to the rear, beside a closed and walled garden. Compared to the rooms kept for noble guests, they were plainly decorated and furnished, the furniture well kept but softened with age.

Olivede Hearne rose from an armchair to greet them with an expression of such naked relief that Telmaine could not help feeling an impulse of sympathy for her. Intimidating as it was for Telmaine to find herself arriving here unprepared, it must have been much more intimidating for the healer mage, who had shared Bal's modest upbringing and had probably never even been past the servants' entrance in a house so grand.

Regaining her composure, Olivede followed the footmen carrying Bal into the main bedroom, and stepped forward to supervise his settling into bed. The footmen tried to deflect her, insisting that doctors had been summoned, but she ignored them, bending to examine her brother gently. She made no overt magical gestures, but Telmaine recognized the sensation of lightness that she was forced to associate with magic being worked nearby. She could not protest, knowing how much it eased Bal. He was resting comfortably amongst an abundance of pillows when the archduke's physicians descended, both impeccably groomed, elegantly dressed, and so elevated in manner that they barely acknowledged the wife and completely ignored the sister. Olivede did not protest her dismissal from the august presences; Telmaine did object, though little good it did her. She found herself banished to the sitting room with her daughter and the door shut firmly against her.

"Arrogant sons of . . ." Olivede muttered, before Telmaine shushed her.

"My apologies," the other woman said stiffly.

"Oh, I quite agree," Telmaine murmured. "But the children do not need to hear it." She heard, too late, the plural, and clenched inside.

Olivede put a careful hand on her sleeve. Telmaine made an effort not to pull away. "They will find her," the mage said. "You have to believe that."

Telmaine swallowed. "Where is Baron Strumheller?"

"Making a report to Lord Vladimer's lieutenant." She shook her head in wonder. "What an extraordinary man Strumheller is.

I'd heard about him—one of the healers I work with trained with him—but I never met him until now."

Telmaine found herself suddenly, inappropriately jealous. "Is he all right?"

"I've done what I can with the lungs and the worst of the burns. The stimulant's going to wear off, and the effects on his mind . . . I don't doubt he's personally experienced worse, though I doubt he's known anything on this scale—I don't think he was in the city during the influenza epidemic, and I don't think it touched the Borders. But you have no idea how terrible the touch-sense makes these kinds of events for a mage." She tilted her head back, loosening her neck. "I *have* to get back to the Rivermarch. It was bad enough to feel it from half a city away—I hardly want to think of the effect it had on mages who were there. I'll want Bal's help, as soon as he's well enough; he's very good at helping people who've survived terrible events."

"I don't think you can go back to the Rivermarch, not while we're in danger," Telmaine said, horrified at the thought of either Bal or Ishmael returning to the Rivermarch. She, too, could still feel it, like an oozing sore in her mind.

Olivede sighed. "We'll be rebuilding for a long, long time, Telmaine, long after whatever was behind this is sorted, and you have gone back to your parties."

"That's not fair," Telmaine said tightly.

Olivede passed an unsteady hand down her face. "No, I suppose it's not. Sweet Imogene, I'm so tired. I hope those buffoons take care with my brother. I don't think I have the strength left to undo any harm they do."

"They are the archduke's own physicians," Telmaine reminded her. "I'm going to put Amerdale down to sleep. I suggest you go back to your rooms and rest, with my gratitude."

"Dismissed, am I?" said Olivede, with a smile so very like Bal's that it drew all the acid from the comment.

"You are Bal's sister. One does not dismiss family."

Olivede's smile was ironic. "If Bal needs me, or if you need me, call me. I am in the rooms next door. Baron Strumheller has the rooms beyond those—the ones nearest the stairs. He insisted on that." She made her way out.

Putting Amerdale down to sleep in the cozy and well-appointed nursery off the sitting room proved impossible, though eventually Amerdale agreed to rest on the sitting room couch, as long as Telmaine herself lay beside her. Telmaine did, stroking her daughter's head and back, trying to use touch to soothe her rather than magic. She listened to the murmur of voices coming from the bedroom, including the occasional distinct phrase from Bal. Presently, the physicians emerged, and the elder of the illustrious two paused to reassure her in orotund and mellifluous tones that her husband was very weak, but would recover with care and time. He did not refer to the magical healings Bal had undergone. She thanked him demurely, reassured him that neither she nor her daughter needed anything besides quiet and rest, and asked him if he would now attend Baron Strumheller. Rather frostily, the archduke's physician indicated that the baron had declined their attentions.

Balthasar's fists released their half clench of his pillows as he sonned Telmaine in the doorway. She could smell the physicians' colognes and the odor of their nostrums in the room, and taste the flavors on Bal's breath as she bent to kiss him. His lips were dry and sticky. She filled a glass with cold water and helped him drink it.

He said irritably, "They accept no efficacy in magical healing, but fortunately they were persuaded that I did not need surgery now." He turned his head and sonned the night table, where four bottles of differing sizes stood in a row. "Could you please take that second bottle on the left and pour it down the sink?"

She opened her mouth to object, but she knew that tone: Bal in a rare uncompromising mood. She did as bidden, returning from the bathroom with the rinsed and empty bottle, running her finger over the soaked label, which meant nothing to her.

Bal sonned the gesture and said, "It contained marcas extract. Works well for nervous agitation, but I've treated too many people unable to break the dependency to risk it. Telmaine, I'm going to need to send word to my patients that I'm laid up. The Rivermarch clinic will know through Olivede, but my other patients won't." She murmured agreement, deciding not to renew the argument about his getting a secretary. He held out his hand for her to take, and she did, settling down on the bed beside him. "I am sorry that this has been your homecoming."

"Bal," she said weakly, and managed to smile. "I must say it's been unlike any other."

"And I hope will remain so." He sighed. "Telmaine, have you heard anything about Flori?"

"No," she said. "But I'm going to ask if Baron Strumheller has."

"Good," he breathed. "I don't like the idea of him refusing to have the physicians attend him. I know from personal experience that when that stimulant wears off, he will feel like death. We should keep aware of him."

"Personal experience?" Telmaine said. Bal seldom drank and never indulged in stimulants.

She read his memory of crouching over the twins with letter opener in hand, the keen, edgy violence, the unwelcome insights. He said, "Something I used to keep myself on my feet after Tercelle drugged me. She slipped me something so I'd sleep through her exposing the twins."

"He didn't tell me *that*," Telmaine said of Ishmael. She marked one more stroke against Tercelle's account, for all the good it did her or the ill it did the dead woman. Then it occurred to her to wonder where her abstemious husband would come by a stimulant that strong. She did not ask; she knew the answer.

Maybe, after this, she would finally persuade him to let that house—and Floria White Hand—go.

Ishmael

Ish's interview with Vladimer's lieutenant, Casamir Blondell, was mercifully brief. Too brief, truthfully, for such a complex and fraught situation, but all either of them could tolerate of each other. Vladimer, unfortunately, was not due back in the city until the next day, and Ish knew he could not delay his report, much as he would have liked to.

Blondell had begun life as a peasant, entered adult life as a factory worker, and come to Vladimer's notice as a successful agitator responsible for a campaign of workers' sabotage against the factories. The young spymaster had even then known exactly how to win, use, and manipulate men with the abilities he needed; he had stoked and slaked Blondell's ambition, diverting it from rebellion into service, and over time came to command Blondell's absolute loyalty. The ex-peasant was several years Ish's senior, bulky with early toil and later affluence, and made even more so by the ornate, quilted jackets he wore as protection against stilettos. He had a horror of assassination, though the only scar he bore, after years in Vladimer's service, had been bestowed by a castoff mistress. They were natural antagonists, he and Ish: the peasant and the nobleman, the unmagical and the mage, the desk worker and the field agent.

Ish gave his report in Blondell's study, a close, cluttered, overdecorated museum to the man's ego. Relics of defeated enemies, sculpture distinguished only by its ornateness, hunting trophies, at least one of which, to Ish's acute nose, had not been properly cured. Ish, after years of roaming, traveled light and collected only memories. Blondell did not invite him to sit, and so he did not sit, though by now the false energy of the stimulant was almost extinguished and he had to make an effort not to sway where he stood. He delivered his report starkly, without speculation or embellishment. Blondell asked some cursory questions and then dismissed him, no doubt to seek further information from his own sources. Ish did not have the strength to ask him what he had found out about the fire, either to cozen the information out of him or to deal emotionally with the death toll.

He trudged back to his rooms through corridors that seemed endless. By the end of the walk, he could only take pride in not having measured his length on the carpet, or not having some servant sonn him hanging on to the ornamental panels like a drunk. As he lurched through the door to his rooms, he registered, too late, the two other bodies in the room. Then two pairs of hands caught him by the arms and steadied him.

"Now, *what* have you been doing to yourself, young master?"

"Lorcas," he breathed, recognizing the voice, the tone of asperity, and the wiry arms as belonging to his elder manservant. The sinewy grip on the left would be his son. The pair, father and son, were supposed to have been waiting in his city residence, where he had told them to expect him one, no, two nights ago, after his meeting with Vladimer. He realized, with remorse, that in the last hectic nights he had not given his household the least thought. "How'd you come—"

"Never you mind about us, for the moment," Lorcas said, as they settled him into a chair. "If you've been up to half the things they say you have, you should be in bed, though I daresay you won't go. They tell me you wouldn't have the archduke's physicians attend you."

"Quacks," he grunted. He started to slump back against the backrest, and then thought better of it. "Now you're here, I'll be fine."

He cast his sonn around the room, noting the presence of four trunks—not the ones with the ornate Strumheller pattern, but the plain trunks he kept for travel in his less public role. "*How* did you come here?"

"We had a message from one of Lord Vladimer's runners that you would be at the ducal palace. So we packed and came over. That was quite a production—two changes of coach and who knows how many so-called destinations." Lorcas appeared beside him with a cup. "Lemon tea, sir."

Ish propped himself on an elbow, cautious of his burns and his unsteady stomach, and accepted the cup. "Nothing should surprise me anymore about the two of you," he said, deciding that the near-instantaneous provision of a cup of lemon tea was no more to be questioned than any other part of it.

Lorcas had joined the Strumheller household with the staff of Ish's city-born mother, and had been Ish's personal servant since Ish graduated from the nursery at the age of eight until his father had turned him out at the age of sixteen. The first night of his return, he had awakened to find Lorcas standing beside Ish's bed with a cup of lemon tea, as if nine years of estrangement had never been.

Years later, when Ish's patrols became too strenuous for the aging Lorcas, one spring evening he had found Eldon waiting beside his horse with saddlebags in hand, stoically enduring the chaffing of the seasoned patrollers. Time after time, the two of them had organized, minded, nursed, and otherwise salvaged him.

Ish drank three cups of tea, each liberally laced with honey and restorative herbs, while his menservants unpacked and installed him in baronial style. With relief, he sonned Lorcas discreetly setting aside a certain small, fabric-wrapped box. For the moment, he said nothing. Father and son each maintained a separate conceit that the other was unaware of Ish's magical practice. Presently, Lorcas would find Eldon an errand to take him away, which would allow Ish to ask for the box, and his store of spicules, each one painstakingly charged with his own vital energy, which he could use to advance his healing. His quick recovery might cause comment, but it could not be deferred.

"What have you heard about the fire?" he said.

"A terrible thing," said the older manservant. "Terrible. The coachman said that nine blocks were burned."

"Were you there, sir?" said Eldon. Ish could no more stop thinking of him as "young Eldon" than Lorcas could stop calling him "young master," though Eldon was married and twice a father. Borders men were not noted for changeability.

"Aye," Ish said. "I was." His stomach roiled at the recollection, the smoke, the layers of fire heat, the sting of sunlight on his skin, the mindless sounds of dying people. But he never stinted telling his people what might, some bitter day, save them in turn. "I'd overstayed in the Rainbow House, after—well, I'll be telling you about that later. Woke with the fire, head already fuddled." It had to have been for him not to have caught up jacket as well as shoes. "I knew th'old houses had first opened underground, which could take us deeper than the basements. So I sought th'old doorway while the others broke down the doors between basements. House started to collapse before I could tell them I'd found it. Couldn't reach them before they got trapped and burned. Bad that," he said briefly, and fell silent.

"I've heard of those streets," said the young man after a moment. "I didn't think anyone could get down there."

"They're foul," Ish admitted. "But that said, if we can't get down this time we're in the city, we'll go down next time."

"Thank you, sir," said Eldon, who had an enthusiasm for city history that Ish liked to encourage, since there was no telling what useful information he'd turn up. His father's aspect was more somber. After all these years, Lorcas would know Ish's habit was to return to confront his horrors.

Ish set aside his tea; it was not sitting well. "How much contact have you with the ducal staff, or are you assigned quarters here?"

"Here, at the end of the hall. We were told we should keep t'ourselves."

Sensible, that, though it would restrict their ability to gather information. "Let's bide quietly for a day or so, then."

"May we let the rest of the staff know?" His daughter, Eldon's sister, and her husband were housekeeper and groom to the staff who would have come north to meet him, and two of their children were pages.

"Aye, do that," Ish said, trying once more to lean back without pressing on the burns. "Circumspectly, though." He moved his tea aside so that he could prop himself upon the armrest. "I can't assure you that there's no danger, or warn you what t'do against it. It'd be best if there's least suspicion th'staff knows anything about what

I've been up to." If it were just his own person he had to consider, he would have told his staff not to hold back the information that he was at the ducal palace, and send the trouble his way, but he had Lady Telmaine, her husband, sister-in-law, and daughter—both daughters—to consider.

Lorcas removed the cup and saucer threatened by his restless shifting. "No need to concern yourself, sir; we'll get it done."

"There's a lady next door, Magistra Olivede Hearne, who's also been caught up in this thing. She's not accustomed t'this style of living, I judge. When you get a chance, find out if she's in need of anything we can provide."

"Yes, my lord."

When Lorcas started "my lord"-ing him, it was a chastening sign. Ish rested his forehead on his folded arms and listened to father and son exchanging quiet words around the message to go to the household. They broke off at a tentative knock on the door. He heard Lorcas open the door, and Telmaine Hearne's soft, disconcerted voice. The exchange was brief, lasting only long enough for him to struggle out of a doze he was not aware of having fallen into. By the time he lifted his head, Lorcas was closing the door.

"What—"

"The lady was inquiring after you," Lorcas said. "I said you were resting; she said not to disturb you. That was Magistra Olivede?"

"No, that was Lady Telmaine Stott, Mrs. Balthasar Hearne, now."

"Ah," said Lorcas. "My mistake."

Ish gathered his thoughts. "I need t'tell you a little more." He gave them a brief sketch of events from his perspective, omitting the nature of Tercelle Amberley's indiscretion. It was enough for them to know that she was a lady with high associations who had compromised herself. He told them of Vladimer's request—both expressions turned grim at that—and his own return to the city with Lady Telmaine to consult her physician husband; of that homecoming; of—omitting specifics—his rendering assistance to the gravely injured physician and setting out in pursuit of Hearne's kidnapped daughter, and how his inquiries led him to the fetid underbelly of the furnace.

There was silence after he finished. "Sir, Father," Eldon said judiciously, "I think I will get that message sent, if you do not need me."

"Aye, you do that," Ish said, recognizing the young man's circumspection.

Eldon went out, closing the door behind him. Ish pushed himself upright in his chair as Lorcas carried the velvet-wrapped box to him. "I'll go into th'bedroom for this," he said. Lorcas helped him rise on jellied legs, supported him into the bedroom, and left him sitting at the dressing table with the box in front of him. Ish opened the box one-handed, supporting himself with the other, sonned carefully, and lifted out a spicule, folding it in his hand and feeling its stored energy drain into him, easing his burns. He used another, and then a third, since they were only as strong as he himself was, tucked the spent spicules into a side pocket for reuse, and closed the box. He knew he should turn some into a small case and carry them with him, as he did while he was patrolling the Borders, but he hesitated to do so while moving amongst his aristocratic peers. It was not a rational caution, but an irrational inhibition. He could readily have found an explanation acceptable to most, and to those who were constantly watching him for stigmata of magehood, the innocent gems on his cuff links and tiepin must all but vibrate with magical iniquity. But there it was. He slid the box into the upper drawer, rose to his feet with some of his old collectedness, went over to the bed, and stretched out on it, prone, knowing that Lorcas would expect it, and would wake him if there was need.

Telmaine

As the elderly servant closed the door, Telmaine dithered. She had done what she had to do, she told herself: She had confirmed that Ishmael was being cared for. Which he surely would be with that formidable old man attending him. She had no business simply wanting to be with Ishmael, to cross words and match wits, to hear his deep, reassuring voice. Perhaps even to touch him again and feel that warming, disturbing spirit of him. She was a respectable married woman and he a mage; she had no business at all.

She heard the door begin to open and shied as the younger servant emerged. Catching her sonn, he turned and sonned her with the briskness of a Borders wind. She need not explain herself to a manservant; without speaking, she turned and rustled back toward her room, aware of him behind her.

She had her hand on the handle when a wash of familiar sonn caught her. "Telmaine!" said Merivan, in her imperious voice.

Her sister swept up to her, tall, heavily veiled, and elegant in a loose, intricately textured gown. Telmaine had an impulse to throw herself on Merivan, as she should have thrown herself on her mother or another of her sisters. She restrained it; Merivan's was not a consoling bosom, and she was far too sharp. "Meri," she said weakly, "what are you doing here?"

Merivan took her by the arm and steered her over the threshold of her rooms, revealing, Telmaine realized, no doubt as to which were Telmaine's. She inspected the plain furnishings. "I suppose you're used to this kind of thing," Merivan remarked, "being married as you are, but it's hardly befitting your station."

"Decor was hardly," Telmaine said, "a consideration. What are you doing here? I thought you were staying at the coast for another several days."

"We were, but Lord Vladimer's illness—"

"Illness?" Telmaine said sharply. "Lord Vladimer is ill?"

"If you'd gone home, as you were supposed to, you would have known. He was taken very ill just after you left—whatever were you thinking, letting that man escort you?—and once everyone found out the house was in such turmoil we decided we should bring the children away. When we arrived home, there was a message from *your* household wondering where you were, because they'd expected you home the night before yesterday, and from mother and Elfreda saying they'd also had a message and did I know anything. So when Theophile had to come over to the government chambers on business, I thought to come, too, so we could go by your house. I hardly thought to find *you* here, and in such state. Telmaine, what have you been up to?"

Telmaine drew a deep breath and let it out. Drew another and let it out, too. She had no idea how to *begin* to answer that question.

"Telmaine, you haven't done anything foolish, have you?"

Telmaine started to laugh, and clapped her hands over her mouth to stifle it.

"Has that man compromised you?"

She shook her head, still struggling to contain her hysteria. "Oh, if only it were as *simple* as that!" she got out.

"Whatever do you mean?" Her sister slapped her, stingingly. "Control yourself."

On the couch, Amerdale stirred and whimpered. Telmaine

pulled her sister through to the little writing room and pushed the door to. Merivan freed herself firmly; she did not much like being managed. "Where is that husband of yours, anyway? If he'd come down for the summer, as he ought to, none of this kind of thing would happen."

"Merivan, *who told you* we were here?"

"That creature of Vladimer's—Blondell. I have no idea why Vladimer regards him so highly. He said you had been brought here by Ishmael di Studier, so I insisted on coming up to you."

"And did he also say that Bal and Amerdale were with me, not to mention Olivede?" Telmaine said tartly. "Or did you just assume you had to rescue me from some adulterous escapade?"

Her sister's bosom heaved dramatically. "Telmaine! With you, I didn't know what to think."

"That," Telmaine said, "is not fair. Bal is in the bedroom, too weak to rise from his bed. Baron Strumheller and I found him nearly beaten to death on the floor of his study. The men who beat him kidnapped Flori. They think that Bal knows something, or has something they want. Baron Strumheller and others are trying to find Flori, and he brought us here because he thought we would be safer."

Merivan absorbed that. "What has your husband got you mixed up in now?" she demanded. "Those Rivermarch dealings of his . . ."

Telmaine chewed on the inside of her lip. She felt no urge to defend the demimondaines, since she felt much as Merivan did, albeit for different reasons. Her Bal was made for better things than the free hospital in the Rivermarch. She had to resist the urge to defend Bal, because in doing so she was likely to let slip more than her sister should know.

Merivan threw up her hands. "I cannot reason with you with that mulish expression on your face."

"You're not reasoning," Telmaine said, provoked beyond circumspection. "You're hectoring, nagging, and badgering. I know it's because you care, but, Meri, I've had a terrible two days, I'm worried about my husband, frantic about my daughter"—*I've used magic to heal my husband and I might be falling in love with another man, and a mage besides*—"and I'm *tired*."

"You should come home with us. Theophile has contacts, and failing that, he would be able to pay for agents."

"Bal shouldn't be moved again until he's stronger, and we're all safer here."

"Safer?" Merivan said. "From what?"

"I don't even know. Ishma—Baron Strumheller—doesn't know."

Merivan couldn't miss that revealing *Ishma*—. "Oh, Telmaine—"

"Yes," Telmaine said in bitter exasperation, "you told me I'd come to a bad end, and maybe this is it. Are you satisfied?"

That checked her sister in midflight. "No," she said in a hurt tone. "It may surprise you to know that I am not."

Telmaine bit her lip. "Please let Mother know that you have found me. I don't expect to stay here any longer than we must—any longer than it takes for the investigations to conclude and allow us to go home and for life to get back to normal. And Merivan—though it doesn't sound like it—I am grateful you came to find me."

"You're right," Merivan said, "it doesn't sound like it. I suppose it is easier for you, with your free and easy attitude to propriety."

"That's an old—"

She stopped, hearing footsteps outside. Not the near-noiseless ones of the servants, but heavy footsteps from men climbing abreast up the stairs in a rhythm of carpet-muffled and floor-resounding footsteps. Her heart rate doubled. The footsteps approached, but did not reach their door. When the pounding came, it was from elsewhere in the corridor. A harsh voice demanded that a door be opened. Neither sister breathed, for listening. Then she heard Ishmael di Studier's distinct, deep tones, suddenly ending in a bark of pain.

Six

Ishmael

Ishmael had only warning enough of his arrest to realize the futility and dangers of flight. When Eldon shook him awake, it was to tell him that the men had already encircled the wing of the house, armed and in force. His servant had heard Casamir Blondell in the side vestibule, talking to the superintendent about a warrant for murder. Tercelle Amberley, almost certainly, if not the man he had shot while escaping—but how had his disguise been penetrated so quickly? Ruthen would not have betrayed him. Was it Blondell's doing, then, and if so, why? There was bad blood between them, but surely not that bad. He swiftly rejected the possibility of testing his luck against their mettle; escape was too unlikely to be worth the punishment that would befall Lorcas and Eldon for forewarning him. He rolled out of bed, shedding his rumpled shirt. "Get my leather vest." The leather vest, with its stiffening of metal links, was armor against knives, and protection for his ribs, at least the first time anyone went at him. "If this goes ill," he said, "y'need t'tell the Hearnes that it's Guillaume di Maurier who's gone seeking their daughter; Hearne knows him, and I'm sure Lady Telmaine knows of him." He pulled on the vest, a clean shirt, and gloves, and when the footsteps and the pounding came, he made his menservants stand well aside, out of the line of any fire, and opened the door himself.

Sonn resolved two heavy pistols, pointed at his head, from the agents on either side of the city superintendent. He wasn't sure whether his nobility or his villainy merited such attention. Behind the double rank of public agents stood Casamir Blondell, his form indistinct amongst the echoes, but his expression twisted in anger and loathing. The extremity of that expression gave Ish the briefest of warning before they laid hands on him—it had, he thought, taken them rather a long time to appreciate that in his shirtsleeves, with his gloved hands spread, he offered neither threat nor resistance. He tensed involuntarily as they hauled him forward, reacting to too many memories of similar manhandlings, but he did not resist as they dragged him into the corridor.

"Ishmael di Studier, Baron Strumheller," the superintendent said, "we are arresting you in the name of the archduke on suspicion of the murder of Lady Tercelle Amberley one night past, and on suspicion of sorcery committed against Lord Vladimer Plantageter two nights past."

He stiffened in their grasp, his mind suddenly locked with horror at the second accusation and its implication. "Vladimer—" he started to say, unwisely, and the men holding his arms turned the joints upon themselves with the elegant efficiency of men practiced in the technique. He cried out once, in agony, and hung between them, gasping.

"Lord Vladimer, as you surely know, lies senseless in the ducal summer house," hissed Blondell.

The superintendent's expression shifted subtly toward distaste. Ish could not allow himself to hope, not with the charge of suspected sorcery against him, but he knew Malachi Plantageter to be as scrupulous in the discharge of his duties as the realities of politics allowed. He had descended from the old nobility—he shared the ducal surname—to this lowly public service, and made it his own. Ishmael said, in a low voice, "I am *innocent*"—a gesture from the superintendent stayed any move to silence him—"of both those charges, but especially of th'last."

"The law grants that possibility," the superintendent allowed, "and ensures all men a fair trial, whatever the charges, witnesses, and evidence. I will ensure you are guarded, until we know the outcome of Lord Vladimer's affliction and know the exact charges to be laid."

He heard the threat and the promise in that, stretched as he was in painful suspension between his guards. Murder was a capital charge, one that would leave a man shackled outside to await the day. Proven sorcery—and there was a conundrum, since the witnesses who could *disprove* it would hardly be considered upstanding citizens and witnesses—could have him exiled, confined to an asylum, or executed. Death by blades of light had last been used twenty years ago, against the mage who'd aided the kidnappers of Guillaume di Maurier and his sisters.

That was always assuming he escaped being knifed or beaten to death in the cells. Lord Vladimer might be feared, but he was also respected for his mastery of the underhanded arts, and he was the archduke's brother. Criminals, Ish had noticed, tended to be traditionalists. His very survival through the next day, never mind to the trial, depended upon the superintendent's readiness to do his duty. And who would help Vladimer, with Ish confined to a cell? Why did they think Vladimer's affliction was magical? Because it seemed unnatural; because it confounded the physicians . . . They'd not let him know or even ask. His mind circled on itself like a mad dog gone frantic with thirst.

The superintendent finished the formal reading of the charges, a ceremony Ish had endured several times before, though never in such august surroundings or company. Setting and sobriety were not as much compensation as he might have thought.

His guards efficiently chained his wrists, but left his ankles free. He was, he thought, rather out of practice in being arrested as a mage, as he did not know whether this represented current thinking on how to contain a mage's power. He hoped it was; he'd no desire to be rendered unconscious, or dosed with some concoction intended to mute his powers, usually by the expedient of drugging him into stumbling imbecility. Flanked by four guards, and led by the superintendent, he was started along the corridor. Imogene's tits, he was thankful that none of the Hearnes, particularly Telmaine, had opened their doors, though they had surely been aware of the affray. He could almost feel the intensity of her listening attention. But only almost—and that was surely imagination alone. She did not know how to reach him herself.

He could change that. He had already worked with her, showing her how to direct her power. He could try, in the few seconds he might sustain such a contact, to convey to her the essence of his own magical understanding, in hopes she could organize and use it. Mind-touching her across distance would incapacitate him, to be sure, and end any chance of escape en route to the prison, if chance there still were for him, shackled and under guard. And if he were to cripple himself mind-touching anyone, he should be getting a warning to Magistra Hearne, or even Phoebe Broome. In short, he was once again being a sentimental fool. But neither of the other women, each a known mage, would be able to reach Vladimer. Neither of them had the loyalty to Vladimer that he had, and Telmaine as a member of Vladimer's own class would have, and Vladimer *had* to have the help of a loyal mage, if this were truly sorcery. Telmaine had the power to help; she should have the willingness; what she lacked was the knowledge. Every step was taking them farther apart, which might not be a real impediment, but *felt* like one, even so. He drew a deep breath, paused at the top of the stairs, as though to catch his balance, and reached into the core of his vitality, tearing loose the largest part of it he had ever committed to his magic. He threw it—vitality, will, magic, intuition—into the strongest mental shout he could summon: <Go to Vladimer! *You* must help him!>

It was all he had to give. The inside of his skull felt as though he'd everted it in sunlight. He was going down. He was vaguely aware of the voices around him shifting from harshness to consternation as he slid to the floor, boneless, and then his awareness went, mercifully, to ash.

Telmaine

One hand pressed to the door, one fist to her lips, Telmaine strained to hear through the heavy doors. They were taking him away. She could hear it; she could almost feel him on the other side of the door, that banked-ember spirit, the rough wisdom she had come so much to rely upon, that had started to tempt her to forget all proprieties, loyalties, and vows.

<Go to Vladimer! *You* must help him!>

And after the voice, which sounded like a shout from far away, all she knew was sudden, scourging pain, followed by an even more sudden, scourging absence. She seized the door handle two-handed; she had the door open and was in the corridor before Merivan's shocked, "Telmaine!" reached her. On the top of the stairs, a huddle of men grappled with a fallen Ishmael, whose unconscious weight threatened to spill them all down the stairs. He lay draped back across their arms, his own bound beneath him, his exposed face frighteningly spent and lax, except where the scars pulled it.

"What is this?" she said, fear lending her voice the ring of imperiousness.

Men's faces turned toward her, men caught going about men's justice and embarrassed at being witnessed doing so. Justice, like all the other worldly affairs of men, was kept out of the sight of women, lest knowledge offend their modesty.

"What are you doing, manhandling one of the archduke's guests so!" she said, her voice piercing.

"This man is no guest of the house," Casamir Blondell said.

She ignored him, the peasant, turning her sonn on the tall, aged man with the distinctive nose of the archducal line, whom she knew slightly as the superintendent of public agents. "What is this, pray tell me?"

Ishmael groaned as the guards settled his awkward weight onto the stairs; the sound, pitiful as it was, weakened her with relief for the indication of life. She braced herself on the lintel; she would not be dismissed as vaporish.

"Lady Telmaine," said the superintendent, "please forgive us for disturbing you, and the peace of the household."

"Disturbing *me*! It is *him* you have rendered senseless."

"It was not our doing. It was a sudden collapse," he said, and gestured with one hand. Obedient to the gesture, his men hefted Ishmael's sagging form and began to lug it down the stairs. "We will have a doctor attend him at the prison."

"How could it not be your doing? I heard him cry out."

"I am sorry, again, that you have been disturbed," the superintendent said, his tone polite, a little chill. "I wish you a pleasant night."

"Wait!" she said. "Why are you arresting Baron Strumheller? I demand to know. He is a friend of my family."

She thought he would appeal to propriety, to charges not fit for a polite lady's ears. He surprised her, saying, "He is charged with murder and sorcery, Lady Telmaine."

At the word, *sorcery*, spoken aloud to her face, her courage left her. She stood gripping her arms as she listened to them carrying Ishmael down the stairs to the next corridor. Their footsteps were faint and hard on the tiling of the vestibule, their passage through the door prolonged. She heard words exchanged below, and then the heavy door closed.

"Telmaine," Merivan said, "have you utterly lost your mind? What do you mean making such a spectacle of yourself, and in defense of an accused *sorcerer*?"

Telmaine found her voice. "This is a *vile* and baseless accusation. You heard him say we must help Vladimer! That's not the assertion of someone who'd mean him harm."

"I heard no such thing," said Merivan sharply. "You are imagining things."

"I am not imagining things. I distinctly—" And as she felt Olivede Hearne's sonn wash over her, she stopped, with the instinct that had let her keep her secret so long. "I thought he said something," she said in a shaken voice. "I must have imagined." She remembered the strange sense of distance in those words, though only a door separated them, and the conviction, before and after, that she had *felt* him. Had he found a way to speak to her without words or touch? Could mages do that? Could *he* do that? *Would* he do that to her, knowing that she felt as she did? Had *he* ordered her to act? She shuddered.

"Telmaine," she heard Merivan declare, "you are not yourself."

Even as she let herself be led back into the guest room, she reached desperately and clumsily out after the vanished footsteps, the vanished sound of wheels on paving, the vanished sense of a presence like a banked fire.

"Tend to your child," Merivan ordered, though Amerdale, exhausted, was unstirring. Merivan swung into Balthasar's room. Telmaine, following, blocked the closing door with an outstretched hand, so that it jarred against her palm. Olivede, who had trailed after them, stood back, seemingly dazed.

"I need to talk to your husband *alone*," Merivan said.

"He's *my* husband. Leave him be," Telmaine growled. "Or so help me, I will remove you from this room myself."

Balthasar cleared his throat. "I heard most of it," he said. "Baron Strumheller has been taken on suspicion of Tercelle Amberley's murder, and suspicion of sorcery directed at Lord Vladimer. You don't think he did either of those things, Telmaine, and you, Merivan, do not think Telmaine should be speaking in his defense, regardless of her convictions, because of the nature of the accusations."

Merivan recovered with her usual swiftness. "I request that you permit Telmaine and Amerdale to come home with me."

"We stay together," Telmaine said. She wrestled a moment with her guilt, but urgency prevailed. "Balthasar, Baron Strumheller needs a lawyer. He had servants here, in his quarters, just down the hall."

His smile was a gift she did not deserve. "Then hopefully they should know his lawyers. We should arrange bribes for the guards to ensure he is well treated in prison. Telmaine, I'm afraid I am going to be talking to your banker."

Merivan said sharply, "Collingwood's will not permit it."

"Everything you need is yours," Telmaine said, ignoring Merivan.

"Then we must find out what ails Lord Vladimer. If we could establish that there was nothing magical about Lord Vladimer's affliction, it would exonerate Baron Strumheller then and there."

"But surely the archduke's physicians would be better able to tell," Telmaine protested, rejecting the memory of that faint mental voice.

"I would like an independent opinion, preferably by someone who knows magic. If this is magic or poison, then someone is out to deprive the state of certain protections. Think of this as if it were all of a piece," he said to Telmaine. "Think of all the people involved, and what it might mean to have them at odds with one another, dead, or otherwise unable to act."

Merivan pulled Telmaine close to her. "We must summon the physicians. He's delirious."

"He's not delirious," Telmaine said. "A lot of things have happened, Merivan. A lot of things . . ." She cast a wisp of sonn over Bal. If he were right, if Tercelle Amberley's sighted children, her murder, the burning of the Rivermarch, Lord Vladimer's sudden illness, and Ishmael's arrest were all part of some terrible conspiracy—to who knew what end—what new danger was Bal bringing down upon them by marshaling forces against it? He was not a powerful man, physically or politically. All he had was his supple scholar's mind, his ability to reach daring conclusions from scattered information, his potent sense of public duty and the respect of other men who shared it. He was such an innocent, compared to herself.

"Merivan," she said. "I have to talk to my husband, alone, if you would."

Her sister hesitated, clearly unsure which one of them was the more unreliable. Balthasar stirred himself to lend his male authority with a quiet, "Please, Merivan."

Breathing through her nose, Merivan left.

Bal said, "She's vexed that she isn't allowed to hear."

"Don't cozen me, Bal," Telmaine said in a low voice. "Please, just arrange for the lawyer. Don't try to do more. You're too weak, and it's too dangerous."

His tone was as gentle as his words were merciless. "You're now asking me not to defend a man we both believe is innocent, against charges that could destroy him socially, if not lead to his execution?"

"Bal," she whimpered.

"I know." He reached out his hand, and she took it, and knew at once what lay behind his words: the fear of a gentle man who knew he had only his wits to serve him and knew they might not be enough. The fear of a man who doubted his own courage—it was not fastidiousness alone that had made him ask her to pour away that marcas-root elixir. And the old fear of a man who had once let justice pass undone that he might do so again.

He had not the least idea that she knew about the girl whose ashes had scattered to the winds.

"You are such a good man," she whispered, withdrawing her hand before she betrayed such knowledge.

"No better or worse than most," he said sadly, "though I am . . . comforted to hear you say it. You understand why we must help Baron Strumheller."

"I understand," she said, resigned.

"I have to speak to Strumheller's servants, find out who his lawyer is," he said, moving his head on the pillow. "And I think . . . I do think you and the children should go with Merivan. Strumheller's arrest has proven that we are within reach even here. I think you would be better protected in Merivan's house, with her husband a judge and a lord, and with your own family's resources to call on—at least better protected from any legal or material threat."

His stipulation made her think, as he was no doubt thinking, of Lord Vladimer's mysterious illness. Her thoughts shied from recollection of Ish's last cry, unheard by anyone but herself.

"I was the one who took Tercelle Amberley in. I—and Olivede—know about her children. There is no reason that you should; in fact, most people will assume that I would not have told you. Delicacy will likely preclude anyone from pressing you—particularly if you are amongst your own social circle."

"Balthasar," she said. "*I* went with Baron Strumheller to interview Tercelle Amberley the morning before she died."

He had caught his breath as soon as he realized what she was saying. His brow drew with worry and discomfort. "That was not wise, Telmaine."

"I was searching for our daughter," Telmaine said in a low growl.

His lips parted; then he released the small sip of breath he had taken. She waited; he did not speak. She gathered up his hand and kissed his curled fingers lightly, feeling his fear for her and their daughters. It was not scruple that prevented him from using them in this argument, but the apprehension that there was truly nowhere safe from the evil that had touched them all.

She welcomed the knock on the door.

Balthasar

Ishmael di Studier's menservants were father and son; there was no mistaking the resemblance. The father was past the prime of life, but straight-backed and alert, while the son appeared a fit and ready thirty. They both wore the practical styles and hard-wearing fabric of the Borders, rather than the livery of the city. They squared themselves before Bal's bedside, their sonn cautiously respectful, their faces guarded. Telmaine sat beside him, not touching him, and Olivede waited beside the door. Merivan had loudly insisted she wanted nothing to do with any of this, but she had not, Bal thought, moved out of hearing.

"I am Balthasar Hearne," Bal said. "Dr. Hearne. Lord Vladimer had, I understand, asked your master to consult with me. He escorted my wife to my door, and there found me beaten nearly to death—"

"He has told us of this," the young man said.

"Good," Bal said, before the older man could reproach his son, or apologize for him. "Then you know I owe your master for my life, his efforts to find my elder daughter, and quite likely my family's present safety. I do not believe the charges against him—I believe they may have something to do with the matter that unfortunately has come to surround myself and my family. I do not care that he is said to be a practitioner; I do not in the least. I am prepared to do whatever I can in his defense, and my wife is prepared to lend that part of her financial resources that is under her control. Her maiden name was Stott; she is Minor Duke Stott's sister and cousin to the archduke."

"That is . . . very good of you, sir, my lady," said Lorcas. He still stood very upright, but his stiffness had perceptibly eased as Balthasar spoke.

"We need to get a message to his legal representatives. We need to find out into whose hands we must lay bribes to make sure no harm comes to him."

"By your leave, sir, the message to his lawyers is already sent,"

Lorcas said. "This is not the first time that the master has met this kind of trouble, though it is the gravest."

"That's most welcome news," Balthasar said. "How did you send the message? By messenger?"

"By messenger . . ." Lorcas said, then, "I understand, sir. Messengers can be waylaid. I should have thought of that."

"I'll send a message of my own," Telmaine said, tilting her chin up defiantly. "Who represents him?"

"Mastersons, my lady. Lord Vladimer gave him an introduction the first time that the master had legal troubles in the city."

"My family also uses Mastersons," Telmaine said. "Bal, if he is accused of harming Vladimer, will they still represent him?"

"I believe so," Lorcas said. "Lord Vladimer has been quite explicit in his expectation that the gentlemen who undertake difficult work in the state's interest receive legal protection, even if the archduke or Lord Vladimer himself should appear unsympathetic or displeased."

Bal appreciated the implications of such an arrangement, both for the kind of work that Vladimer's agents undertook, and for their master's integrity. He had met the famously reclusive Vladimer only briefly and not drawn his attention then. "Then the essential task now is to make sure that the message gets to Mastersons, and let ourselves be guided by them. Telmaine, I would ask you to do it on your way to Merivan's. It would ease my mind greatly."

He squeezed her hand, reaching for reason to persuade her—and knowing that all he was doing was layering word over emotion. To this day, he did not know what moved and persuaded his wife. But he tried: "A respectable lady, perhaps known to be softhearted and more open-minded than is good for her, can interject a voice of moderation. And, as cousin to the archduke and Lord Vladimer, sister-in-law to Lord Theophile, she is in a position to obtain information that might not come to the defense in any other way."

Ishmael di Studier's servants softly withdrew with that studied unobtrusiveness that experienced servants had.

"I've never been able to argue with you," she said, her voice trembling. "Shall we have quarreled?"

"I'd . . . rather not," Bal said. He had had that very thought, to increase her protection, but now that she had offered it, it repelled him. "No, best you seek the comforts of your family home after a distressing experience. Later you can become appalled at my activities, if need be."

She took a breath, audible in her tight throat. "I remember how you used to pay for your studies by playing cards. I'm told Lord Vladimer is a consummate cards and games master."

"It wasn't for my studies that I played," Bal said with a reminiscent smile. "It was for gifts and favors for my lady."

She leaned toward him and stroked a finger gently from his forehead down to his chin. He rested in the last fading harmonics of her sonn, feeling a remarkable ease come from her touch, and the brush of her lips on his forehead. They lay a moment, side by side, in precious contentment, before she abruptly slid from the bed.

"Telmaine," he said, his sonn bursting forth to outline her. "If you need me, if you need anything . . ." He knew even as he spoke that he was opening himself for the answer that would reveal his promise a lie: *I need you to come with me.*

She did not give it, whether out of anger or scruple. She just said, in a stifled whisper, "All I need is things as they were. You will tell me if there is word, will you not? Of Flori?"

He listened to the women's voices outside as they gathered up their baggage and Amerdale. It was testament to Telmaine's state of mind, and perhaps her anger at him, that she did not contradict Merivan's pronouncement that waking Amerdale to say good-bye would only upset the child. Merivan did not believe in a father's attachment to his children, having in her possessiveness blighted her husband's. He heard the outer door closing behind Telmaine, Merivan, Amerdale, and the servants Merivan had mustered. The sound pierced him so intensely he was hardly aware of Lorcas's return for willing himself to believe that he had done the right thing in sending them away.

"Sir, I thought you should know: Your sister insisted upon leaving. She says she knows the area near the prison, and the people in it, and is going to learn what bribes can be laid. She said I should tell you that she would then go on to the Rivermarch."

Guiltily, Bal realized that he had not even noticed his sister slipping away. Lorcas continued, even more formally. "I could not dissuade her, I regret, sir, but I sent my son with her. He will not leave until he is satisfied she has found protection. I trust that this meets with your approval, sir."

"Your action does," Bal said, feeling beset. "Not hers."

There was a brief hesitation. "She is a mage, sir," Ishmael di Studier's manservant said. "They are not always sensible people."

Bal was startled into a laugh, which cost him in pain, though less than hitherto. Lorcas moved around him, straightening his blankets and ordering his pillows, helping him lie more comfortably, in body if not in spirit. The man had clearly had a certain amount of practice.

"Perhaps you would care for some soup, sir? I do not doubt the kitchen could be persuaded to produce something suitable."

"Thank you," Bal said, made hungry by the very mention. "I would very much like some soup." Hunger engaged duty in a brief struggle before he said, "And if you could please let Mr. Blondell's staff know that I would like to speak to him at his earliest convenience, I would appreciate it." He could only hope that the soup and Vladimer's lieutenant did not arrive together, and make the first wait on the second.

As it transpired, they did not. He was two plates of soup—a savory consommé—and a roll ahead on his hunger when Lorcas announced that Mr. Blondell was asking to be received. Lorcas covered the bread dish, stacked the soup plates, and carried them away.

"You have no one from your own household to attend to you?" Blondell said, head turned suspiciously after Ishmael's manservant.

"It was a hurried departure."

There was a silence. Bal recognized the waiting game, and decided he'd gain rather than lose by promptly conceding it. "The baron's servants have been good enough to wait on me, as I am still not able to rise from my bed."

"I had the physicians' reports on your injuries, before they went on to attend Lord Vladimer."

Unhappy Lord Vladimer, Bal thought disrespectfully of his illustrious seniors in the medical arts.

"A most unpleasant and unfortunate experience," Blondell remarked, "to come from an act of such simple decency as giving a lady succor. I had an account from Strumheller, though his had a number of elements I personally found implausible."

Well, if he had sought the measure of Blondell's attitude to Ishmael di Studier, he had it there. "If you mean the infants' sightedness, I can tell you that I am fairly confident that I am right in my inference—I have an interest in the properties of sight. There was no mention in my training or even in my reference books of sight among the Darkborn. I had meant to consult the Physicians' College library, but was struck down before I had a chance. There are always speculations about forerunner persistence in Imogene's land, or this 'third race.' "

"Speculations, you say; wild rumors, I say." The tone of voice conveyed a closed mind on the matter.

"How is His Grace, Lord Vladimer?"

"He has lain senseless for two nights now."

"Is there truly evidence of sorcery?"

"When a man as careful of his safety and cautious in his diet as Lord Vladimer is stricken senseless within hours of spending cloistered time with a known mage, it is sufficient for suspicion, and suspicion is a legal charge. Ishmael di Studier has been confined so that evidence may be sought."

"My wife returned from the ducal estate the very next night, and there had been no mention of Lord Vladimer's illness then."

"It was kept from the staff and guests at first. Then, of course, the gossip and uproar started. Very poorly managed."

Yes, Balthasar thought, and were he in Blondell's place he might inquire as to the source of that mismanagement. "How do you plan to disprove the charge? Are there other mages in Lord Vladimer's employ who can testify?"

Blondell stiffened, and fleetingly Bal thought he might have to press for an answer. "Lord Vladimer has no other mages in his employ."

Interesting, Bal thought. "Then how," he said, "can the charge of sorcery be proven or disproven? Do you plan to engage outside talent?"

Blondell rose, offended. "Sir, I bid you good day. I do not believe you can give me the help I require."

"Sorcerous harm is a capital charge," Balthasar insisted politely.

"I am not easy with the thought that a man might be put to death on mere surmise by those who have no means of *knowing* whether magic is involved or not. Would Lord Vladimer accept that his loyal servants might be convicted on such scant evidence?"

"I don't need t'be told my trade by a noble parasite who lives off his wife's fortune," Blondell said, stung, his accent lapsing.

"I am a trained physician and a scientist," Bal said, intrigued rather than provoked by the insult. He diagnosed an afflicted conscience. "I believe in observation and evidence. You know, I presume, the identity of the lady involved?"

"I know it. I know, too, why she came to you. I would have a care, sir, for the peace of your marriage."

That made Bal flinch involuntarily. Blondell smiled slightly, and Bal realized he had interpreted the flinch as the noble parasite imagining being plucked off his comfortable latch.

He said evenly, "And guilt for her death, too, has been laid at Baron Strumheller's door."

Blondell's sonn, deft but oddly sour in its timbres, swept over him, probing, Bal thought, for something. "Yes," Blondell said. "There is a witness, and the witness places Strumheller in that house at the time of the murder. I believe, also, that Strumheller had visited the house earlier, in the company of a lady whose identity I expect, presently, to discover."

Balthasar kept his breathing steady and his face unchanged with an effort. "If your witness bears burn marks across his face or body, then he is one of the men who battered me. Any testimony he gives will be suspect."

"He bears no such marks."

Bal breathed out, admitting his relief that he must not yet confront his assailants. "Those men—"

"I have di Studier's description."

"And I may be able to verify that description. As a physician, I am a trained observer of human traits."

"I will send a clerk to collect your testimony," Blondell said, stepping back.

"One last question," Bal said quickly. "The fire in the Rivermarch. Were there many casualties?"

He touched Blondell lightly with his sonn and for the first time recognized a deeply worried man. Blondell gripped the back of the chair he had risen from, leaning upon it, the knuckles of his hands prominent with work-hardened bone and tendon. "If you call a hundred fifty, hundred sixty, many."

"I do," Bal said. "Too many."

There was a silence; then Blondell said, "You've been an Intercalatory Councilman, I understand."

"I'm due to sit again in the winter."

"There are ugly rumors directed against the Lightborn. It's said they wanted that land for themselves, to build on, and the council did not agree."

"That's entirely wrong," Balthasar said, growing chilled. "There's been no such request entered in the annals of the council in the last thirteen years."

"You've not served that long."

"Even before my first sitting, my father had me following the proceedings."

"Well, that's what's said, and worse."

"Building toward violence, do you think?" Bal said, pushing himself up. "There's been peace in the city for over a hundred years, peace between our races. We cannot let that lapse."

"There's no 'letting' about this, Hearne. There's ugliness about, plot and rumor. His Grace was working against it, and now he's down, and I've got to do whatever I can—" He broke off, then said heavily, "If Strumheller is deemed innocent, the Lightborn themselves will be the next accused, and the city will crack, from prince's palace to ducal estates."

"Sir," Balthasar said somberly, after a long moment, "I have misjudged you."

"Y'thought it was because I'd taken against Strumheller personally that I arranged that he be arrested," Blondell said, unsurprised. "Better one man suffer than the peace of the city—and I think my lord and master would agree."

You have misjudged me, Bal thought, *if you think I would collude in an injustice, even for the sake of peace.* He weighed his next words carefully. "I will give you all the help I can, as an Intercalatory Councilman, to keep the peace."

Balthasar

Bal found Ishmael di Studier's lawyers a study in contrasts, when Lorcas showed them into his bedroom. The senior was small and rotund, with a shrewd, complacent face. His clothing was well tailored though plain and well-worn, the clothing of a man confident in his station and frugal by habit. His junior was taller even than young Guillaume di Maurier and much healthier-seeming, with a sharp-planed, handsome face, and the broad shoulders and lean hips of an athlete beneath an elegantly cut frock coat. Whoever he was, he was not subsisting on a junior's stipend.

"Thank you," said Balthasar. "Thank you for coming so near to sunrise. I am Balthasar Hearne."

"I am Preston di Brennan," said the senior lawyer, his name and faint accent betraying origins in the interior, "and my junior is Ingmar Myerling." The tall youth bowed his head very slightly.

"Archipelagean," Bal said; that explained the distinctive cast of face and athleticism; the Archipelago valued physical prowess. "You share the name of the dukes of the Scallon Isles."

"I am the youngest son of that family, sir." He spoke with precision, forming his vowels to match those of the city, as he had no doubt learned he had to do to carry authority in court. The passionate, unruly Scallon Islanders were the butt of many jokes, particularly now. Bal, hearing the diction, hearing the resonant voice—surely he was a singer, like many of the islanders—appreciating the physique, doubted that they would mock him long.

"Have you been able to speak to Baron Strumheller?"

"We have inquired for him, but were told he had not recovered his senses. There seems no reason for concern; he has long been prone to sudden bouts of extreme lassitude, from which he recovers completely."

"You know him, then," Bal probed.

The lawyer replied blandly, "I have represented his family's interests in the city since I was a young solicitor; I expect to continue doing so until I retire. I have known the baron all his adult life. Tell me, sir, what is it you believe you can add to the case?"

"What is the case?" Bal said. "What I have heard has come to me secondhand."

The lawyer considered a moment. "The case, sir, is that Baron Strumheller is charged with the murder of a lady in the Lagerhans district, and with malignant sorcery against Lord Vladimer, who lies mysteriously stricken in the ducal summer house. There is a witness to the murder, who has testified to having been elsewhere in the house when the murder was committed, and to having heard Baron Strumheller's voice raised in argument with the lady, on behalf of a child who had disappeared. Shortly afterward the lady screamed, and when her staff entered the room the baron shot one, though that is not part of the charge as yet, and fled. The lady was newly dead. There are, however, some irregularities about the charges laid that make one wonder, and I expect an interview with my client to be illuminating."

"Perhaps I can help you, too," Bal said. "I know who the lady was, and the missing child is my daughter."

Preston di Brennan's sonn washed over him. He had a touch that was almost feminine in its lightness. "Pray continue."

"You may have to decide what of this to use," Bal cautioned, "because it may come to touch on affairs of state." He laid out events for the lawyers, starting with the arrival of Tercelle Amberley on his doorstep and the birth of the children, omitting, once more, the mention of their sightedness, and not naming the midwife he had called to attend her. As a respectable physician and a man, he would take responsibility before the law, and the case was not one of malpractice. He described Tercelle's attempt to drug him and expose the newborns, and her flight, and the assault on himself two days later. With great care, he qualified his impressions of the next day, emphasizing his own pain, weakness, and disorientation, and therefore his unreliability, and taking up the narrative with authority only with the return of Baron Strumheller from the burning Rivermarch and his evacuation of Bal and his family.

"Mm, interesting," said di Brennan. "Most interesting. And with Lord Ferdenzil himself arriving, there will be much pressure to resolve the murder of his intended in a way least embarrassing to him. Though I cannot understand how the trial of a fellow peer would achieve that." To his junior he said, "Do you know anything of this, Ingmar? Your circle has an interest in Ferdenzil Mycene's doings."

The young man stiffened. It was, after all, his home and inheritance that Ferdenzil Mycene's ambitions threatened, and there was a growing clique of islanders in the city agitating for support against them.

"Think on your answer, and give me your best," said the older lawyer in a mellow tone. "If you feel you have a conflict of interest, you must tell me. And you will hold this information in confidence until it is brought forward in court."

"I will, sir," said the young man, bridling at the suggestion against his honor, for all the meek acquiescence of his words. The older man leaned over and patted his arm. "Forgive me lad," he said. "I do trust you, but it must be said so that this gentlemen knows he can trust us. He means well toward Baron Strumheller, and has valuable information for us. Sir, you are prepared to testify to this?"

"Yes," Bal said.

"Well, if the lady were indiscreet, then it will be worth inquiry as to who else may have an interest. It is most unfortunate that the infants cannot presently be traced, although examination of the lady's body will confirm that she bore a child very shortly before her death. Still, we must move along; I judge we have half an hour before we must leave, or have to impose upon the archduke's hospitality for the day. And then there is the second charge," he said in a more delicate tone.

"There are," Bal said quietly, "many reasons for a man to fall unconscious that have nothing to do with sorcery, many of which, again, we would consider natural. A cerebral stroke, for instance, can produce sudden and profound unconsciousness."

"We will, of course, produce witnesses to that effect," the lawyer said, his tone once more bland.

"I did not mention until now how Baron Strumheller came to

be at my door," Bal said after a moment. "It was a very fortunate circumstance for myself, since his timely arrival prevented my assailants from returning and may have saved my life. But I understand from my wife that Lord Vladimer had in fact sent him to me. I can only surmise why at this moment, but you may not be aware that I specialize in the care of people with disorders of thought: addictions, compulsions, and delusions. The delusion that one possesses magic is not a common one, but it is not entirely unknown, either."

The delicate sonn washed over him once more. "Again, sir, this conversation is proving surprisingly interesting; do go on."

"It is widely rumored, I believe, that Baron Strumheller is a mage," Bal said carefully. "Indeed, he seems to believe so himself. However, the archduke's physicians, upon examining me, asserted their opinions that, although my injuries were painful and debilitating, I must not have been as badly injured as my wife and I believed. They do not recognize the efficacy of magical healing, you realize."

"And why should a man choose to believe himself a mage?" probed the lawyer.

"There is little choice in delusion. Again, I have not spoken to Baron Strumheller, but in such cases it can arise out of a great loss in his early life, a sense of powerlessness or insignificance, or perhaps neglect and a need for attention, even negative attention."

"His mother, to whom the family was much devoted, died when he was sixteen, bearing a premature child. He claimed to have healed the child, his sister."

Bal nodded. "That might indeed have been it. I suppose the family did not receive the claim particularly well."

"His father threw him out of the house. Disinherited him completely. He spent the next nine years a vagabond, and took to the trade, such as it is, of Shadowhunter."

"But not magic?" Balthasar said.

"Not magic, not then. He returned to the family when he did the barony the service of ridding them of a glazen, and the old baron's friends persuaded his father to reinstate him. The scars on his face—he got them then."

"That he carries them still argues against him having much in the way of power," Bal remarked.

"He didn't stay in the Borders: There'd been a woman killed by the glazen, whom he'd loved as a girl. He came into the city and made contact with the mages."

"A similar impetus as before, the death of someone dear to him," Bal murmured, nodding slightly.

"Supposedly, he trained his magic then. Lord Vladimer took him on somewhat later, and for the next few years he went hither and yon on Lord Vladimer's account, up and down the coast, into and out of the Shadowlands, Shadowhunting when there was need. Then, when his father died, he returned to the barony. He's done well there; he's well regarded by his tenants and his peers, and he has organized and built up the Borders defense against Shadowborn so well that the number of deaths from incursions has steadily declined. This year, there were none."

"And once again, the claim to magic is in abeyance," Bal noted.

"He wears gloves all the time," the lawyer said, testing.

Bal said, "My wife wears gloves in public. It is, in her case, a harmless phobia about infection."

"He claims these collapses of his are exhaustion of his magic."

"Neurasthenic collapses," Bal said. "Not at all uncommon, either, though he should be examined by a physician to rule out a physical cause."

"And you believe Lord Vladimer might have sent him to you for the treatment of this delusion."

"I am aware that professional discretion should have imposed silence on me, except that Baron Strumheller's life could be in far greater danger from this charge than from a relatively mild delusion—I would not say benign, because it has obviously had great consequences in his personal life—that he possesses magic."

There was a silence. Bal did not dare sonn the lawyer, shrewd as he was.

"You are a clever young man," di Brennan observed, by way of acknowledging the question evaded. "Were you to go onto the stand, you could testify to all this?"

"I could testify to all this."

"Even though you yourself were ostensibly a recipient of Baron Strumheller's healing."

"Sir, I was injured and in great pain. Indeed, I believed I was dying, and so I must qualify my own reliability."

"Yes, I noted that. And what of his menservants?" he asked, with a cast of sonn toward Lorcas, who had been standing quiet and tense throughout.

"They must tell the truth of what they have witnessed, of course," Bal said. "It is for the defense to frame their testimony as suits their case. Baron Strumheller, I understand, has never claimed to be a mage of great power."

"And is that characteristic of such a delusion?"

"It depends," Bal said carefully, "upon the nature and severity of the delusion. Baron Strumheller's condition seems to me mild, though of long duration, and potentially curable, should he so choose. Lord Vladimer's wish may well have been enough for him to consider treatment, and Lord Vladimer's trust—and the relationships he now has—could prove most helpful."

There was another silence, and then the rustle of clothing. Bal sonned the two lawyers in the act of rising. "A most interesting discussion, Dr. Hearne, but we must go now; the sunrise bell will be tolling soon. You will be available for further consultation, I trust."

"I will be, certainly."

"Then we will bid you good day, with our best wishes for your recovery."

Bal lay back on his pillows, limp and aching, and did not sonn around him when he heard Lorcas approach.

"You realize why?" he said.

"To undermine the charge," Lorcas said, "but sir, we *cannot* go on the stand. Our experience—" He stopped, unhappily.

"As I said, you must testify according to what you yourself have witnessed and believe, and let the legal gentlemen frame your testimony. I am afraid that you may come off seeming credulous—though they will have to be careful, because we cannot insult the whole of society, which ostracized him because of this claim of magic, because we cannot risk their turning on him. High society's attitude to the Borders will help, I fear. It will be delicate maneuvering, but I do believe Mr. di Brennan can do it. You realize that I still have no idea whether or not he himself knows or believes that Baron Strumheller is a mage. But it does not matter; he can guide us through the pitfalls without our perjuring ourselves."

"It is clever," Lorcas said. Bal's sonn showed his tight, unhappy face.

"It troubles you," Bal said quietly, "because it does a disservice to your master, who is a man who lives with courage and integrity and who faces complex and painful realities squarely. The very last man, I would suspect, to succumb to a delusion."

"Yes," Lorcas said. "You . . . know him very well, it seems, already."

"And hold him in high regard," Bal said quietly. "Tell me, has your son returned or sent word? It's very close to sunrise, as di Brennan said."

"Not yet," Lorcas said. "Best you do not worry yourself over it, sir. He'll not leave your sister until he's assured of her safety."

Ishmael

The Darkborn prison was adjacent to the city's main bell tower, so that the thick stone walls twice daily reverberated with the tolling of sunrise and sunset. All its inmates could not but know, on execution days, the moment that justice was done. Justice, Ish had long ago decided, served a barbarous and bloodthirsty god. It was a conclusion he had reached lying in a prison cell much smaller and cruder than this one, listening to the curses, sobs, and pleas of the two men and one woman chained to the execution post outside. He had been barely seventeen, in the first year of his exile, before he learned which company to keep and which to avoid: The three outside had been the leaders of the gang who had taken him up. The county judge had been merciful to the terrified boy, and lectured him, pardoned him, and told him to go home to his family. Ish had not, of course, told the judge that he was a mage.

The tolling fell silent, and no screams and prayers of the condemned followed after. Ish did not allow relief to alter either his breathing or posture. Since he had been practically unconscious when they carried him through the doors, he had missed knowing whether or not there was to be an execution, and had been lying in dread of this moment. On the other hand, being practically unconscious had likely saved him from a beating. Prisons abounded with men to whom any or all of his scarred face, his title, or his reputation were welcome provocation—and that did not include his fellow prisoners. Against those, at least, he'd be permitted a knock or two, until the guards decided whether or not they cared for the way the bout was going. But that he'd been spared, too: He was alone in his cell.

From the corridor, beyond the bars, he heard boots scuffing in the corridor, and harsh sonn blasted over him. He amused himself briefly thinking of Telmaine's reaction. "Ugly brute," he heard a voice remark from the bars beyond his feet. "You'd think if he were such a mage, he'd fix those scars."

He heard a sound he identified as rough fingers scratching a stubbled chin, and a slow voice with an East Borders accent. "Aye, well, I reckon he hasn't fixed those scars for the same reason he's not stirred a finger since they dumped him here." A meaningful pause. "To make y'think he's not what he is."

Good thinking, Ish approved. Maybe incorrect in this particular case, but in principle, it was a sensible philosophy. He carried these scars because he deserved them; they were a brand of memory for a time he had been foolish and others had paid for it. And he had not stirred a finger because, although he might be able to summon the strength, he would not much like the consequences. If he sat up, he would be sick, and go on being sick for several hours, that being his frequent reaction to overreaching himself. Which was unpleasant enough when done in baronial comfort, never mind when crouched over the open toilet of a prison cell, to the mockery of guards and prisoners alike. So he would just lie here, limp as boiled leather, and go back to sleep. When the prison settled would be time enough to crawl to the water jug on the floor beside the bars.

"We could wake him up," the first voice said.

"And then again," the second voice said, "we could just do what we've been paid to do: let him lie quiet and make sure he comes to court with no marks on him."

Interesting, thought Ish, as the guards moved on. And encouraging, if this implied bribes moving in the right direction. He tracked the scuffing boots and occasional clink of a key down the corridor between the cells. He had already started to place the location and temper of the occupants by their voices, and now he added a few more, uncovered by the silence that fell after the sunset bell. He would not be the only prisoner who remembered the screams and cries of the condemned and had opportunity to consider his situation.

Murder was a grim enough charge, but one that, after the aborted trap at Tercelle Amberley's home, he had half expected. For the accusation of sorcery, he had been in no way prepared. Ostracism was the worst penalty he had come to expect from the Darkborn, since Darkborn polite society preferred to ignore the existence of magic. The Lightborn Temple Vigilance, against whom he had warned Telmaine, would hardly take notice of a mage as weak as he. But their justice would not misfire. Amongst his own, he could be accused, tried, and convicted by those ignorant of all aspects of magic. Others had been, in years gone by.

Had he known about that second charge, he might well have attempted to flee. That mental cry to Telmaine had been an act of desperation and, likely, futility. If she had heard it, would she have heeded it? If she had heeded it, what could she do, an untrained mage fixated on concealing, if not outright denying, what she was?

Moreover, she was an aristocratic lady, educated to passivity and accustomed to a public stage in which the men around her were the actors and she merely audience and decoration. He would have been better off to have cried out to Olivede Hearne or Phoebe Broome, and even better off not to have spent himself so. It would be two or three days before he had his full strength back, though he'd be fit to stand by nightfall, for all the good it would do him. The guards had taken his shoes and, with his shoes, his lock picks and concealed knives. Though they had left him his body armor.

He was puzzling over the meaning of that when he realized that there was someone outside his cell. He heard a key scrape in the lock, and willed himself not to stiffen, not to betray his awareness by even the twitch of a muscle. The key turned—the lock clearly better made and kept than those of other cells he'd been in—and he heard a shoe scuff nearby.

"You've overspent yourself," the voice said from close to his level and in the manner of one long accustomed to being heard no farther away than he needed to be. It was a young man's voice, with the accent of the Rivermarch lightly overlaid by erudition. Ish did not respond, but his heart, over which he had no control, quickened, and he was sure the pulse in his throat betrayed itself to the man's sonn.

So he risked a feather touch of sonn, enough to reveal the man as he moved the water jug to the head of the cot, where it would not be obvious to casual inspection, but where Ish need not rise to reach it. He was a narrow-faced, canny fellow, wearing a fashionably styled jacket that was clearly secondhand and altered to fit. To Ish's keen nose, a faint medicinal odor lingered around him. The prison apothecary, then.

"Magistra Hearne said to give you these and bid you use them."

Ish caught the scent of the herbed lozenges mages used as a restorative, which were often charged as spicules by their makers.

"No one's in the cells opposite," the apothecary continued. "You're good for the day. You'll have to be chary with the night watch, but they'll be kept busy, and there'll be people in for you soon as the sun sets; she said to tell you that." Ish heard him shift away, and rise, and move to the door. The key turned. "He'll be no trouble," he heard him say to an approaching set of boots.

Ish disciplined himself to lie quiet as the prison settled around him for the day, before he risked feeling beneath the cot for the flask and lozenges. There were six, each one big as his lower thumb, and he knew, with the first touch of them, that they were charged and who by; the character of each mage's magic was distinctive, and Olivede Hearne's was unmistakable in its brisk focus. So he had a conduit to the outside as well, and friends already working on his behalf. He slid the first into his mouth, and let the sugar and stored vitality start to dissolve away the sickly lassitude of magical overuse.

He had mentioned marriage to her in whimsical relief at surcease from pain, and she had treated it as such. If he survived this, then perhaps he *would* lay his suit at Olivede Hearne's door. Her bloodline was older than his; she could not yet be much over thirty; she was unmarried; and she was at peace with her magic. She was no society lady, but she might well suit the Borders, and the Borders might well suit her. Lady Telmaine—married or otherwise—had beauty, spirit, and power, but time would erode the beauty, society would stifle the spirit, and her own will would smother her power. Lying in a prison cell, at peril of life and reputation from a charge of sorcery, only an impractical fool—as his father had so often called him—would grieve the waste of it all.

Seven

Balthasar

The sunset bell, and his last dose of soporific wearing off, woke Balthasar. Not quite awake, he reached for Telmaine and found only a wasteland of luxury, a smothering desert of pillows and quilt, with only a single stuffed toy to mark the place of his daughters. He drew it to him.

Lorcas rose from the chair he had been sitting in. "Good evening, sir."

He took efficient charge of Balthasar, helping him out of bed and to the toilet. "You seem stronger this evening," he observed, while Bal concentrated on placing his feet just so, so that his knees, which seemed made of pure milk pudding, would not collapse under his weight.

"Any word?" he said, as Lorcas spread the covers over him again. "Olivede? Baron Strumheller? Your son? Baronet di Maurier?" *Florilinde,* he wanted to say, but shrank from the answer.

"One moment," Lorcas said. From the doorway, he beckoned in his strong son. "He set foot on the doorstep as the sunrise bell stopped," the old man said, with a lingering note of censure for such risk taking. "You were already asleep; I decided to hold word until you awoke."

Bal decided it would take a better man than he to argue with that decision.

"I delivered Magistra Hearne to the home of Magister Broome," Eldon reported.

"Was his son or daughter there?" he said. He would trust either one of them to protect Olivede before he'd trust the father. Had Farquhar Broome not been a mage of extraordinary strength, Bal would have diagnosed him as deranged. But since he was such a mage, he was rightly out of touch with common limitations and vulnerabilities.

"His daughter was, and much relieved t'greet Magistra Hearne. Your sister is very well respected, sir, amongst her own." Bal recognized this as intended reassurance. He sighed and said, half to himself, "Olivede's an adult, and responsible to herself. Did she give you any message for me?"

"She said the very thing, that she was adult and responsible, and that I should give you her love and promise that she would be back in a few days."

Bal drew a slow breath, bracing himself against the stab of pain from his ribs. "How bad is it in the Rivermarch?"

"Nine solid blocks burned, and th'people are still searching the ruins and numbering the dead. There's ash and water ankle-deep in the streets all around, and folk moving through it like they're sick to death. It grieved me not t'have stayed and helped, and if the master had been free, we'd have been down there wi' them. Still have a few people every hour coming out of the understreets, too, same way the master escaped, but it's half-flooded in there wi' the Lightborn's rain, and there may be some drowned. Magistra Olivede said that the Lightborn weather-workers were keeping a land breeze going t'blow the worst of the smoke and stink downriver. She also said you weren't t'think of coming down there in your present condition. There'd be a need for your help for a long time after you'd healed."

"She's one to talk," Bal said, past a lump in his throat. "And the mages, how are they managing?"

"Weary, sir. I could almost be glad the master isn't there." He said no more, whether out of habitual or new circumspection, his father no doubt having briefed him on Bal's discussions with his lawyer.

Bal's clinician's mind briefly diverted itself by wondering what compelled Ishmael di Studier to so recklessly overspend his slender magical talent, when he had so many other resources at his command.

"There's been . . . no word of my daughter, has there? Or Baronet di Maurier?" he said, his hand moving slowly over the furred head of her toy.

"I am afraid not, sir."

"Imogene's bane, I can't lie here and do nothing!" he said, aware that sounded like an invalid's fretfulness. "There's been no word from Floria—Mistress White Hand?"

"No, sir."

Lightborn messages traveled through the day, and Floria knew, she *knew* he would be half out of his mind with worry and would want to know even if nothing had happened. "Why haven't the Lightborn found her?" Bal fretted. "With their mages . . . I have to get a message to Floria, find out what's happening. I can't ask anyone to take it to the house; it's too dangerous. I can't trust Casamir Blondell—he'd sooner have Strumheller burn for sorcery than risk interracial strife." He stopped, remembering their loyalties. "I'm sorry—I'm speaking out of turn. The Intercalatory Council," he said, more quietly. "I will send the letter to Mistress Tempe of the Intercalatory Council; as a member of the Prince's Vigilance, she will ensure Floria gets it. Except I need *ink*, ink and a guide frame." Which he had not thought to bring. He was ready to weep, overwrought by that petty obstacle.

Lorcas left the room on silent feet, returning with a small case containing the very materials he sought. Bal said, "The baron . . . ?"

Answer to that seemed unnecessary. Lorcas occupied himself with propping Balthasar up and organizing him with ink, pen, and guide frame, which would let him trace, by feel, the Lightborn script neither he nor any other Darkborn could visualize. But he'd doubly secure the message by ciphering it in a code only he and Floria knew. It had been a game between them in childhood, and the language of his romance in youth.

Floria, Baron Strumheller has been arrested for Tercelle Amberley's murder and for sorcerous harm to Lord Vladimer, who has fallen mysteriously ill. Casamir Blondell is prepared to have Strumheller executed rather than have suspicion fall on the Lightborn, for reasons of public order. If sorcery is behind Lord Vladimer's illness, then I would urge you to urge the Temple to consider intervention—for the peace of all and the life of a decent man. I have sent Telmaine and Amerdale to Merivan's house, where I hope they will be safe, but I am desperate—we are all desperate—for any news of Florilinde. Please send me something, anything. Always yours, Balthasar.

He felt his way to the top of the sheet and wrote a note to Mistress Tempe in plain script, asking her to ensure that the letter reached Floria, urgently. Lorcas relieved him of the ink before he sluiced it over the bedclothes. "Wait," said Bal, as he felt the manservant lift the frame, paper and all. "Now I need a stylus and punch frame. I have to write a cover letter."

Stylus in hand, Bal let his mind empty. What could he possibly write that would convince any Darkborn who laid hands on the letter that they had the true message? He'd been so *good* at this, once, when all his concerns were the world-shaking ones of a sixteen-year-old boy in the flush of a hopeless crush.

Lord Aversham, he decided at last. Haven Aversham currently chaired the Darkborn membership of the mediating council. *Dear Haven*, he began, *I am writing to express my concern about the recent tragic events, and to reiterate my willingness to serve . . .* Aversham had an aversion to brevity that made the council minutes tedious reading and the meetings themselves tedious listening, but which Bal knew to be tactical. Bored, impatient people grew careless in their words and listening. It meant, though, that Bal could readily cover a page with elaborations of his opening sentiment. He punched his signature—he had left his personal seal behind—and turned to the envelope. He addressed the ink to Mistress Tempe, the punch to Lord Aversham. Even if the letter did wind up in Aversham's hands, it would do no harm; the desire to help was honest enough.

"This has to go to the chambers of the Intercalatory Council, over by the prince's residence. There are two slots side by side for communications, and it must go into the left-hand slot—that directs it to Mistress Tempe's secretary and thence to Mistress White Hand. Tell the messenger that, if possible, no one should observe it going into left as opposed to right. It should be in Floria's hands before sunrise."

"I will ensure it is done," Lorcas said, and passed it off to his son. "Forgive me for saying this, sir, but you seem to have a certain facility for this."

Bal laughed. "The influence of Mistress Floria White Hand. She taught me a little of her tradecraft. We used to correspond in this way, and still do, from time to time."

"Very good, sir. *Now*, may I get you something for breakfast?"

"Yes, and the morning papers, please."

He was just finishing off a plate of soup, this one with egg vermicelli, and trying to read the headlines without smearing grease across the front page, when Lorcas reappeared in the doorway. "Sir," he said. "A gentleman is asking to speak to you. Would you prefer to receive him here or—" But the newcomer had already pushed past him.

"I'll announce myself," he said, his sonn rippling over Bal. "Hello, little brother. It's been a long time, hasn't it?"

He did not move, could not speak as, unbidden, Lysander Hearne drew a chair to Balthasar's bedside and sat down. "You can go," he said, dismissing Lorcas. His sonn washed over Balthasar, raising blurred echoes from bedclothes and draperies.

Lorcas leaned over him to clear away tray, plates, and papers, setting his body between Bal's face and his brother's sonn. In doing so, Bal vaguely realized, Lorcas was offering him a chance to gesture, or signal, or otherwise communicate. But what? *Help*? *Call the guard*? *Throw him out*? "Yes," Bal managed. "Thank you, Lorcas. Thank you."

"Will that be all for the moment, sir?"

"Yes," he heard himself say again. "Thank you."

He heard, rather than sonned, the manservant leave.

"Have you no greeting for me?" Lysander said from closer, startling a burst of sonn out of Bal. The sonn outlined the fine-boned face that so distinctly resembled his own. Bal said, with a steadiness that surprised him, "I'll thank you to come no nearer, sir."

"Come no nearer?" Lysander said. "What am I, suddenly turned mage?"

It was not that; he simply did not want Lysander near him. He still feared him, feared his repertoire of petty physical torments and larger mental ones. And there was the way they had parted, over the ashes of the girl Lysander had murdered. His skin recoiled from the man as it had from the corpse. He managed to resist the urge to wipe his hands to clean from them the touch-memory of dead, chilling skin, coarse canvas of stretcher and shroud, and the damp predawn earth he and Lysander had laid her on.

"Balthasar," Lysander said, sounding weary and a little wistful, "I've wanted all these years to tell you how sorry I was that I involved you that night. I panicked, you understand; I was afraid for Father and Mother. I thought it would kill them. Ruin our family name. Ruin your prospects."

Such a glib and ready apology, and at the same time a subtle threat of implication. And no acknowledgment of the girl. No, he would not give this man any hold on him. There had been no witnesses and, beyond that sunrise, no body; there would only be, as there had always been, brother's word against brother. That was his protection as much as it was Lysander's. "I do not believe," he said steadily, "that I know what you are talking about."

He heard Lysander draw breath, hesitate, and then say, "It does not matter. It was all so very long ago. And I have . . . I have more recent wrongs to exculpate."

Balthasar tensed; he could not help it. "Then might I suggest you take your confessions to the rightful authorities."

"Bal, this concerns your daughter."

Bal caught his breath, painfully, and then pushed himself up and reached for the chain, jerking it violently once before Lysander could catch him, and it. "I want a witness."

"You do *not*," Lysander said, a hiss, and as Lorcas opened the door he spoke in a very low voice: "Send him away, brother, as you value your daughter's safety."

Bal struggled with himself a moment, frightened, furious, and in pain. His instinct to bring in a witness was the correct one, he knew. But his instinct to protect his daughter was stronger. "Lorcas," he said. "I am sorry. My mistake. My . . . my visitor has offered to attend to my needs. Thank you."

"That was clumsy," Lysander noted, once the door had closed.

"It was the best I could do," Bal said. He wondered if Ishmael's servants were in the habit of listening through walls. They seemed to have latitude enough, and he hoped, even on such little acquaintance, that they would sense his duress.

"What do you know about my daughter?" he said.

"That she is the elder of two, and six years old, by your wife, the former Lady Telmaine Stott," Lysander said. "Whom I do not recall having had the pleasure of meeting, since she moved in much more elevated circles than ours. Rich blood to mingle with ours, brother mine. Your daughter has been missing since the night before yesterday. I do understand how you must be feeling. My children are missing too. My twin sons, by Tercelle Amberley."

His sonn washed across Balthasar, probing every nuance of Bal's expression. Bal kept his face utterly still.

"The sons she delivered in our family home," Lysander said. "The sons our sorceress sister took away. Where are my sons, Balthasar?"

And I should say what? Balthasar thought desperately. Whatever stories Tercelle elaborated, her sons' sightedness testified to something other than an origin in common infidelity. Who was the most deceived here? Ferdenzil Mycene? Tercelle? Lysander? . . . Himself?

If he said he did not know, he risked Olivede. Though he recalled that, from the moment she demonstrated her magic, Lysander had never again laid his cruel hand on her, and even his mockery and harrying had been wary. He had feared her—it had, Bal realized, forced him to gratify his cruelties outside the family, led him to discover new license, and led, in the end, to that murder. Lysander still must fear Olivede, if he knew she had taken the children but still sought out Bal by preference.

If only Olivede or Baron Strumheller were here now. He was fiercely glad that Telmaine was not. "Tercelle did not tell me who had fathered her children," he said steadily.

Lysander confessed uneasily, "Tercelle became rather . . . strange as she neared her time, Balthasar. I was not as . . . patient with her as I should have been. Which is why, rather than be confined as we had planned, she ran away. To you."

I remember your impatience, Bal thought, and noted that Lysander had shown no grief for the woman whom he claimed as the mother of his children. "How did she become strange?"

His sonn caught a restless motion, as though of unease. "She was convinced that the child—our sons—were in some way unnatural."

Sonn came so swift after that that Bal knew his brother was probing for some revelation about his sons' nature. He did not know whether to lie then or not, whether Lysander knew, or merely suspected, that the infants he claimed as his sons were not pure Darkborn. And on what grounds he might know or suspect. Balthasar might dare to test his lie against Lysander's suspicion, but not against his certainty.

It occurred to him, though, that Lysander might be similarly uncertain as to what Balthasar knew, and similarly cautious of arousing suspicion.

"A woman can have such strange thoughts at such a time, yes," Bal said.

"Would that I had been more patient with her," Lysander said. "What do you know about my sons? How did she come to leave them with you?"

"I believe she planned it that way from the first," he said. "She brought with her a quantity of hypnotic, which she used on me and on the children." He had decided not to tell Lysander that Tercelle had tried to expose the children, though whether his impulse was to protect himself from further questions, or not further damage the dead woman's reputation, he did not know. "She crept away while we were sleeping. I knew I could not keep the children—she had not, remember, told me there was any connection between myself and them—so I took the first steps in arranging for them to be fostered."

"But you do not know where?"

"No."

"But you can find out, can't you? You would wish to ensure they were well treated." That with only a trace of his former sneer at Bal's mush-heartedness.

But the sneer was there, and suddenly Balthasar remembered lying against the paper wall, voiceless, in agony, in shock from his internal bleeding, while the man with the aristocratic accent, who had directed the assault, stooped to pull his hood from his head.

He remembered: *He said this one was weak.*

Weak was the epithet Lysander had hurled at both his siblings, and their parents, whether they tried to placate or resist his will.

"Lysander," Bal said, "you have not asked how I came to be in this bed. Two men invaded my home and tried to beat out of me the whereabouts of the infants. When I was lying on the floor, nearly unconscious, I remember that one of them said: 'He said this one was weak.' Those were *your* words, weren't they?"

This time his sonn aggressed, capturing the betraying twist of Lysander's expression: anger, not remorse, at being balked. For a moment, Lysander hesitated, as though toying with the lie, and then he said carelessly, "Right up until I left, you were a whining, belly-aching brat."

"That was seventeen years ago."

"Very well, Balthasar," Lysander said. "I'll grant you've grown a spine. So I'll put it to you man-to-man. Give me back my sons, and I'll give you back your daughter."

"Why should I trust you?" Bal cried, in a sudden outburst of anguish that was less than half calculated. "You have never spoken a single word that did not advance your own interests. Tercelle Amberley is dead, and you've barely acknowledged that, or acknowledged *her* except as someone who inconvenienced your plans. She was to be married, Lysander. How dare you compromise her?"

"She loved me! I would have married her but that you drove me out of the city," Lysander said. "She was the only person who ever loved me, and her sons are mine, and the only thing I shall ever have of her. But why should I *bleed* before you, who love your daughter so little that you sit here—"

"Lie here," Balthasar corrected sharply.

"—bandying words with me, while your child suffers."

How very Lysander, Balthasar thought, *that even as he blackmails me, he seeks to persuade me that I am in the wrong.* It was potent still; he was fighting for composure.

Sensing his vulnerability, Lysander leaned closer. "Balthasar, we are both fathers concerned for our children. I know I won't persuade you that I love mine—I'd never even held or sonned them. But they are *my* children, Balthasar."

"I did not drive you out of the city," Bal said harshly. "You fled in fear of justice. But you are right." He forced the words through a tightening throat. "You seem to know . . . rather a lot. I have to believe it is real and you are not just using it to your advantage. Please . . . bring me back my daughter, or tell me who has her. I will do whatever is within my ability to find your sons for you."

Lysander leaned back, smiling slightly now. "I want mine first. Then you can have yours."

"I don't know where they are," Balthasar said.

"You are in no position to bargain, Balthasar. But I will take evidence of your goodwill."

"I will find *out*," Bal said, his voice shaking. "I need time."

"Balthasar. Ishmael di Studier murdered the woman I loved. I was there, in that house, when he tried to bully from her the knowledge of your daughter's whereabouts; I was there, listening—to my eternal regret too late in my intervention—when he murdered her. I know you and our beloved sister have helped arrange bribes within the jail. I know you are planning to use your wife's money in his defense. All that has to stop. If it does, I will give you time." He rose. "And if it doesn't, be assured I will know. And if my sons have come to harm, harm *you* sent them into, you will never know what happened to your daughter, except that, believe me, it will be worse than anything you can imagine." He waited a moment longer, and then, satisfied that he had rendered Balthasar speechless, he said, "I don't suppose that I need to tell you to discuss this with no one."

The door closed behind him.

Balthasar rolled onto his side, curling up, as he had lain against the paper wall, as he had lain in his bed for days after he and his brother laid out the murdered girl. He knew now why Lysander's grief had seemed as shallow and false as a glass lake in a model garden, his declaration of other wrongs to exculpate merely mockery. He had not changed.

Lorcas announced himself by a light brush of sonn and a chinking of bottles on the bedside table behind him. "Here, sir," he said, arriving on the near bedside with a glass. "Get this down you." He steadied Bal with a wiry arm and forced the draft down him, with the indifference to protest of the experienced nurse.

"It's mostly not . . . physical," Bal whispered through sticky lips.

"I know, sir. It was plain that you feared that your visitor did not mean well, so I presumed to listen at the door. I apologize if I have given offense."

No offense, just a desperate sense of relief that he did not have to choose to tell or not to tell. "That . . . was my brother. Seventeen years gone and still a monster. And he has my daughter, or knows who does. Lorcas, you know what he asked of me; you know I have no choice but to comply, though if anyone should burn for the murder of Tercelle Amberley, it should be Lysander!" He shuddered. "But I suppose it would be brother's word against brother again; there's no ash, even." Bal whispered, an abject confession, "I cannot continue to help Baron Strumheller. He insists I . . . not."

"I fully understand, sir, and so would the master," said the manservant quietly. "I think we should ask the ducal staff to attend you now. It could endanger your daughter if he learns of the connection between us and the master. My son and I will return to the city residence. There will be correspondence to manage and transfers of funds to arrange; if we are not to have the support of Lord Vladimer's local network, then we must use paid agents in our inquiries. If I may be so bold, though, I think my master would recommend that you go to your wife's sister's as well."

"I . . . can't," Bal said. "Lysander will be back." Which was the least of it, he knew, sick with shame. He did not want to expose Telmaine to Lysander, did not want to witness Lysander's manipulations bent on her. He did not want to have to tell her *why* he was withdrawing their support from Baron Strumheller, though he knew she would understand and forgive it as being for their family. She had already opposed his becoming involved, and he had argued oh, so eloquently in favor and sent her away.

Sweet, cursed Imogene. He thought—he'd sworn—he'd never again be bent to Lysander's will, made accomplice to his appetites and his corruption. He had never imagined that he'd be party to the suffering of innocents at Lysander's hands. What he would do to Strumheller was betrayal enough, given Blondell's willingness to have him made scapegoat, but Strumheller still had loyalists and resources; he was not helpless. But Tercelle Amberley's infant sons were helpless, if they were even still alive. Whatever Lysander's true relationship to them, he could only do them harm. It was not in his nature to do otherwise.

Perhaps Lysander already knew about them; perhaps Tercelle had told him . . . what? Of that Lightborn lover . . . but why should Lysander believe it, much less be incited to murderous rage? Or perhaps the conviction that the children were *other* was his, not hers, and she had fled him in terror—but why then not confide in Bal? Except she had known him when he was in thrall to Lysander—but why then would she flee Lysander and come to Bal? It was all contradictions, and his agitated mind could find no purchase.

Telmaine

Several times in the night Telmaine woke to the sound of a child crying. Twice it had been Amerdale; the other times she had been certain it was Florilinde, until that leaden instant of realization that it could not be. Betweentimes she'd been tormented by bizarre dreams: dreams of streets she'd never walked and people she'd never known; of a strange old man in an ornament-filled home; of laying hands on a man's swollen leg, feeling and easing its pain; of crouching in stony rubble amongst gnarled trees, with open space beyond the reach of sonn all around; of running for her life, pursued so close she dared not turn. This last time she woke, trembling, to the tolling of the sunset bell.

Amerdale was asleep in the cot beside her. Florilinde . . . Florilinde was somewhere out there in the city, alone, and crying in Telmaine's dreams. She muted her sonn and lay in stillness, remembering her firstborn as the midwife lifted her, squalling, from between Telmaine's thighs. Even as Florilinde declared herself in the world, she was still bound to Telmaine by the fat umbilical cord. If only there were still such a cord binding heart to heart, mouth to ear, eye to eye.

Who was to say there was not, for a mage mother and her child? She might have asked Ishmael di Studier that—she might have asked Ishmael di Studier many things, but for her aversion and his importunity. Her vagrant thoughts lingered on that kiss, and the emotions it had aroused in her, and in him, and in her again. How *could* she, said the inner voice of censure, how could she think of such a thing at such a time? But she was, she was, and she was also thinking, if she were more powerful than he, *was* her magic truly contained within her skin, when his, it seemed, was not?

She breathed slowly, extending her awareness, slowly pushing outward the skin that was so exquisitely sensitive, seeking the distinctive essence of her elder daughter's consciousness, seeking the child's voice that wept in her dreams. Silent as mist, her awareness pervaded the room; as though her fingers had brushed her daughter's skin, she sensed Amerdale's dreaming presence, had a sense of a soft dog's muzzle nuzzling her face, of kitten fur fluffing under her fingers. She let herself diffuse farther, beyond the walls of the room. Here was Merivan, lying wakeful, seething with frustrated energies, and here her husband, his half-awake thoughts an erudite babble, and there each of their children. And there the servants—a fierce burst of furtive sexual passion that reminded her of Tercelle Amberley's impressions. And elsewhere a drearier coupling, the man's imposition as resigned as the woman's submission, the affection between them gone as barren as the Shadowlands. Here were the nearest Lightborn, outside under the sun. She lingered a moment, fascinated. It was not simply that they were awake, but that they were *different*, like hard crystal to her mental touch. A voice whispered, <Who?> She shied away, mindful of Ishmael's warning. Beyond were more Lightborn, some watery, some fiery, some crystal, some stone, and some that felt as though her drifting consciousness had brushed leaves or grass. Other voices whispered, <Who?>, and went unanswered. She spread her awareness farther, drifting through isolated points of water, fire, stone, leaf. Lightborn and Darkborn, she knew the difference, though her sense of individual essences was growing less distinct the more she gathered within the radius of her awareness, and she worried that she would find Flori and not know it.

The fringe of her consciousness brushed something, like a great smoldering ulcer in the tissue of the city. Grief, pain, fear, misery. It was the burned quarter, and the houses and hospitals around it in which the grieving and suffering lay. Her spirit shuddered back from it, and for a moment she lost herself, lost direction.

And then she felt a banked-ember heat she recognized. <Ish-

mael?> How else could she call him, here? But he was dreaming, a familiar dream of running and being pursued.

"Telmaine! Telmaine!" Far, far in the distance, a body was being shaken, a face slapped over and over again, ice water splattered on a head and chest. Far, far in the distance, a desperately attenuated tether was tightening. She clung for one more terrifying, uncomprehending moment to her sense of Ishmael's presence, and then was back, furious and unwilling, in the bedroom.

The voice, the shaking hands, the slaps and pinches, were Merivan's, Merivan barefoot, bareheaded, with a rumpled nightdress. Amerdale was howling. Telmaine sat up, reeling, her bones bobbing like bubbles, her head floating on her shoulders. She realized her nightgown and bedclothes were soaked. "What'sha *doing*?" she demanded in groggy outrage. Merivan had never been given to this kind of nonsensical prank, unlike her brothers, who had tormented Telmaine to the screaming point.

"You wouldn't wake up!" Merivan accused. "The maid"—she was a quivering girl clutching a bowl—"came in to conduct your morning toilette and you wouldn't wake up."

"Oh, for pity's sake!" Telmaine said, toppling over on one elbow. "I was asleep."

"You were unconscious. What did you dose yourself with?"

"*Nothing!* My husband works with addicts. Sweet Imogene, Meri, I have had three indescribable days. I was utterly exhausted." She threw back the wet sheet and swung her legs over the edge of the bed, leaning forward, tugging the soaked nightgown away from her breasts. "There was absolutely no need for all this *hysteria*."

The particular accusation made Merivan draw herself up. "I do apologize," she said icily. "And I will leave you to dress. Breakfast will be in an hour." She turned and, straight-backed, left the room.

"And you, too, you blithering ninny," Telmaine snapped at the hand-wringing maid. "Don't you dare come into this room again unless you're called!"

Amerdale scrambled into Telmaine's arms, sparing the maid her further wrath and Telmaine later repentance. Telmaine gathered her sobbing daughter to her, feeling the child's fright and disorientation at wakening in yet another strange place, to yet another rumpus. "Shh, shh," she murmured, while she struggled to comprehend with her rational mind what had seemed so plausible in that dream-walking state. Had that truly been Ishmael di Studier she had touched? What did it mean that they had nightmares in common? Had he fashioned some kind of connection between them yesterday? How *dared* he! Or had she simply been overwrought, as Merivan asserted she was, overwrought in her imagination and troubled in her conscience? She wavered, divided as to what she wished were so. If she truly had power, if she truly had extended her senses over the city, then *she* could find Florilinde. But in doing so . . . in doing so she would violate her compact with the natural order, and would become . . . She did not know what she would become.

Curse them for interrupting her! Curse them, too, for giving her a chance to think.

"You're wet, Mama," Amerdale complained, cheek against her wet nightgown.

"I know. Those silly women half drowned me."

"I want to go home. I want Papa."

Telmaine gently drew her fist away from her mouth. "Don't do that, Amy. It's babyish. We'll go and visit Papa after breakfast." Surely Bal would have heard from somebody by then, even if that somebody were Mistress Floria White Hand. *Give me her back*, she whispered to the Sole God, *give me her back and my world, your world, will be back in order. My magic will lie still within my skin, and I'll think no more of the feeling—all the feelings—of Ishmael's lips on mine.*

And if you don't . . .

Ishmael

The first attempt on Ishmael's life came just after the sunset bell. The night shift came barging along the cell block, hammering on bars and jabbing recumbent feet or heads with their batons, bellowing to the prisoners to stand for inspection. The manner of their address to the other prisoners warned him what to expect. Face impassive, hands slack at his sides, shoulders held in a prisoner's stoop, he endured their stripping sonn and foulmouthed commentary on his mother's morals, his father's identity, and the perversions of lords and mages. He heard with a sour appreciation the suggestion that his mother had copulated with a Shadowborn. If they had ever been within the glamour of a glazen, they'd have learned that men could abjectly desire Shadowborn. Brave men, strong-willed men, righteous, moral, and upstanding men, men who spit when they spoke of Shadowborn—no man was immune to the glazen's allure. Women, however, were, a trait to which he never forgot he owed his life.

Rather to his surprise, they confined their bile to words and, when they had had their sport, moved on to the next imprisoned wretch. Experienced in prison rituals, he did not sink back onto his bunk, and sure enough they were back, swift as adders, ripe to abuse those who had lain down again.

When they moved on, Ish considered the little he had learned so far about the layout of the prison. If he'd had any foresight, he should have had himself arrested for public drunkenness last month to allow for scouting of the exits. And he should have thought to move his lock picks from his shoes, which were always ripe for confiscation. By the direction of the guards' movement, the exit seemed to be to his right, and the guard post and most of the remaining cells to his left. It might be a touch early to abandon hope in the process of law, particularly with Preston di Brennan as his advocate. But experience had taught him it was never too early to start planning escape.

The returning guards shouted at the prisoners to put their water flasks out for replacement, or go thirsty. With much clanging of metal bottles, it was done. Ish pitied those who had come in drunk and were now suffering sunrise-head. Noting how the guard who set down his bottle selected and checked it, he fully expected to receive urine or something equally noxious instead of water—it was amazing how many buffoons thought that their *original* trick—but the liquid in the flask lacked that distinctive odor. Accustomed to drinking from dubious sources, he took a very small sip.

It stung his tongue. Two heartbeats later, tongue and lips were numb. He spit, sucked saliva into his mouth, and spit again. Did *not* swallow. He recognized the poison: scavvern. He went down on one knee to set aside the flask with utmost care, since the poison could also be absorbed through skin, though less efficiently. He had the two remaining spicule-lozenges tucked under the rumpled collar of his shirt. Rising, he pulled the first out and pushed it into a mouth that could no longer feel it; he caught it between his teeth, afraid it would spill from his enervated lips. He reached the bunk as the tinnitus and vertigo began, and rolled into it, cursing himself for the wasted movement, for being too damned effete to stretch his length on the filthy floor. Civilization would be the death of him. Belly-down on the bunk to avoid choking on the lozenge, he pulled vitality from it and poured it into his numb mouth and ringing ears, while at the same time he concentrated on neutralizing the poison, thanking his Drunken God it was scavvern, and something he'd met before. He was aware of distant shouts, of jolts and jarring, but numbness and ringing ears were fine protection against distraction—until someone lifted him up from the bunk, dangled him briefly like a shot weasel, and then let him slam down. The lozenge hopped from his mouth and skittered across the floor.

"The coward's poisoned himself!" Someone clouted him, hard, on the side of the head. He'd laugh later, he promised himself.

"Give him water," someone else ordered crisply.

Sweet Imogene, no. The same hand as before dragged him up, but this time an arm went around him. His head lolled so he could not sonn the flask, but he got a hand up, somehow, in what felt like the right direction. He nudged something hard to his gloved touch, braced, and thrust it away with all his remaining strength. Someone yelled a warning; there was a violent jostling and a clatter near him. Ish's wavering sonn picked out the outlines of the men around him. Two of them pressed up against the others in an almost comic impression of panicked retreat. The man holding him said in sudden alarm, "My arm's tingling."

"Get away from him," said one of them, and pulled the other away, leaving Ish to flop sideways, half on and half off the bed. He had lost all sensation in his face and all control of his sonn, which pulsed in erratic, unfocused bursts. He sonned his own hand, bent upon its wrist beside a puddle on the floor, protected only by its thick leather glove; he sonned milling footsteps; heard, through the clamor in his ears, the shouting. If they chose, through anger or spite, to pitch him onto the floor, he would be dead as soon as the spill soaked through his shirt. And there surely would be retribution on his fellow mages, if any of their own sickened or died of this "suicide attempt."

Nothing he could do about any of that. He turned his attention inward once more. Vaguely he heard the door to his cell slam, the nearby voices recede into the general bedlam of a prison roused, as the prisoners added their barracking and heckling to the guards' panic. He regained enough control to retrieve the last lozenge from his shirt and fumble it into his mouth, nearly losing it when his cheek brushed a sodden spot on the pillow—drool, he realized a moment later, not poison. He hoped, for the sake of the man who'd been about to give him the water—in all innocence—that the prison apothecary had his wits about him and knew how to support breathing. Scavvern poison was short-lasting; there was that to be said about it. And then a surge of utter fury drove the worst of the numbness away. He hauled himself upright, using wall, bed, and rage as crutches, and reeled against the bars. Gripping the bars with one gloved hand, he spit the spicule into the other and yelled—or tried to yell, with his voice a wheezing growl and his tongue flapping like a lone sock on a laundry line—"Was'n the *water*, curse you. 'M no sorcerer and no suicide." He slung an arm through the bars, dangling by his armpit, and pointed at one of the men who had so conspicuously scrambled away from the water. "Ask'm why he *knew* h'couldn't let th'water touch'm."

Madness, he knew: The guards would never accept the logic of his accusation. Even if they tore him apart, and in the process landed two or three more in that deadly spill, he would still be blamed. The man he'd accused was overset enough to be babbling denials that would surely have been suspicious to anyone whose reason was engaged, but were going unheard. Half a dozen guards started toward Ish, enraged. He pushed himself back from the bars, lest they start by using the bars as leverage to dismember him, and lurched back against the wall.

Bracing himself, he heard a man's voice say, "What is going on here?"

The voice was that of the superintendent who had arrested him, the middle-aged man with the distinctive nose and a reputation for principle above all. With him, he recognized di Brennan, his lawyer. His knees caved in beneath him—he told himself that it was not relief, merely the wearing off of that wildman's rage—and he slid down the wall to sit curled up against it and simply wait out the shouting.

Ishmael

Guards took him from his cell, fearfully and none too gently, and dragged him to an interview room at the far end of the hall, beside the guard station. He had by then more or less regained the use of his limbs, and was striving not to shake too openly with reaction. Di Brennan and his student were allowed to join him, but only in the presence of a guard. He supposed each was meant to neutralize the biases of the other. Save for an inquiry into his recovery, he and his lawyer did not speak. The student he recognized immediately: He had heard one of the ducal sons of the Scallon Isles had turned to law, as an alternative strategy for defending their sovereignty. Try though the young man might, he could not entirely contain his curiosity when he sonned Ish, or his distaste when he sonned their surroundings.

Malachi Plantageter returned somewhat later. He dismissed the guard, turned the chair and sat on it, sonned Ish with a deft, civil touch. He wasted no time on pleasantries.

"When we went back to your cell, there were three rats lying dead in that puddle on the floor. Come out to drink, I suppose, after the commotion was gone. Your lozenge was gone, carried away by a rat, I would presume. That, at least, was not death to the touch." He offered no interpretation of the facts so suggestively juxtaposed. "I've ordered it cleaned up. Carefully."

"And the guard—the one it spilled on?" Ish said.

Malachi turned on him an expression of surprise that he should ask, and then irritation, at himself, Ish thought, that he was surprised. "Doing well enough. Our prison apothecary's a cut above the usual incompetent sot."

"Tell him that the poison was scavvern, and wears off rapidly with no aftereffects."

Di Brennan stirred. "Baron Strumheller," he said, "have I not previously advised you against spontaneous contributions when you are in legal jeopardy?"

Ish was still gripped by that mood that counted self-protection secondary. "What else d'you know? Did you question th'man I marked?"

Di Brennan turned a severe expression on him, one reminiscent of long-ago tutors of the baron's unruly son.

Plantageter sonned them both. "I questioned him, yes," he said judiciously. "He claimed he feared that a sorcerer's affliction would be catching. I do note, however, that he was in the party that arrested you, and showed no fear even when you collapsed."

"He was also th'one who ordered them to give me th'water when I was stricken. I marked th'voice."

"I questioned the others; they gave me a clear account of everyone's response to your extremity, and to their reaction to the spilling of the water."

"And your thinking?"

"I am assigning two members of my own force to guard you—by lot, so there can be no fixing—at all times. It is, I am afraid, the best I can do. I will also ensure that the prison physician attends you."

"No need," Ish rumbled. "Mightn't have studied at any Physicians' College, but I know healing. Th'poison's almost out of my system."

He had asserted himself once too often, it seemed: After all, Plantageter was an official. "Nevertheless," the superintendent said, "your lawyer has requested it. I will also arrange a new cell." He rose, and with a, "Good day, sir," to di Brennan, left, taking the guard with him.

Ish suppressed his inclination to say, "I need no doctor," since the apothecary was clearly already in Olivede Hearne's pay, if not di Brennan's. "Well, di Brennan. What can you do for this pretty fix of mine?"

The lawyer turned his tutorly expression on him. "I can do more if I understand better. You might start by briefly telling me your version of the events that have led to your imprisonment."

"I wish," Ish said ruefully, "I knew." Di Brennan shifted in his chair, preparatory to making what was no doubt a cautioning remark. Ish raised a hand. "People have wanted me dead before, but usually have the decency t'issue the odd threat first. My troubles started with Balthasar Hearne. And Hearne's troubles started with Tercelle Amberley. Whom I most definitely did not murder. Th'body was warm, though, as I was no doubt meant to find it."

Di Brennan considered that. "Her fiancé is due to return to the city tonight. Doubtless that will inflame the passions surrounding this case."

Ish could well imagine that the story would jostle with the Rivermarch fire and the di Masterson divorce case for the front page on the broadsheets. *Notorious Mage Baron Arrested for Murder of Heiress Bride! Shadowhunter Accused of Murder!!* And so forth, with sense degenerating as exclamation marks accumulated.

"There will be pressure to settle the case quickly, before the scandal spreads," di Brennan noted.

"And before inconvenient truths are revealed," Ingmar Myerling added. "Like who got Ferdenzil Mycene's fiancée with child."

"Seems you know some of't already," Ish noted.

Di Brennan sonned his junior and said, "Take notes, please, Ingmar." *And listen*, was implied in his tone. Myerling opened up the case he had been carrying and produced one of the miniature keypunches that had become the fashion in efficient offices.

"Well, that was none of my doing," Ish said, to the accompaniment of a soft staccato of *pock-pock-pock* as the pins struck the paper. "Nine months ago I was as conspicuous about the Borders as she was in Minhorne society. I never met th'woman before this."

"There is a witness who claims that he heard you arguing with her about the whereabouts of a missing child, before she shrieked and fell silent. When they burst into the room, they found her newly strangled."

He sighed; it was all very nice and tight, the exact story that would have been used to account for his bloodied and bullet-ridden corpse. "Th'first time I called on her, it was plain t'me that Tercelle Amberley knew nothing of th'child—Florilinde Hearne. Y'should know that Mrs. Telmaine Hearne was with me th'first time—Lady Telmaine Stott, that was—she was the one who knew where we would find Tercelle Amberley, since she knew Lysander Hearne had given her the house. But it was searching for her child she was and nothing else."

"*Lysander* Hearne?"

"Aye, brother of Balthasar Hearne. A bad lot, and not heard of in the city for the last seventeen years." Lysander Hearne would have been little older at that time than Ish was at the start of his own exile. Given Ish's narrow survival, Hearne likely never would return. He would be long dead by accident or his own folly, and scattered by the wind.

It occurred to Ish to wonder how a youth of perhaps twenty, and not from a wealthy family, came by a house to make a gift of to his paramour.

"I doubt we will be able to summon Lady Telmaine to the stand to testify."

"I'm glad of that," he said honestly. "She has troubles enough."

Di Brennan made a noncommittal sound that Ish had no difficulty deciphering. His lawyer claimed little sentimentality about womanhood after decades before the bar, and the rearing of five spirited and spoiled daughters. "I'd have to get past that brother-in-law and that dragon of a sister of hers."

Ish decided to change the subject. "How is Lord Vladimer?"

"He breathes, and will swallow liquid, but other than that, he is unresponsive. The archduke's physicians are in attendance."

Unhappy Vladimer. Expensive physicians tended to want to prove themselves worth their fees, if not by curing the patient, at least by persuading him he had been treated.

"Who brought th'charge on me?"

"That was Master Blondell. He harbors no love for you, I am afraid, my lord."

"If I'd false charges laid by every man who has no love for me, I'd be the whole of your practice, Barrister. There's a sour note here. Blondell detests magic. It's the peasant in him," said the border baron.

"Then he would be readier than most to attribute an unexpected, unwelcome event to unnatural causes," di Brennan said, his voice a warning. "The charge is only suspicion, but by old laws still in our statutes, suspicion alone is sufficient for arrest, pending investigation."

"And who'd be doing th'investigating, since they'd sooner have magic not exist?"

"In law it still exists," di Brennan cautioned. "However, it will be to our advantage as we deny the charge. It has been suggested to me that a man, for complex, psychological reasons, may be persuaded that he is able to affect events around him. By magic, if you will."

For a moment Ish did not understand. Then, "So it's mad I am? Seduced into a delusion of my own magical powers?" He laughed at the sheer irony of it. "So I am t'enter the broadsheets as th'Notorious Mad Baron, rather than th'Notorious Mage Baron."

"It is the court we must persuade," di Brennan said dryly, "not the press."

"And you think you can." There was a ghastly fascination to the notion, he had to admit. He'd never have thought of it himself. His magic, meager as it was, was fundamental to his sense of himself.

"If need be, yes. We will require, as part of our preparation, to review all circumstances in which others might interpret your actions as magical. Please organize your thoughts and recollections in preparation. Now, I'd appreciate a narrative of recent events, from your perspective. Why were you in the city?"

"Lord Vladimer had asked me t'come for a meeting."

"Excellent. Let us begin, then, with that meeting."

"Some details touch on the work I do for Lord Vladimer, so I might needs be vague." Di Brennan alone he might have trusted, but the dukeling was largely unknown, and inevitably a partisan unknown. "You should know, Lord Vladimer wanted me on a mission that I'd likely not survive. This may be taken as motive for murder."

"Let me worry about what may be construed," di Brennan chided. "Please continue."

Ish did, in an account that was becoming increasingly polished in the repetition. He'd have to watch that, because overpolished reports tended to lose details, particularly details that were not self-consistent, and in a situation that made as little apparent sense as this one, inconsistencies could be revelatory. The dukeling hammered keys with enthusiasm; the islands had a storytelling tradition rich in fantasy and wild adventure. Di Brennan was more phlegmatic. "Well," he remarked at the end of it, "if I didn't know you, I might have doubts about your sanity. I wonder what young Gil di Maurier's investigation has discovered."

Ish said slowly, "Take care in asking him. The last mage convicted of malignant sorcery was the one that allowed Gil's and his sisters' kidnapping. I don't know how he'll greet this."

Di Brennan said to Ingmar Myerling, "Archduke's prosecutor versus Peregrine di Maurier, Givaun di Chamberlin, Marilla di Chamberlin, and Dianna Scarlatti, all for child abduction and murder, and the last for sorcery. Pull and review it, if you would."

"Do we know how long it will be before I come to trial?" Ish said.

"Weeks, maybe. I'll be setting a dedicated guard on you. I'm not easy at all in my mind that someone has already tried to poison you. You take care."

"Trust me, I will."

Telmaine

"I believe," decreed Merivan at breakfast, "you are in need of distraction."

She ladled honeyed mint jelly on a large slice of toast with a liberal hand. Mornings were her best time of day, and in her loose morning dress dense with lace, she appeared dignified and energetic, very much the mistress of the breakfast table.

Telmaine for her part felt as though she had been dragged along the railway tracks without a train. She had made an effort to put her appearance in order, but the time she'd have used for her toilette had been needed to settle Amerdale for the children's breakfast in the nursery, since the child objected to being separated from her mother. Merivan, sonning her sister, had compressed her lips, but in charity to the distraught mother had refrained from comment.

"Do you not think so, Theophile?" Merivan said to her husband, who was reading the newspaper, his fingers moving even more swiftly along the punched rows than Bal's when he read, his face wearing the slightly stupefied expression of deep concentration that had fooled advocates and criminals alike. He roused himself. "Pardon, my dear."

"I was saying," Merivan said, "that I believe Telmaine needs distraction."

Distraction, Telmaine thought savagely. Rides in the park, visits to the dressmaker, country outings, dances, parties, salons and concerts, novels to read, letters to write, gossip to exchange . . . society's anodynes for the worry for an absent parent, the grief for a dead sibling, the anxieties of an impending confinement, the shame of a husband's infidelity, a family's money worries, an in-law's scandal, the fears of a husband's illness or a kidnapped daughter. Adding to the burdens of life the burden of social pretense.

"Mm," Theophile said, his sonn brushing her obliquely. "Wouldn't have said that myself. Would have said she'd be wanting to get on with finding her daughter. I've asked three of the inquiry agents I'm accustomed to using to come 'round after breakfast."

Telmaine melted with gratitude, remembering why the formidable judge was her favorite in-law. He *noticed* things.

"Must she distress herself?" Merivan said, bridling with protectiveness. "Surely those inquiries should be made of her husband, whose foolishness brought this about."

"I'd like to do that," Telmaine spoke up for herself. "Thank you."

"Well, it will not take very long." Merivan regrouped. "And then I think you should go and visit—"

This was unbearable. "There is no one I wish to visit except my husband," Telmaine snapped.

There was a pause, and Merivan said in a hurt tone, "I received a card from Sylvide di Reuther this morning, asking if she might call on us." No doubt she interpreted the twinge of guilt on Telmaine's face as due herself, rather than Sylvide, for Merivan continued inexorably, "I think it would be more appropriate were you to call on her."

Of course, Telmaine thought: While Lady Telmaine Stott might have social precedence over Lady Sylvide di Reuther, Mrs. Telmaine Hearne did not.

"Can't understand the difference myself," Theophile murmured to his newspaper. He did, Telmaine knew, perfectly well. It was his subtle reproach to his wife.

Merivan opened her mouth, closed it. "You will do as you will," she said to Telmaine, in a tone of concession. "You always do."

Telmaine, her mouth full of ash-dry toast, knew of no reason to answer. She wished she dared ask Theophile what the papers were saying about Ishmael's—Baron Strumheller's—arrest. She must school herself to think of him with more detachment. But she dared not ask in front of Merivan, and she dared not take the paper. She finished her toast, ate another small slice, and finished the lemon tea she'd had an inexplicable craving for, and then excused herself to host and hostess. After she had spoken to the inquiry agents, she would take Amerdale to visit Balthasar, with as little prior discussion as possible. And she must write a note to poor forgotten Sylvide, asking her to meet them at the ducal palace. Sylvide would surely be as desperate to escape her mother-in-law's domain as Telmaine was to escape her sister's. She would ask her to bring the newspapers. Maybe after she had visited Bal she would know what to do, aside from seethe and bate like a mewed falcon.

Go to Vladimer. You must help him.

She chewed the inside of her lip and pushed the intrusive thought away. Helping Vladimer was not her *part*, particularly when she was afraid she knew what kind of help Ishmael—it surely was Ishmael—intended. She was a wife, a mother—a respectable woman. She would tend to her family, as she should.

Ishmael

The second murder attempt came as Ishmael was being escorted from the interview cell to his new cell, adjacent to the guard station, where they kept all the troublemakers. Farther from the exit, to his regret. He could hear the profane heckling, and the shouts for silence, even before they turned the corridor, and both redoubled as soon as the first sonn caught their approach. Vicious as the harassment was, there was a peculiar forced quality to it, which he attributed to the fundamental hollowness of men who were compelled to fight all comers to prove they existed, had consequence, *were* men.

They were level with the cells when a prisoner reached through the bars and grabbed at the nearer guard's belt. The guard was young, or slow-witted, or . . . for whatever reason, he reacted too late, for his backward lunge against the grip coincided with the prisoner's push. He stumbled into Ish, thrusting Ish against the second guard; the guard twisted, seizing Ish, and shoved him hard against the bars of the opposite cell. The prisoner's arm snapped up like a bar across Ish's throat; a knife—he did not need to sonn it to know—was driven with killing force through his shirt and against the rings of his armored vest. His assailant swore. The guards shouted and tore him away before his assailant could deliver a second stab to his unprotected armpit or throat.

A seemingly random cast of sonn told Ish there was no hope of a dash for the exit. He let himself pitch forward into their arms, impersonating the stab victim he was meant to be. They lugged him into his appointed cell; there were shouts for the apothecary, amongst the greater cacophony of a triumphant prison kill. None of them attempted to open his shirt or examine his wound, clearly averse to touching the mage more than they had to. He lay inert, considering the choreography of the assault. The more he thought about it, the less accidental it appeared. Two prisoners, surely, the guard maybe, and whoever had contributed that knife.

All prisons were bad for a man's health. This one promised to be exceptionally bad for his. He breathed steadily, knowing calmness was his best ally now.

The prison apothecary arrived, demanded in his thinly veneered accent that they leave one guard with him, one *competent* guard, please, and give him room to work. He'd let them know if he needed help to move his patient. Ish let the apothecary discover for himself the dry shirt around the knife tear and the hard carapace of the ring-stitched vest. He snorted and announced, "This one's no more dead than I am." He lifted Ish's shirt, revealing the vest to those he'd banished outside the bars. "Don't you even *search* your prisoners these days that one's got a knife and another's got armor? You're lucky the one met the other. Come, your lordship, sit up. Enough malingering."

Ish sat up as bidden, taking the opportunity to inspect the man he'd sonned only obliquely the night before. He was above average height, wiry, and slightly stooped, even at his young age, with the hollow chest left by a childhood of deprivation and its maladies. He would have been handsome were he not so thin. He wore a different coat than last night, another of the dandy's castoffs. That accent said Rivermarch, the dress said Rivermarch, and with those origins he'd have come by his education through the indulgence of a rich protector, whether his mother's or his own. Ish was long past judging men for what they did to survive, only for what they made of their lives beyond survival. The apothecary had had the nerve and gumption to save the poisoned guard, and he'd helped Ish last night.

"Magister di Studier," the apothecary greeted him, startling him. A sonn revealed bare hands—not a mage—and an urchin smile on the narrow face. "Y'don't remember me. I ran your errands when I was a street rat and you an apprentice. If I'd known you were a baronet, I'd have held out for three coppers."

Ish laughed in surprise and recognition. "You'd not have got them, Kip."

"Wouldn't I?" he challenged with a familiar tilt of the head. "How many'd you pay two coppers to, Magister Tightwad?"

"None of th'rest could read, and half would garble a simple message. You'd your letters and your wits, both, for all you were a chancer. And I wasn't a baronet then; I was an ex-Shadowhunter, living on his earnings."

"You haven't lost the hunter's habits, I note, moving in high society."

"There are daggers there no less deadly. You've done well for yourself; I'm glad of it."

"No thanks to you, Baron Tightwad." Ish smiled a little; so, the tutor he'd covertly paid to give the boy the little education he'd take back then had never let on.

Kip leaned forward to ask intensely, "What's this about poisoned water?"

"I'd just taken a small mouthful before I felt the effect. The guard got more."

"When you spilled it on him."

"He was about t'pour it down my throat. All unwitting, of that I am sure. It goes in less easily through skin. The superintendent told me that he lived."

"Aye, he did. Which is as well for you." This was said without the least inflection. "He's a mate of mine, and well liked. You know this poison?"

"Scavvern venom."

"Any aftereffects to expect?"

"None; it's quick-onset, quick-offset. I've met it before."

Kip crouched, quickly sliding up Ishmael's sleeve to take a pulse, his movements sure and competent. Ish caught the flavor of his thoughts: amusement at Ish's predicament, speculation without malice as to how to turn it to his advantage, and a hoist-of-the-finger defiance toward Ish's magical insights.

"Someone not convinced their case will hold?" Kip murmured. He was, Ish realized, largely untroubled as to Ish's possible guilt or innocence. "You burned this arm," he observed distinctly. Ish was impressed; he himself had barely heard the stealthily approaching step.

"I escaped the Rivermarch with my life, not my shirt."

Kip's hand closed hard, almost brutally, on his wrist. "My woman didn't," he said flatly. "Nor her youngest."

"I am very sorry."

"She was a shrew, but burning's a bad end, and the child had done no one harm in all its short life." Ish had a moment's impression of a child's high giggling, a squirming weight sprawled across his chest, the feathery touch of soft curls on his chin and nose—all that remained of the infant Kip had loved and, despite his cynical posture, yearned to avenge. Ish wondered how many like him there were in the city tonight.

"They say this was Lightborn set," Kip said grimly.

"No," Ish rumbled. "No Lightborn. Or Darkborn either. Say Shadowborn, if you must give them a race. They've put themselves outside race and law by this act. I know the spoor of them." Kip's quick wits, he trusted, would make the connections Ish intended. "Where are you living now?"

"Other wing, so long as there's an empty cell," said Kip, after a moment's pause. His thoughts had grown wary; he lifted his hand away. "How's your chest wi' the smoke? You seem to be breathing well enough."

"For now I am," Ish said dryly. He lowered his voice. "Can you get me my lock picks? They went with my shoes."

"I likely can, or a set as good," the other man said in a voice as low. "It'll cost you, for all those times you should have paid me three coppers."

Ish grinned; he was on sure ground here. He would need to sweeten his offer enough that it, and old district loyalties—such as they were—would outweigh any counteroffer. The erstwhile street rat would warn him of the need to raise his bid. "You need somewhere to stay. There's a boardinghouse run by Ruthen di Sommerlin up on Perlen Street. It's on the north side, well clear of the burn. Tell him I sent you." Nobody raised in the Rivermarch would be offended at the house lifestyles, and he rather thought the faded glamour of its burlesque past would appeal to Kip. Kip would suit the old men, and he'd care for them, in his own way, if Ish did not survive these toils.

"Seems to me," Kip said softly, "next time they try you should let them succeed. Feet first's the easiest way out of here." The prison apothecary rose and ran his sonn over Ish. "Think about it," he added casually.

Telmaine

Telmaine did not recognize the manservant who showed her into the apartment and Balthasar's room. Neither Lorcas nor Eldon was present, and nor, to her relief, was Olivede Hearne. Her husband was lying in his bed surrounded by unread newspapers. She knew them to be unread because Bal habitually reduced newspapers to a shambles that was the despair of every conscientious housemaid. His face was taut with strain, even as he smiled and opened his arms to Amerdale and herself. She was immediately frightened he might have relapsed, but when she slid her hand behind his neck she felt no greater physical duress. Emotionally was a different matter. She sucked in her breath at his emotional storm: He was trying and failing to avoid thinking of something, and all that did was fragment it. He made an effort, a valiant effort, at lightheartedness for their sakes.

At last, she coaxed Amerdale to agree that she would like to visit the menagerie in the central garden, and asked a manservant to find a nursery maid to take her. They sent her off with the young girl who appeared, and Bal sighed with audible regret. "She needs the distraction," he said, unwittingly echoing Merivan's unappreciated offer. Telmaine concealed a wince and slipped into the small, warm place left by their daughter, lay down beside him, and laid her arm across his chest, sliding her bare hand under the yoke of his shirt to rest on his shoulder. "Something's wrong," she risked asking. "I can tell it. What is it?"

The surge of utter, impotent hatred in him made her recoil, even so far as to pull her hand away. He did not notice. His thoughts, normally so orderly and engaging, were a hard coil of anger. After a long moment, he said in a soft, strained voice, "Telmaine, I'm sorry. But I can't . . . I haven't the strength to keep doing this. I've . . . withdrawn my support from Baron Strumheller. I've lost my nerve. I'm hurt and I'm worried and . . ." And to her touch, to her magic, his jagged memories of the night before told her the truth behind his lies, that his supposedly dead brother Lysander, the one who'd made him accomplice to murder seventeen years ago, had claimed to have their daughter, and was threatening her life.

"I'm sorry," he said. "I know you'll be ashamed of me."

She could not speak, horrified at what her touch was revealing, horrified at the lie in his words. He had never lied to her, not like this. She knew Lysander had hurt him, but not that Lysander would exert such control over him.

She sought truthful words, to fit between his lie and her knowledge. "My love, my cherished, I understand. Don't hate yourself."

"I won't," he said, another lie. He felt so frail in her arms. She held him as tightly as she dared, sinking her awareness into his body and sensing the slow, natural healing of his injuries. She longed to inject her own vitality into the still-fragile bulk of the spleen, the delicate matrix of the broken rib, the clot-stiffened areas in the lungs. There . . . there was a small foul area, like the rotten spot on a peach: the beginnings of pneumonia. He'd not know that was gone, and it was so *easily* brushed away, as though she had been doing this for years.

"I haven't had any word about Florilinde," he said, resting his cheek against hers. "Or Baronet di Maurier."

She broke off her examination to remember that yes, she should have asked that question. "Theophile called in three inquiry agents. I spoke to them this morning, told them everything I knew. They said they would come and speak to you later on. They seemed very competent." Which she could not believe of Guillaume di Maurier, social scandal that he was. One of the agents, fortunately, had reminded her of Ishmael, a seasoned man with a brusque but gentle manner.

"Good . . ." he murmured. "Telmaine, I am worried about Olivede. She went back to the Rivermarch to help. Eldon says that she had company, a guard, but after everything that's happened . . ." *They are* my *children, Balthasar,* Lysander's voice spoke through him. "And I'm . . . I can't help thinking about the twin babies. I don't know whether they're alive or dead, Telmaine. It's all mixed up in my mind with Florilinde. . . ."

She stroked his forehead, though his memories and guilt and lies lacerated her. "Bal, no one can care for them all at once. Your sister is a grown woman, responsible for her own well-being. No one can know better than she does what the dangers are. Baron Strumheller is a great landowner and a Shadowhunter; he has money and lawyers and powerful friends. Yes, it would be terrible if anything happened to the twins, but you have done your best for them already. We *must* think first of our Florilinde." Deliberately, she added, "I cannot think of anything that I would not do to get her back safely."

And she knew, as she said it, that it was the truth, should and had to be the truth. She pushed herself upright, tucking her legs under her beneath her hampering skirts, and put a hand on the table beside the medicine bottles. "Which one of these helps you rest?" She would use her magic to help him sleep, but with his experience, he would surely know.

"It's all right," he said. "I don't need—"

"You don't *need* to lie here and fret. I'm going to go and pay a call on Mistress White Hand."

"I sent her a letter."

"A letter's too slow. Then I am going to call at the rooms of Guillaume di Maurier and find out what he knows, and then I . . . well, what I do next depends upon what I find out."

"It's not safe," he protested.

She allowed a moment for him to tell her the truth as to why it was not safe, and then leaned over and kissed him lightly, a blithe wife disregarding her husband's fretting. "I'll not use my own or the ducal carriage: I've asked Sylvide to call on me. I will start by taking hers, as far as I think it's safe for her to go. Then I'll hire."

"Telmaine—"

"I can do this, Bal. You can't. Baron Strumheller can't. Did I not hear you say, just before we left the house, that whatever condition we find ourselves in, we are the ones to fight this evil? You made no distinction then between Baron Strumheller and yourself, and your sister and me."

"I do not think," he said, after a long silence, "I could live if anything happened to you."

She swallowed. "I thought the same. But we have children, and we cannot be so selfish. Promise me that if anything does happen to me—anything that forces us apart—promise me you will still live for, love, and care for the children. And I will make you the same promise."

"Kiss me," he whispered. She braced herself against his profound unhappiness and sense of inadequacy, but drew strength from his unexpected admiration. She did not press him for his promise, knowing by the kiss and the emotions that, consciously or otherwise, it was given. Despite her better wisdom, she pressed healing on him through the kiss.

"Better than any medicine," he breathed, his hand curling around the back of her neck as she drew away. They smiled at each other, each wreathed in secrets and unspoken truths.

Eight

Telmaine

Telmaine's conscience twinged as Sylvide peered from the carriage, her flowerlike face creasing in worry as her sonn brushed Telmaine. "Dearest, what is it? Your note was very strange." The ducal footman came forward to open the door, and Sylvide gathered her extravagant skirts to rise, but Telmaine forestalled her, hitching hers up to climb aboard. She had dressed plainly, in a style that would let her move as freely as possible. "Let's go," she said to Sylvide. "Anywhere."

Her friend's expression was one of hurt bewilderment at her abruptness. Not clever, and made well aware of it by her brothers, Sylvide hated the sense of events moving too quickly for her to understand. Telmaine shuffled forward to take both her hands in her gloved ones, across the space between them. "I'm sorry. I had to get us moving while I explained."

"Explained what? Why did you have me bring a pistol? Why aren't you at your town home? What has happened to Balthasar? Where are your children?"

"Amerdale is with Bal. Flori . . . Flori is part of the reason I asked you to come here. I need your help."

"Telmaine! Are you in trouble?"

"A great deal of trouble," Telmaine said grimly. "Until this moment I thought it was a good idea to . . . to use your coach. Now I am not sure. Could I have the pistol, please?"

Sylvide pulled the box from beneath her full skirts and handed it over. She nibbled on the index finger of her fine glove while Telmaine unboxed the pistol, checked that it was unloaded, and confirmed that she understood the loading and safety mechanism. She left it unloaded for the moment. It was designed for a lady's hand and taste, but the di Reuther holdings were still close enough to the Borders and the Shadowlands that even ladies' weapons had heft to them. It also came with an ornate holster sash, another practical accommodation of the Borders, since a gun in a reticule or saddlebag could be more useless than no weapon at all. She settled the sash across her shoulder and laced the waistband, resting the weight of the gun on her hip. She would practice drawing it when she was indoors. She had once been a reasonably sporting shot, but the last time she had held a gun of any kind had been at a target competition just after her marriage—one of the times she had unwittingly colluded in her family's humiliation of her husband, who had proven to be one of the worst marksmen she'd ever met.

She'd felt Sylvide's tentative sonn rippling over her as she completed her preparations. "Tellie," she said in a small voice, "I don't understand."

Telmaine drew a deep breath and put her head back. "I'm sorry I wasn't there to meet you at the town house. I . . . admit I forgot about inviting you. It was quite driven out of my head. You know that I accepted an invitation from Baron Strumheller to escort me to the city."

"Tellie, haven't you heard? Baron Strumheller has been arrested for murder and sorcery."

"I know. I was there when it happened."

"You were there! How . . . ?" Her suddenly appalled, guilty expression was enough to almost make Telmaine laugh. She said gently, "So was Bal."

"Tellie, I never—" Sylvide said, her voice nearly a sob.

"Shh, it's all right. I'm past being offended by any of the simple things. To begin at the beginning, when we—the girls and I, and Baron Strumheller—arrived at the doorstep, two men came out of the house. One of them picked up Florilinde and"—her voice thickened—"carried her away. We don't know where she is."

"Abduction! How horrible! But why?"

She had given some thought as to what to say to Sylvide and others she had to protect, for their lives, from the truth. "Bal had treated a patient. They wanted information about that patient—I think there was a great deal of . . . an inheritance riding on that information. He had refused to give it to them. They'd nearly . . . they'd beaten Bal unconscious: He's still in bed. They took Florilinde to force us, but we haven't even had . . . haven't even had a ransom note from them." She was not going to talk about Lysander Hearne's visit. "Baron Strumheller was helping us find Florilinde when he was arrested."

"How horrible! Can't your family help? What about the public agents?"

"What all has been done, I don't know; I'm merely the mother. My brother-in-law, may he be blessed, had me speak to private inquiry agents this morning. I know Bal asked Mistress White Hand to find out what she could, and Baron Strumheller spoke to someone else, whom I will also visit. I hope they might have found out something and we've just not heard. I'm hoping that you can drive me at least to Bal's family home. I'm going to start with Floria White Hand."

"Of course!" Sylvide said. "You poor dear."

Telmaine

"I'll wait here," Sylvide said as the carriage drew up behind Ishmael's automobile, scattering three of the neighboring boys, who had been scrambling over it, crowding into the seat, pulling at the levers, and impersonating its noises. Telmaine relaxed slightly, and realized that she interpreted the children's presence as evidence of no danger. She reminded herself that danger could stay concealed.

"If it seems dangerous," she said to Sylvide, "and you have to leave, then do. If you hear me shoot, go. If you hear me shouting, go. If anything . . . if anything *strange* happens, *go*."

"Tellie," Sylvide protested at such an ominous litany.

"You have to promise, Sylvide. I've taken shameless advantage of you so far, and I'll never forgive myself if I've brought you into danger."

Sylvide's face set in mutiny, and she slid her hand under her skirts and brought out a second box, identical to the one she had given Telmaine. "I know you think I'm a feather-wit, Telmaine, but I've *lived* near the Borders. My coachman is armed, too."

Telmaine opened her mouth, closed it. Sylvide said, "We'll be in less danger if you get on with what you have to do." Her sweet, light voice trembled.

Forceful sonn cast along the street to either side, as the baron had cast, outlined nothing to alarm her. She could not help realizing that his sonn had revealed a greater distance, far more crisply than hers, but his sonn had been refined in the Borders and Shadowlands. That made her think, fleetingly, of the landscape of her dreams, and she shuddered.

The steps of Bal's home felt strange underfoot, almost as though she walked on ice and at any moment they would shatter underfoot, or tip and slide her over their edge. She had had no idea, when she scrambled from the ducal side door into the carriage, that this evening was so intensely *cold.* Or why she should be shaking so with fear that she had to brace one hand with her other to fit the key into the lock. It was absurd. The last time she had felt fear of this irrational intensity was . . . was in the garden. Where she had been drawn by the sound of a voice that was not her husband's, and where she had been brushed by an aura of fear and chill given off by a woman no one else perceived.

She clung to the door handle, panting and sick. She *must* go on, *must* speak to Floria White Hand, *must* know what the Lightborn had found out about Flori. As she clumsily twisted the key, she felt sudden searing agony across her fingers, as though a branding iron had struck them; she shrieked aloud and flung herself away in an instinctive recoil, trod heavily on her hem, and pitched down the steps, arms thrown over her head to protect it, ribs unspared. Sylvide and her coachman had dismounted almost as soon as she landed, Sylvide crouching beside her in great distress. "Tellie, Tellie, what is it?"

The pain of the bruises and scrapes inflicted by the steps went unfelt beside the agony in her hand. "Light!" she gasped. "The house is full of *light.*"

"Light? But—"

"The *wall's* gone. The paper wall. I *told* Bal. My *hand*—" She half shrieked, sure now that if she unclenched her hand, it would crumble into ash. "No, don't touch it."

Sylvide's hands fluttered over her, brushing her down, feeling for injury. "Shall I go for a doctor, m'lady?" said the coachman, a thought that horrified Telmaine; all she wanted was to get away from here. By then several passersby had gathered; one brought her the key, lost in her fall. Sylvide took it and uncertainly sonned the door. Telmaine struggled up to a sitting position, still near retching from the pain and the horror of the touch of light. "Mark the door! Light breach." The witnesses, whom she perceived indistinctly, recoiled; suddenly, instead of half a dozen, there were only two. One was a public agent, wearing the uniform of the city's law. He said, "Do you know this house, missus?"

"This is Mrs. Telmaine Hearne, and that is her husband's house," Sylvide said in her best great-lady tone. Her hauteur might not have been convincing, but her cultivated voice was. The agent, chastened into caution if not civility, said more politely, "Mrs. Hearne, could your husband be . . . ?" he faltered.

"No!" she said, in reflex rejection of the very thought. Imogene's Curse, was that what was *meant*, that the light was meant to immolate whoever next opened the door . . . ? The ground rocked beneath her. *I am going to be sick,* she thought, and then, *No, I'm going to—*

Someone was bathing her face with cool, scented water. She was lying, awkwardly, on a padded bench that was too short for her, which was jolting and rolling in the familiar coach-over-cobbles rhythm. She brought her throbbing hand before her sonn, too confused to remember why she did not want to know. Sylvide captured it, folded her own hand carefully around it, cradling its hurts. "It's all there, Tellie, dear, but you're going to have a nasty scar." She could feel, through the brush of skin on skin, Sylvide's shock and anxiety. "I'll never call your gloves silly again, Tellie. Your hand could have been burned right off."

"I thought it was," she whispered. "Where are we—where are we going?"

"You have to visit a doctor. It's still a bad burn. I thought . . . well, I didn't know whether to take you to your sister's or to Bal."

"Don't . . . tell him."

The carriage lurched, and Sylvide released Telmaine's hand to brace herself on the decorative arm of the bench. "I'm afraid, dear Tellie, that that agent seemed to have a very florid imagination. I believe he was working up a little story about how you had immolated your husband, though how he thought you might have done so without burning yourself up, I don't know." Sylvide was an avid reader of murder melodramas, and well acquainted with the logic of literary murder. "So I daresay he will be inquiring as to Bal's whereabouts and well-being."

"Ah," said Telmaine, half a groan. "I didn't want Bal to know. Did he . . . did the agent . . . mark the house?"

"Yes. Once I put on my mother-in-law's voice."

She tried to straighten her fingers. The pain was excruciating. Was a wound left by the light different from other wounds? Would it heal? "Maybe he'll finally have that wall closed up properly. He loves her, you know," she confessed with a sob. "Always has, as long as I've known him. I don't think he even admits to himself how much he loves her. But I know. I tell myself it could be worse: It could be a Darkborn mistress. Someone he could *touch*."

Sylvide crooned wordless sympathy and reassurance. The lurching of the coach was making Telmaine nauseated, lying down. She hauled herself upright with her sound hand and elbow, holding her injured hand to protect it from jarring, and was almost pitched to the floor by a particularly violent lurch. Sylvide's quick brace steadied her.

The coach had stopped. Sylvide unlatched and slid down the side panel. They had been too absorbed in their own conversation, the sound of wheels on paving too close for them to have heard the crowd outside, but now they did, an excited hubbub around them with a murk of sonn too dense for theirs to penetrate. Telmaine realized that they were in the Lower Archduke's Mile, near the courts and the main newspaper outlet, and opposite Speaker's Square. Speaker's Square was the place where the proselytizers and rabble-rousers of the city traditionally had their public say. One of the latter was in full volley. He had a powerful voice, and had drawn an unusually large crowd, which had spilled back onto the roadway. ". . . this is *our* city. *We* founded it. *We* built it. We made it what it is today. *Without* magic. *Without* making our women dirty their hands and strain their soft bodies. Without endangering our sons' and daughters' health and morals."

At the end of each statement he paused, inviting low surges of muttered agreement that rose and fell like the sea. "We built this city with honest labor. It was safe, and peaceful. Now what do we have? Great fires killing hundreds. Magical storms killing who knows how many hundreds more. Our archduke's brother magically sickened. A lady murdered. A mage accused of murder and sorcery." The rumbling surged in outrage. He spoke more swiftly now, building momentum. "One of our nobility shot down in the street. That's the way *they* behave toward each other. It's not the way *we* behave. Let them take their poisoning magic and their poisonous women and their barbarous ways and go back where they came from. Let them go back to live amongst the Mad Baron's kind. Let them go back to the Shadowlands, among their foul brothers and sisters."

The muttering surged into a muted roar. A thin, anonymous

voice yelled, "Break in their doors. Turn out their lights!" Other voices took it up. "Send them back to the Borders. Melt them all."

Sylvide said faintly, "Oh dear."

There were laws against the fomenting of race hatred, violence, and revolution from Speaker's Square, albeit laws too often more honored in the breach than the observance. The authorities were alert to such instances, and would shortly move in to quiet if not arrest the speaker and disperse the crowd—but the crowd was surely of a size and volatility to be teetering on the verge of riot. Telmaine could feel the seething violence around her, as febrile as the miasma over Balthasar's door had been chill. The coachman redoubled his efforts to clear the rippling fringes of the mob, people too concerned with getting close enough to hear to attend much to their surroundings, even had the density of sonn allowed it. The coachman must be proceeding as much by feel and sound as by sonn now, desperately trying to bring them out of the crowd before it turned on them, while doing no injury that would make them turn—a near impossibility in a press like this. There'd be at least one person crushed under hoof and wheel today, if not several. And still the speaker railed on, a celebration of vitriol. "Burn the mages!" she heard him scream, and experienced a sudden, furious wish that he *lose his voice.*

He croaked to a sudden silence in midrant. Her mouth opened at the beginning of a shocked protest. She had not . . . She could not . . .

Then she heard the overlapping clatter of multiple hooves, shouts, shrieks, and several shots. Sylvide scrambled her pistol out of its box. A man's voice bellowed orders, followed by a curse and a whip slash as someone challenged the orders. The carriage lurched forward, erratically gaining speed under an unknown escort. Sylvide clung with one hand to the seat arm, with the other to her pistol.

Telmaine held on to the seat arm with her unburned hand. The coach swung through a turn into a side street and stopped. They heard a man's vigorous voice giving directions to their driver. Sylvide said faintly, "That's Ferdenzil Mycene."

A moment later, they resolved movement outside the still-open door panel. The man himself leaned forward along the neck of his tall horse to sonn inside, in a fashion too crisp to be entirely gentlemanly. "Are you ladies all right?"

She had always thought that the sculptor who created his statue—one tended to think of statues with Ferdenzil around—would need genius, or be driven mad with frustration. He was overmounted, as usual, on a tall, powerful horse that stomped and snorted under his hand and crop. His physical appearance was commonplace: a little less than average height, his strength wiry rather than sculpted, with a face assembled from off-the-shelf features, its only distinction the distinctive asymmetry of his cheekbones. His allure was all intangible: the abundant energy, the intelligence, the will. In any room he drew and held attention as he pleased, and every adventurous woman in the city schemed for him to notice her. He had paid court to Telmaine before she married, but she had found the devouring ambition beneath the charisma frightening.

"Are you ladies all right?" he said again, while each waited for the other to speak, whether as a result of their tangled state of social precedence, or profound uncertainty as to whether they were all right, Telmaine did not know and was too weary to wonder. "Yes," Sylvide said at last. "Yes, thank you, Lord Ferdenzil."

"I can't spare you an escort; the situation's going to . . . downhill too fast, and we'll have to turn it in the next few minutes if we're to turn it at all." He lifted his head at a new wave of shouts and heckling and the sound of a horn. "Good day, ladies."

"Wait!" Telmaine said, pulling herself forward to the window. "He—the speaker—said there was a nobleman shot down on the street."

"Guillaume di Maurier," Ferdenzil said with dispassionate impatience. "They found him alive this morning, but they say the wound's mortal." Refusing further questions, he swung his horse and disappeared out of range of sonn.

Telmaine felt chill, as chill as she had standing on the steps of that cursed and light-filled house. Ishmael had sent Guillaume di Maurier searching for Florilinde.

Telmaine

Guillaume di Maurier's close, overheated bedroom was fetid with the stink of blood and infection. The large young man lay gasping with agony and fever amidst disarrayed sheets on a bed whose ornately erotic carvings would have otherwise overwhelmed Telmaine with embarrassment. As a frame to his mortal suffering, they seemed merely pitiful and grotesque. There was a broad bandage over his exposed lower abdomen, where the sonn echoed crisp with sweat saturation; he'd been shot in the lower belly, and while he lay hidden through the day, peritonitis had set in. A stiff-lipped doctor rattled a dense clutter of hypodermics and bottles—a scene too uncomfortably reminiscent for her—and a starched nurse bustled by with basins and cloths. Both exuded disapproval that family had been banished to the antechambers while strangers were admitted to the sickroom. The stoic manservant, who seemed to have taken charge of all, acknowledged them, but ignored their mood.

Sylvide, who had insisted on coming with her, gripped Telmaine's arm with her nails in silent distress. The manservant moved to the bedside and ordered the sheet decently, and firmly deflected the patient's attempts to toss it away. "Lady Sylvide and Mrs. Telmaine Hearne are here, sir, as I told you."

There was a long silence broken only by Gil's harsh breathing. The bloodless flesh had sunk between the bones of his face. "Hearne," he croaked at last.

"Mrs. Balthasar Hearne, sir."

"Tell her . . . I . . . *found* . . . her."

Telmaine pressed forward, pulling Sylvide after perforce. "Tell me!"

His hand came up, groping air, and then locked into a fist as a spasm of pain brought a new shower of sweat to his skull-face. The muscles around his neck stood out as hard and sharp as blades. The doctor stepped forward, hypodermic in hand, wrestling Gil's rigid arm away from his side. With a fastidious finger he probed the entire length of the scarred, knotted vein. Telmaine muttered, "Get on with it." The doctor jabbed with the needle. Sylvide whimpered and swayed on her arm. Telmaine steadied her, irritated at the interruption. "Go outside," she ordered. "I won't be long."

The nurse helped Sylvide out of the room.

Forcing herself to use her burned hand rather than her teeth, Telmaine slipped her glove off, and, bracing herself for what she would feel, folded her hand around Guillaume's clenched fist.

It was worse even than Bal, who though beaten and bleeding had been almost unconscious. Gil was in agony, consumed from within, fully aware he was dying. Prepared, she resisted an outcry. She released her magic, let it flood him, praying the witnesses would take the surcease of pain for the effect of the drug.

His gasping breaths steadied. "Lower Docks. Pier thirty-one. Lower level. Left-hand warehouse. There's a door—"

"I know the place," she said; from his memories she knew it.

"Shouldn't have let them surprise me. I know better." Voices behind him, a pile-driver blow in his lower belly, men kicking and taunting him as he writhed on the ground and then pitching him into the empty street as the sunrise bell fell silent. He'd dragged himself into a cleft that he could seal with rubble, and lain throughout the day beneath the burning flagstones—as he'd lain in the hot, dark place of his confinement with the rotting bodies of his dead sisters. Even with her vicarious experience of so many kinds of inner torment, she had never imagined torment like this.

"Tell . . . tell your husband"—the rictus of his smile was ghastly—"he saved me . . . for a better death than . . . the one I sought." Through his memories, she glimpsed her Bal, a gentle and inexorable healer, banisher of monsters, hunter of demons, giver of hope. It wasn't just for Florilinde that Gil had lived out the terrible day.

She lifted her head and sonned the doctor. He was no one she recognized, but she said crisply, "My husband is Dr. Balthasar Hearne. This young man is a patient of his. If my husband were here, I suspect he would tell you Baronet di Maurier needs much more of that than you are giving him. It does not matter whether you, personally, disapprove or not. You have a duty to relieve suffering."

The doctor's face was tight with disapproval and resentment. Gil croaked a laugh. "No use, there. He's my family's."

Telmaine bore down on the doctor. "You took an oath, did you not? The same one my husband took."

Grudgingly, the doctor began to prepare another syringe. "Is that enough?" she challenged, the moment he hesitated. Grudgingly, he yielded, drawing up what seemed to be a frighteningly large volume. She fervently hoped she had remembered correctly Bal's explanations of addiction and tolerance.

She felt the needle punch through his scarred vein and, unnervingly, Gil's rush of gratification at the sensation. She'd needed that dose to be given to cover what she was about to do. She had a sense that Ishmael di Studier was crouched beside her, his hand over hers, his awareness overlapping hers, giving her insight. The heavy bullet had torn the bowel on its entry, and lodged deep in the pelvic cavity; in its removal, more damage had been done. The bleeding had been severe and critically weakening, and the spilled bowel contents had started a raging peritonitis. Delicately, she knitted together the torn bowel, sealing its poisons within. Then, as she had done with Bal's incipient pneumonia, she swept away the infection clawing at the raw membranes. That was all she could do; he was still dangerously weak, though the drug had finally eased his agony. An even more potent analgesic was his profound relief at having delivered up his message, at having not failed at his appointed task. She leaned over and brushed his burning cheek with her lips. "Thank you," she whispered.

"Tell Ishmael," he rasped, his breath foul. "Bastard mage or no, he's a great hunter. He'll find her for you."

"*You* found her," she said, ignoring the chill that that "bastard mage" gave her. Gil di Maurier had better cause than most to hate magic. "And you'll find and save others." She straightened, laying his loosening hand back onto the covers. If he lived, they would simply call it a miracle, which suited her fine. If magic couldn't ever return what it had taken from him, surely she'd added something to the balance.

For the first time, she truly understood why sixteen-year-old Ishmael di Studier, of high birth and slender talent, had exchanged his birthright for his talent and thought the bargain sound.

She found Sylvide in the sitting room, quietly sobbing in an armchair, the only one of the dozen or so there, men and women, who was. Telmaine acknowledged Guillaume di Maurier's kin with the necessary civilities, but no more; she had no desire to talk to them, gathered like carrion birds at the deathbed of a son and nephew they had shunned in life. Though, she thought with a rising blush, if the carvings on that bed were anything to go by, Gil was hardly the blameless victim of social disapproval.

"Oh, Tellie," Sylvide said with a hiccough as they climbed back into the carriage, "that was so sad. I know he was dissipated and a great disappointment to his family, but I knew him as a boy, and he was . . ."

"Rather horrible, I suspect," Telmaine said, as her friend faltered. "Most little boys are, at least to little girls. Let's pray for him, Sylvide. He's had so much suffering in his life; surely there should be some redress." She drew a deep breath. "I need you to take me to the prison."

"To the *prison*?" Sylvide said, incredulous.

"Baron Strumheller asked Guillaume to search for Florilinde, and Guillaume *found* her just before he was shot. If the people who have her think he died before he could tell anyone, they won't have moved her, and that's our opportunity to get her back. But the man who knows best how to rescue her is in that prison."

"Tellie, he's held for sorcery and murder. They won't let you visit him."

"On false charges, Sylvide," Telmaine said in a voice hammered hard with anger and resolution. "False, foul charges."

"Tellie . . ." Sylvide wrung her hands. "You can't go rushing off to the prison to visit a sorcerer. It doesn't matter if you think he's innocent; other people don't. Think of your reputation. Think of mine, if you don't care about yours. Your sister will . . . she'll eat me alive!"

"I don't"—*care*, she started to say. But she did care about the opinion of a society in which she had been embedded since birth. And about her friend's safety and life. Gil di Maurier might be dying because Ishmael had involved him. Ishmael was in prison, surely, because he had been drawn in. Bal . . . She drew a deep breath, thinking swiftly, and then released it in a sigh.

"You're right. I'll go back to Merivan's, tell the inquiry agents. But you must go to Bal for me. He should know about Guillaume. He'll know someone he can send over there, someone who can treat his pain properly. If you set me down at Bolingbroke Circle I'll be able to get a carriage from there."

Sylvide argued, without effect. She set Telmaine down at the interchange, protesting still, while Telmaine reiterated the message she was supposed to give Balthasar. She sonned Sylvide's worried, unhappy face, framed in the window of the departing coach, as she climbed aboard the hired carriage and gave her true destination, the Lower Docks.

Nine

Ishmael

To Ishmael's mind, the riot was a mixed blessing. It kept the corridors full and the prison staff busy—too busy earning their licit pay for their thoughts to turn to earning their bribes, and constantly within play of one another's sonn. On the other hand, it made escape well nigh impossible, even without taking into account the two-man guard on his cell, the private agent engaged by Ish's lawyer, and the single prison guard whom the superintendent couldn't really spare, but did, now that his honor was staked on Ish's life. There wouldn't be another attack like the first two, but given the burning of the Rivermarch, Ish found that the thought of spending another day confined made him profoundly uneasy, both for himself and for the thoroughly mixed bag of his fellow men who'd share his fate. So.

He shifted his fingers, feeling the lock picks slide inside his gloves. A couple of hours before sunset would be the best time. If he couldn't escape by stealth, taking advantage of the guards' confusion, fatigue, and dilution by inexperienced men—and his little scrap of magic—then he'd trust Kip's cunning and plan to leave feet-first, a victim of unexpected delayed effects of the poisoning. As a mage, he'd the body control to enact a fatal collapse most convincingly, with Kip there to deny the remaining suggestions of life. It would be chancy, since nothing held the young opportunist to his course but the promise of a reward, and Ish might be at any moment outbidden. Except that he had, implicitly, promised to enact Kip's revenge for his lost child, Shadowhunter that he was. So he rested, sitting on top of his bunk with his back propped against the wall, listening carefully to the voices and sounds around him, the feet hurrying and shuffling past his cell, and waiting.

<Ishmael?> The mental whisper was as clear, suddenly, as if Telmaine were there in his cell with him. <Baron Strumheller?> It wavered with her uncertainty that she should be able to address him so intimately. Defiantly she claimed his name and hurled it through his mind like a shaft of fire. <*Ishmael*!>

He jolted upright. <I hear you!> Sweet Imogene, she was powerful! His sense of her was as acute as if she were sitting here on his lap, and his body responded to that thought. He tamped down his response; he didn't want to frighten her into retreat. <Telmaine, I didn't expect>—*you to be able to do this*, seemed insulting, and perhaps disingenuous.

There was a pause. He felt the simmering of her personality, and her power. <You did something to me, didn't you?> She sensed his immediate impulse to dissemble; her thought stabbed him. <Don't you dare pretend that you didn't.>

He formulated his thoughts carefully. <I gave you the way I think of my magic, the way I . . . picture it. That won't be the way you think of yours, ultimately, but it's a start. For some mages, it works. Creates a connection, too. Makes things like this easier.>

He sensed her remembering dreams not her own, spun out of his memories. <Rat bastard.>

Ouch, he thought, though if she was dreaming of *that*, she'd every right.

<Where are you?> he asked. <You're hurt. I can feel it.>

<I'm in a coach, bound for the Lower Docks. I went to talk to Floria White Hand, but . . .> The memories spilled into him, swirling around that single moment of searing heat and horrified realization at the touch of light. His horror mirrored hers, the visceral horror of the Darkborn contemplating light, and the horror of knowing how near she had come to death. In this intimacy, there was no deceiving either of them about how he felt about her. Or she about him.

In his distraction, the chill and terror she had experienced on the doorstep nearly passed him by unnoticed. But not quite. He had felt hot horror at the possibility of her burning. Now he felt the cold horror of recognition.

She sensed that. <What is it?> He did not respond, remembering barren lands, twisted bushes, and that chill sense, like a miasma over it all. Inside his mind, the Call throbbed, stronger than he'd ever felt it this far north.

<Ishmael! What is it?>

Reluctantly and full of dread, he responded, <Shadowlands magic.>

<The Shadowlands have mages?>

<Some of th'Shadowborn work magic. By instinct, we've thought, not as we do. Seems we might be wrong.> *Vladimer was right*, he thought. *Vladimer was surely right, by whatever uncanny instinct he possessed. The Shadowborn have elevated their attack on us beyond the crude marauding*

that already has the Borders in constant skirmishes. And I never even recognized it. <Telmaine,> he said. <I will do anything you ask of me, anything, if you will only go t'Vladimer. He's th'only person I know to do something about this.>

<I have to get my daughter,> she said, and once again her unschooled impressions crowded in on him: of Lysander as perceived through Bal's thoughts, of Gil di Maurier, suffering in his sickbed.

<Gil di Maurier, dying?> He remembered all the other men and sometimes women who had died while he sat or lay helpless beside them, his meager power spent. *How many more must we lose?* he thought achingly. He felt her reach out to him, and it was as though she cradled his head gently in her hands.

<I did what I could for him.> Diffidently, as a student seeking approval.

He inspected her memories, surprised that she could have done so much. But maybe he should not have been: She was the mage wife of a fine young physician. She'd been learning from her husband, too, all this time.

If he'd been in the least inclined, he'd have been jealous. As it was, his heart wanted to open up and fold her in. <You've done fine,> he said. <Fine.>

<If they have not moved my daughter,> she said, <how do I get her out?>

His thoughts split, one path a swift flow of possibilities, the other eddying in conflict and self-contradiction. She snatched at the flow, vexed by the distractions of the latter with its mingling strands of protectiveness, desire, envy of, and pride in her. <I know I haven't been willing to do this before, but I am now. I have power, you say, and if I have to use it now, I will.>

And at that, the resentment and fury beneath her defiant willingness flared up to scald him. She had seldom used her power, and never without furtiveness and guilt. She had given men their due in submission, and society its due in conformity. In exchange, men and society were supposed to give her their protection, not submit to blackmail or scheme to use her powers or censure her for something she had never wanted and could not prevent. He realized he had curled up on his bunk, arms uselessly over his head, instinctively trying to shield himself from the intangible.

The awareness of the pain she was causing shocked her into remorse. <I can't do this, Ishmael,> she said, her mental voice a tiny whisper.

<Yes, you can,> he said firmly.

There was no answer, no sense of her. He wanted to reach out, though it would render him helpless once again. *She* had been sustaining this contact entirely by herself, following a magical healing of a mortal wound and who knew what else. She was a powerhouse.

And, he thought, she was the wild card in the pack, the gaming piece their enemies did not know was in play. They'd—those mysterious, powerful, frighteningly organized Shadowborn—they'd taken down Vladimer. If they hadn't yet killed him, it was only to extract maximum benefit from the disarray that his incapacity had caused. As surely as Vladimer had planned around his own death (as he planned around others'), he had not planned around his incapacity. He found it too unthinkable.

He'd not make the same mistake again, if he lived.

But he might well not live, because so far his loyalists were losing the field badly. The enemy had taken down the mages, who'd be grieving and drained by the aftermath of the burning of the Rivermarch. Who knew what havoc they were already causing amongst the Lightborn. They'd taken down Ishmael himself, and seemed determined to eliminate him entirely, presumably for his role in the Borders defense, possibly for his magic, possibly because, in the course of the last few days, he'd simply *annoyed* them too much. Alive or dead, he'd annoy them further. Any enemy who assumed the Borders defenses depended on him or on any one man would be deservedly sorry. He was ten years older than Vladimer and had spent enough time laid out flat, whether from wounds or from over-spending his powers, to make full provision for that in *his* plans.

The person they hadn't known to take down was Telmaine Hearne, gracious lady and mage of precocious and surprising facility.

The moment they knew they had to, she was going to be in mortal danger.

<I don't care,> she said in his mind. <I'm going to find my daughter. Will you or won't you help me?>

He had no idea when she'd started listening to his thoughts again. Her emotions told him that there was no purpose to argument, whether concerning the risk to herself or the cost to others if she were hurt or captured or even killed. And the sooner she had her daughter, the sooner he could persuade her to go to Vladimer.

<The simplest thing for you t'do is to put everyone t'sleep. That would let you just walk in and take her. I suspect you already know how to make others sleep, even if y'don't know you know. You've had children. And you already know how to reach a familiar mind at a distance. I know how t'identify unfamiliar minds around me, though once I've done it a minute or two, I'm useless. You'll not be.>

<All right. We do it that way,> she said, with a determination and trust in him that was so innocent it frightened him. He felt a clench of apprehension at the thought of her wounded as Gil di

Maurier was wounded, counterpointed with a kinetic memory of a desperate sideways lunge to escape a snarling shadow.

<What was that?>

<Memory. Run-in with a Borders lynx,> Ish said. <Female, protecting her cubs.>

The lady was not flattered by the association. <What else?>

He'd have to get control of his thoughts. Couldn't risk distracting her, or spilling something he didn't want spilled, or she didn't need spilled on her. Their thoughts came together so easily, so fluidly, it was the not-doing that was difficult, not the doing. He'd never worked with so congenial a mage.

<What else depends upon what we find? What are you wearing? I've a reason for asking,> he said, in response to her sense of pique. <The docks are a rough area; y'don't want to be sticking out. Anyone who troubles you amply deserves what he gets, but you'd be using energy y'might need later.>

She visualized her dress for him. He feared that, plain as it was, its quality would be immediately apparent to the habitués of the docks, who had a sense as fine as gold measures for the coin worth of anything. <Take the jewelry off.>

She did, readily for the earrings, more reluctantly for the pendant around her neck, an intricate love knot in silver. She held it in her hand, thinking of the young student who had given it to her, and how he had paid for it. Hearne was evidently an accomplished cardsharp. Sweet Imogene, Ishmael thought, if he could only be going with her. Even her husband would be better than having her do this alone.

<I'm not stopping now,> she said, sensing his dithering. <And I'm not alone.>

<There's a boardinghouse . . .> He tried to avoid thinking in

detail of the habits of the residents, except to say, <They're good people.>

<And if her abductors move my daughter in the meantime? I'm not going to waste this chance. You think I'm powerful. You think I'm dangerous. Then show me how to do this. If you argue rather than help, you're a liability.>

She had a way of coming to the point. He yielded. <Leave the pistol, too, and its holster; it's the wrong kind of weapon. As soon as you get out, take off your veil—that marks you. Telmaine, you clearly don't belong here—>

<I'm a once-respectable lady with a shameful habit who has come to the end of her contacts, but not yet her money—or at least the money she's been able to purloin.> From Balthasar, she knew such unhappy people existed, and how they might behave as their craving induced them to ever more desperate attempts to avert withdrawal.

<That may work,> Ish said. <Last thing, tend to your hand.>

<I don't want to waste the energy.>

<You're wasting vitality talking to me,> he said forcefully. <Tend to your hand. You may need it hale.>

The coach drew into the Upper Docks Circle, as far into the docks as any coach from the center of town was willing to go, and the coachman fulfilled his social duty by descending to open the door. Slipping into her intended role, she offered him a hand that trembled slightly and let him steady her down. "Wait here, please."

<Show him the money, and give him a third. It might be enough t'hold him, if nothing happens.>

She fumbled out the money, gave him three coins, and clenched the others tightly, swallowing as though in the grip of anxiety or nausea. What she felt was neither, only a sense of profound unreality, as though she moved through a story she could not even imagine wanting to read. <We'll worry about that later.>

<You don't leave worrying about your line of retreat until later.>

<And this is supposed to help how?>

Reticule clamped under her arm, she slid off her veil. With quick, nervous steps, she started along the long road toward the Lower Docks. In his cell, he braced his back against the wall, knees drawn up. His heart was beating so hard he was dizzy, beating harder with her in danger and he a vicarious mind-rider, than it ever had when he was on foot in the Shadowlands.

<Stop panicking, Ishmael,> she said sternly. <Help me.>

<Cast harder,> he advised her. <You need to know what's around you.>

He knew the Upper Docks well, and the Lower Docks better than he cared to. Here, in the Upper Docks, which thumped with industry, the danger was more the danger of meeting with an accident rather than mischief. There were sidewalks along the wide boulevard, clear of the main tram tracks that grooved the paved road and made walking treacherous, but every side road and every major warehouse and dock had its own side branch of the tracks, to allow the trams to move in and out. Most were still drawn by draft horses, but some were pulled by the internal combustion engine, which added its own unique contribution to the cacophony. On the docks, onloading and off-loading proceeded from the barest interval past sunset to the barest interval before sunrise—there'd been recent worker agitation against owners working them through the sunrise bell, ended by an archducal edict that no one was to be denied immediate shelter. From the waterside, she could hear the grinding of pulleys, the bellowing of foremen, the crash of cargo roughly handled. Packing, sorting, and loading were carried out by the day shift within the light-sealed warehouses on either side of the boulevard, loading the trams for transfer to the huge covered station. Already there were four tracks engineered for day trains, with two more under construction.

<Where does it all come from?> she asked, bewildered.

<Along the coast, south of the Shadowlands. Trade from the isles and from the Unsundered Lands is increasing yearly. Smell . . .> Obediently she breathed in the scent of raw spices in abundance so vast as to be smothering. Ishmael, in his cell, luxuriated in them.

<You like the isles?>

Her mental voice was still as fresh now as when they had established the connection, though she alone was sustaining it. They could risk a little conversation that had nothing to do with her errand. <If I'd no lands or provenance, I'd live there, grow spices, and wax plump and complacent. There's nothing large enough even on the largest island to kill or maim a human.>

<And the waters?>

<I didn't say I'd fish.> Indeed, the Shadowborn had ravaged the waters around the Scallon Isles until the massed fleet of the islanders hunted them down. Past invasions by sea had suffered badly at the hands, cutlasses, pistols, and cannon of those ships. Ferdenzil Mycene seemed well aware of that; his buildup of men was gradual and inexorable.

<Ferdenzil Mycene's back,> Telmaine said, stepping sideways to evade a cadre of briskly moving factory women being quick-marched between sites by a loud-voiced supervisor.

The supervisor accosted her. "Where's you supposed to be, then?"

<Macavere's Textiles,> Ish quickly prompted her; she repeated it. The woman, hearing the distinctive upper-class accent, said, "It's over there," in a tone that was marginally less abrasive, but much more curious. Telmaine thanked her civilly, and continued on.

<You were saying about Mycene?> Ish said.

She recalled the encounter for him; in his cell, he shifted a hand to hide a grin at her irreverent reflections about statues. <He's going to want my hide.>

<He won't get it,> Telmaine said. <Once I've got Florilinde, Lysander no longer has a hold over Bal, and Bal can tell the superintendent that he's back, that he claims the children were his. They'll want to investigate *him*.> He felt her push down a thought, bound up with loathing and protectiveness: the loathing toward Lysander Hearne, the protectiveness toward her husband.

<Macavere's Textiles,> Ish noted, tactfully, of the nearest warehouse. <We're almost at the bridge into the Lower Docks. That's . . . rather a different proposition than this. They're th'older docks, can't handle the large barges and cargoes, so they've had to make do with the smaller, poorer cargoes. Some of th'warehouses aren't used. They were run by organized crime for most of th'last century. Th'only way th'city authorities could break th'hold was build th'new docks, near th'train terminal, and starve them out. It was Lord Vladimer and his people made sure they didn't get a similar hold on the Upper Docks, though he was little more than a boy at th'time. Someday I'll have to tell you the stories.> Those ranged from sunset raids that involved dozens waiting through the day in shelter, to audacious burglaries of the houses of the then-richest in

the land—some attributed to the sixteen- and seventeen-year-old Vladimer himself—to months and years of careful analysis of the movement of goods and moneys to discriminate legitimate trade from graft, blackmail, and peculation. The trials that had ensued had occupied the tabloids for months, and the courts for years. They had sent dozens to prison and a handful to the shackle posts, and driven several more to choose suicide over disgrace. The consequences had shaken the foundations of three aristocratic dynasties, and ruined several large merchant houses. But the operation had secured the city's economic health, and established the career and reputation of the archduke's young half brother.

<What is that horrible smell?>

<Th'old canal. Used t'be flushed daily with the opening of the upstream locks, but now there's so much traffic going through the new canal, they do it weekly, if that. Breathe through your mouth.> He carefully did not think of the human debris that the flushing of the canal also removed. That foul stench was likely to include one or more rotting corpses; for all that the great criminal dynasties had been vanquished, their lesser offshoots remained.

<Where's thirty-one?>

<Second from the end. Start paying attention t'your surroundings. The warehouses at the other end, near the main road, are still being used; these aren't. At least, not for anything legal. So don't dally. Someone tries to stop you, put them out before they're within a dozen strides of you. Y'don't realize how fast they could have you pinned.> *Cut your throat*, was the thought he kept from her. <When you're close enough to the warehouse, that's the time t'sense who is in there—you shouldn't act until you *know* Florilinde's there. If she's not, promise me you'll leave, go t'your brother-in-law, and get him to organize a search of those warehouses. If they have moved her— What is it?>

He had felt her suddenly halt, but even as he asked the question, he had the answer in that flush of chill and terror he felt sweeping over her, the unmistakable sense of Shadowborn magic emanating from the warehouse ahead.

And Telmaine pulled up her skirts and ran. He started—<Telmaine!> The faint sense of a reply came back that she *must* move now, or stop, rooted, until they came to hunt her down.

Ish twisted on his back on the prison bunk, gripping the side rails in anguish. He reached for her—surely it would be easier now that they had spent so long in rapport—but the pain of the futile exertion was like a sheet of fire through his skull. Oh, sweet Imogene, this could not be happening again.

Telmaine

Telmaine reached the wall of warehouse thirty-one, slapping against it with both hands, and bent over involuntarily, breathless. She hadn't run like that since her girlhood; indeed, she'd never run like that, even in her girlhood. Horror stories were to be shared huddled with her cousins in the library. Those cousins seemed to have an endless supply of the kind of magazines that her mama forbade her to read. There'd be hot cocoa to warm chills, cream cakes to stifle shrieks, and the certainty that squealing aloud meant possible confiscation of the magazine and heaped scorn from the elder cousin she worshiped. Worlds away from standing with the cold horror of the Shadowborn magic streaming down on her like an icy rainfall. She reached through it with longing: <Ishmael.>

She found him immersed in his own horror, remembering a Shadowhunt long ago, and a woman who died saving his life when he fell in thrall to the Shadowborn himself. She had been his first love, the woman he should have married but for his exile. The scars on his face were a brand of grief and shame.

She hardly needed Bal's insights to tell her why Ishmael should be thinking of this now.

She withdrew her awareness from him and, leaning against the wall beside the door Gil had told her about, sought her daughter. Found her, immediately, just within the walls. Florilinde huddled on the floor of the corner of her room beside her chamber pot, knees drawn up to her chest, weeping silently, sick and frightened. She had vomited on herself and on her bed, and dreaded her captors' punishment.

Telmaine felt her power surge with murderous rage. She swept the interior of the warehouse, seized the four minds therein and slapped them down into unconsciousness, twisted the door handle and threw her shoulder against the door.

And the magic surged as the interior of the warehouse exploded into flame.

"Ishmael!" she screamed.

Florilinde's terror became absolute as her bed erupted with fire. She scrambled to her feet, beating upon the locked door like a little bird against a cage. Telmaine reached in with her will and seized upon the nearest man to her—<Free my daughter!>—but he was already burning in the fire that had bloomed from the fabric and springs of his chair, writhing mindlessly in the flame's embrace.

<Telmaine!> Ishmael's mental voice was raw with the effort of projection. <Push the flames and heat *back*. Push them back like *this*—> A mental gesture, a demonstration of something he hadn't the power to do himself. She caught his gesture and cast it out into the real world, and a still cavern opened up in the midst of the flames. <Yes!> said Ish. <Open it up more. There's too much turbulence, too many reflections, and you don't want to trip.> Behind

that calm, calm mental voice, he was fey with terror for her. <You'll not keep this up for long. Go, go quickly.>

She stepped forward, into the cavern within the flames, and let flames sheet down behind her. She was aware of the heat, but at a remove. Steadily, hardly daring to think lest the bubble enclosing her life burst, she walked forward, following her sense of Florilinde. She was blind to sonn with the chaos of the fire, nearly deafened by its raging. Around her, timbers creaked and burst. She heard Ishmael's stifled thought that with this heat, the warehouse would not stand for long without collapse; she felt his desperate need to not distract her, his certainty that if her concentration wavered, she would be dead before she could draw breath to scream.

Within the roil of flame reflection, something solid loomed: a door. Ish said, <It's a bolt, blessed be. . . . It will be hot.>

<Can I cool it?> Without even waiting for his answer, she reached out and thought of ice, thought of cool mountain streams, thought of ice cream, thought of cold pouring from her hand upon it. When her fingers touched the bolt, it was dewed with condensation. She forced it back and opened the door.

Florilinde threw herself against her, beating at her in a frenzy of terror. Ish said, <Sleep her, quickly.> Telmaine held her daughter against herself, hand across her forehead, until she went limp. She staggered as she hefted her, realizing as she buckled under the small weight of her child how little physical and magical strength remained for her for the return journey. Ish said, <Use her if you have to, but carefully. And use me.>

<I don't need . . .> She was straining now, feeling the effort of pushing back the flames, and carrying her daughter, and setting one foot before the other.

She felt his fear for her intensify; his mental voice was fierce. <You must. I am not losing you.>

She caught the vitality tendered, drew on it, even as she felt the weariness growing in him. Step by weary step, she retreated through the fiery chaos, guided now by Ishmael's sense of direction, since there was no child's presence to steer by. Her skirt caught on something; she sonned the obstacle, dragging it free. It was a burned, bent stick, jutting at an angle from a larger mass within the flame.

Ish said urgently, <Keep moving!>

One more step and she realized what it was: the charred remnants of a man's leg. Her concentration failed. The bubble burst. Ish screamed in her mind as he reached across the distance between them to, for a heartbeat, hold away the inferno alone. She seized the burden from him, her magic tearing at his, and felt his consciousness go out like a candle, leaving her utterly alone in the midst of fire.

She never did remember how she took the remaining dozen steps to the door. She stepped out of the doorway into the air, into the fine spray of the fire hoses, the globe of flame unraveling upward from around her. Through the wild ripples of heated air and water, she perceived the crowd, and for a moment felt sheer social panic at the thought of so many witnesses—and then realized that they must sonn her against the turbulence of fire even more poorly than she sonned them. With a steadying step, now that the immense drain of magic had ceased, she angled her walk along the side of the building and out into the milling gathering beyond the edge. No one accosted her; their faces were all turned to the fiery chaos of sonned flame. In her arms, Florilinde stirred and whimpered, and she touched her lightly with magic, soothing her, as she continued to ease through the crowd. Several sonned her, smelling smoke, she realized, smoke and the charred and scorched places on her dress. She did not return their sonn, did nothing except navigate through the crowd, Florilinde held tightly in her arms. Anyone who accosted her, she thought, would regret it.

She crossed the bridge against the press of spectators too excited by the fire to pay much attention to her. The trams seemed to have halted with the sirens, and walking the pavement was much easier. Florilinde stirred again, whimpering, and suddenly she vomited over Telmaine's bodice. Telmaine paused, laid her chin against Flori's clammy forehead, and sank her awareness into her daughter's body. She found no injury, no inflammation, only a residue of wrongness—they'd fed her spoiled food.

And if they had not, she would have been lying on her bed when the Shadowborn trap exploded, and Telmaine could no more have saved her than she could have saved those men.

She reached the Upper Docks Circle unmolested, and—*sweet Imogene*—the carriage was still there, with the coachman standing in his seat and straining to hear what was outside his sonn. Telmaine said in a hoarse rasp, "Help me."

He nearly refused, concerned for his upholstery; a brush of her fingers through her burned-away glove told her of the conflict within him, between a father's compassion for a sick child, and a breadwinner worried about feeding his own children from his slender profits. She realized she had no reticule; she had dropped it—she did not know where. The loss of Bal's love knot pierced her, but dimly. She said, "I've lost . . . my money. But if you get me to the ducal palace, I'll ensure you're paid. I need to report to . . . I need to report to Master Blondell." It was a threadbare inspiration, but it sufficed. The coachman hesitated, and then shed his cloak and laid it inside the carriage—a gesture of kindness, she realized, warmth for the whimpering, trembling child. He helped her lift Florilinde and then herself aboard, and asked no questions, for which she was deeply grateful. As the carriage began to move, she rocked her bundled daughter gently in her arms, ignoring the slime of vomit covering her bodice, and waiting for Florilinde to know her once more. And tried desperately not to think of that last sense of Ishmael, suffering her draining, making that impossible reach to save her, and going to ash in her mind.

Ten

Balthasar

Bal was relieved when loyal, anxious Sylvide di Reuther left. He had been hard-pressed to talk her out of going to search for Telmaine, particularly since he would dearly have liked to do so himself, and if she'd said one more time, "I shouldn't have let her go," he might have said something he would regret. He was exhausted with reassuring her when he had no such reassurance to give himself, no matter how often he told himself that Telmaine was not yet overdue, that she might have had to wait for the inquiry agents, that . . . The broadsheets under his fingers were little help, filled as they were with speculation about Ishmael di Studier's arrest and reports of the riot. They still lacked the name of Ishmael's alleged victim, which merely gave them license to couple his name to the most celebrated corpses and unsolved disappearances in the last twenty years: the Three Headless Women of the Lower Docks, Beven Imre's vanished mistress, and a dozen others. Bal should have followed it all with clinical fascination, had he not been involved, compromised, bound to stand by when a decent man was rent and scalded by public opinion.

The papers crumpled under his clenching hands as he heard the outer door open, and his borrowed manservant's agitated voice. A woman's voice, husky and strange, spoke sharply to him. Balthasar pushed himself up on his pillows, wondering what new incursion he faced now. Through his door came a whiff of smoke, sweat, perfume, and vomit, and someone kneed it wider with a thud. Telmaine entered, her face ghastly with strain, arms full of a cloak-wrapped bundle. He scarcely dared breathe for shock turning to hope. Staggering, unspeaking, she laid the bundle on the bed, and Balthasar sonned the sleeping or unconscious face of their elder daughter.

"Flori," he breathed. "How?"

"By the grace of Gil di Maurier," said Telmaine in a thick voice. "I need to give the cloak back to the coachman. I need to pay him." She seemed unable to do either, though she protested when Bal called in the servant to lift Flori from the cloak, roll up the garment, and carry it and her generous fee down to the waiting coachman. She protested again when he pulled himself up onto his knees to examine Flori, who was stirring now.

He discovered the vomit on Florilinde's clothes. "Was she injured? Has she been drugged?" he said, carefully examining the child's head for swellings, her abdomen for tenderness.

"I think it's food poisoning. It's all right, Bal. She'll be fine."

His gently probing hands elicited no complaint. Florilinde's sonn wavered over him. "Papa . . . Mama . . ."

It would have taken a sterner physician than he to resist the arms lifted to him. He folded Florilinde in his embrace, heedless of her fouled dress. "Sweet Imogene, Telmaine, you are the most . . . the bravest . . . How did you find her?"

"It was Guillaume di Maurier who found her. Sylvide—did she tell you?"

"Yes, but . . . but she told me you were going to tell the inquiry agents."

"I decided Florilinde didn't have time," she said flatly. "And she didn't."

Telmaine's veil was gone. She stank of sweat, vomit, burned fabric, and smoke. Holding his daughter close, he whispered, "Fire? Oh, sweet Imogene, Telmaine. You could both have died."

"Papa," Florilinde said, her voice rising to a panicked pitch.

"Take hold of yourself, Balthasar!" Telmaine snapped. She pulled Florilinde away and curled herself around her, stroking her forehead.

He fell back on his pillows, trying to master his reaction at the risk his wife had run. "She's dehydrated," he finally managed. "Did she vomit on the way here? Has she had diarrhea?" He thought he could smell feces. "We have to start getting fluids into her, try to keep pace with the fluid loss."

Telmaine seemed oblivious to his voice as she cradled her daughter.

High, childish sonn pinged him. Amerdale, entering unnoticed, scrambled onto the bed with a glad, "Flori!" which changed swiftly to an, "Ugh!" as she smelled her mother and her sister. "Papa, is Flori sick?"

"A little, I think," he said shakily. "But we'll make her well."

"Where's Fuzzbear? Do you still have Fuzzbear?" She scrambled amongst the bedclothes until she retrieved the stuffed toy he had carried with him throughout, and thrust it toward her sister. "Here's Fuzzbear, Flori. Papa brought him all this way. He knew you'd be back. I did too."

Flori's arm crept around the toy, and she smiled tentatively at her sister and father. "Mama," she said, in a small, somewhat smothered voice. "Mama, I'm hungry. . . ."

* * *

Balthasar

Malachi Plantageter arrived late in the night, in response to Balthasar's urgent note. The superintendent appeared weary, as well a man might who had the responsibility for public law and order on a night like tonight. It was a mark of Bal's elevation by marriage that he merited a personal visit and not a deputy.

"Thank you for coming," Bal said. "Sit down, please. Can I ask for anything for you to eat or drink?"

Plantageter lowered himself into a chair. "Thank you, but my wife would not forgive me; she has my dinner kept for me, no matter how late I arrive home. Before we come to the substance of your note, I heard that your daughter had been found, alive."

"Yes," Bal said, letting his natural joy sound in his voice.

"That must have been a great relief to you."

"It's a very great relief, not only for the sake of my daughter and wife, but because it frees me to . . . do what is moral and right."

A brief silence. "I may need to talk to your wife," Plantageter said in a warning tone. "There were some additional disturbing events tonight." His heart rate picked up. "She is resting next door at present, with our daughters. I would much rather she not be disturbed."

"I understand. I would prefer not to impose on her." The tone made that, unmistakably, a warning. Bal wondered what Plantageter already knew—more than himself, he feared. And for the first time, he wondered if Telmaine were trying to do more than simply protect him from knowing what dreadful risks she had taken.

Sweet Imogene, had she *set* that fire?

He said, too urgently, "I believe I know who killed Tercelle Amberley. I have only circumstantial evidence, but I do know that he has killed at least one woman in similar circumstances."

Plantageter waited a moment. Bal could almost feel him deciding whether to pursue the first topic, or let himself be distracted by the second. Then he said mildly, "Let me decide what is circumstantial and not circumstantial."

Bal faltered. He had resolved upon doing this, fiercely resolved upon doing this, even before Plantageter had begun asking questions around Telmaine. Even so, it was disconcertingly hard for him to find it in him to betray Lysander. But if he hesitated too long, he thought desperately, Plantageter might start asking again about Telmaine and the fire.

"I have a brother, Lysander Hearne, with whom I had not spoken for seventeen years. I was considerably surprised when he called on me last night. He wanted information about the whereabouts of the children Tercelle bore—he claimed, in fact, to be their father. In exchange, he offered me my daughter, missing these three days. He threatened her life if I did not comply with that and with his other demands. Thanks to the courage of Gil di Maurier and my wife, Florilinde has been found. I am therefore no longer bound to silence. I suspect him of the murder of Tercelle Amberley."

"And why do you suspect your brother?" Plantageter asked, intent, but revealing nothing.

"Seventeen years ago he killed a young actress he had made his mistress. He did not intend to, but he took her by the throat during a quarrel, and when he let go, she was no longer breathing." He paused, then made himself go on. "He came to me and begged my help in concealing the murder. He invoked the health of our parents, the reputation of our sister, my own prospects, and his horror of the end he would meet if convicted of murder. I helped him take the body, in secret, out of the city. We left it off the road for the sunrise while we took refuge in one of the wayfarers' shelters. After sunset we came back to confirm that it was gone."

"This was never reported, I presume."

"I can give you the girl's name and description and the day we left her outside the walls. You should find her in your records as an unsolved disappearance."

"You do know that if there were charges, you would face them also, though your youth—you were what, fourteen?—would be offered in mitigation."

"I was well aware, even then, that what I did was wrong," Bal said. "I will always regret—for the sake of the girl's family—that it has taken me so long to admit to the doing."

There was a silence, broken at last by Malachi. "No body, no evidence, only a long absence and the word of brother against brother. I doubt there would be charges merely on the basis of your confession." Bal drew breath, sensing the shroud of respectability drawing in. Malachi confirmed it, saying, "Your parents may be dead now, sir, but you have a wife and daughters. Consider them." He did not let Bal remonstrate; he continued, "How in particular does this relate to the death of Tercelle Amberley?"

Bal struggled with his thwarted need for restitution. Plantageter let him, his face implacable. He was not offering to spare Bal, that face said, but leaving him to his conscience.

"From the experience of living with my brother, I developed my professional interest in pathology of mind. Lysander Hearne, I believe, was and is pathologically narcissistic and devoid of conscience. Tercelle Amberley crossed him, perhaps by conceiving by him in the first place, but certainly by not remaining where they, or he, had planned she would have his children, and then by putting the children in my hands. I believe that it was Lysander Hearne, and not Baron Strumheller, who quarreled with Tercelle Amberley about the whereabouts of the twins, and in the midst of that quarrel took her around her throat and strangled her."

Malachi Plantageter said mildly, "Where did you learn the cause of death was strangulation?"

There was nothing to do but admit it. "Baron Strumheller said so. I presumed—since he found the body—he could tell."

There was a silence. "It is possible that you may be right. I have gained a certain facility in recognizing the criminal mentality myself, and I thought I recognized a type when I questioned your brother about the statement he had given impugning Baron Strumheller—it being no light thing to charge a border baron with murder."

"My testimony should surely help exonerate Baron Strumheller, should it not?"

Pantageter appeared even wearier. "It is immaterial now. I would much prefer you kept this to yourself for the moment, but it will be all over the broadsheets soon: Baron Strumheller died in his cell this evening."

"Died?" Bal said in disbelief. "Of what cause?"

"He appears to have suffered some kind of seizure, was heard groaning, the prison apothecary was called, and shortly afterward he expired."

"Had he . . . had he been ill?"

"He was brought into the prison in a state of collapse, though he seemed to recover well enough. His lawyers were going to arrange for a physician's examination." He seemed about to say more, then stopped himself.

Bal tried to steady his voice. "When did that happen?"

He got the answer he feared. "Around two of the clock. Why do you ask?"

At the very time Telmaine was carrying Florilinde out of the blazing warehouse. Bal struggled to keep his responses predictable; this information he *could not* give Plantageter. "Will there be an autopsy?"

"If the family chooses. The prison has no jurisdiction over the body of a man who dies while awaiting trial, only over those who die after conviction. We have released the body; it will, I understand, be transported back to the Borders for the final ceremonies."

"Surely the charges will not be allowed to stand now?"

"I think it likely that petition would be made to the court to have the charges set aside. I would support that."

"You don't believe the charges, do you?"

Plantageter hesitated, then said, "Certainly not the second, which seemed to me . . . well, desperate opportunism seems the least of it. As to the charge of murder, I will investigate it to the fullest ability of my department, pressed though we are. May I count on your assistance in that, if need be?"

"You may count on it," Bal said, hearing the grimness in his own voice. "It is my own and my family's best protection against further threats from that quarter."

"I will speak to the ducal guard and let them know that I wish to interview your brother, and moreover that he should not be granted admittance here."

"Thank you," Bal said, and then, "Wait. Has Lord Vladimer awakened?"

"No."

"Then that exonerates Ishmael di Studier of the charge of sorcery!" Bal said, pushing himself close to a sitting position. "Magical effect is sustained by the life force of the mage. When the mage dies, the magic dies. If Lord Vladimer is still affected, Ishmael di Studier was not responsible."

"I have heard that said, yes, but what then of Imogene's Curse, laid by mages eight hundred years dead?" He paused, but Bal had no answer for that one incontrovertible exception. "And not only has Lord Vladimer not awakened, he is said to be sinking." Wearily, he pushed himself to his feet. "My best wishes for your recovery, and your daughter's. Assure your wife that I will be speaking to her only if it is unavoidable."

Balthasar fell back against the pillows as the echoes of their sonn faded to the vague, constant shimmer of sound. A thump and rustle in the doorway to the inner bedroom brought his head up. Telmaine was there, supporting herself with a two-handed grip on the doorjamb.

"Ishmael is *dead*?" she said in a raw whisper. *"Dead?"*

"I fear so," he said.

He pushed himself up, bracing his straight arm behind him, and held out the other arm to receive her stumbling rush across the room. She fell across the bed, face in his chest, and began to cry. He let himself down onto his elbow, then his back, and took her in his arms while she sobbed as though she would never stop.

In the early years of his marriage, he had wondered why Telmaine had encouraged his suit, had waited out the years of her father's resistance, and had married him with such apparent satisfaction at her choice. She was so beautiful, and so highly born, cousin to the archduke himself, and on intimate terms with those of his circle. Whereas he himself might be able to trace his own lineage to archdukes, that lineage was filtered through a long succession of younger sons. Hearne might be a name of note in the public service and intellectual histories, but was attached to neither title nor property. He was uncomfortable in the elevated society of her birth, while her readiness to play hostess at his gatherings of scientists, physicians, and councilmen put him to shame. All he had to offer her was his love. He had wondered at times what would happen to make her regret her choice, if she met a man of her own class whom she could love. Had Ishmael di Studier been that man?

Telmaine's wretched sobbing finally abated. He shifted her on his chest—she was leaning on his still-tender left ribs—and said quietly, "There was something between you, wasn't there?"

She pushed herself up, dismayed; she seemed hardly to register his involuntary grimace of pain. "I have never been unfaithful to you, Balthasar! Never!"

He had his answer. "But there was, nevertheless, something between you. Something that will burden your spirit if you do not admit it, at least to yourself."

"Bal," she said in a voice thick with sobs. "Bal, don't."

He wondered if he had a right to go on. As her physician, he would have. As her husband . . . "I won't, then," he said quietly. "I don't need you to tell me anything. But promise me you will be honest with yourself. I've known too many people damaged by the guilt of losing someone whom they had unresolved feelings for. I don't want you to be one."

He was proud of the steady compassion in his voice. Quite unlike his conflicted feelings as he took the measure of the intensity of her grief. Immeasurable gratitude for his own life and Florilinde's; admiration for the man's competence and selflessness; curiosity about and appreciation for Ishmael's complexity; a sense of inferiority, less to the breeding than the stamina, courage, and resolution. Guilt: for surrendering Ishmael to Lysander's blackmail, even though it had likely made no difference, and for being, in some small part of him, relieved at the passing of a rival.

"Bal," Telmaine wept. "Bal, I think I killed him."

He took her face in his hands, lifting it so he could brush it lightly with sonn. He smelled smoke on her hair, smoke on her skin, the scorched fabric of her petticoats. She had simply lain down in them, shedding the soiled outer garment, but otherwise too exhausted to change. Despite his grief, and despite the knowledge of the price Gil and Ishmael had both paid, he found himself angry at both of them for the way they had exposed her to danger. It was unconscionable. And even more unconscionable that she should believe herself in any way at fault.

"No, Bal," she said before he could speak. "You don't understand. I . . . Oh, sweet Imogene, I can't . . ." She caught him behind the neck and pulled his lips to hers in a desperate kiss. He felt a sudden shock of lightness, a sudden release of pain, a sudden surge in well-being. He recognized the sensation. He knew it was impossible.

His sonn rang against her face, revealing for an instant the fine bones beneath the skin. She rolled away from him and lay curled up, gasping, with her back to him. <It's not impossible,> her mental voice said, sweet and clear as the sound of a knife on fine crystal.

If he thought the realization that she had been falling in love with Ishmael di Studier had tested him, he had been much mistaken. This was the test. She was a mage. She knew, she always had known, everything he felt. He rolled toward her, the painlessness of the movement a revelation, rested his forehead against her back. "I did wonder, once or twice," he breathed. "But I . . . I could not be certain."

He drew a deep breath and slid his hand down to cover hers—a more intimate touch seemed an imposition—and yielded himself up to her. Yielded up his shock, awe, disconcertedness, satisfaction at the confirmation of odd moments of half suspicion, the fierce debate between defensiveness and rationalization. Yielded up the triumphant, "She *knows* me," of the lover, vying with, "She knows *everything*," of the man, and a quick, scrambling turning up and pressing down of all those embarrassing or venal impulses, thoughts, and memories that burden every man's conscience. She rolled over and clung to him, whispering, "I love you, I love you, I love you." And finally, he yielded up Lysander and the memory of his own crime.

"I knew," she whispered. "When I came this morning, it was all you were thinking of. That was why—"

Why she went after Florilinde, alone except for Ishmael di Studier. Now it was his turn to be pierced by guilt, and hers to say, "Don't."

"Who else knows?" he said.

"Only Ishmael," she said, and began to weep anew.

He knew she felt that ripple of jealousy from him, jealousy, remorse, and relief that his rival was gone before Balthasar had learned anything. Sweet Imogene, this was harder than anything he'd done before. She flinched back from him.

"Bal, I'm sorry. I never wanted to deceive you—"

"Yes, you did," he said. He was not going to let her lie to either of them. "Anyone who deceives themselves cannot but deceive others. And I think you did deceive yourself, all these years. With good reason; this must have been a terrible burden." His hand started toward her cheek, and hesitated. He shied from new self-exposure. It had not taken long. He had reacted as bravely as he could, but he could not but admit to himself that he needed time to reconcile himself. She was not the woman he thought she was, and he was trying not to condemn her. He was not the man he thought he was, and he was ashamed.

"Say . . . what you're thinking," she whispered.

"I'm going to need . . . a little time to find my balance, Telmaine," he confessed. "We're going to need time to find a new balance, in our marriage."

She pressed a hand to her lips. "I have so dreaded this happening, ever since you asked me to marry you."

"Was that it?" Bal said, remembering. In her beautiful young face, he had sonned dismay undercutting a palpable joy. He strove for transient lightness, though it had been deathly daunting at the time. "I thought I'd offended you and was about to be horsewhipped down the drive."

"I know," she said with meaning. Before she answered, she had leaned in to kiss him, her lips soft and uncertain on his, her elegantly gloved hand sliding hesitantly behind the nape of his neck. She would have felt all the uncertainty of the young suitor reaching high, the young man committing himself irrevocably to that state that young men uneasily disparaged as the end of their freedom, the young lover whose senses were nearly overset by her nearness, her softness, her fragrance. He'd been too nervous for physical arousal, at least then, but there had been other times when he had not been so inhibited. And she had known. As she had become surer of him, she had *teased* him with it, the vixen.

Her sonn washed over him, finding him in the best of all possible states, with a reminiscent smile on his lips. She let out her breath and rested against him, careful that only their clad bodies touched. The smoke lingering around her was acrid in his throat, but he did not draw away.

She whispered, "I thought . . . how could I marry you, when you did not know? I thought, How could you marry me if you did know? I wanted you, Bal; I wanted you as much as you wanted me. When I kissed you . . . when I kissed you and felt you offering up that gentle heart of yours, I knew I could not bear to lose you."

"It was your magic, as well as Ishmael's, that saved my life," he said.

She nodded.

"You will not lose me," he said quietly. "That I can promise. I grew up with a mage for a sister; I can get used to a mage wife. I've already learned some of the advantages."

She gave a choked, exhausted chuckle.

"Although with my sister it was a little different: With training, Olivede did learn to cloak her touch-sense."

"*Cloak* her touch-sense?" she said, lifting her head.

He remembered how Telmaine had maintained a studied ignorance and studied dislike of all aspects of magic—protective coloration, he realized, along with her "phobia" about microbes that let her remain gloved. He wondered how else she had sustained her masquerade—and laid aside the questions, lest a chance touch expose her to the wondering and the resentment. He, after all, well knew what it was to keep a secret rather than risk losing her regard. She had merely been much more successful at it than he.

"She's a third-rank mage," he said. "Lower-rankers are involuntary touch-readers. Upper-rankers can control the sense. It takes considerable practice; she told me it's like learning to ignore one's skin."

She gasped, started to laugh, and started to weep once more. "He never told me it was possible! That rat bastard!"

He was, absurdly, shocked at hearing his genteel wife express herself so.

"It takes a certain strength—"

She propped herself up on her arm. "Balthasar, I *have* that strength. He told me I might be a fifth- or sixth-rank mage." The terrible, stricken expression came over her again. "He *warned* me about my strength. He *warned* me that I might kill if I drew on him too hard—and I did. Bal . . ." She was shivering violently. "I want to die. And if the Lightborn find me, I will die, or be driven insane."

He had her in his arms, an instinctive reaction, before he fully appreciated what it was she had said. She cried more wildly as she sensed his alarm, all self-control abandoned. That self-control must be quite formidable to have enabled her to conceal her reactions all those years. "I think," he said, "you must tell me everything you remember."

"*Why*?" she sobbed.

"Because I know quite a bit more about the practice of magic than you do, unless you have been studying it in secret. I suspect, rather than you overdrawing him, that Ishmael di Studier sacrificed himself for you and Florilinde. And that is a noble gift, Telmaine, not a crime." With his cheek resting against her head, she would know how much he believed and how much he simply, desperately hoped was true.

She eased out of his arms and curled up beside him. In a quavering voice, she told him of the psychic conversation in the coach, and the plan she and Ishmael had formulated. Which made him unfairly furious with the dead man all over again; the plan was *insane*. Ishmael must have loved her beyond all reason to believe that with no training she could safely approach the warehouse and rescue Florilinde. Her description of her walk through the flames left his heart hammering with terror. She told him of the momentary distraction and fatal collapse of her shield, and how she had felt Ishmael hold back the flames for an instant, and then . . . go out like a snuffed candle.

"It is as I thought," he said softly. "He offered up his life freely. I think, from what I know of the man, he would consider it well given."

"That makes it so much worse," she whispered, and wept again.

"As to why he never told you about the cloaking of touch-sense," Bal said, drawing her to him again with care, "two possibilities come to mind. He had too little time to teach you much beyond what was necessary to survive the moment. Or, because he never had the strength to master the touch-sense himself, and learned to live with that, it didn't occur to him that it was a skill you *could* master." He paused, then said mildly, "Calling him a 'rat bastard' seems a touch strong, my dear."

She snuffled a laugh, still trembling. "Oh, Bal, you have no idea. He has—he had—the idea that there are Shadowborn involved in all our troubles, and that Vladimer is in danger. He wanted *me* to go to Vladimer, to help him."

Balthasar's immediate impulse was vehement and protective rejection. He controlled that, recognizing that the woman shivering in his arms was in some ways beyond his protection. Fifth- or sixth-rank mage; there might be only ten or twelve Darkborn mages as powerful. It was a profoundly unsettling realization.

"Why do—did he think that?" he asked.

"Because of what I sensed outside your parents' town house. He said that was Shadowborn magic."

"And a very little while later," Bal said slowly, "Lord Vladimer becomes desperately ill." Her hair tickled his chin as she moved her head. He moved his, very slightly, to prevent their skin from touching. She seemed unaware. "Telmaine, what did di Studier have time to teach you?"

"Some healing, but a lot of that I already understood from you. Oh, Bal, Gil di Maurier—I did what I could for him, repaired the bowel damage and cleared out the infection."

He jerked his head backward involuntarily and sonned her. That casual description, even more than the fire, shocked him. He knew about the efficacy of magical healing, and how it far exceeded the present capabilities of physicians such as himself, but to hear her so blithely . . . They *had* to, he thought, suddenly and passionately, they *had* to break magic free of the stigma that was smothering it, of the barriers placed around it. He'd had such arguments with Olivede, where she had pointed out that mages were too few and in the main too weak to work routine miracles, but in alliance with physicians' scientific understanding, surely . . .

"I don't know whether I did enough," she said. "I knew they'd not accept my healing—"

"Telmaine," he said, realizing what she meant. "Don't tell me." Cowardly of him, perhaps, but he knew Guillaume di Maurier's horror of magic was as deep-rooted as the survivor's guilt that had so nearly destroyed him. Perhaps had destroyed him. If Gil died, that, "Tell Balthasar . . . he saved me for a better death" would haunt him for a long time.

"I should not have, I know. I just couldn't . . . He'd *found* Florilinde."

He tucked her hair back. "I know. I understand. Gil would not." He paused. "If we leave soon," he said quietly, "we can catch the day train to the coast. The ducal station is underground, and there's a courier's entrance to the house itself from the concourse, as well as the main guest entrance. I delivered a few messages there myself, when I was acting as an amateur courier in Flo—Lightborn—business. We could be in the house itself by midafternoon."

"Bal, I can't—"

"Lord Vladimer is failing, Telmaine. The superintendent told me so. If his affliction is not magical, you can do something about it. And if it is . . . Do you remember what I said just before we left the town house: that we were the ones who must resist this evil? If not ourselves, then who?"

"What . . . what about the children?" she pleaded.

"We must leave them here, in the nursery," he said, his voice thin but resolute, "under guard by the household agents, who are already aware of the risk to us. I will send an urgent note to your mother to come. If all goes well, we will be back before tomorrow's sunrise. If the worst happens, to both of us, our wills are in order; she will stand as guardian, and they will not want for love or comforts."

"Bal, we cannot leave them like this! What about Flori? I've dealt with the food poisoning, but she's been horribly used. And Amerdale, what she's witnessed . . ."

He hesitated: It was another unconscionable act to desert children as traumatized as theirs. She sensed his wavering. "We're ordinary people, Bal, ordinary parents with little children who need us. Surely there's someone . . . Casamir Blondell. The mages. Even the Lightborn."

"Casamir Blondell chose to sacrifice Ishmael to keep the peace. The mages . . . this accusation of magical sorcery will have terrified them, and they'll be overspent in healing survivors of the fire. As for the Lightborn . . . I fear they may be as beset as we are. I have not heard from Floria. The light breach in my house may not have been a trap for us, but the result of an attack on her." His voice shook; he'd not fitted it together before this moment. Telmaine's anguish over Ishmael di Studier found new resonance in him.

"The archduke!"

"And say what to him? You know Sejanus Plantageter; would he believe even a quarter of this farrago?"

"Ferdenzil Mycene then!"

"Had Ishmael di Studier not been accused of murdering his

intended, then yes. But we don't have time to overcome his resistance."

"Balthasar," she said, palpably angry now, "Floria White Hand might have encouraged you to play at being a courier and agent as a child, but you are a grown man now, and it is time to put away those boyhood games."

"Do you really think this is a game?" he said, knowing it an unfair answer: Her point was that *he* did not belong in this, not that the conflict itself was a game. He was aware of her struggling to recognize his tactic, despite her tiredness.

She said in despair, "If you insist, husband, I will go, but you *have* to stay. You're barely healed, and the children need you."

Now it was his turn to struggle. He might be physically healed from the beating, but he was emotionally far from ready to confront the men who had beaten him, or their masters. She would know that. If fear paralyzed him, it could be the death of them both.

"If there were anyone else I could ask, I would," he said shakily. "If I could reach Olivede in time, I would. But Lord Vladimer may not have *time*. And someone must go with you, to watch your back." He was at the end of his words and, knowing that, reached out, laid the back of his fingers against her cheek, and, through that, poured all his understanding, conviction, and fear—for her, for himself, for their children, and for their world. She recoiled with a cry. They crouched in shared silence, and then she rolled off his bed and stumbled out of the room, leaving him aching with remorse.

She returned just as he finished writing the letter to her mother, washed and dressed in a plain traveling outfit and cloak, precariously composed, gloved, and perfumed to cover the lingering scent of smoke. He should have warned her against the perfume, he thought too late, but likely the small disadvantage it placed them at would have no effect in the end. He said nothing; there was no sense to it. He held up the letter for her; she shook her head, refusing to read it.

"I've told the maid that I am taking you out for a short drive," she said. "She will call the nursery staff to attend to the children. They will assume when we do not arrive back that we were caught short by the sunrise bell and took shelter."

He said, "Since I'm not sure how much we can trust Lord Vladimer's other agents to help rather than hinder us—never mind what our enemies might do—I think we should time our arrival at the station as close as we possibly can to the doors being closed for the day."

She tugged his collars straight and held his jacket for him, just as though they were embarking on an ordinary late outing. "You'd better not seem too spry outside," she said with a brittle briskness.

He leaned on her arm as they went along the hall, walking slightly hunched and slowly as an invalid, and letting her sonn guide them. They passed the rooms so briefly occupied by Ishmael di Studier. He did not need to be a mage to know she knew it; the catch in her breathing told him as much. Down the stairs, across the hall, where she gave a few orders to the staff, as her role required. To his ears she sounded strained and unnatural, but perhaps to people who knew her only as one of the archduke's many visitors, she did well enough. It was still a relief for them to be in the carriage.

At his murmured direction, she instructed the coachman to take them to the botanical gardens. "Why there?" she said.

"We'll get off at the west side of the fountains, run over to the stand on the east, and catch a carriage to the station. That should be literally moments before the sunrise bell begins to toll. We should take anyone following us by surprise, and the traffic flow around there is such that they won't be able to follow us in a carriage."

"There won't be any carriages there this late, and they won't take us."

"They will, for a surcharge and the surety that we're going somewhere they'll be able to safely overstay the day and pick up a profitable fare right after sunset. But anyone who transfers to follow should have trouble, not knowing where we're bound."

Her expression was skeptical, but she confined the skepticism to: "Can you run?"

"I'll have to," he said. "Be ready." He leaned forward and lowered the carriage window, calling up to the coachman to stop at the fountains. The carriage stopped with a sudden and unnecessary lurch that nearly landed him on Telmaine's lap and reminded him that his healing was still very fresh. He opened the door and half slid down the stairs. Telmaine followed with ladylike grace. She passed the coins for their fare to him, and he took her hand firmly in his, while he reached up to pay the coachman. To his left, he heard the slowing clop of a horse and the creaking of an undercarriage. His heart rate surged. "Now!" he said, and cast sonn before them, outlining the shimmer of falling water from the huge fountain, the scatter of starlings and pigeons, the empty seats set in a wide curve.

They ran, she snatching her hand from his to be able to hitch up her skirts, he holding his side. Birds scattered around their feet. Someone said, in a woman's voice, "Well, really!" as he skipped over a shape that he realized belatedly was a small dog. Sonn laced around them, but thin sonn, as from a very few people. At this hour, the fountain square would be nearly deserted, and in the quiet Bal could hear running footsteps behind them. He cast sonn wildly ahead, trying to visualize the standing coaches and guess from the postures of the coachmen who would be most curious, least wary. Telmaine did not hesitate; she dashed for the nearest. "We're just going to Bolingbroke Station," he heard her gasp out, keeping her voice from carrying. "Please, quickly. That's my guardian behind me; he's trying to stop our wedding." Then, without waiting for any assent that Bal could hear, she hitched up her skirts and scrambled up into the coach, stooping to help him heave himself aboard. The coach started with a lurch, pulling out and gathering speed. Bal lay half-on and half-off the seat, his side searing with every heaving breath. Telmaine crouched beside him. He felt her gentle fingertips on his forehead, and the pain eased. "Do you think he heard where we are going?" he asked huskily.

"I don't think so," she said, and risked leaning out of the window to call up to the coachman: Were they being followed? He thought not. She slid up onto the worn bench facing him and sonned Bal. "Whom do you suppose?"

"Let's assume foe. Friends you can always apologize to later."

"Can you?" she said dryly.

He decided to let that pass. He pushed himself upright, shifted across the carriage to her side, and slipped an arm around her. "I never knew you had a secret hankering to elope," he remarked.

She made a noise of disdain. "Every girl reads the same silly novels. What do we do when we get to the station?"

The sunrise bell began to toll. They felt the coach pick up its pace. Balthasar said with relief, "We'll be in time. Buy the tickets, get on the train."

"A day train," she said. "Bal, if we're right about these people, day will not stop them."

"I know," Bal said. "I hope that we can outrun them."

"Why? If . . . Ishmael and I could speak at a distance, why not them?"

The thought chilled him; he had no answer for her.

They arrived at Bolingbroke Station without further incident, pulling in as the sunrise bell stopped tolling and the station attendant called a warning for the closing of the doors. The coachman received their ample payment, saluted them with a knowing grin, and wished them good fortune. He flicked his horse into a trot, bound for the closed garage and its amenities. Balthasar followed Telmaine with all haste, but paused inside the door to wait on its closing.

"That's it," he said. "You realize we are quite a cliché. Two decamping lovers traveling by day train."

Telmaine sniffed. If one were to believe the melodramas of the day, the sealed trains that traveled by day were full of spies, conspirators, jewel thieves, and eloping or adulterous lovers, all dashing to meet their deserved ends in fiery crashes and immolation by daylight. The reality, as experienced by Bal in his student days, was usually more prosaic. The Lightborn ensured that the Darkborn's day trains traveled safely along cleared tracks, because they must of necessity travel sealed. In the twenty years since the first day train, there had been only one disaster, resulting from unanticipated mechanical failures.

Upper class of the coastal route, at the safer rear of the train, was occupied by ducal couriers, civil servants, and nobility on urgent business. Lower class, at the front, was occupied by students, servants, and other holidaymakers taking advantage of the cheap fares. The journeys were sometimes raucous, with drunkenness and the occasional brawl, but each carriage had one or more public agents present to impose order, and penalties for reckless conduct during daylight hours were high.

He had never before traveled at the rear of the day train, and as soon as they were shown into their luxurious private compartment, he realized that it would be a very different experience from his student days. He sank gratefully into the soft seating.

Telmaine said, "Are you all right?"

"Too much excitement," he said, more lightly than he felt. He did not want her expending herself on him any more. She settled herself in, deploying skirts, hat, and reticule with her usual grace, leaned her head back against the plush headrest, and sighed.

"I think we should have something to eat," he said.

"I'm not sure I could," she said.

"Then you should, because that is exactly how I feel, which tells me I need it to keep going."

He rang the bell for the steward, who came promptly, suggesting that the carriage was not overly busy. They discussed the menu, and he pressed Telmaine to expand her choices beyond the insubstantial soup she first requested. The steward joined him in solicitude; Telmaine yielded. Once the steward had gone, she frowned. "Are you going to help me eat all that?"

"I am. Merely discussing it makes me hungrier. You do good work, my love."

She shifted a little, unhappily, in her seat. He drew breath, but it seemed not the time to press her, much as his impulse was to explore her unease.

"We're moving," she observed. "I've never taken one of these trains before. I'm not sure anyone I know has."

"I've traveled this route a half a dozen times at least, as a student, though never before in such style."

Over their meal, he gave her an account of one particular journey spent in the company of a traveling theater troupe whose writer-manager was clearly suffering from the kind of mania that was almost indistinguishable from genius—or vice versa. They had barely pulled out of the station before he had the entire troupe and most of the other passengers improvising a melodrama in the grand style under his direction. By the end of the journey, one respectable matron and her spinster daughter had vowed to join the troupe, two students were planning a duel over the ingenue, who had obvious designs on a third, and the railway's public agent—*not* a flexible character—had threatened to impose a daylight travel ban on the whole pack of them. When Telmaine choked on her soup and set to coughing and laughing at the same time, he was satisfied. He did not even have to persuade her to eat an éclair, while she intercepted his reach for his fourth with a crisp tap of gloved fingers on his wrist. "Some protector you'll be if you're too sick to move."

When the steward returned to clear away the dishes, Bal remarked that the train seemed not to be particularly busy. This proved so: There was only one other pair of gentlemen in upper class, a gentleman traveling to the coast for his health, and his personal physician. The steward had put them at the far end, so that his coughing would not disturb the other passengers.

"That wasn't a casual inquiry, was it?" Telmaine said softly, when the steward had left.

"No," Bal said. "Though I'm not sure what I could have learned by it. I'm somewhat reassured that he seems to find them quite ordinary."

"I didn't have that sense of chill and horror when I came on board," Telmaine said.

Her little frown made him say quickly, "No, don't try. I thought about making a call—one physician to another—but if we were to provoke a confrontation, we risk being stranded until nightfall." *Or not getting there at all*, he thought. "It's to our advantage to wait. And it's most likely that they are what they seem to be." He shook his head a little ruefully. "Three nights ago, all I'd have been worried about would have been the risk of infection."

"Mm," she said. "Three nights ago I was on my way back to Minhorne with Florilinde and Amerdale, with Ishmael as escort."

The silence was heavy with grief and unsaid words.

"Why don't you put your head down," Bal said at last. "You'll need your vitality."

She nodded wearily and got up, steadying herself against the rocking of the train. "And you? Will you join me?"

"I'm going to write those letters I said I would, and then I'll join you. I'm feeling much better for those éclairs."

She made a small sound in her throat that might have been a laugh. "Don't you *dare* give the children the idea it's possible to eat three éclairs at one sitting."

"Nobody needs to give a child that idea," Bal said. His sonn followed her as she made her way into their stateroom and lay down.

He called for the steward again, to bring him a writing case, stylus, and paper. How to write a letter to a six-year-old that could contain the sum of everything he had hoped to say to her over an entire lifetime? That would explain his, or his and Telmaine's, sudden and catastrophic desertion? He held his stylus poised, struggling with the density of his burden and his recognition that what he wanted to do could not be done. In the end he wrote each of his daughters a letter much like the ones he had written them the past two summers, while they were on the coast and he in the city, missing them, keeping it simple and fond for their present understanding. Then he wrote a third letter, one he hoped they would read in fifteen or twenty years. He asked for their forgiveness, reassured them of his and Telmaine's love, and wished them joy. The words did not say a fraction of what he wanted them to say, but he knew he could do no more.

After that, he fitted another page to his frame and addressed it to Olivede. He had been negligent in not telling her about Lysander's reappearance, and he must repair that. Of the leavetaking—well, she was a mage, and he her loving younger brother. Love needed but to be reaffirmed, not averred. He folded and addressed the letter and set it atop the others.

The fifth letter . . . He weighed his options for a long spell, while the train clattered on, whistling shrilly. He steadied his pen until the train had finished dancing through a complicated series of switches, smiling wryly at the memory of the discussions that had taken place over training and employing Lightborn switchmen, when the Lightborn's idea of nonmagical fast transport was still post-coaches. He decided to stick to Darkborn text, since Floria had the advantage of being able to see the punches, but ciphered. She'd never forgive him otherwise. But he could say good-bye, and write what he felt. If it came into her hands, he'd be dead, and past caring if she dismissed it as Darkborn mawkishness.

And last . . . Telmaine. If she outlived him, as she might well do—as he *intended* her to do, if it came to that—then he wanted her to know that what he felt for her was unchanged by the brief transit of Ishmael di Studier, and by her long deception. He admitted to himself that there was something appealing in knowing he would be represented by his written words alone, and that her touch on paper would never tell her what ambivalence or dissimulation lay behind them.

Over an hour remained once his letter to Telmaine was done. He started to fold up the frame, and then had the thought that if he and Telmaine both died, Vladimer would not know who held each accurate piece of the story they had so carefully scattered around, and would lose valuable time resolving the inconsistencies. With a cramping hand, he carefully began another sheet, addressed to Lord Vladimer, and summarizing events as he knew them. He hardly needed encryption, he thought, lifting his stylus for the last time; his punching seemed little more than random.

He felt the train slowing, and remembered the tunnel it passed through before beginning its final descent to the coast. Since the Lightborn could not comfortably enter its darkness, and the Darkborn could maintain it only by night, the train crept through at barely more than a walking pace. The addition of doors was one of the recurrent questions before the Intercalatory Council.

Sonn washed over him. "I thought," said his wife, "you were going to lie down."

He carefully folded that last letter, addressed the envelope, and tucked it into his jacket. "I was. But one letter led to another. I wrote the children . . ."

He held out the single letter for their daughters of the future; this one she consented to read, and handed it back with a subdued, "It's perfect, Bal. I'd not change a word of it."

He sensed her curiosity as he gathered up the other letters and slipped them into their folder in his writing case, but she did not ask to whom he had written. He would leave the case in the custody of the steward; if he lived, he would retrieve it later, and if not, the letters would find their way to their destinations.

He wrote a quick note of instruction and tucked it into the case, then set it on the table before him, and reached over it to take her small, gloved hand firmly in his. At their reduced speed, even inside a tunnel, the pulse and rattle of wheels on tracks was muted.

As the sound changed as they approached the end of the tunnel, they heard a heavy thud from overhead, as though a body had landed on a hollow box, feet first. Telmaine's breath whistled in; her grip on his hand was suddenly crushing. Bal reached across with his left hand to grope for the pistol in his pocket, though the reflex was irrationality itself—a pistol ball through the wall would kill them as surely as any assault from without.

Telmaine said a single, imperative, "*No*," and there was a second, sliding thump, and a falling-away screech. Telmaine's mouth and blind eyes went wide in a silent scream of anguish.

"It's all right," Bal said, not knowing whether he spoke truth or falsehood, but responding by reflex to that expression. He returned her grip as firmly as he could without returning the discomfort. "It's all right. Slow, deep breaths. Breathe in, breathe out. You know how." If his own heart were not beating like an overwound clock, he would be far more authoritative. As the train gained speed he strained to hear any extraneous sound over the pounding pistons and rattling undercarriage.

Telmaine gave a stifled sob, pulling his crushed hand to her lips. "I had to," she whispered against it. "I had to. He wanted us dead. I felt . . . He had something with him that would . . . Oh, by the Sole God, Bal, I killed him."

He slid from his seat, handling himself around the table to kneel beside her and gather her to him, burying her forehead in the crook of his shoulder. She was shuddering, fighting hysterics. He tried hard not to give way to his impulse to offer pure comfort to his wife, the lady he had sworn to love and protect for a lifetime. She was no longer just his wife. He said quietly, "Do you sense anyone or anything else?"

She gasped, swallowed, and said, "No. Just one."

"Was it Shadowborn?"

"Lightborn, he felt Lightborn."

Bal swallowed and kept his voice steady with an effort. "And what did he have with him?"

"It might . . . have been explosive. It was going to . . . going to break open the carriage. Oh, Bal."

"Shh," he said. "You did what you needed to." He tried—since her forehead was resting against his neck—to contain his curiosity as to how. She answered his unvoiced question in a muffled voice: "I made ice under his feet, the same way I cooled the handle down in the warehouse."

He could not spare her his quixotic but profound relief that she had not corrupted her healing talents, and remembered his own jagged thoughts as he crouched beside the sleeping babies, holding the letter opener and rehearsing its placement in a human body.

She trembled. "What's this doing to us?" she whispered. "Is it going to end if we save Lord Vladimer?"

"I don't think so," he whispered, because he could not lie, touching her.

He held her until he felt the train begin to slow. By then she had relaxed a little. "We need to collect ourselves," he said softly. "I'd still like not to draw attention, but we need to be prepared to run. I want you to promise me that if you have to leave me, you will leave me."

"No," she said, lifting her head, showing a face shaken and fierce. "I offered you the chance to stay behind and you did not take it. Now we're going together, or not at all."

Telmaine

The thud of the post-bags striking the platform behind her made Telmaine jump and blurt sonn in that direction. The station doors penned in the engine smoke, and the murk was dizzying. She started unthinkingly toward the gate that, for the archducal guests, led directly toward the main guest entrance of the archducal summer estate. Bal caught her and steered her toward the gate into the main concourse. "If anyone's expecting us, they're expecting us via that entrance."

As upper-class passengers they were allowed to disembark first, so they were first through the main entrance into the station concourse. It was a huge, domed building that lay adjacent to the tracks and offered refreshments, seating, and entrance to hotel accommodation for early-arriving and late-departing passengers, as well as more extensive entertainments to those traveling at more usual hours. The younger visitors to the archducal summer house amused themselves here, in the fashionable afternoon.

From behind them came a harsh cough. She swung, barely restraining sonn. By Bal's casual cast, she caught an impression of two figures nearby, one heavily muffled, leaning on the other. Bal murmured, "Our fellow first-class passengers. I hate to think what that smoke is doing to a bad chest. Very carefully now, do you sense anything from the rest of the train?"

She extended her awareness into the mill of people now disembarking from the lower-class coach. For an instant she thought she had a sense of a presence like spent embers, but when she groped for it, it was gone. She drew back, afraid to attract attention to herself, and reminding herself that in the months after her father died, she had sonned him at the oddest times, and in the oddest faces. "No," she breathed. "Not among them."

Bal took her arm, leaning toward her like a wooer. "If I can get us in through the courier's entrance, and account for us to the guard, it'll be up to you to get us into Vladimer's rooms. I realize that if

I had been planning ahead, I should have married an adventuress who'd know these things as a matter of course."

Behind her the great concourse doors ground closed, shutting with a final reverberating slam. Through the solid walls, they felt the vibrations of the engine as it built up steam. More faintly came the feel and sound of the outer door opening. Bal's head twitched toward the sound and she sonned the fine flicker of his pulse in his throat. She lifted her gloved hand and laid the beaded back of it along his cheek briefly. "You're trying too hard, my love. But I appreciate the effort."

She let him set the pace as he led her along the concourse, trying not to be obtrusive, but ever wary and starting at sounds. They drew away from their fellow passengers, who chose to linger amongst the early-opening shops and cafés. She realized he had his hand in his pocket, where the pistol rested. "Here it is . . ." he breathed, as they drew level with a huge bas-relief mural depicting a bucolic midsummer's night on the beach. It was a style of art that had been highly fashionable when the concourse was built, that had been inspired by Lightborn descriptions of their visual art. Balthasar traced a finger along the ridge depicting the horizon, something, she thought, he no doubt had little difficulty imagining, for all it lay far outside the reach of sonn.

Bal's hand spanned a flock of seagulls, fingers coming to rest on three of them. He pressed, dropped his hand and slipped his fingers underneath a ridge of rock, and pulled. Found a depression in the sand. Leaned. Tapped a quick pattern on the cards held by a quartet of players in the right foreground. There was a muted hiss, and to the right of the mural, a panel opened. He caught her hand and pulled her inside, and the wall swallowed them up.

The space was meant for only one, or two who knew each other as intimately as husband and wife. "What now?" she whispered.

"Shh," he said, "I have to get this right." She felt him grope along the wall, touch something there, press. Nothing happened. He drew a cramped breath; she could feel his heart beating hard against her chest. "What is it?" she said.

"I have three tries to get the sequence correct," Bal said.

"Or else?"

"Or else we'll be trapped here until the guards come to let us out."

She didn't need to touch him to know the implication of that; she could hear it in his voice. Already she could feel the air becoming close.

"And if they've changed the sequence since you carried messages?" she said.

"That is not a helpful suggestion," he muttered.

She quelled her sense of claustrophobia and panic, trying to find reassurance in the thought of her magic. She could smell her own perfume overlying her sweat, and his. He drew a breath like the one he had drawn before he asked her to marry him, his hand moved again, and the inner wall swung open, spilling them into a larger room. Her coldness resolved abruptly into the familiar chill and terror. "It's here."

"I know," he said, in a very different voice.

Her impression of a large room had been through his sonn; now she cast her own, and perceived the three men sprawled in and around a card table: the guards to this couriers' entrance. Bal moved toward them, his impulse a physician's; she caught his arm, remembering explosions of flame. "Don't . . . don't touch them."

He heard the panic in her voice. "Can you go on?"

"I must," she said breathlessly, but she could not move.

He took her by the shoulders. "Let me hypnotize you."

"Now?" she half gasped.

"You've always been a good subject," he said. "You know it can be effective."

"For childbirth, yes," she said. "But this . . ."

"Listen to my voice," he said in a measured tone.

"It helps if I touch you."

"Does it? Do what you have to, though I'm not . . . as calm as I would like to be."

"Hypnotize yourself as well," she said, a little tartly.

"It's a thought . . ." He began to speak the familiar phrases, the ones he'd taught her as Flori's birth loomed and he could not change her vehement rejection of magical or chemical relief of pain. Now, as then—he had read far too many medical textbooks to be a calm expectant father—the words calmed him as much as they calmed her.

"That's better," she breathed. "You're *good* at this." She felt his pleasure. "Whatever happens now," she said, softly, taking his hands in hers, "you are the finest man I have ever known, and I have had great joy and pride in being your wife."

"Telmaine," he said, very low, "you are brave, beautiful, and versatile, and a constant surprise and delight, and I am . . . I am amazed to have been your husband."

As a compliment, Telmaine thought, it wasn't like any she had ever received, but then there were fine liqueurs she had never tasted, either.

If she lived, she thought, she would make it her business to.

"I . . . don't think I'd need to know the way," she said. Hand held tightly in hand, they moved quietly through the stunned halls of the ducal estate. She had at times to lift her skirts and step carefully over the sprawled body of a maid or secretary. If she could prevent Balthasar from touching them, she could not prevent his lingering over one—a young housemaid—probing her fragile chest deeply with his sonn. She visualized a flicker of motion within the girl, and realized that Bal had imaged her beating heart, confirming that she was alive.

"How long?" she breathed. "How long could they have been like this?"

"I would think . . . shortly after sunrise," Bal said, stopping again beside the body of a young man who lay beneath a ladder in the main hall. He must have been climbing it when stricken; from the angle of his head, the fall had broken his neck. Bal's expression was distraught and resolute. "There are too many people about for it to have happened during the day, but if it came on during the night, people outside would surely have noticed that the coming and going had stopped."

She gripped Balthasar's hand more tightly thereafter, pulling him along with her, deeply disturbed by the evidence of her adversary's—and it had to be *her* adversary's—power.

I beat him once, she thought. *I was not meant to rescue Florilinde, with those traps laid around her.* Ishmael di Studier had thought her a powerhouse, had *envied* her power. She warmed herself with the memory of his banked-ember presence in her mind, his smoky desire for her, his admiration and concern. It was not infidelity, she thought, to use all his gifts to her, even the one of understanding of his magic and, through it, something of hers.

Lord Vladimer's apartments were in a secluded corridor far from all public entrances, behind a minimally ornamented door. She and Bal groped their way slowly along the corridor, feeling with their toes for fallen bodies or sculptures or ornaments, using their hands on the wall to guide them. She caught Bal's arm as she judged him to be nearby, and they listened hard, hearing nothing. He eased himself out of her grip, and, an instant before she reestablished it, he stepped clear of the wall. His first cast showed the door slightly ajar. Committed now, he leaned around the doorjamb and cast into the room. She heard him draw a sharp breath—and then that alien magical aura surged around her, like polluted ice water. She crushed her lips with her fist so as to make no sound.

"Do come in, brother," said the half-familiar voice.

She sensed no sonn, smelled only a strange scent like melted wax. Bal's outstretched hand found her near shoulder and pressed her back. She caught at him, horrified at his recklessness, but he had already moved forward.

"Lysander," he said steadily. "I did not expect to find you here." He sounded almost detached, with his scholar's mind engaged to purpose. "Is this all your doing?"

"Crude, little brother," Lysander remarked. "I don't need to ask you if you are alone. I can sense her. I've been waiting for—"

Telmaine grappled for the mind and magic in the center of that chill, found it, as alien and hating and foul as Ishmael's had been familiar and loving and brave. She bore down on that mind with all her untrained power, and all the force of her rage over Ishmael's disgrace and death, Florilinde's suffering, Balthasar's torments of body and mind, the many unknowns slaughtered in the Rivermarch, and the intolerable shattering of her own innocence. Lysander Hearne's arrogant assertion ended in a groan that gladdened her; she wanted him to suffer before he yielded.

Then she felt that mind slither from beneath the pressure of hers, a repellent sensation that made her, fatally, flinch. Like cold, foul mud, his magic rose around her, folded over her, and began to bear down on her in its turn.

<That's not the way, Magistra,> the voice in her mind mocked. <But you're not a magistra, are you? Merely a student with an incompetent master. I could do better by you, I am sure.> She felt him—it—forcing into her mind, her magic, his own vile seed. <This will—>

A pistol sounded, with shattering concussion. She felt from him—it—searing pain—a wound, though not a serious one—outrage at the effrontery. For an instant his mind was unguarded, the impression of it, and of its power, open to hers. She was too clumsy and off balance to thrust at it. Then his magic lashed back at her, and the next she knew she was sliding down the wall, vaguely aware of the sounds of physical struggle from within the room. She struggled onto her knees, battling her full skirts, and half dragged herself, half crawled into the doorway.

Sonn showed her the bed, with a still form laid thereon, chairs, a discarded pistol, and two figures wrestling on the floor beyond it. One reared up and lashed talon-tipped fingers across the face of the other, who screamed in Balthasar's voice. Telmaine seized the spent pistol and hurled it with all her strength at Lysander and, with a nauseating effort, hurled her magic after. Lysander snarled and twisted toward her, his face and form rippling as though his skin were dissolving. She still sensed no sonn, but the magic rent her, no sense of avuncular mockery remaining, no words between them, only a bestial savagery. She felt her own magic beginning to shred beneath the assault, and realized with horror that her magic was rooted down at the base of her being, and there was no way of escaping it before she and it died together.

Overhead, a heavy revolver boomed, two shots close together, two blows felt deep in chest and belly. She screamed with Lysander Hearne, tasting his blood in her throat, curling up with his agony, writhing on the floor as he writhed. The hem of a cloak brushed her face, and her wild sonn imaged an immense, striding figure stepping over her. Then, with an immense concussion, pain, cold, consciousness all ended at once.

Except for the one frail, tattered, whimpering part of it that was still Telmaine. She became aware that she was lying on the floor, contorted with recent agony. Her mind felt lacerated, her magic shriveled.

"Telmaine!" Ishmael's voice said urgently. "Telmaine, I need some help here."

She pushed herself up on her arms and cast a wavering sonn in the direction of that impossible voice. A broad, cloak-and-scarf-draped figure crouched beside Bal; beneath the wide-brimmed hat, Ishmael's familiar face turned toward her.

"Ishmael," she whispered.

"I'll explain shortly, but your husband's bleeding badly, and I've nothing t'give."

Beyond them, she sonned the booted legs of another figure. The feet were splayed, quite still. She struggled again to hands and knees and dragged herself across to their side. Ishmael was pressing his folded scarf against Balthasar's right cheek and jaw as an improvised compress. She could smell the raw, metallic odor of fresh blood.

"You needn't do anything," Ish said, his voice hoarse. "Just help me get the bleeding stopped."

She recognized what he was trying to do and spared him the effort. "Bal knows; I told him."

She laid her fingers on Balthasar's throat, feeling tacky wetness and a strong, very fast pulse. Ishmael laid his hand over hers, and she caught her breath at the feel of him, like the crumbling ash left by fire. "It'll come back," he said—as though she could not know the depth of his fear that it would not. With an effort, he visualized nerves and arteries and veins of the face for her, and she roused the dregs of her own magic for the weaving together of tissues. It was slower work than she thought; throughout, Balthasar lay quite still, shivering, suspended between terror and triumph at his own survival. Presently, Ishmael peeled away the soaked scarf, revealing the three long, closed slashes from Balthasar's ear to his jaw. "A few inches lower, Hearne, and you'd have been dead."

"If he'd wanted to kill me outright," Balthasar said huskily, trying not to move his jaw, "he'd have taken those few inches." Very carefully, he sat up. "I'd rather not speculate as to what he might have spared me for. Let's . . ." He turned his head and cast an unsteady sonn over the corpse that lay beside him. "Ah," he said. Shaky or not, it was the sound of intellectual satisfaction.

" 'Ah,' indeed," said Ishmael.

He eased back so that Telmaine could direct her own sonn over the corpse, a manly courtesy she little appreciated, as she realized Ishmael's killing shot had shattered its skull and spilled its brains in a soft scrambled pudding. She apprehended few details beyond that before she reared back, retching. "Get it away," she sobbed, doubled over. "Get it *away*."

Sonn blazed over them with stripping force. There was the click of a drawn-back hammer. Vladimer Plantageter's voice said, "Do not move, any of you, or I will shoot. And I will shoot to kill."

Telmaine started to lift her head. Ish's broad hand landed hard behind her neck, pinning her down. There was a crack of a revolver, and a bullet struck the floor near enough for her to smell singed carpet and burning wood.

"Ishmael di Studier," Vladimer said. "Explain."

"I am delighted," Ishmael said, "t'be in a position to. But first might I let Lady Telmaine sit up?"

"Telmaine?" Vladimer said. "My cousin Telmaine . . ." For the first time he sounded less than authoritative and certain. "There was a woman. . . ." His voice shook. The warning pressure of Ishmael's hand on the back of her head did not ease. "Yes," Vladimer said at last. "Let her up."

She dared cast sonn as she sat up, catching Vladimer in the act of sliding his long, thin legs off the bed and pushing himself to his feet. One leg was noticeably atrophied, the ankle twisted and scarred. Even so, barefoot and in a long nightshirt, Vladimer commanded the room. "Who," he said, tilting his head toward the corpse, "is *that*?"

"Likely one of th'breed of Shadowborn you spoke of when we last met." A slight, deliberate pause. "Four nights ago."

"Four nights? But—" He checked himself, and firmed the gun on the three of them. "What happened to my attendants and my household?"

His attendants, Telmaine realized, were the physician and nurse sprawled in ungainly unconsciousness on the far side of the bed, beside a spilled tray of bottles and instruments. And Vladimer would surely have expected his household to respond to the sound of that shot; perhaps, besides intimidation, that was his intent.

Ishmael said steadily, "You fell into a coma four nights ago, with rumors of sorcery. We came down here t'undo that if we could, found your staff unconscious to a man, and this one waiting. It tried t'kill Hearne, and Lady Telmaine, but I got a fair shot at it. Now you're awake, that means it was th'one that ensorcelled you. And whatever form it came t'you in was likely not its true form. Until it died, it held the shape of one Lysander Hearne, who'd a close likeness to his brother here. Then it changed to what y'sonn now."

Vladimer shuddered perceptibly. He cast sonn across the corpse, his expression deeply disturbed. "So you say. Can you prove it? Can you prove *you* are who you claim to be?"

Ishmael hesitated, as well he might, given such a conundrum. Vladimer had no magic, so he could not detect the absence of that monstrous aura. "At worst, you could shoot one of us—best that be myself"—Telmaine could not stifle an involuntary sound of protest—"and learn if that one changes shape."

Sudden movement from where the nurse and physician had lain made them all tense, though Vladimer and Ishmael least of all. "Lord Vladimer!" gasped the nurse.

"Sweet Imogene, what has happened here?" said the physician, his sonn washing over the corpse.

Vladimer smiled thinly. "That is what I am presently trying to establish. Kindly satisfy my curiosity, Doctor. Have I indeed been unconscious for four days?"

The doctor—one of the imperious pair who had attended Balthasar—was clearly more accustomed to having patients satisfy his curiosity than the other way around. Waking up on the floor in his noble patient's bedroom, entangled in his nurse, seemed to have subdued his imperiousness, for the moment. He said, "That was what I was told, when I was called to attend you."

"And you could find no reason for the unconsciousness?"

"No, my lord," the physician said grudgingly.

"And what is the last thing you yourself recollect. Specifically, what *time* do you yourself last recollect?"

"My lord—" protested the physician.

"I remember hearing the sunrise bell," supplied the nurse.

Vladimer walked slowly forward, limping on his lamed leg, but the disability made him appear more sinister and threatening, not less. He leveled his revolver at Ishmael's head, choosing his line so as not to uncover either Balthasar or Telmaine. "Shoot you, you said? That seems drastic."

"You'll not think it drastic, my lord, when you hear what we have to report. So if that is what you need for proof, shoot me."

"My lord," began the physician, authoritatively.

"Doctor, if you feel yourself recovered, I would like you and your nurse to check the other members of the household, as I have reason to suspect them of having been similarly afflicted."

"But—"

"I feel quite well, Doctor, and I am increasingly coming to think that the cause of the immediate trouble is dead. You may tell the household staff that—"

"My lord," the physician broke in, "that man there cannot be Ishmael di Studier. Di Studier is dead."

The revolver came up, Vladimer's expression settling into a mask of suspicion; only then did Telmaine realize how much he had softened. "No!" she cried out. "Vladimer, hear us out, please!" She realized, with dismay, that her intervention had, if anything, worsened their predicament. Vladimer held the revolver steady on Ishmael's head. Her and Balthasar's overlapping sonn caught the tightening of his finger on the trigger. Ish did not sonn; he knelt very still, hands upturned on his thighs.

Vladimer abruptly released the trigger and stepped back, a decision made by whatever obscure calculus he had applied. "If you'd been in a position to defend yourself, you'd have done so. So, yes, I'll hear you out."

"Thank you, m'lord," Ishmael said, the huskiness of his voice finally betraying strain.

From outside came the sound of confused voices, footsteps, and bodies bumbling against one another. Everyone tensed again. The main bedroom door opened, and half a dozen men in house-guard uniforms forced in a seventh—the narrow-faced young man from the train station.

"This," Vladimer muttered, "is starting to resemble a bedroom farce."

"My lord," said the chief guard in delighted surprise, and then took in the tableau: Vladimer with revolver in hand; Ishmael, Telmaine, and Balthasar in various positions on the floor; the sprawled corpse; the doctor and nurse. He cleared his throat and reported, "We found this man outside, my lord."

"He's with me," Ishmael said evenly.

Four pistols were immediately leveled at him. One side of Vladimer's mouth quirked. "Your vigilance is appreciated; however, I am increasingly convinced that these three pose no immediate threat. About the fourth, I do not yet know. Bring him 'round, and do not let anyone else into this room."

"Lord Vladimer, Baron Strumheller was charged with sorcery—against yourself—and murder. He was reported to have died in prison."

"Doubtless the broadsheets got their facts wrong again, a saving grace on which I often rely. Bring the prisoner 'round."

The narrow-faced young man was marched to face Vladimer, who considered him. "Your name."

"Kip. Nothing else. M'mother didn't know which son of a bitch to blame."

"Rivermarch," Vladimer noted. "Not a physician, I suspect, for all your fine clothes."

"Prison apothecary, sir—my lord. Ex, now, no doubt, since I can't tell a live 'un from a dead 'un. I'll be in need of work."

"Will you now?" Vladimer said, his quick wit readily connecting the foregoing. "I'm not sure whether it's work in my service or a cell that awaits you, but it'll be one of the two, surely. Trevannen"—this to the commander of the guards—"lock this one up until I decide what to do about him. I want the household checked; ensure everyone recovers well. Take the doctor and nurse with you. Reassure the staff that I am awake, but do *not* tell them who is here, and do not allow anyone else in here. Be assured that if any whisper of these events that I have not authorized reaches me, the person responsible will be dismissed without references at the *very* least, and quite possibly charged with treason. Am I fully understood?"

A chorus of *yes, my lord*s answered him.

"Good. Then I will need chairs for all my visitors." A slight, malevolent smile. "Low, *comfortable* chairs, such as will discourage any sudden moves. And a blanket, to cover *that.*"

"My lord," Ishmael rumbled, "we're so cursed spent, we'll fall asleep on you."

"I'm sure I can keep you stimulated," Vladimer said. "You can get up." He held the revolver pointed loosely at them as they helped one another to their feet. Telmaine leaned against Balthasar, smelling sweat and blood from the closed lacerations of his face.

"Lord Vladimer," she said, "please, might someone dress my husband's wounds?"

Vladimer considered, his face guarded, and then allowed, "When my brother's physician returns, he can do that. In the meantime, I have not eaten for four days, and before I find myself set on a diet of nourishing broth and clear tea, I am going to find out what the kitchen can muster."

Balthasar

The kitchen delivered its first installment of cold meats, cheeses, and assorted biscuits, with joyful promises of more, much more. Balthasar watched with some apprehension as Vladimer bolted smoked meat and cheese, since he could anticipate the house guards' and staff's response to a digestive upset in their newly recovered lord. Ishmael purposefully chewed a slice, eating with mechanical efficiency and scant appetite.

Bal eased sideways in the deep and capacious chair to let Telmaine slide down beside him. She lay against him, the crown of her head against his cheek, suffering him to feed her small slices of meat, and sips of broth and sweetened tea. She was too tired to insist he eat in turn, which was as well; he did not want to find out, just at the moment, what chewing would do to his aching face. He settled for tea and broth.

With an abrupt expression of inner unease, Vladimer set aside a half-eaten slice of pungent cheese and took a stomach-quelling sip of tea. "Now," he said.

"Hearne," Ishmael said. "I know it's an imposition, with your face and all, but I think you'd tell it best of th'three of us. I'm too spent for wordcraft."

By Telmaine's stiffening, Bal realized that she also had caught Ishmael's intent: to have Balthasar tell it, and give into Balthasar's hands the decision of how much to tell of Telmaine's involvement, and the opportunity, if he could, to veil it.

"My part of it begins," he said, speaking cautiously for his closed wounds, "four days ago, just before sunrise. A woman came to my door, seeking shelter. . . ." Indigestion or no, Vladimer followed with a keen wit, probing for further details with pointed questions. Bal explained his own survival after the beating as he had first had it explained to him, as Ish's own doing, aided by Floria's spicule; that passed. Ishmael then took up the thread of his own investigations, from his and Telmaine's visit to Tercelle Amberley, through the burning of the Rivermarch—Vladimer called in his staff with an urgent request for confirmation—to his arrest. Vladimer's fingers tapped lightly on the edge of his chair, his only betrayal of temper. Casamir Blondell was due an uneasy interview with his master, Bal thought. Bal took up the story after Ishmael's arrest, his legal defense strategy greeted by Vladimer's dry approval and Ishmael's discomfiture. He described Lysander's reappearance, or seeming reappearance, and blackmail. Ishmael then told him about the two attempts on his life, drawing a stifled gasp from Telmaine, and the encounter with Kip, with the plan for escape that spun from it.

"Chancy," Vladimer critiqued.

"Aye, but it worked," said Ishmael matter-of-factly.

"What was the third attempt on your life?" Vladimer said. "Since it was your intent to escape then."

Ishmael hesitated, and Vladimer perceptibly stiffened. Propped against Bal, Telmaine stirred and spoke for the first time. "Lord Vladimer—cousin—do you believe what you have heard so far?"

His face guarded, Vladimer said, "I expect to hear the sum of it before making up my mind."

She eased herself more upright. "We are coming to a part of the story that concerns something that no one but these two men know about me. It's not . . . not a state secret—it's personal, but the kind of thing that . . . makes for juicy gossip and social ruin. I'd like everyone else to leave." She swallowed audibly. "Balthasar and Ishmael would try not to tell you, for my sake, but I don't think there's any way to explain without this—and we'd wind up with you holding a revolver on Ishmael again."

Ishmael had drawn a breath; he let it out slowly. "I fear she's right."

Vladimer sonned them again, that disconcertingly focused cast. "My staff does not gossip."

Telmaine said wearily, "I grew up in a ducal household; things get known, nonetheless."

There was a silence; then Vladimer waved a hand. "Leave us, please. Ensure we are not disturbed."

With a brief remonstrance, the remaining guard left. Vladimer toyed pointedly with his revolver. "Continue."

"My husband did not tell me about Lysander Hearne's threat—I presume we will continue to call him that—but I knew nonetheless." Her throat tightened. "I knew as soon as I touched Balthasar."

She hardly dared sonn the expression on Vladimer's face, but she forced herself to. It was deeply analytical, and disturbed. "Explain."

"Since the age of five, I have had the . . . gift . . . curse . . . whatever you would choose to call it, of magic. It was something I never wanted and tried not to use. The gloves, the phobia about infection, those were a means of putting a barrier between me and others."

There was a silence. "You married."

"Yes, cousin. With a confidence in my husband's goodness not given many women."

"That would be an advantage in a courtship, true. But you did not tell your husband, did you?"

"To tell him might have been to lose him," Telmaine said

staunchly. "I was wrong about that. Even though I knew my beloved intimately I . . . still underestimated him."

His heart stirred by the gift, Balthasar stroked her cheek, so that she could know his gratitude and his appreciation of her courage at this moment. Vladimer's sonn washed over them. "You learned this when?" he said to Balthasar.

"Yesterday evening, shortly before my wife and I decided to come down here and try to undo the sorcery affecting you."

"Decided," said Vladimer with precision. "Your wife assures us that she never wished to be a mage."

"Hear the rest of our story," Bal said. "Then you may judge."

Telmaine said, "Since there was no one else able, I took my own steps to find my daughter." In a flat, steady voice, she detailed events from the moment she climbed into Sylvide's carriage to the moment she laid Florilinde down on Balthasar's bed. Vladimer simply listened intently, asking no questions. At the end he said, "Strumheller?"

Ishmael seemed to rouse himself from trance or half doze, his expression somber. "I went down harder than I'd ever gone," he said. "Kip can tell you his part in it, but in short he realized that though I wasn't quite dead I'd not be long so—no wrist pulse and barely a throat pulse. He declared me dead and got me out of the prison and into the hands of my own people. Lorcas sent an urgent summons to Magistras Olivede Hearne and Phoebe Broome, who managed to get me more or less back on my feet in time for th'day train. Wasn't enough time for anything fancy in th'way of disguise, so I swaddled myself up and declared myself an invalid, traveling with my doctor. I figured nobody'd connect Kip with me, whereas they would have connected my menservants, and most people would stay clear of a man with a lung complaint."

"Why didn't you tell us at the station?" Telmaine said, a half whisper.

"When you didn't sense me, I'd the thought th'Shadowborn mightn't, either. I'd have been little use t'you as a mage, better as a stalking gun. You held it; I got a bullet into it."

Vladimer shifted impatiently. Balthasar, reading his impatience, took up the thread of the story. "My wife told me about the conversations she had had with Baron Strumheller, and that he'd tried to persuade her to help you, so we decided that we must try to do what he would have done."

"He convinced me," Telmaine said, head on Balthasar's shoulder. "Convinced me that it was our duty."

"We drove to the station to catch the day train, and spent the entire journey in suspicion and apprehension of the other first-class passengers," he said.

"I slept," Telmaine said, with a trace of bitterness. "And he wrote letters to our children, in case we did not come back."

Vladimer was unmoved by sentiment. Together, they finished the story, describing the incident at the tunnel. Ishmael's expression was horrified; he reached out a hand to Telmaine and she gripped it, and Balthasar could not find it in himself to begrudge her the comfort of someone else who understood. Vladimer and Ishmael both shook their heads dubiously when they heard how close Bal had been when he fired Sylvide's pistol at the Shadowborn, merely to graze its arm. Both were men who considered marksmanship as fundamental a skill as writing. Telmaine described confusion and a sense of great pressure and foulness in her magical duel; Ishmael supported the description from his own encounters with Shadowborn, and whether he found Telmaine's account incomplete, Bal could not say, but he wondered about her slight hesitations, when she had been so bleakly candid otherwise. Ishmael described his own pursuit of them through the concourse and corridors, leading to his timely intervention.

Vladimer rose and limped over to the corpse of the Shadowborn, stooping to lift the thick blanket that covered it. "If he fathered those twin infants, and it appears he—or one of his race—did, *why*, when their birth would require concealment by mass murder?" At their uncomprehending expressions, he said impatiently, "The Rivermarch fire."

"Accident," Bal said. "Intimacy. Experiment. To name three. I wonder how much Tercelle Amberley did know, or whether she was as deceived as the rest of us. Did she know him in the guise of Lysander Hearne? I think she must have done. Else why come to me, of all people? But his chancing the day made her wonder, and fear."

"Indeed," said Vladimer. "The next question that comes to mind is, Are there more nearby, or is this the only one?"

"There are at least two," Telmaine said unexpectedly. "The night of the last party at the summer house there was a woman in the garden. When she came near me, I felt—though I did not know it then—Shadowborn magic. She was not alone; there was a man with her, a man who spoke in a voice that sounded much like my husband's."

This seemed to be news to Ishmael as well.

"And you did not report this?" Vladimer said tautly.

"What would I have said?" she demanded. "I'd no idea what it was I was sensing. And you wouldn't have believed me."

The shift in Vladimer's expression toward deep suspicion made Balthasar say quietly, "Lord Vladimer, your distrust of my wife is evident. Do you suspect that she might be the woman who committed sorcery on you?"

Telmaine's body stiffened beside him. He was aware of a similar tension in Ishmael's, at no more than arm's reach away. Vladimer's expression was hard, almost masklike, with the effort to contain his emotions, not to reveal weakness. The effort was, to Bal, conspicuous. He said, "I have no reason to believe that my wife is not, in fact, my wife. Everything she has said and done has been consistent with the speech and behavior of my wife of over ten years."

"You would vouch for her?"

"More than that: I traveled with her by the day train. Had she not been who she seems, I would not have reached my destination alive. I was there when Tercelle's children were born, and the little that I could have contributed to any Shadowborn's errand would have been offset by the threat that knowledge represented. No, sir, if you reason this out, this is my wife."

"Unless you are not who you seem," Vladimer pointed out.

Bal said, "Lord Vladimer, you chose to be alone with us, without protection aside from that revolver. Which, I can assure you from very recent experience, would offer little defense against a Shadowborn. Those were not human nails that laid my face open. Please, follow your demonstrated conviction the rest of the way. We may not have much time, and Baron Strumheller felt very strongly that you were essential to our cause—and that our enemies knew it."

Vladimer's brows rose; Bal had the sense that the man was reevaluating him. "Have the three of you anything else to tell me?" he said.

"Telmaine," said Ishmael, "what did the Shadowborn say t'each other?"

She told him, finishing with, "I nearly asked you, there in the gardens, what that aura was. But I didn't know how to, and not make you suspect."

"My dear lady, I started to suspect the moment we met."

She sighed. "How much would have been different had I spoken up."

"That is often th'way," Ishmael said, and beneath the weary wisdom, Bal heard long experience, which had saddened and scarred, but not embittered the man. He eased his chin away from Telmaine's ear and indulged himself in a momentary wish that the other man who had entered his wife's heart was one of the many gadflies who frequented high society, rather than one of courage and moral substance. But that would have been unworthy of Telmaine, and of himself.

He returned his attention to the present and the place. "Lord Vladimer, could you tell us about your experience with the Shadowborn?"

"There is not much to tell," Vladimer said, but his terse, sickened manner said otherwise. Bal remembered the reports of the effect of glazen on their victims, and what Telmaine had sensed from Tercelle Amberley. Even a libertine would be shocked to be so used, and Lord Vladimer had the reputation of being deeply private, and a celibate.

He considered probing deeper and decided against it; now was not the time. "If you are able to give your agents a description, it would help trace the woman's movements backward from your meeting at least, if not forward, since we are dealing with a shapeshifter." He hesitated slightly, but this he could not defer, whatever its effect on Vladimer's hidden wounds. "The woman who was with you four nights ago, the man I met as Lysander Hearne, and the man on the floor behind us are almost certainly one and the same."

Ishmael cleared his throat. "My lord, he's right. I've told you that magic is sustained by the vitality of th'mage. You woke once it was dead, which suggests that it did this t'you. And we know already they've a great liking for magical firetraps, but nothing has happened, which may mean any trap died with th'mage."

"We may be wrong in assuming this particular Shadowborn to have fathered Tercelle's twins, since Telmaine described hearing the woman talking to a man who sounded like me," Bal said. "It may have been another one with the same gifts, using the same semblance of my brother. Who I presume, at some point during his exile, strayed into their territory." He felt a surprisingly sharp pang at the thought that he must count Lysander dead—and at the same time, it lifted a burden on his own heart. The little boy in him who yearned for a brother to adore could still keep faith that his brother had gone out into the world and become a good man.

They waited, while Vladimer considered. Abruptly, he swept sonn over Ishmael. "Do you remember the discussion we had, last time we met?"

Ishmael cleared his throat. "Aye, my lord."

"I want you to leave for the Borders by the express train this evening. Dr. Hearne will accompany you. I will commission an express for Minhorne for myself immediately. I will get Sejanus to issue a ducal order that you muster forces in the Borders to resist a possible Shadowborn incursion. Once you are satisfied you have done that, and if no such incursion has materialized—if they have not come to us—you will scout the Shadowlands, as we discussed. Dr. Hearne, your part in this is to prepare Baron Strumheller to enter the Shadowlands. I know of no better agent for this task than he, but he has previously been wounded by Shadowborn, been . . . ensorcelled by them . . ." An expression of profound unease came to his face, and he stopped.

Ishmael rasped, "Vladimer, if they'd laid the Call on you, you'd know it already. Hearne, if you're willing, I'm willing. Telmaine told how you were able to steady her; y'might be able to do it with me. If I've got to go into the Shadowlands, your help would make it more likely I'd come back."

"I will do whatever I can," Bal said, though he would not have needed to be a mage to hear Telmaine's horrified, silent, *No, no, no*, voiced in only a tiny throat-sound of protest.

"So be it," said Vladimer. "I will also take that scheming apothecary of yours into my service. I have worked with enough men of negotiable loyalty to trust that I can use him well."

Ishmael murmured his thanks. Balthasar said, "What about the charges against Baron Strumheller, and the fact that, at present, he is believed to be dead?"

Vladimer waved a hand. "Leave those to me."

Ishmael said, "There may be some difficulty over the inheritance. M'younger brother's been waiting a long time for this."

"Settle it," Vladimer said tersely. "Anyone who hampers your work, I'll have up for treason."

Ish dipped his head. "Aye, m'lord."

"Lord Vladimer," Balthasar said, "what about my wife?"

Vladimer waved a dismissive hand. "I have no doubt that my dear cousin is sitting there furious at me for sending her husband away; it cannot be helped. She is free to return to her children."

Ishmael chewed a moment on his temper. "Don't be a fool, m'lord," was what escaped. "Y'need to be guarded, and she's the best possible guard y'can have: a mage who can sense our enemies, who can move through society at your side, and who is, above all, loyal."

"You advise this, Strumheller?" Vladimer said dangerously softly.

"I most strongly advise it, m'lord. We know there's at least one more out there, and whatever else y'can do, you've no defense against their magic."

That was, Bal thought, more bluntly put than he would have dared phrase it himself. Vladimer drew a thin breath, his face chill with anger and, Bal feared, revulsion. But when he spoke, it was to accede. "So be it. She may accompany me." He rose. "Say your farewells; we will be leaving immediately the train is readied."

"Do you mean this seriously?" Telmaine demanded of Ish, as the three of them were shown into a side room for a final moment of privacy.

"Very seriously," Bal answered for him. "For the moment, you are the one remaining here who knows the stakes and the score of this game, and it is progressing both swiftly and lethally. We can only hope the danger lessens once Vladimer has had a chance to broaden our defense."

"You're a mage, and Vladimer trusts you," she said to Ishmael.

He shook his head and said heavily, "Even if he'd not ordered me south, I'd be scant use t'him now."

Telmaine raised a hand, hesitated, and then tentatively laid it on Ishmael's chest. "How much has it hurt you, to push back the flames?" she said in a low voice. "Tell me truly."

There was a long silence; then he said, reluctantly, "Th'magic may come back, it may come back partly, or it may not come back at all, Magistra Broome says. Time alone's going to show."

"Oh, sweet Imogene, Ishmael, I am so very sorry. I know how important your magic is to you." She reached up to brush his face gently with her gloved hand, as she had Bal's on the concourse. Bal wrestled once more with an intense—but for the moment private—ache of jealousy.

"Aye, well. I'd been warned often enough. I don't regret it going this way, if gone it is."

"I do," she breathed. "I'm so afraid, Ishmael."

"I wish I could tell you the fear goes. Y'learn to use it, though. Everything you survive teaches you more. And you'll not be alone. You can still speak t'me—t'us." He drew a deep breath, its self-consciousness at odds with his jesting of days—only days—ago, and stepped back. "Lord Vladimer'll not be long. I'll be leaving you. Hearne, I'll meet you on th'platform for th'express."

His footsteps, leaving, were inaudible beneath the industrious clatter of the reawakened household. Neither of them heard him close the door.

"I don't believe this," Telmaine said in a low voice. "I don't believe Vladimer has ordered you to do this, and that you're doing it." Bal did not answer; he hardly believed it himself. "Promise me you'll come back safe to me and our daughters. Please," she added with what tried to be a smile, "if there's any shooting, let Ishmael do it."

Bal put his arms around her, for the moment little caring that she knew everything he felt: his barely contained fear for her; his uncertainty whether he could do what Vladimer asked him to, and whether Ishmael could trust him enough; his disorientation at so hurried a parting; his dread of losing her. All personal, even selfish concerns, but all he could grasp of the unfathomable future.

"I'll be back as soon as I can," he said, settling his unwounded cheek against her hair. "Promise me that you'll take care of yourself and our daughters. Guard yourself around Lord Vladimer, too. The effect of this experience on him concerns me. He may react unpredictably."

"This . . . creature seduced him, didn't she—it?" she whispered, remembering the deeply embarrassing—and arousing—memories she had drawn from Tercelle.

"I fear so. I would have liked the chance to speak to him, but it's not to be, at least now. Be careful."

Telmaine said faintly, "Not a week ago I was here, at the summer house, with no thought on my mind but the night's party."

"I know," he murmured. He, he thought, had been feeding sweetened and watered goat's milk to Tercelle's abandoned twins. "It's . . . one of the consequences of power, my love. Responsibility."

"Bal," she whispered, her forehead resting against his chest as the seconds counted away. "The only power I'd wish for is the power to turn back time."

About the Author

Alison Sinclair is the author of the science fiction novels *Legacies*, *Blueheart*, and *Cavalcade* (which was nominated for the Arthur C. Clarke award). *Darkborn* is her first fantasy novel, which began with a meditation on the light-dark motif as it is used in fantasy, met up with years of eclectic reading and cities remembered and imagined, and took flight in directions almost as unexpected to the writer as to the characters. Alison Sinclair presently lives in Montréal, where she is working on the sequels to *Darkborn.*

Read on for an excerpt from the next fascinating novel in
Alison Sinclair's stunning fantasy trilogy

Lightborn

Coming in trade paperback from Roc in May 2010

The first tapping of raindrops on the taut fabric just above his face awakened Ishmael. He lay listening, frowning a little. He had known rain was coming, had felt it on the wind, but he had hoped it would hold off until after sunset. He'd reached Renmoor, as he had intended, but had decided against the public shelter and spent the time before the sunrise bell finding the ideal spot to stake out his hide. He'd placed it so that it would catch the late-afternoon sun, having learned to use that warming touch that once so unnerved him. But with the rain, his sunset signals—the birdsong and animal activities, and most of all the cooling of his blind and the rocks around him—were all muted. He must wait on the sunset bell itself, though he had hoped to be on his way before the workers went into the fields, harvest not being over. The fewer people he met, the less likely one would report when the word came through that a wanted man with a scarred face was traveling through the area. He doubted the notice would publicize his name.

He wondered how Balthasar Hearne was faring, in Strumheller amongst his kin.

And Telmaine . . . He'd not heard a whisper from her since their brief conversation on the train, and he feared he knew why. She would have felt the onset of that attack that had so perturbed her astute husband, and she had been in mental contact with him when he came close to killing himself with magic. She would be too afraid for him to try again.

Phoebe Broome had explained that he had not ceased to be a mage. He could still draw on his own vitality to extend his senses and agency beyond the strictly physical. But the penalty would be so much greater that even a small effort risked killing him outright. She had grimaced at his translation of that into engines, fuel tanks and valves, but she had agreed—the valves in the fuel lines were broken. The attack he'd suffered from speaking to Telmaine had proven it.

When he reached Stranhorne, he must risk sending a message north. Explaining, for one, that he now knew better than to exert his damaged powers. And counseling her as to what she must and must not do with her own emergent ones. He could almost wish that Balthasar's uxorious impulses would overcome his sense of duty and turn him north tomorrow. Hearne was no mage, but he surely understood something of magic, with his keen interest in all things. Likely he understood more than Telmaine did.

Ishmael shook his head wryly. A man with his reputation, hankering after a married woman, ought not to let himself like her husband.

From the nearby village, the sunset bell began to toll. Ishmael rolled himself up on his elbow, listening hard. He'd known of villages changing the timing of their main sunset bells to trap fugitives or raiders, and it would be ironic if he were immolated in a trap meant for a local troublemaker. But between the heavy strokes of the main bell, he could hear the dull clanging of the bell from the fieldworker's barracks, and a third, sweeter chime he could not identify. He relaxed. If it were a trap, it would be just the one bell.

A rustle of claws and sudden exhortation of birdsong from directly overhead made him start, and he smiled toward the night diva as he reached for the light-tight flap. *That* was a sign he trusted.

Camp was swiftly broken, hide and sleeping roll slung on his back, and his waterproof cape draped over it and himself; good, then he'd not be too obviously sleeping rough, which was uncommon enough to raise questions. He'd break his fast on the track as he worked the stiffness out of his joints. Too much civilized living, of late—if he discounted prison beds; he was getting soft. He bypassed Renmoor by the farm tracks, bidding an amiable good evening from behind his scarf to the first harvesters emerging, grumbling, into the rain. He accepted a mug of hot cider and a roll from a woman who took him for one of their own, and drained the mug as he followed the harvesters up the westward road. He left the mug with others discarded by the field gate and continued to the first crossroads and then south, once the rain had veiled him from sonn.

He had thought, if the rain held off, that he could make sufficient time on the tracks, but with the rain he would need to use the roads if he were to reach Stranhorne manor by sunrise, and even then he'd have to eat and drink on the move. Horses behind him he *would* hear, but an ambush, men waiting still and silent in his path, he would not. The greatest danger was from the warning that went before him.

He paused to shake out his dripping cape, and listened. This road was the best compromise: quiet since the post road had been built from the railway station to Stranhorne, but faster walking than the tracks. He could do nothing about what went before or came behind him, and he must pay attention to what lay around him. Just because he was in the Borders did not mean he had left the Shadowborn behind.

The rain did not let up, and he hoped, deeply hoped, that the harvest was well on its way to gathering in, because this could be the crop-spoiling storm they dreaded every harvest season. Mile upon mile he tramped into the wind, his hat little sparing him the rain that streamed down his face and seeped into his collar. The best that might be said for the storm was that he had traveled through worse, and only the reckless or very experienced would ride in it. The murk of tiny echoes limited sonn, and while Darkborn horses were bred for night riding, even they had difficulty on a night as thick as this.

His Borders-bred stubbornness would not let him carry a watch. He'd feared he would come to rely on it, and broken watches killed a handful of trusting travelers every year. But without a watch, knowing the mud and rain were slowing him and he'd not have precise signals of sunrise, he would have to stop early, set up camp, spend another night in the rain. And the temperature was definitely falling.

He stretched his stride, teeth gritted against the wind, sonn blurred by the rain, listening past the patter on his hat. He should be within a few miles of the junction with the post road, the best maintained road in the entire barony—the postal service would have it no other way—and the busiest. There was a post station near the junction, a place to change horses and overnight for the post riders and couriers, with an attached coach stop and day shelter. Should he chance still being ahead of the alarm, and catch a public coach into Stranhorne village? If the coaches were still running, in this deluge. He stumbled and lurched against the grassy verge. A few more steps took him to a cairn, and he leaned upon it, catching his breath, and fighting off vertigo. Fatigue, he told himself, but he realized he was shivering, and not only because of the rain.

He had sensed such a cold though Telmaine, as she approached the warehouse set with Shadowborn firetraps. He had sensed it again in Vladimer's bedroom, where Vladimer's Shadowborn assassin waited. He had sensed it during his encounters with magically gifted Shadowborn, mostly, as he had told Vladimer, too late for it to be other than a distraction.

And the vertigo—he knew the vertigo of old, too, from the time he had tried to live in the Broomes' communal mansion. It was the way powerful magic affected him. He had felt the same vertigo while he sheltered in the underground streets of the old Riverwalk, while overhead Lightborn mages twisted atmospheric energies into a storm to douse the burning city.

This was no natural storm.

And he doubted whether, amongst the few dozen low-rank, untrained mages in the area who worked as healers or fortune-tellers, or had nothing to do with magic, there were *any* could recognize or articulate what he or she would be feeling now. Baron Stranhorne's objections to magic kept its roots shallow in his barony.

That settled it: the post road, the post house. He had to raise the alarm, no matter the risk to his liberty. He did not know the purpose of this storm, whether to ruin crops, to conceal hostile movement, to prevent an alarm from spreading, to kill travelers. Sufficient magic could raise floods, turn rain to snow, snow in late summer, paralyze the area . . . Chaos had seemed their enemy's ruling plan to date, chaos, death and suffering.

Ishmael braced himself against the cairn, acknowledging the cold, acknowledging the vertigo, and setting both aside. He pushed off his hat, letting it flap on the end of its tether, baring his head to the elements. Not wise, for the long-term, but the shock of cold seemed to abate the vertigo, and he would need to hear if anything were coming at him through the storm. He'd set one foot before the other until he reached the post road, and if nothing ate him, or he wasn't run down by a post coach, he'd manage the few hundred yards to the post station.

Shivering, his steps weaving, he resumed walking. The vertigo came and went, came and went, and at its worst he lurched against the verge every dozen steps. In the driving rain, with the land heaving beneath him, he might as well have been in a storm at sea.

Except of this ship, he was captain, and navigator, as well as sorry passenger. When he tripped and fell, and struggled from the mud with the rain driving against his back, he realized that he had turned completely around without knowing it. His sense of direction was gone. Except . . .

Except for that constant, aching pull southward, in the direction he needed to go.

For eleven years he had resisted it, with all a Bordersman's stubbornness, refusing to take a single unnecessary step in its direction. Of the three other men he knew who had been similarly afflicted, one had put a bullet through his brain to end the torment, the one had moved to the north most tip of the country, and the third was in an asylum. Intransigence and constant vigilance had kept Ishmael sane and on this side of the Border.

If he let it guide him, even to the post road, could he force it to release him at the end?

But if he did not, would he reach the road before he lost his bearings entirely and turned back without knowing it? In this state, he'd not sense the sunrise.

And if he tried to reach anyone with magic—Telmaine or Magistra Broome—he would die in the failing.

He sent up a prayer, his first genuine prayer in years, to the Mother of All Things Born. Then he turned into the rain, turned as the Call bid him, and began to walk.